LEGIONARY

DARK EAGLE

by Gordon Doherty

www.gordondoherty.co.uk

Also by Gordon Doherty:

THE LEGIONARY SERIES

1. LEGIONARY (2011)
2. LEGIONARY: VIPER OF THE NORTH (2012)
3. LEGIONARY: LAND OF THE SACRED FIRE (2013)
4. LEGIONARY: THE SCOURGE OF THRACIA (2015)
5. LEGIONARY: GODS & EMPERORS (2015)
6. LEGIONARY: EMPIRE OF SHADES (2017)
7. LEGIONARY: THE BLOOD ROAD (2018)
8. LEGIONARY: DARK EAGLE (2020)

THE STRATEGOS TRILOGY

1. STRATEGOS: BORN IN THE BORDERLANDS (2011)
2. STRATEGOS: RISE OF THE GOLDEN HEART (2013)
3. STRATEGOS: ISLAND IN THE STORM (2014)

THE EMPIRES OF BRONZE SERIES

1. EMPIRES OF BRONZE: SON OF ISHTAR (2019)

GORDON DOHERTY

For Eileen.
You thought of everyone else first.

The Roman Empire, circa 382 AD

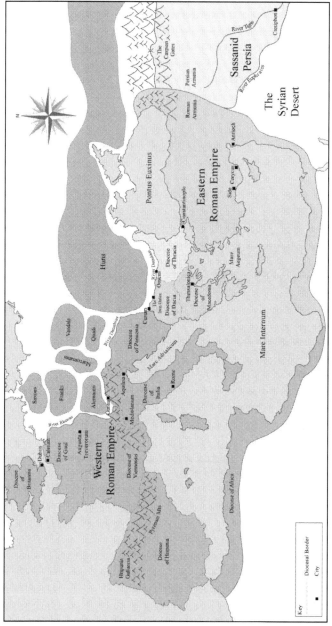

Note that full and interactive versions of this and all the diagrams & maps can be found on the 'Legionary' section of my website, www.gordondoherty.co.uk

Thracia circa 382 AD

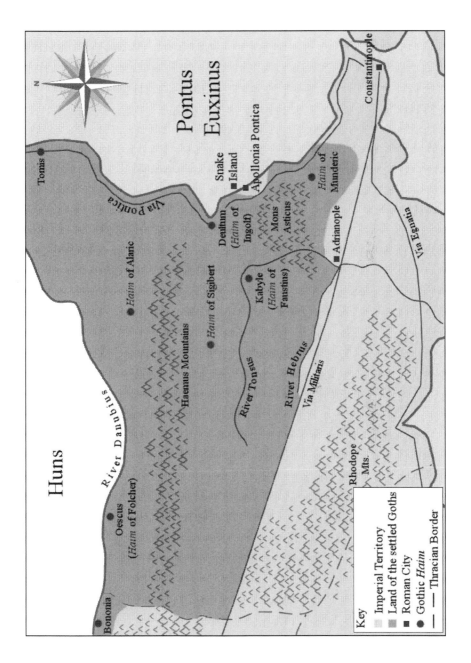

Gaul circa 382 AD

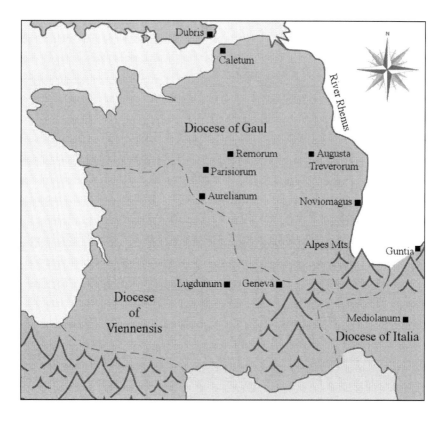

Structure of Legio XI Claudia Pia Fidelis

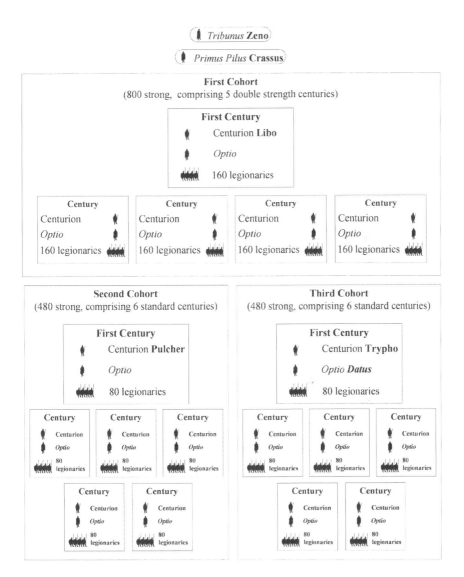

Tribunus **Zeno**

Primus Pilus **Crassus**

First Cohort
(800 strong, comprising 5 double strength centuries)

First Century

Centurion **Libo**

Optio

160 legionaries

Century	Century	Century	Century
Centurion	Centurion	Centurion	Centurion
Optio	*Optio*	*Optio*	*Optio*
160 legionaries	160 legionaries	160 legionaries	160 legionaries

Second Cohort
(480 strong, comprising 6 standard centuries)

First Century

Centurion **Pulcher**

Optio

80 legionaries

Century	Century	Century
Centurion	Centurion	Centurion
Optio	*Optio*	*Optio*
80 legionaries	80 legionaries	80 legionaries

Century	Century
Centurion	Centurion
Optio	*Optio*
80 legionaries	80 legionaries

Third Cohort
(480 strong, comprising 6 standard centuries)

First Century

Centurion **Trypho**

Optio **Datus**

80 legionaries

Century	Century	Century
Centurion	Centurion	Centurion
Optio	*Optio*	*Optio*
80 legionaries	80 legionaries	80 legionaries

Century	Century
Centurion	Centurion
Optio	*Optio*
80 legionaries	80 legionaries

The Western Imperial Army circa 382 AD

See glossary (at rear of book) for a description of terms

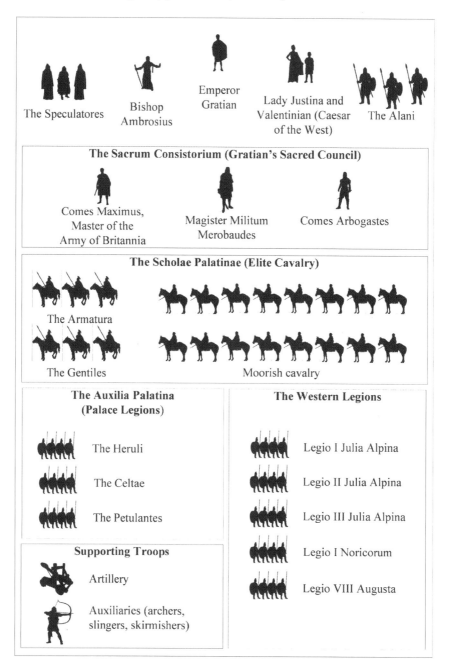

The Speculatores

Bishop Ambrosius

Emperor Gratian

Lady Justina and Valentinian (Caesar of the West)

The Alani

The Sacrum Consistorium (Gratian's Sacred Council)

Comes Maximus, Master of the Army of Britannia

Magister Militum Merobaudes

Comes Arbogastes

The Scholae Palatinae (Elite Cavalry)

The Armatura

The Gentiles

Moorish cavalry

The Auxilia Palatina (Palace Legions)

The Heruli

The Celtae

The Petulantes

Supporting Troops

Artillery

Auxiliaries (archers, slingers, skirmishers)

The Western Legions

Legio I Julia Alpina

Legio II Julia Alpina

Legio III Julia Alpina

Legio I Noricorum

Legio VIII Augusta

The Eastern Imperial Army circa 382 AD

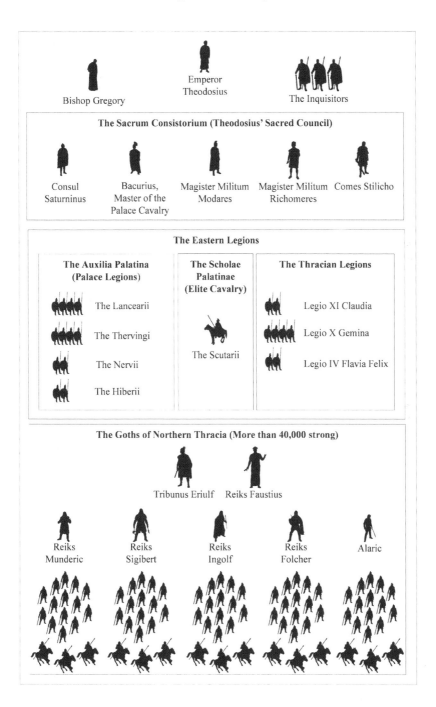

Bishop Gregory

Emperor
Theodosius

The Inquisitors

The Sacrum Consistorium (Theodosius' Sacred Council)

Consul
Saturninus

Bacurius,
Master of the
Palace Cavalry

Magister Militum
Modares

Magister Militum
Richomeres

Comes Stilicho

The Eastern Legions

**The Auxilia Palatina
(Palace Legions)**

The Lancearii

The Thervingi

The Nervii

The Hiberii

**The Scholae
Palatinae
(Elite Cavalry)**

The Scutarii

The Thracian Legions

Legio XI Claudia

Legio X Gemina

Legio IV Flavia Felix

The Goths of Northern Thracia (More than 40,000 strong)

Tribunus Eriulf   Reiks Faustius

Reiks
Munderic

Reiks
Sigibert

Reiks
Ingolf

Reiks
Folcher

Alaric

Part 1

Exile

GORDON DOHERTY

Chapter 1
Late October 382 AD
The Syrian Desert

Three dozen Romans padded across the searing wilderness, the air dry as salt and crawling like the breath of an oven across their skin. The first six of the party rode on the backs of camels, and the thirty behind were escort legionaries, trooping two-abreast, their ringmail armour glinting like white flames in the dazzling sun. Every so often the sound of popping corks and glugging water broke the shrill song of nearby insects and croaking desert toads.

The men saddled upon the two foremost camels were *dromedarii* scouts, draped in white robes, bronze scale jackets and iron helms. With the lands of Sassanid Persia just days ahead, these expert desert watchmen were supposed to be leading the way, alert and vigilant, but one of them was clearly drifting into a heat-induced slumber. He listed backwards in the saddle until the scales of his bronze vest – hot as coals – sizzled against the camel's hump. The beast grunted and groaned, then shook its great body, throwing the scout. The man woke as he fell, screaming. He threw out a hand to break his fall and instead broke his wrist. With much grumbling and sighing of hot and exhausted men, the column slowed.

Ambassador Sporacius guided his camel carefully around the fallen man then looked back down the column. His chiselled face was streaked with sweat, his deep-set eyes like vaults of wisdom as he scanned the small party before settling on one of the marching men near the back: a low-ranking type, going by his scarred helmet, poor-quality ringmail, tattered boots and the way he marched with his head down – a soldier yet to win confidence.

'You, Legionary,' Sporacius called. 'Help him.' It was a command that was not his to give, for he was not a military man, but he delivered it assertively, the demand clear but respectful.

The legionary mutely jogged forward, helping the injured dromedarius to his feet. The camel-scout, ashen-faced with pain and embarrassment, cradled the wounded wrist under his opposite armpit and coyly glanced up at Sporacius. 'I will lead my beast on foot from here on in.'

'Probably for the best,' Sporacius said, again, with a well-measured tone selected to reprimand but not humiliate. He mopped at his neck and short silver hair with a damp cloth then turned to the legionary who had helped. 'It's Urbicus, isn't it?'

'Yes sir,' the legionary muttered in reply.

'Good work,' Sporacius said, flicking his head towards the column's end. 'Now back to your place.'

'Yes sir,' the legionary replied mutedly, his head still dipped.

With that, Sporacius circled his camel again and swished a hand. 'Onwards.'

As the column crunched ahead once more, Urbicus the legionary held back, shoulders rounded, head dipped. After years of leading men, where eye-contact and a proud stance had been essential, this false name and pretend posture felt strange to Pavo. But it had to be this way. Exile and anonymity.

Only when the rear ranks of marchers – two abreast once again – came by, when every strange face was past him, did he tilt his head up just a little, the shade of his helmet peeling back and the sunlight spreading across his eagle-like face and hazel eyes.

He fell into place alongside the unpartnered legionary at the tail end of the party, who marched with that same head-down posture. This man's emerald eyes were rolled up a little in their sockets, scrutinising the column, particularly the riders. 'He was watching you,' Sura said quietly, the words disguised by the thump and grind of boots on dust and sand. 'Studying your face when you were helping the fallen scout.'

Pavo followed his oldest friend's gaze. Behind Sporacius, guiding his camel alongside the remaining dromedarius scout, rode a young officer in a white tunic spotted with two large purple decorative circles and arrow-stripes at each shoulder. He wore a black felt cap from the rim of which short brown curls sprouted, and he sported a thick, curly beard. This was General Stilicho, half-Roman, half-Vandal – and most importantly a military man of growing repute, sent on this sortie to aid and learn from Ambassador Sporacius. He was a few summers younger than Pavo and already he was Emperor Theodosius' *Comes Stabuli* – master of the imperial stables – and husband to the emperor's adopted niece.

'Not him,' Sura said. '*Him.*'

Pavo followed Sura's slight tilt of the head to see the silver-cloaked man riding alongside Stilicho. *Trierarchus* Ripanus, captain of the vessel that had brought them here to what felt like the edge of the world. Ripanus was staring off to the right of the column, scanning the desert wastes, his pinkish face pinched against the sun's glare and one arm – bare apart from the leather bracer on the wrist – raised to shield his deep-set eyes from the light. He wore an *intercisa* helm with a jutting and sharp fin-like ridge similar to Pavo's and Sura's, but made distinct by the opals inlaid in the two eye motifs above the brow. 'He was watching me? Are you sure?'

'As sure as cock-rot in the island brothels. Do you think he suspects?'

'No,' Pavo muttered. 'We played our part well on his boat. As far as he's concerned, I'm Urbicus and you're Mucianus – nothing but a pair of low-ranking swords.'

'He was smiling when he was watching you... but his eyes weren't. And what about the thing the oarsman said when we were at sea?'

Pavo chewed his bottom lip and stared at the swaying supply pack of the legionary in front of him as he replayed the memory. One of the rowers on Ripanus' vessel had been particularly friendly – bringing Pavo water during his bouts of sea-sickness. One night, as the others slept, the fellow had shared wine with him and Sura. Pavo, irked by Sura's suspicions about Ripanus, had asked the rower what he knew of the captain. The rower had laughed wryly, and answered in a way Pavo had not expected. *'There is a statue of Neptune in the Rhodos docks. One night, years ago, I made love to a beauty of a woman at the foot of the statue. It was one of those moments you know you'll remember forever. I recall thinking at the time that I'd never forget the statue's bright red robes and golden trident. Yet the next time I put into port there, the robes were blue and the trident silver. The locals swore to me that nobody had repainted it. It was the same statue, no doubt. But at the same time, it wasn't.'* He had swigged on his wine a few times before continuing. *'What do I think of Ripanus? He is a fine captain. Loves his ship and his men as if they are his brothers. I'd row into a storm if Ripanus asked me to.'* He had sucked on his wine again and exhaled contentedly through his nostrils, before holding up a finger and wagging it towards the figure of the trierarchus, sleeping near the helm. *'But that... is not Ripanus.'* Pavo felt that same shiver now as he had then. *'He's wearing Ripanus' cloak and helmet. Looks very similar... similar, but not the same. Maybe it's just age; before this voyage I hadn't seen him in years. I don't know...'*

Something yanked Pavo from the memory. Two small, simultaneous flashes of reflected sunlight, just ahead. He looked up, realising the flashes had come from Ripanus. Yet the captain was still staring out across the desert wastes on the right. But Pavo's gaze was drawn to the inlaid opals on the man's helm. Two polished gems, two flashes of light. Had the man just snatched a rearward look at him and Sura? The croaking of insects rose into a shrill, almost deafening sound, and the beat of footsteps seemed to quicken and quicken. He felt his sweat-soaked tunic and his ringmail tighten around his chest like a shroud.

'You're probably right,' Sura exhaled. 'I'm making too much of it. The heat is cooking my brain. Nobody here knows who we really are,' he tried to reassure.

Pavo sighed, the tension easing a fraction.

'We are two escort legionaries. The lowest-ranking men on this mission,' Sura continued as he peered ahead through the silvery heat in search of some sign that they were near their destination. 'Our job is to stand around in a Persian palace while that lot at the front flap their lips at the new King of Kings.'

Pavo took a few dried tarragon leaves from his purse, popped one onto his tongue and offered Sura the other. The texture and earthy flavour conjured a little saliva into his dry mouth, and the herb was always a good source of energy on a march such as this. As he chewed, he mulled over their role. The Persian King of Kings, Aradashir, was dead. His successor, Shapur III, needed to be persuaded that the recent peace between his empire and that of Eastern Rome was worth preserving – formalising, even. The division of Armenia between the two states had been agreed in principle. Now it was time to thrash out the detail.

'Right *now* things are not ideal,' Sura continued, gesturing to the marching men and animals ahead. 'The aroma of thirty-four sweaty crotches and six camel arses is,' he paused to pluck the perfect word out of the air, 'diabolical! But give it two more days and we'll be in the cool and shady halls of Ctesiphon. I heard stories from escort soldiers who travelled there before. Apparently the Persian women like us 'exotic' westerners... and General Stilicho reckons these talks will last for some time.'

Pavo tried to smile, but it was a feeble attempt.

'Come on, Pavo,' Sura continued. 'Thracia may be a thousand miles behind us, but our homeland is at peace, at long last. The war is over.'

Pavo slid his eyes round to meet Sura's. 'But the wrong man won.'

Sura's lips moved a few times before he fell silent.

There was no argument to counter this, no platitude to lessen the truth of it. The Gothic War was over, but Gratian, Emperor of the West, had claimed it as *his* victory, securing and reaffirming his position as senior emperor over Theodosius and the still-weakened eastern realm. Gratian, the man complicit in the terrible military disasters that had crippled the Eastern Empire, was now effectively its master. Worse, his agents – the *Speculatores* – were still crawling all over their distant homeland. They came in many guises – artisans, entertainers, riders, soldiers, friends, beggars – but every one of them was a highly-trained killer. All Speculatores were marked somewhere with that wretched emblem of their secretive school – a single, staring eye.

Checking nobody was watching, Pavo reached into his purse and lifted out a leather strap, from which two lead tags hung, bearing his true name and that of his beloved legion back in Thracia. He traced a finger over the etching, *Legio XI Claudia Pia Fidelis*, and sighed: 'Be watchful, Brothers.'

'The Claudia lads will be well,' Sura said.

'Even with their new commander?' said Pavo, tucking the *signaculum* tags away again.

'I only *heard* about the man chosen to replace you. I don't know for certain that-'

'You said he was a Western officer.' Pavo cut him off.

'That much is true, but that doesn't mean-'

'If he's from the West then he's Gratian's man. Gratian knows that the Claudia lads were behind us in everything we did to defy him,' Pavo said, staring at the ground before them.

'Doesn't mean this new tribunus is a bad man. Gallus came from the Western Empire,' Sura said quietly. 'Sebastianus too, and Geridus.'

Pavo tilted his head to one side in agreement. 'Aye, you are right, and they were golden. I just can't help but taste danger for our comrades back there.'

Sura spat into the dust. 'What can we do? We're supposed to be dead men, Pavo. If we show our faces in the Eastern Empire anytime soon, Gratian's Speculatores will peel them off, and if we go near the Claudia then they will suffer too. We can't go back,' Sura finished.

'Exactly. We're at the wrong end of the world, in hiding, in failure.'

'So why torment yourself? Think of what lies ahead,' Sura said, then batted the rear of one hand across his chest, his neck suddenly lengthening. 'Look, we're almost across the desert.'

Pavo peered ahead to see a shimmer on the horizon – some four miles away. A great river, which from this distance was merely a vague green ribbon, glittering where the sunlight caught the rippling current. 'The Euphrates,' he said almost in unison with every other man in the party. Beyond was ancient and fertile Mesopotamia, the heartland and bread basket of Sassanid Persia.

One of the legionaries in front of Pavo and Sura smacked his dry lips at the sight of the broad and flowing fresh water. 'My drinking skin is warm and flat. Little more than spit left in there. When I get to the river, I'm going to drink myself sick,' he said with a cackle.

'Idiot,' Sura whispered.

The legionary swung round, his bulbous nose scrunched up in anger. 'You got something to say, *tiro?*'

Sura balked at the term. 'A recruit?'

The legionary snorted. 'Looks like it to me.'

Pavo noticed his friend's fair skin reddening with ire. 'One day we'll be veterans like you two,' he said before Sura could reply.

'Wasn't talking to you,' the bulbous-nosed one sneered, then jabbed a finger at Sura. 'This one was whispering about me.'

Mercifully, while Pavo had been talking, Sura had used the few heartbeats of respite to calm himself. 'Just wanted to offer you some advice, that's all. The trick with marching in hot lands is to drink water carefully. Small and controlled sips,' he reasoned with Bulbous-nose in a friendlier tone. 'Back where I come from, I was famed for my ability to march for days on end with just a single drinking skin. You know what they used to call me? The Camel. The Camel of Adrianople.'

Pavo nudged Sura discreetly, stopping him before he said too much. The legionaries for this escort had been scraped together – some from Thracia, some from the island ports they had stopped at during the voyage to Antioch, and some were already aboard Sporacius' vessel when Ripanus' ship had rendezvoused with it in the southern Aegean. None of them really knew more than a few of the others, or their backgrounds. *Best it stays that way,* Pavo thought.

'Anyway, we don't need to stay thirsty till we get to the river,' the bulbous-nosed one shrugged and pointed, 'look, a village... and a well!'

All heads in the column rose, dry voices croaking in interest. A short way ahead, and to the right of their route, lay a desert settlement. It was a small and random collection of white-walled houses, lying like dice that had been tossed absently across the dust. Villagers sat on the flat roofs, sheltered under the shade of awnings. One man, painting a clay pot, looked up lazily, then carried on about his business. Bright robes and skirts hung from washing lines stretched between the homes and the few palm trees sprouting here and there. A dog lay in the shade of one building, scratching madly behind its ear. The village centred around a low circular stone well with a windlass and leather bucket positioned over it.

Sporacius saw it too. The ambassador eyed the well and the village for a moment, before raising a hand. 'Halt here,' he said. 'Go, take water in the village. Bring full skins back for us riders too.'

At this, General Stilicho sat upright in his saddle as if hearing a distant rumble of thunder. He heeled his camel round to Sporacius and the two entered into a sudden duel of words, a contest of leadership.

'The escort is under *my* command,' Stilicho snapped.

'And this is *my* mission,' Sporacius spat back.

Regardless, the soldiers were already peeling over towards the village.

'Us two should stay back and guard the embassy,' Sura reasoned, watching Stilicho and Sporacius, now left with just Ripanus and a pair of camel scouts to protect them. Still, he couldn't resist a fond look over at the village and the well, nor a lick at his dry lips.

Just then, Ripanus' gaze fell upon them, his face pinching with interest at the two men refusing the chance to drink.

'We can't afford to stand out,' Pavo murmured to Sura, elbowing him and shoving him towards the village. 'Come on.'

The two jogged on to catch up with the other legionaries moving towards the well. Bulbous-nose, now childishly-excited at the prospect of water, turned to backstep so he could talk to Pavo and Sura, his face bent in a grin. 'Mucianus, isn't it? You said they call you The Camel?' he asked. 'Well back in Thessalonica, they call me the horse.'

Sura feigned deafness.

'I said they call me *the horse*,' Bulbous-nose roared so he would hear this time, grabbing his crotch. 'Because I've got a massive co-'

Thrum...whack!

Wetness, blood.

Bulbous nose halted, statue-still, an arrow tip sticking out of his left eye socket like a pointing finger, the milky liquid of his eye and pinkish-grey chunks of brain gently pattering down on the desert floor between him and Sura. The legionary's body swayed, then crumpled. Some of the others had slowed, looking around in confusion, some still ambled on towards the well, oblivious to the silent strike.

Stunned, Pavo's eyes swept like a hawk's, across the desert village, then snapped onto the one thing that had changed. The man who had been painting a pot was now winking behind a bow, ready to loose another arrow. More, he now saw the similar shapes on the other roofs, and the bandits hiding in the doorways of the houses, betrayed by the blink of their steel blades.

'Ambush!' he cried as best as his parched throat would allow. Sura's shoulder crashed against his, knocking both of them clear of the potter's next arrow. All at once, his world was a tumbling chaos of dust, whizzing arrows and the punches of steel meeting flesh. Footsteps pounded and a desert battle cry rose as the hidden assailants sprang from the doorways. Pavo righted himself. Where was Sura? Some way behind them he heard the camels grunting in panic, heard Stilicho blaring orders from distance. But there was no imperative here other than survival.

A dusky-skinned bandit bounded towards Pavo, his loose robes flailing, his yellow-tinged eyes mean and his black beard wildly overgrown. The man had all the advantages: surprise, speed, weapon drawn. Pavo frantically grabbed at his shield strap, pulling the scarred, pale-blue screen from his shoulder and swinging it in front of him just as the bandit's broadsword swished round. The blade sliced into the leather edging and bit into the wood. Pavo grabbed the shield edge with his free hand and pivoted on his heel, the movement yanking the wedged blade from the bandit's hand. Before completing a full turn, he dropped his free hand to his scabbard and clasped it around his *spatha* hilt, drawing the legionary sword in one move and chopping it round into the bandit's neck. The man stumbled away in a fit of grunting and slapping at the lethal wound, dark blood sheeting out between his fingers. At once, Pavo sensed the whirr behind him, swung once more and fell to one knee, bringing his shield up to catch two more arrows.

'There are scores of them!' Sura cried from nearby.

Pavo saw his friend, splashed red, working his sword free of another bandit's body. In every direction, clusters of these mean-eyed robbers closed in. Fourteen of the escort legionaries lay dead or twitching. His heart pounded in his throat as he realised that he, Sura and the other fourteen remaining were trapped. His eyes swung to the potter's house, closest of the white-walled homes. The archer-bandit up on its roof was dead thanks to a thrown legionary spear and he now hung like a wet drape over the roof's edge, staining the white walls red. 'Inside!' he cried to Sura and the surviving legionaries. He unclipped a *plumbata* – one of three lead weighted darts secured on the inside of his shield – and hurled it in the general direction of the nearest bandits, causing them to slow and duck. It would buy them a breath of time.

Lunging up from one knee like a sprinter, he charged for the potter's house, the others converging there with him. Three more legionaries fell as they ran but, in a metallic thunder and a chorus of gasping, the men barrelled into the house – a well of cool shade. Colourful rugs lay on the floor and a scented oil burner glowed. Nobody else inside. An old cane ladder led up to an open square hatch of sunlight.

'Onto the roof,' Pavo bawled, waving each man up.

Pavo and Sura's heads flicked from the bandits outside, coming for the door, to the last of the legionaries speeding up the ladder.

'Go!' Pavo demanded of Sura.

'No, you go!' Sura barked back.

'Go… and that's an order,' Pavo snarled.

Sura sped on up to the roof, then, just as the bandits spilled inside, Pavo clambered up, feeling a broadsword hack through the cane rung his boot had just left. He scrambled onto the roof and kicked the half-broken ladder down into the house interior, then swept his eyes around the low white mud-brick lip of this roof, ears pricking up at the rising clamour of bandit shouts and curses rising from inside and those gathering around each of the house's sides. Scores of them? There were more like a hundred, he realised. Against thirteen legionaries. His mind spun like a falling sycamore key, searching through moments in the past, moments like this, in search of a way out. He shot looks in every direction: nothing but pan-flat golden dust and calm blue desert sky… apart from just south of the village where a low set of golden hills rose – but they were too distant to attempt any sort of fighting retreat there.

'There's no way out,' he said quietly. He looked northwards, seeing that Sporacius, Ripanus and the camel scouts had backed well away – rightly, for it would be madness should an ambassador be hurt or killed in a futile attempt to save the men who were supposed to be guarding him. Regardless, Stilicho had dismounted, anguished. The general's sword was drawn, his chest heaving as he took a few steps towards the scene. Yet he did not approach any further. A soldier right enough, Pavo realised, but not a fool.

His thoughts were scattered by the *clack* of a new cane ladder swinging up against the lip of the roof beside him. 'I'll empty your purse, Roman,' said a voice in broken Greek. 'I'll sell your armour and your clothes.' The bandit's fiercely ugly head appeared over the roof's edge, his broadsword glinting. 'I'll feed your heart to the desert dogs.'

Another ladder clacked into place next to this man, and then another three on the opposite roof edge.

'Together!' Pavo roared. The thirteen legionaries backed up against one another, the reverberation of their panicked breaths and pounding hearts binding them at the last like a sheaf of wheat about to be ripped apart by a hundred scythes.

A long, low groan of camels pierced the air over the village. It came not from the few beasts in the north with Ambassador Sporacius, this was a chorus of many, coming from those southern hills. Pavo saw a dark jumble of silhouettes appear at the crest of the low hills then spill down towards the village. More desert warriors – camel riders, coursing between the houses like the waters of a burst dam, coming to help finish the job the bandits had started. He could not see much of them thanks to the sun at their backs, but there were eighty or so. Many of them stretched in their saddles, lifting bent bows into the air.

Thrum… whoosh.

At the same time, the ugly bandit scrambled up onto the roof along with three fellow thugs.

'*Mithras*, it has been good fighting alongside you,' Sura said quietly as he and Pavo braced and watched the storm of arrows and bandits speeding towards them.

Whump, whack, whack!

A mist of blood floated through the hot, late-afternoon air, settling on Pavo, Sura and the others. All of them stared as the ugly bandit shuddered, mid-stride, before crumpling, dead, an arrow quivering between his shoulder blades. The others who had climbed up with him fell too, riddled with shafts. Screams rose from the desert floor around the house, as the camel riders swept around the building like a tornado, swishing and stabbing with spears and curved blades at the men who had ambushed the legionaries. In a blur of noise and stampeding feet, a few dozen of the bandits fled, and half of them were struck down by arrows in the back. As quickly as the desert had exploded into life, the din of battle faded to just the sawing of exhausted breaths.

'What just happened?' said one legionary, still pressed tightly beside Pavo and Sura, his sword drawn and trembling.

Pavo lengthened his neck to see over the roof's edge and stare down at the camel riders. They were now milling slowly, checking that the stricken bandits were all dead and despatching those who were not. He saw that the riders wore light robes like the bandits, but they were also armoured in dark-brown, hardened leather cuirasses, and many wore iron helms, some plumed. A chill breath puffed from the vaults of memory as he realised who they were. 'Maratocupreni,' he whispered.

'Maroto... Marama... what?' the shaking legionary beside him stammered.

'It is the Maratocupreni,' Pavo said, his voice full now. 'Sheathe your swords.'

When the legionaries did not obey, Pavo's face bent into an evil scowl like an eagle spotting its prey. 'Sheathe your *fucking* weapons, *now!*'

The men were quick to obey this time. None questioned this man they had up until now considered to be some hopeless recruit.

Pavo gestured to the north, waving to Sporacius and Stilicho to indicate that the danger had passed. They hesitated, but when he repeated the gesture they began to walk cautiously towards the village. Pavo approached one ladder at the roof's edge and descended. He found himself stepping down onto a carpet of bloody bandit bodies, surrounded by a forest of camel legs. The beasts milled around him, lowing and grumbling, their stink horrific. The fawn-skinned riders glared down at him with hard eyes, underlined with thick stripes of kohl, their mouths cruel, faces framed by their long, charcoal locks. Most telling of all, their bows remained nocked, and their spears and swords were not sheathed. One rider – a man built like a god with a sculpted face, limbs corded with muscles, hair hanging in sweeping, long dark locks to his broad shoulders – ambled over... and raised his bow, the arrow trembling at full draw, trained on Pavo's chest.

Pavo realised he had made a fatal mistake. These were not the same Maratocupreni he had once known. These men were robbers just like the bandits. They would slaughter the legionaries on the roof *and* the ambassadorial party unwittingly coming back towards the village. He would die out here, as an anonymous, forgotten fool.

'Darik, no!' a voice called out.

Another camel rider broke through. Their leader, Pavo realised as the figure placed a hand on the big warrior's bow, gently pushing it down. This one sported a helm with a long, trailing plume and a face veil. With a nimble swish of one leg, this lead rider dismounted, landing almost without a sound.

Between the brow of the helm and the top of the face veil, sky-blue, almond-shaped eyes assessed Pavo.

Pavo held this one's gaze, then realisation tolled within him like a hammer striking a bell. 'Izo... Izodora?' he stammered.

The leader unclipped the face veil and lifted off the helmet. Her pursed lips were humourless for a moment, but then they quirked at one side. The barest hint of a greeting.

'By the *Djinns* of the Desert, Pavo, you have aged,' she replied.

After they had buried the slain legionaries, Izodora, leader of the Maratocupreni, offered the services of her band as an additional escort for the Roman party. She led them to the Euphrates, where the arid golden nothingness began to sprout with patches of greenery – first hardy camelthorn here and there, then swaying grasses. Cicadas rose in a trilling song all around them. More, the air here seemed to be spiced with the scent of crops and woodsmoke – aromas of life. They reached the Euphrates' western banks and boarded a flat-hulled ferry. The crossing was short and pleasant, the downriver breeze welcome. As they stepped off of the timber ferry and onto the river's eastern banks, Pavo gazed across this 'Land Between the Rivers', spellbound. In contrast to the barren desert they had just crossed, it was so fertile, carpeted in lush, shimmering green clover fields, criss-crossed with sparkling brooks and irrigation canals, stretching all the way to the eastern horizon. Bees and insects hummed all around, and the air carried a sweet scent from the many date-palm orchards lining the south.

With a few clipped commands from Stilicho – clearly rushed so Ambassador Sporacius couldn't deliver the orders first – they set off through this fecund land. Pavo took up his position once more at the rear of the surviving legionaries, Sura alongside. Izodora barked orders to her camel troops, sending them out wide to screen the party on either flank. The impossibly chiselled Darik, who seemed to be her second-in-command, led the leftmost screen.

Pavo eyed the Maratocupreni leader furtively. Back at the village, she had been abrupt with Ambassador Sporacius and General Stilicho, explaining plainly that she and her people served the Persian *Shahanshah* as outlying watchmen to keep the desert routes clear of bandits, and that they should thank not her but the King of Kings for their rescue. She had said just enough to gain their trust, and had mentioned nothing of her past with Pavo. Indeed she had not yet let on to them that she knew him at all. He watched as she roved up and down along her own riders, talking to some, then came over to the Roman column to ride level with Ambassador Sporacius and his officers. He observed carefully, trying in futility to read her lips – but he guessed she was talking about the ambush. If she even once spoke his real name it would ruin everything.

Near dusk, he prized off his helm and raked his fingers through his sweat-damp, short dark locks, the pleasant coolness of the coming night soothing on his scalp and neck. He closed his eyes for a few moments as he walked, taking a handful of deep breaths. When he opened his eyes again, he found that Izodora had fallen back and was walking her camel alongside him. For a while she remained silent, staring directly ahead. But he knew she was watching him from the edges of her eyes – like a huntress.

'You should see this place in high summer,' she said at last. 'These clover fields are ablaze with purple flowers.'

He shot her a sideways look, flummoxed by the banality of the statement.

'Do not worry, *Urbicus,*' she said in a tone lightly-mocking his choice of name. 'I found out from the men ahead that that is what they call you. I have not told them who you really are,' she added, quietly, once a small gap had grown between them and the legionaries just ahead.

Pavo nodded stiffly.

'It takes a brave man to cross that desert,' she said.

Pavo tilted his head a little to one side in the way he had seen gnarled veterans do in an effortless show of heroic modesty. 'Brave, hmm, perhaps,' he started.

'-and a fool to cross it twice,' she finished.

He sighed in defeat. 'And both times you have saved me.'

The two fell silent again, and Pavo wondered how much she remembered of their previous meeting. Six years ago, as a mere *optio*, he and a detachment from the XI Claudia had been sent on a covert mission across the belly of the desert, tasked with infiltrating Persian lands and finding a lost scroll that documented the old King of Kings' agreement to a lasting truce between the Empires of Rome and Persia. Along the way, the Maratocupreni had saved the Claudia from a marauding desert tribe.

'Did you find what you were looking for all those years ago?' she asked.

'The scroll was not what we thought, but we obtained peace nevertheless, a peace that the ambassador is here to reaffirm.'

She smiled sadly. 'I wasn't talking about the scroll.'

Pavo gulped, caught off-guard for the first time in many moons by that desolate beast, grief. 'I found my father in the depths of the Persian salt mines. He... he...' a stinging, invisible hand choked him and pricked sharp needles into his eyes as he remembered Father's final moments.

'You found him, and that is what matters,' Izodora said softly.

Pavo carefully rubbed his eyes as if he were only wiping tiredness away, then cleared his throat and flicked his head towards the outlying screens of Maratocupreni camel riders. 'You rove far from the crescent valley,' he said, thinking of the sunken crevasse to which she had taken the Claudia men for shelter all those years ago – the valley walls lined with cave-homes and the floor blessed with a natural spring.

'We had to leave it behind three summers ago,' she said quietly. 'The spring dried up and the place became no more than a parched grave.'

'Where is your new home? Where are the others?' he said, thinking of the many hundreds of families who had been living in that crescent shelter.

Now it was Izodora's turn to struggle with words. 'There is no new home but whichever patch of desert floor we find ourselves upon come nightfall. There are... no others. This is all that is left.'

Pavo's heart plunged. He dared not ask what had become of the non-fighting Maratocupreni – the elderly and the children – for he feared he knew the answer. The desert was a cruel mistress: if thirst or hunger did not steal the lives of wanderers, then bands of raiders like those today would be quick to do so.

In the last hours of light, they passed wandering bands of shepherds, ancient mounds, fire shrines and shady palm groves. When the day finally faded, each screen of Maratocupreni riders settled in a tight circle, resting their backs on their dozing camels, eating and chatting. Meanwhile, General Stilicho ordered the legionaries to prepare a camp of sorts between the two camel groups, near one of the many brooks. Given that there were just thirteen legionaries, three dromedarii scouts, three officers and six camels, it was a somewhat pathetic camp, but nonetheless it offered a degree of familiarity and a little protection. The desert moon rose fiery and huge, a glowing coal that hung just above the horizon, the sky flaring blood-red around it. They cooked and ate a filling and salty wheat porridge, washing it down with cool, fresh draughts of brook water. Pavo more than once glanced across to Darik's camel camp. The Herculean warrior stood, braying in his native tongue as he acted out some past heroic deed. The watching Maratocupreni were entranced by the tale. Izodora too. It was this last fact that needled at Pavo just a little.

'Have you heard this?' Sura said, backstepping across his line of sight, breaking his train of thought.

Pavo turned to see the object of Sura's bemusement: the escort party's lone *contubernium* tent. The goatskin was sagging in the middle, patched-up badly and emblazoned with more than a few dubious stains.

'One eight-man tent, and thirteen of us are supposed to share it?' Sura stared at the limited space inside the tent, then at Pavo and the eleven other sweating, filthy legionaries, before glaring at one who broke wind for the hundredth time since eating. Even with two men on watch, this would still be a horrific experience. 'This is a joke, aye?' Sura asked.

He had directed the question at the legionaries, but General Stilicho overheard, and paced over from the spacious dignitary tent nearby. 'The other tents were ripped apart by the bandits,' Stilicho shrugged. 'I sympathise, I really do.' He stroked his curly beard for a moment, then clicked his fingers. 'In fact, here's what I'll do: I'll squeeze in there with you lot.'

Sura's face fell. 'What? No... n-'

But Stilicho carried on enthusiastically: 'It is an officer's duty to share the hardships of his men, eh?' he said, dropping to all fours and squirming inside. 'Come on, it'll be nice and snug,' he called from within, patting a space of ground for Sura. Pavo could not help but smile. The man was sincere yet affable – with the wits of a statesman but the manner of a soldier, unbothered by the superficial things most high-ranking imperial men obsessed over. When Pavo had first encountered him, the general had been playing knucklebones with the escort men, crunching through hardtack and enjoying their ribald humour. Pavo wondered if it was for show, but in the days since he had been equally ascetic: happily lacing his food with olive oil from the third-press, preferring sour soldier wine over the finer stuff, and – seemingly – relishing the opportunity to sleep in a cramped tent with stinking legionaries.

'I'll take the first watch on this side of camp,' Pavo volunteered quickly, turning away to stifle laughter at the whole scenario. He limited himself to a gentle chuckle as he strolled over to the small break in the square palisade enclosure and planted his spear haft in the dust.

He heard the men in the overcrowded tent shuffling, grunting and complaining. A few threats were issued, then apologies from those who realised that in the darkness their threats had been directed towards Stilicho. A furious volley of farts conjured a resigned chorus of groans, a final sheepish apology and then, at last, there was silence. The only noise to be heard was the sound of night crickets, the gurgling brook, and the gentle chatter of Sporacius and Ripanus, still awake by the officer's tent, sitting around their fire and drinking hot brew.

Pavo stared out into the night, the day just gone seeming hazy and unreal – like an entire moon rolled into a handful of hours. His legs ached and his feet pulsed with hot-spots, and his eyelids felt as if they were made of lead. He felt the dreaded hands of sleep crawling up his body again and again, and resorted to the usual tricks to stay awake – hard-learned in his seven years in the army – such as biting his lip or digging his nails into his palm. But after the long march through the infernal heat and the strain of the bandit ambush, sleep found a way through. His head nodded forwards.

He stared up, entranced. The sky was pure black one moment, then sheet lightning flickered, betraying roiling storm clouds, tinged purple and green. There was something else up there too... something huge.

Boom! the thunder roared and again the lightning flashed. This time he saw them: a pair of giant eagles, soaring across the heavens. Both beasts had wings like sails and talons the length of men. One shrieked and then the other replied, the noise tearing the sky in two.

He sensed a presence next to him, and turned to the withered old crone standing there. She might have been there all along; he could not tell. In many ways, she had been there by his side since he was a boy. Still now, in his twenty-sixth year, she looked just as ancient as that first time he had seen her: her hair like wisps of web, eyes milky and sightless, face puckered and sad.

'What do you see?' she asked him.

He gazed around him, seeing a dark and strange land. Not Rome, nor Persia. It was like night in every direction and even under his feet, nothing but pure, Cimmerian blackness. So he looked up again. The eagles were circling one another, he realised, each beast's great head turning to keep track of the other. One was white as virgin snow, the other black – blacker than the land and the sky. The malice between the two was unmistakable.

Pavo felt a childish urge to demand answers from her. What was this? But the need faded. She had never given him answers, but she had taught him how to find them for himself. In the vision, he thought, the answers were always in the vision. He gazed up at the skies until he felt a deep, cold twist in his stomach. Such hatred between the two eagles. The certainty that they would fight. The great birds were symbols of Rome, and they could mean only one thing.

'A great war looms for the empire,' he said sadly.

She said nothing in reply, and he knew he was right.

'Yet the war in Thracia is over. How can another threaten so soon afterwards?'

'Thracia is but a small patch of land.' She held out her hands as if cupping an apple, then spread her arms wide. 'This war will change the entire Roman world.'

He raised a mirthless smile. 'I will have no part in it, for now I am in exile, beyond Rome's borders. Here I will live out my days and die.'

'Is that so?' She stared into his eyes as if she could see again.

'I don't see how it can be any different.'

'If you want to see, Pavo,' she said, 'then you must open your eyes.'

His ears pricked up, hearing only the roiling of the storm above and the shrieking of the eagles. 'I don't understand, my eyes are open, I have seen all there is to see here.'

Her lips parted again, her age-long teeth in a cage as she hissed once more. 'Open your eyes!'

He jolted awake with a croak and a gasp. Asleep on watch? For a moment, he was riddled with shame and shock, before he realised – with a glance at the dripping water clock – that he had been asleep for but a blink, rocking a little forward on his spear. All was the same: the quiet Persian night, the gentle chatter of the officers behind him, the chirruping crickets...

'Trouble, watchman?' Ambassador Sporacius called from behind.

Pavo turned to look over the legionary tent towards him, where the ambassador and Ripanus were finishing the last of their root drinks. The ambassador's regal expression was tinged with concern.

'No, Ambassador,' he replied, 'I just... just choked on some blown dust.'

Ripanus, sitting beside Sporacius and sipping on his cup of brew, eyed Pavo. It was a look that seemed to reach inside his veneer as a lowly recruit, and it lasted an uncomfortably long time. At last, the captain picked up a water skin and tossed it across the small camp. Pavo caught it.

'Drink,' Ripanus said, 'clear your throat.'

Pavo muttered in gratitude and turned away. But throughout the remaining hours of his shift, he was sure he could feel Ripanus' gaze on his back.

The following day, they trooped eastwards along The Persian Royal Road – a wide and ancient highway that spliced the endless network of shimmering grain fields and gurgling qanats. The route led very gradually downhill, until, near noon, the eastern haze sharpened and took shape. At first, they saw another huge, pale river winding across the land, north to south. The Tigris, Pavo realised, sister-river of the Euphrates, broad and endless. Next, they saw a sprawling city hugging the river on the near side and far. Pavo had to sweep his eyes across it three times to be sure it was not a trick of the heat – the place was huge! There were wards of pale-stucco houses, towers and manors, games arenas, stable yards and majestic bathhouses. Squares and avenues stretched, bronze monuments rose into the sky and a great barracks dominated a huge quarter of the place. Grand Fire Temples winked at the approaching party like the orange eyes of strangers offering just a tantalising hint of some forbidden secret. All of this was in a style vaguely reminiscent of imperial architecture but with curves, twists of colour and flair that made it seem magically different, mystical. On the sun-splashed far banks stood the greatest structure: a huge white palace that soared like a mountain and shone with the lustre of snow, surrounded by giant arches. Every single street and space within the city teemed with moving throngs of people and animals. Streams of them poured to and from the many gates around the city's lengthy defences. Pavo had never believed there could be a place to rival Constantinople, but his eyes made war with his beliefs now.

'Welcome to Ctesiphon,' Izodora said. 'They call it *The Cities*, because she has grown so large.'

'Emperor Julian once fought here,' Sura mused.

Pavo pointed to the ward on these near banks, wagging his finger as he recalled the scrolls he had read in his childhood. 'That district there – that was once a city in its own right: Seleucia. One of Alexander's jewels... he must have thought he had built a great metropolis, yet look at it now: swallowed up like a crumb – a mere ward of Ctesiphon.'

'Listen to officer clever-bollocks,' said Clodus, a weathered legionary with a permanently ruddy face. It was meant in jest – for this one and the other escort soldiers now treated Pavo and Sura with respect following their vital words of encouragement during the desert ambush. But to Pavo the joking use of the term 'officer' sounded like the crack of a torturer's whip. He half-laughed, half-grunted, then dipped his head a little.

They followed the royal road down towards Ctesiphon's western gates – a monumental arch supported on the backs of two winged bulls with human heads and Persian-style beards. Sentries lined the high gatehouse, their breastplates shimmering like gold, watching the in and outflow of people, wagons and animals. The Roman embassy merged into the incoming stream. It was like stepping into a river with an unexpectedly strong current. Sun-burnished strangers bustled and barged all around them, jabbering in a polyglot babble, shouting over the din of hooves and footsteps. There was a new mix of smells too: fragrances, spices and 'interesting' body odours. The people wore bright gowns and most of the men sported long, thick beards. The more affluent ones travelled in sedan chairs, bathed in shade, draped in silk and dripping with jewels.

As they passed into the shadows of the huge gateway, Pavo noticed one guard posted at ground level wearing a tall helm and a scale vest, scanning each and every face entering the city. His beard and tumbling mane of hair glistened with oil, and his bronze earrings juddered whenever he moved his head to watch any particular incomer more closely. Unnervingly, he continuously flexed his fingers on his spear haft, as if eager to use the weapon. Pavo sensed trouble before it happened. The guard spotted the paler-skinned Romans amongst the many others coming in and bawled something. Instantly, five more dressed and armed like him came spilling from a doorway in the gate-arch. They spread out across Ambassador Sporacius' path while the lead sentry held his spear out like a barrier, then barked something in his native Parsi tongue. Pavo could not hear what the demand was, but he could guess. Equally, he did not hear Sporacius' reply, but he could detect that it too was spoken in Parsi. Yet it was not enough to appease the guard. General Stilicho tried next, unfurling and showing the guard one of the many scrolls he carried in a leather bag. The guard glowered at the scroll then shrugged and snapped at them once more, refusing to let them pass.

'He can't read Greek,' Pavo sighed.

'And he's an arsehole,' Sura added.

Pavo watched with interest, noting how Ripanus said nothing, sitting back on his camel and watching the struggles of Sporacius and Stilicho.

The belligerent guard became more and more animated, and his five charges began to puff themselves up like angry cats. Seeing this, Izodora groaned, then heeled her camel forward and spoke to the lead sentry, vouching for the Romans and their scroll.

Bitterly, the guard acquiesced, hectoring his five now-deflated charges back to the side of the gate arch then – with a grumble – beckoning the embassy inside.

The guard led them inside the city, through the windless streets and sweating, jabbering crowds. In a market ward, an older man, resting by a blue-tiled fountain, plucked on the strings of a *setar*, and a fellow sitting on an adjacent roof, legs dangling over the edge, slapped his hands on a *tombak* drum, lending the great flow of the city some sense of rhythm. Traders threaded this with regular piercing monologues about their spices, silks and jewels.

They passed a temple district and came to a vaulted bridge spanning the Tigris, the waters dotted with trade ships and fishing skiffs, the banks packed with women washing garments and drawing water. Finally, they peeled away from the masses and onto a broad, largely deserted avenue, lined with palms and statues of ancient Persian gods – the approach to the great White Palace of the King of Kings, Pavo realised, eyeing the great structure that he had first seen from miles away. He saw silvery sentinels lining the palace roof and dotted all around its exterior walled gardens.

'Mithras,' Sura croaked, seeing two of these guards standing either side of the entrance to the gardens. 'It's *them* – the *pushtigban*.'

For a moment, Pavo's mind was thrown back to the desperate desert clash he and the Claudia had fought against the Persians, six years ago. None were more ferocious than the pushtigban, the Shahanshah's personal guard. From the belt of each hung a *shamshir* – a long curved sword with a hilt marked in a honeycomb pattern for expert grip. They held bronze-coated spears and wore polished iron helms adorned with finely crafted bronze wings. But most of all it was their steel masks that roused fear in the pit of one's stomach: expressionless iron plates, hiding all but the glint of baleful eyes. Pavo felt his stomach twist in anticipation, fully expecting another challenge from the two elite sentries. But the grumpy gate guard muttered something in Parsi, and they were allowed through.

Inside the gardens, the scent of the cascading flowerbeds, the playful whistle of waxwings and the babble of stucco fountains effortlessly settled each man's nerves. When they came to a decorative moat hugging the palace's southern walls, a canoe drifted serenely towards their march, pulled along by some weak current flowing from a culvert in the palace foundations. Pavo glanced at the canoe – really just a halved, hollowed out log – and the man lying in it. Basking in the garden paradise and bright sunshine, he guessed. Then the smell hit them.

Faeces, vomit, decay.

'Urgh,' Sura choked.

The drone of flies rose like a thousand rasping saws, and Pavo noticed the black cloud of insects hovering around the boat.

'Mithras!' the red-faced Clodus croaked, covering his nose and mouth.

As they filed past the canoe, Pavo saw the awful state of the man aboard. Yes, he was lying on his back, but that was because he had been bound that way, with ropes as thick as ships' rigging strapped across his ankles, knees, waist, chest and forehead. His face was blistered and weeping pus, his lips half chewed off, purulent and bleeding. His eyes were obscured by unctuous globules of yellow, blood-streaked pus. And his belly... his belly was *writhing*. It took Pavo a moment to comprehend what he was looking at: the skin was gone and a mound of maggots were twisting and wriggling in the cavity where his guts should have been. In the places where his skin was intact, translucent grubs moved underneath, working to break through. Worst of all, the wretch's chest still moved with desperate, shallow breaths. He was still alive.

'*The boats*, they call it,' Izodora said quietly as the canoe drifted past and the smell with it.

Pavo realised she had fallen in to walk alongside the escort troops. Stilicho too.

'They force-feed the bound man honey and milk every day, so that he soils himself as he drifts around hopelessly. Next, the insects come, attracted by the stink, lay their eggs in him and when the young hatch, they eat him alive...'

Stilicho issued a strangled gasp of disgust. 'Shapur wanted us to see this,' he said with a sly look up at the magnificent palace and its many galleries – its every shady window like a watching eye. Indeed, the grumpy gate guard leading them was barely disguising a triumphant smirk at their reactions.

'I don't like this, not at all,' Sura whispered so only Pavo could hear.

'Best get used to it. This is our lives now... maybe forever,' Pavo replied.

As they trooped on towards the palace, a soft hand rested on his shoulder. He twisted to see Izodora. While she continued to walk with him, Darik and the others had slowed, as if afraid to approach the palace. 'You're not coming inside with us?' he asked her.

'I cannot. I must return to the desert, to watch those approaches as I promised the Shahanshah I would. But I will be back here, from time to time.'

'So this is goodbye?'

She checked nobody in the Roman column was looking back, then leaned close to him as they walked. He felt her robes brush on his forearms, smelt her scent – some washing oil spiced with frankincense, felt the shock of her wet lips at his ear. 'Someone in your party betrayed this mission. Someone who didn't want this embassy to reach the Shahanshah.'

Pavo peeled his ear from her lips, staring at her. 'How can you possibly know this?'

'I could not sleep last night. And all this morning my mind has been combing over the events of yesterday. That ambush. There was something wrong with it. It was too... too perfect.'

'It was, until you arrived.'

'But she seemed lost in thought. 'We were tracking those bandits for days. They did not know we were following them. They took a very deliberate path upriver to reach that village. I crept close enough to their camp one night to hear their leader berating them. He was telling them they were behind schedule – that they had to be there in time.'

'At the village? In time for what?'

Her eyes darkened. 'In time for your lot to wander past.'

Pavo's eyes shifted left then right. 'How would they even know we were coming? How would they know our route?'

But she fell away now, slowing while the legionaries moved on towards the palace. 'I don't know, Pavo,' she whispered to him as the distance between them began to grow. 'All I can say for sure is that you must be watchful in there. Do not let your guard down.'

With that, she turned away and made for Darik and her men. He kept his head twisted round to watch her go, her hips swaying as she walked, the contours of her body changing gracefully underneath her robes and armour, her long tail of hair swishing at the small of her back.

Sura batted him across the chest to return his attentions forward, just as the shadow of the Persian palace crawled across them. The pushtigban pair watching the grand doorway straightened with a *clank* of iron armour to greet them. He gazed up at the palace and then across the men of the small embassy, knowing not which held the greatest threat. The only thing he did know for sure was that he would right now give anything to be far away from here, with his legion … back home in Thracia.

Chapter 2
November 382 AD
Thracia

Thin vapour rose from the hills and meadows as the midwinter sun gradually burnt off the shell of morning frost. The first parts of ground to thaw revealed hoof-shaped divots, made during the Gothic War by the many frantic imperial and Gothic scouts who had sped across this land in every direction. The scars were wide and deep, but the grass was closing in around those tracks… time *was* beginning to heal the land. More, the fields at Adrianople and Ad Salices, the heights of the Scupi Ridge and the cliffs at Dionysopolis – sites of the great battles, once sepulchral and littered with the bones and rusting armour of Romans and Goths alike – had now been cleared, the dead laid to rest at long last. For the first time in more than seven years, Thracia knew peace. As if in celebration, doves swirled around the blue sky like strokes of an artist's brush, their flapping wings like a round of applause.

But another sound emerged, threatening the bucolic serenity. Like an echo of the recent past: the dull rumble of soldier boots. Legionaries, marching; yet they were not men on the way to war, they were keepers of the newfound peace, on patrol to ensure the recent accord remained intact. A moment later and the sound of their boots was joined by a jaunty song.

'Can you hear the sound of soldier boots,

walking proud and tall on the ancient routes?
See a silver eagle gliding low,
and a great red bull on a legion pole?
We are the Claudia, sworn to Rome,
to guard this sweet, green land that we call home.
We shine and clatter like soldier kings,
With the wind of Mithras under our wings...
A pause, then a swell of breath and a huge chorus:
'...for we are the watchmen of Thraaa-cia!'

From the brow of the hills and as if filling the prophetic verse, a silver eagle ascended like a miniature dawn, catching the sunlight. It sat upon a crossbar, with a ruby banner hanging from it, a bull emblem woven into the fabric.

Opis, the handsome and broad-shouldered young *aquilifer* used the standard like a walking pole as he breasted the hill first, his mouth wide with the closing words of the song. His white tunic, fin-topped helm and ringmail vest glinted in the sunlight. He scanned the land ahead and waved a hand, encouraging the rest of his legion to keep pace with him. In days past, 'the rest' would have meant three replete cohorts, over seventeen hundred men: scouts, baggage handlers, technicians and artillery experts. Today, just one hundred and sixty seven men rose into view behind Opis, each carrying a ruby-red shield etched with gold and black motifs of the old gods and personal symbols of fortune. Libo, the one-eyed, wild-haired Chief Centurion of the First Cohort marched ahead of the sixty men who remained from his unit. Big Pulcher was now an officer too – Chief Centurion of the Second Cohort, of whom just thirty nine men remained. The brutish, pox-scarred officer scruffed at his short, black oily curls of hair and brayed at his few charges. A rabble of sixty eight came last – the Claudia's Third Cohort, composed almost entirely of soldiers only just old enough to serve, led temporarily by the earnest and enthusiastic legionary, Trypho, with his jug-eared friend Datus serving him as an *optio* of sorts.

Libo snorted and spat into the grass, his good eye swivelling across the crisp, green land, the wooden false eye fixed and staring wildly skywards. Happy that there was no sign of bother, his lips peeled apart in a smile, revealing his motley array of teeth – little more than small yellow pegs.

'All clear?' Pulcher said, marching level with him.

'Not a speck of trouble. No smoke on the horizon. Nothing.' No sooner had he said this than his smile slid away.

Pulcher frowned. 'So why do you look as if someone's just shat in your porridge?'

Libo lifted a hand behind his ear and scratched like a dog. 'Because... that waystation we camped at last night. I swear those pillows they gave us were riddled with fleas.'

'Oh, the *pillows* had fleas, did they?' said Rectus. The legion's lantern-jawed *medicus*, saddled on his mule – Balbina, a gentle creature older than the hills – rode level with Libo and Pulcher, his swept-back strands of hair and bear fur cloak tossing and rippling in the winnowing wind. 'So that would explain why you were scratching like that yesterday morning, *before* we got to the waystation?'

Libo's good eye swivelled to Rectus. 'They itch on my head and down below. One more word from you and I'll have you tend to my nether regions, medicus.'

Rectus suddenly fell silent. Opis disguised a laugh behind a cough.

The four moved at the head of the others for a time.

'I've been thinking,' mused Pulcher.

'Dangerous,' quipped Opis.

Pulcher shot him a flinty glower, before continuing: 'These parts are quiet. There is no need for us to move in unison. If we divide the route into three sections, and assign one cohort to each, we can carry out this patrol in half the time allotted. Or even less.'

Libo nodded as he began to understand Pulcher's idea. This broad stripe of countryside that they had been tasked with patrolling ran east to west, just above and parallel to the *Via Militaris*. To the south of that great military road lay the imperial cities and waystations, while the Goths had been granted the majority of the lands north of here, all the way to the River Danubius. Tasked by Emperor Theodosius with restoring the war-torn farming regions, the Goths had divided the land up into a number of *haims*, each governed by a tribal *reiks*. Since the peace had been struck, the Claudia alone had patrolled this notional border, sweeping endlessly from east to west and back again. During their time on this route, they had only visited the most southerly of the Gothic *Haims* sparingly, being careful to treat the Goths as equals. Policy was to leave them to their task and let the delicate peace settle and harden like molten wax cooling to take shape. His mind returned to Pulcher's suggestion about honing the patrol pattern. 'Quicker, more frequent patrols mean less chance of trouble taking root,' he agreed.

Rectus mused over it for a short time then suggested: 'Perhaps we should ask *Tribunus* Pav-'

He fell silent again. All four slumped a fraction, each privately thinking of Tribunus Pavo and *Primus Pilus* Sura. Libo's mind flashed with images of Sura's death, the officer driven from the cliff edge at Dionysopolis like so many others during the terrible press of battle. It was a sad but noble memory. But Pavo? Nobody knew what had become of him. He had survived the battle and he had been present at the parley tent for the peace talks that followed. Then he had gone to the cliff's edge to mourn the death of Sura, and the many other loved-ones he had lost during the war. Nobody had seen him again. Libo knew, deep within, that his old commander had most likely taken his own life. 'This is how it is,' he said quietly. 'The way of the legions. Don't get too attached to your comrades. They don't often last for long.'

'Aye,' Rectus sighed, then sucked in a deep breath to try his sentence again. 'But as for Pulcher's idea about the scouting route, perhaps we should ask Tribunus... Zeno.'

A rapping of hooves sounded from behind. All three twisted to see the lone officer riding on a pale mare. He was a vision of imperial splendour: the white plume on his gemmed bronze helm thrashing, his red cloak billowing likewise in his wake, his golden greaves sparkling. He slowed to a canter then a walk as he drew closer.

'Sir,' the three saluted, squinting up at him.

He untied and slid off his helm to reveal a boyish, heart-shaped face bright with enthusiasm, his black hair swept back and glistening with oil. 'You make good time,' Zeno grinned at them, arching one eyebrow. 'Too good, I might say – I had to ride like a Hun to catch you up.'

'We could be even swifter,' Libo said, gesturing towards Pulcher. 'The big man here has a good idea about future patrols. It would mean dividing our already sparse ranks, but-'

Zeno held up a palm to interrupt. 'I waited back at the waystation this morning because I was expecting an update to our orders. Instead, I received a missive from Crassus, my primus pilus.'

All looked bemused. None had yet met this Crassus. Apparently he was off organising things that Zeno could not attend to.

'It seems he has managed to gather reinforcements, and soon they will be sent to replenish our ranks – almost to full strength.'

The news rippled back down the column and the men yammered in excitement.

'Full strength?' said Pulcher. 'With that many bodies, we could patrol the route in dozens of small sections. Do it twice or more in a single day.'

Libo reflected Zeno's smile – albeit a lot less handsomely. 'In all my time with the Claudia, we have rarely had more than half-numbers.'

'Those were times of war, Centurion,' Zeno said. 'This is a new age of peace.' He heeled his mount a few strides ahead and swished a hand overhead. 'Onwards.'

With a blast of *buccinae*, the Claudians trooped on, stirred and strong. After a time, they reached higher, snow-coated ground. Without the lee of the hills, a bitter winter wind sparred with them, casting up flurries of white at them, numbing Libo's brow and giving him a stinking headache. After a solid hour of this, he heard chattering teeth and glanced to one side to see Pulcher, scowling into the gale, teeth battering together. 'Keep it down,' he snapped.

Pulcher's big, pitted face swung round and shook a little – like a Labrador hearing its master's call. 'Eh?'

'The teeth,' Libo grunted. 'It's cold, aye, but you don't hear my teeth chattering, do you?'

'Cos you've hardly got any, sir,' a voice said from behind.

Libo's head swung round, good eye wide with fury. All of the legionaries – young ones and old hands – were blue in the face and shivering in the perishing wind, but the cheeky comment from the unknown speaker had them all stifling laughter. Libo's lips rose at one edge, and he let it go.

He faced forward again, and watched the swaying, mounted Tribunus Zeno, seemingly unaffected by the cold.

'When we next stop to eat we'll probably find he's been dead for the last six miles,' Rectus chuckled. Balbina the mule nickered as if amused by the dry joke.

A few hundred strides later, they heard the drumming of hooves. Libo, Pulcher, Opis and Rectus shared a knowing, steely look, all aware that there were no other Roman soldiers or riders in these parts. Each of them unconsciously let their sword hand edge towards their scabbard.

But then a herd of riderless horses burst across the hills – powerful sorrel-coloured beasts. There was just one man, riding the rearmost steed. A Goth, wearing a red woollen tunic, his golden hair in a tight topknot, the tail flicking and swishing in the wake of the ride as he shouted jagged commands to bring the herd round in tight turns. The man slowed a little when he spotted the Romans, but only for a moment before he carried on with his duties, cantering off, snow flicking up in his wake.

This is a new age of peace, Libo recited Zeno's proclamation as he and the others sagged in relief. They moved onwards until they came across a tract of flat land pricked with timber posts and twines, marking out huge new crop fields to be sown for the spring. At the end of these fields stretched snow-blanketed pasture meadows and a long line of barns. The lowing of cows, the bleating of goats and clucking of chickens rose from within. Gothic women and children peered out from those shelters, holding half-full milk urns and baskets of eggs, looks of curiosity on their faces as they beheld the legionaries.

Finally, the puffing, panting, sniffing, shivering and chattering of the Claudia men ebbed as they came past the *Haim* of Munderic. This – one of the most southerly of the Gothic settlements – was huge, as big as the palace ward of Constantinople and growing, unwalled but nestled within a crescent of low grey bluffs lined with conifers. A halo of grubby tents formed an outer district of sorts, where men and women wandered to and fro in the bitter wind and swirling snow, carrying freshly-sawn timbers and buckets while others knelt over benches hammering and chiselling. Teams pulled on ropes and hoisted wooden pillars that were taking shape as the skeletons of new barns and huts. Within this outer ring sat a smaller circle of recently-completed stallhouses, the wattle and daub walls gleaming white and the roofs thatched and bearing openings from which smoke plumes puffed out into the sky. But it was the centre of the place that was most eye-catching of all, for something new had been erected since their last time past here: a citadel of sorts, ringed with a wall of sharpened stakes – not in the style of a camp palisade but higher and stronger, with many thick trunks strapped together. Built to last. Timber towers rose every forty paces or so along the length of the stake-wall, with a larger one either side of the single gatehouse. Guardsmen in long blue cloaks, wearing visored iron helms paced on the platforms up there – with slow, steady steps and keen-eyes. Gothic elite guards, Libo realised. He could see little of what lay inside this fortified centre, apart from the high thatched roofs of a colossal hall.

'Munderic's hall?' Pulcher mused.

'I'd say so,' Libo replied. 'Looks a little too much like a *king's* hall for my liking.'

'They can have their tribal chieftains,' Rectus argued, 'as long as they leave it at that.'

Libo and Pulcher grunted in agreement at this. The war had stolen untold lives, Roman and Gothic, amongst them *Iudex* Fritigern, Master of the Horde and in Roman eyes, King of the Goths. Even those of his kin who had murdered and usurped him had fallen in battle. The terms of the peace deal had clearly demanded that no Goth should seek to resurrect that post or attempt to unite the settled tribes again. Indeed, the highest-ranking tribesmen had even buried Fritigern's royal battle helmet as a show of good faith.

The marching legionaries skirted so close to the *haim* that the Gothic teams working on the new buildings stopped and stared. Dogs barked, children pointed and shouted in fear and excitement. But amongst them were darker-haired and darker-skinned peoples. Romans. Some were living here, while others were visiting from outlying farms – like the man and his sons who rode in on a wagon heaped with felled timber to trade. The sight warmed Libo's frozen body like a roaring fire. The first signs of integration. The peace *was* working.

'All we went through… it was worth it,' Pulcher said with a rarely-heard gentleness.

'Ha! I never thought I'd see the day,' Rectus chuckled, nodding towards the narrow, sheltered gap between two stallhouses where a tall Roman boy stood pressed against a young Gothic woman, just a little older than him. The pair were locked in each other's arms, the boy kissing her neck, her eyes closed as she whispered in his ear.

They were just about to pass by the *haim* when the glacial wind picked up to new heights, and then hail came battering down upon the Claudians. It was heavy at first, then it redefined the meaning of heavy.

'What price mercy, Jove?' squawked Betto, one of Pulcher's young charges, prematurely bald and with a delicate, sculpted face, always eager to show off his glittering vocabulary. 'Thy hibernal squall does cut deeper than the keenest blade.'

'What?' Libo and Pulcher grunted in unison, hunched against the sudden icy storm.

'I think he m-means that,' Durio chattered, 'that it's bloody c-c-c-cooold.'

The hail grew ferocious, stinging, the chunks as big as sling pellets. 'Mithrasss!' Indus wailed.

'Sir,' Libo called ahead. 'This is brutal. And the light's fading. I know we're not supposed to impose on the Gothic villages, but perhaps we could take billet here?'

Zeno twisted in his saddle, hail bouncing crazily from his armour. He beheld Libo and the men for a moment, then the town of Munderic, then tilted his head a little to the left. Finally, he cocked an eyebrow. 'Aye,' he conceded. 'Hot meals and dry, warm beds. Fall out.'

The hail hammered down upon the longhouse tavern roof, ice-particles smashing down relentlessly near the threshold. Libo and Pulcher cradled their cups of barley beer lovingly, enjoying the heat from the roaring fire as it gradually dried their damp hair and tunics. They had dropped their armour and weapons at the billet house given to them by the Gothic guards and now they basked in a rising wooziness from the drink and a sense of contentment from the meal of bread and warm, fatty venison stew they had just devoured. Goths spoke in jagged tones all around them, seated along the timber benches, laughing, slapping the tables and in the main caring little about the Romans in their midst. A dozen other Claudians sat at an adjacent table, telling bawdy tales, each one wilder and wilder until men were spraying drink from their lips, doubled over, broken with laughter. Tribunus Zeno was with them too, Libo noted with interest.

He and Pulcher listened in as Indus told a tale of a Rhodian shepherd who had no wife yet one day it was discovered that he had children. More, the children had fleece instead of hair and ate nothing but grass. The others mocked the tale playfully, then all eyes shifted to the legionary next to him: Betto was wont to spend his moments of free time either playing his flute or reading the bag of scrolls he carried with him like a treasure – copies of the great plays and poems. He rather overreached by reciting a passage from Horatius' Satires, only to be met with blank expressions from his comrades who were primed for some tale of sexual or latrine-based depravity. Undeterred, Betto rolled his syllables and gesticulated like an orator, before noticing that a sizeable group of those around the table had spotted a striped insect and were now, making a 'hurdle' out of empty cups and trying to entice the creature to jump over it. With a disgusted sigh and a swish of one hand, Betto gave up, tucked his scroll away and muttered something about Philistines. A few more tales of a more fitting and vulgar nature followed as each man took their turn. Zeno seemed a little awkward, chuckling now and then but still not at ease around his new charges.

He's trying, Libo thought, *but he's not Pavo*. How many leaders had he marched under throughout his years, he wondered? None had been as selfless or inspirational as Pavo. Sura too – unhinged but vital. Courage in a shell of skin and bone!

'What d'you make of him?' Pulcher said, his face flushed around the cheeks from the beer.

'Zeno? He's a bit green – not sure how much of the war he actually saw, or if he's been in much real combat. But he's learning with every day he spends with us.'

'Aye,' Pulcher snorted. 'Learning to stay upwind of you after meal time.

Libo rocked with a canine grunt of amusement, proud of his own legendary reputation for stench.

'I should have taken the opportunity to speak to the lads of the X Gemina, before we left Constantinople,' Pulcher said, gulping down the rest of his beer and signalling to a buxom Gothic maid for another.

'The Gemina?' Libo said, thinking of the legion stationed near the Golden Gate guard house back in the capital. 'Why?'

Pulcher's face crumpled in slight annoyance at having to explain. 'Well, Zeno came from their ranks.'

Libo frowned for a moment. He had spoken with a few soldiers and messengers on the day Zeno had arrived at the Neorion Barracks to assume command. Much to-ing and fro-ing, lots of babbling, not a lot of sense. 'I thought he was from the Flavia Felix?'

'Eh?' Pulcher scowled, then he pinged the side of Libo's cup and chuckled. 'You've had too much of that stuff.'

'I'll be the judge of that,' Libo spluttered, raising a hand to attract the maid's attention.

The thunder of hail changed slightly then, growing into a splash of hooves. Libo lowered his hand. He and Pulcher looked towards the tavern doorway. Blaring, excited voices sounded as Goths emerged from adjacent houses to stand in the porches and watch some procession coming down the street.

'Topless Gothic women on horseback?' Pulcher guessed, absurdly.

The image had Libo entranced for a moment, then he shook his head and batted Pulcher on the arm, rising. 'I doubt it, but let's check – just in case.'

They staggered over to the tavern doorway with a few dozen Goths, all with their drinks in hand. Libo looked up the narrow street – a winding lane of semi-frozen mud and mushy hail. A lone horseman came charging down from the fortified town centre, his red leather vest gleaming wet with half-melted hail. The black mare he was riding thrashed and whinnied as if it was struggling… and then Libo saw why.

A taut rope extended from the rear of the saddle, the other end bound around one ankle of a naked man, who roared and gasped as he sliced through the mess of mud and hail like a blunt harrow.

'Gods,' Pulcher gasped, seeing the streaks of the man's blood staining the lying hail. 'Is this what they do for entertainment?'

When the man was dragged at high speed over a lump of exposed bedrock, a stark *crack* of bone rang out.

'What did the poor bastard do?' Libo winced.

'I love her,' the man cried.

Libo heard the words, then realised they were conspicuous for some reason… spoken in perfect Greek. The Roman lad from earlier. 'Mithras, no…'

The horseman circled a few times near the tavern before stopping. The many Goths watching on from their sheltered doorways carried on braying and cheering, while the tall Roman boy spasmed, weeping. His thighbone was poking from his leg at a horrible angle.

'Irma,' he cried, reaching out blindly in a direction whence he had been dragged.

With a splashing of feet, the young Gothic woman with whom he had shared a tryst earlier that day came running, the hems of her long brown robes filthy with dirt, the rest soaked through. 'Cassian!'

Two red-vested Gothic spearmen stepped out to catch her by a shoulder each.

The horseman slid from his saddle and drew his longsword, slicing the rope. Another pair of Gothic soldiers – this time wearing salvaged Roman ringmail – hurried over and hoisted the boy up. The boy cried horrifically as his ruined leg twisted and dangled.

'Set him down,' a new voice cried from the direction of the billet house.

Libo and Pulcher's heads shot up. Rectus was there, blinking from sleep and dressed only in his tunic, Balbina the mule by his side. Zeno stepped out from the tavern and towards the lad too, face etched with concern, his helmetless head soaked and his dark hair hanging to his brow in points. Scores more Claudians emerged into the freezing hail – some from the tavern, some from their billets, all shivering, staring, confused.

'Set him down,' Rectus said again, he and the tribunus striding closer. 'I'm a medicus.'

The two Goths holding the Roman lad looked at Rectus, then at one another, smirked, and dragged the boy away, towards a dead oak. The pair took the end of the cut rope trailing from the ankle of his broken leg and threw it up over a branch. In unison, they heaved. The boy was torn from his feet and dragged upside down by his shattered limb. His screams were animal-like, his free leg kicking uselessly as the two tied the rope to a stump to suspend him there.

'Cassian!' the Gothic girl wailed, struggling in the grip of the two who held her.

'What are you doing?' Libo cried at the Goths, striding out into the hail, tossing his beer away. Pulcher strode through the tempest with him, fists balled.

A *shush* of steel halted both of them.

Libo looked down to see the longswords that had swung out like barriers before each of their necks. He rolled his eyes left and right, seeing two of the visor-helmed ones there. The elite guards from the citadel, Libo realised.

'Don't tell me you've forgotten already,' said a new voice. A corpulent Goth draped in Roman scale and a golden cloak. His flat face was marked with cruel eyes, a thick red moustache and framed by long, flowing hair. His teeth were stained with wine. He walked with his thumbs tucked into his swordbelt, examining Libo and Pulcher as if they were rogues.

'Reiks Munderic,' Libo said. He threw out a hand, gesturing towards the Roman lad – now vomiting and spasming. 'What is this? What has the boy done?'

Munderic's glare hardened. 'He has spat on the very treaty our peoples agreed not two months past.'

Libo didn't understand, until he heard the Gothic girl's sobs. He thought of their tryst earlier that day, and his eyelids rolled down. 'Oh, shit…'

'Your negotiators stated that there must be no *conubium*,' said Munderic. 'No carnal relations or intermarriage between Gothic and Roman subjects.'

'But… but this is different?' Pulcher reasoned.

'Is it? Is it not simply the laws we agreed upon being followed in full?' Munderic smiled triumphantly.

Libo and Pulcher both groaned. The clause had been added to the peace treaty because some thought that Romans were too good to breed with Goths. It had been crafted with the intent of punishing Goths who broke this rule, without ever being explicit enough to protect a Roman involved in such a dalliance.

'Language is a slippery beast, is it not?' Munderic smiled, then flicked one finger.

It happened so carefully and with so little thought for the dangling lad's life. The Goth standing beside him drew his blade and sliced it across the young man's belly. First a sheet of red soaked the lad from his chest to his face, then an awful tangle of grey-blue gut ropes slipped from the wound, slick with a pearlescent fluid, tumbling to hang like awful garlands. He shuddered a final few times before he breathed his last. At the same time, the Gothic girl screamed as a spear burst through her breastbone like the finger of an escaping demon. Her scream fragmented into animal croaks as she swayed and then slapped, face-forward, into the freezing slush.

'You wish to make an issue of this?' Munderic challenged the small Roman party, facing them with his feet wide apart, hands now clasped across his thick leather belt, his elite guards and murderous sentries gathering behind him. 'You contest the treaty?'

A silence built, before Zeno replied. 'I appreciate your hospitality, and recognise your authority here. Most of all, I respect the peace treaty.' His voice was even and measured.

Libo turned a black look on the Tribunus. Crawling to a murderer?

But Zeno then squared his shoulders in the same commanding way as Munderic, before edging over to stand almost nose-to-nose with the reiks, as if his elite tribal guards were nothing. He was a good hand's width taller than Munderic too. 'But that treaty was written to allow you and your people to be part of the empire. Part of my world. And in this world we do not drag young lovers out through the night and slaughter them... like *cattle*,' he spat, meltwater spooling from the end of his hate-wrinkled nose. 'All have a right to a trial, to have their case heard. If they are found guilty then they shall be punished as such. This?' he stabbed a finger in the direction of the two corpses. 'This was murder, and you will answer for it in an imperial court.'

Libo's top lip rose in an appreciative dog-like growl. With that action, Zeno became something golden. A true leader, fearless, selfless. A worthy heir to Pavo and to that iron eagle, Gallus, who went before.

Munderic's cheek twitched and his eyes betrayed a cold fear, before he stepped back from Zeno with a contrived scoff. 'Well... I will wait for the next passing legion to take me to trial,' he said, grinning as he swung his gaze around the many onlookers, who rose in uproarious laughter at the notion of a replete Roman regiment in these parts. 'Unless your paltry band would like to try to put me in chains and drag me south, all the way to Constantinople?'

The word *try* was a clear threat, read by the elite tribal guards, who edged into a semi-circle like a hand about to clamp shut on Zeno.

Libo saw the two flanking the tribunus edging their hands slowly down their lance hafts – a classic tell of a spearman on the brink of striking. His stomach twisted like a sack of snakes, realising that he and Pulcher had no weapons, seeing the other woken Claudians mixed amongst the many Gothic watchers, equally unarmed and confused. This would be a slaughter – and one that would suit Munderic perfectly. The Claudia would be butchered and his crime would be buried with them. 'Sir,' he said. 'Perhaps... perhaps we should be moving on.'

Munderic smiled triumphantly at Zeno, flicking up both eyebrows. 'Listen to the one-eyed, ugly dog. Go...'

They marched from the *Haim* of Munderic in the freezing darkness of night, the men to the rear keeping a close watch in case Munderic should send out a party to follow and fall upon them. but no such attack came. Instead, the elements were their enemies. The hail stopped but the cutting winter wind sliced through their damp clothes and chilled them to their marrow. None spoke for those hours of darkness, all exhausted and troubled by what they had seen. Libo thought again and again of the dead lovers, of the soaring tension, and hated himself for having been the first to stand down.

'It's not easy,' a voice spoke beside him. Zeno was scowling straight ahead as he spoke, swaying on his mount. 'When the heart thunders and the blood runs hot. When another is jeering and spitting on everything you believe in. To have the coolness of mind to step back, that is the mark of a good officer. I can see now why your old tribunus valued you so highly as to put you in charge of the First Cohort.'

Libo – never the best at accepting compliments – grunted, shrugged and hitched his crotch for good measure.

'Gods,' Zeno scoffed at himself, 'I am your new leader and I almost forgot myself back there. I was willing for the fight! One man with no weapon, ready to take on a village of vindictive Goths.'

'You wouldn't have been alone,' Libo rumbled. 'Had it come to it, then me, Pulcher – all of us – would have fought with our fists and our feet, with whatever we could use. That's what being a Claudian means. We are unbreakable. We weather hardship and loss together.'

'Loss,' Zeno repeated with a sad smile, 'is it not the cruellest of torments?'

Libo recognised the tribunus' distant stare. The war had stolen many loved ones. 'Who... who did you lose?'

Zeno took a moment to compose himself. 'My father,' he said, his voice thick with emotion.

Libo sucked in a breath and sighed. 'Nobody can replace a man's father... but this ironclad band walking with you, they are now your brothers.'

Zeno's smile changed, the sadness fading. He swirled a hand overhead and boomed to his charges: 'Onwards!'

Chapter 3
December 382 AD
Ctesiphon

A month passed, each day of which felt like a year. Every night since arriving, a round of talks had taken place. 'Talks' was very much a loose term – for in reality every session had been an overblown feast, with a few verses of overly-poetic rhetoric exchanged, and absolutely nothing decided. On the thirty-third night, Pavo and Sura waited in their quarters in the White Palace's cellars – a bare and simple vaulted stone chamber. Both wore just their legionary tunics and boots – foreign visitors were not permitted to wear weapons or armour in the Shahanshah's home. From the doorway, the sound of descending footsteps echoed. Two of the escort legionaries – Porcus and Clodus – trooped in, weary-eyed and clutching their lower backs, sore from standing.

'Oi, Urbicus, Mucianus… your turn,' Porcus muttered to Pavo and Sura, jabbing a thumb over his shoulder in the direction of the doorway and the stairs, before flopping face down on his shabby box bed and snoring violently.

With a shared sigh, Pavo and Sura left the chamber and climbed three flights of increasingly grand steps. The last set was fashioned from marble, as wide as a street. The high walls were adorned with stucco reliefs of hunting scenes and Persian legends, the grandest of all being a giant emblem of a broad-winged and soaring guardian angel, half eagle, half man; this was the *Faravahar*, the sacred image of the Zoroastrian faith. The huge doorway at the top of the stairs was flanked by two statues of prowling griffins, tongues extended as if tasting the air for nearby prey. Even more disconcerting was the masked pushtigban pair standing guard, one beside each statue like griffin-keepers.

The sound of flutes and laughter and the frequent splashes of rich wine being poured tumbled from the doorway and down the stairs, washing over them as they ascended. Sura sniffed the air, basking in the aromas of freshly-baked flatbread and pistachio-topped honey cakes, roasting meats spiced with sumac and saffron. However, the truth was he and Pavo would get none of this. A bowl of weakly-spiced soldier stew seemed to be the staple for the palace guards and for the visiting legionaries. 'Ah, what I'd give to sit at one of the feasting tables,' Sura grumbled. 'And I've forgotten what it even feels like to be drunk.'

'But the Halls of Ctesiphon,' Pavo said in a weak impression of Sura, 'feasting and wine, girls, dancing – *every* night.'

Sura shot him a sour look. 'Well it's true… just not for us.'

They entered the circular hall, moving in behind the broad crescent of tables. There sat Persian Satraps – each a lord of one of the Sassanid Empire's many regions – along with noblemen and less-than-noble men, courtiers, military officers and officials, all facing the dais at the hall's far end. Just before the dais, a fat, wheezing old Persian orator waddled slowly in tight circles in the centre of the floor, spitting and blowing his way through an ancient Zoroastrian poem, stroking his waist-length beard as he spoke as if it was a pet. Cheering and laughter greeted his every inflection. Flanking the dais, two tongues of flame licked at the air, rising from gemmed, gilt sconces held by dark-robed *magi*, the holy men of the Sassanid realm. Between them and in the centre of the dais itself sat Shapur III, King of Kings, seated upon a golden throne from the back of which sprouted a splendorous fan of peacock feathers. For a crown he wore a tall puffed-out purple hat, the brow fashioned from gold and studded with a dark-red gemstone on the forehead. He was dark skinned and blue-eyed. Not young, as Pavo had assumed he might be given that he was a new king; fifty, perhaps – his thick, curled mane and magnificent, oiled beard were both silver, trailing over his broad shoulders and down his jasper-coloured silk robe. He wore a few golden rings upon his fingers, and finely-made soft calfskin slippers. Knots of advisors hovered either side of his throne.

As they had learned to do in this last month, Pavo and Sura quietly parted and moved over to the positions in the hall they had been shown on that first day. Each stood by a stone pillar, near enough to the table where Sporacius, Stilicho and Ripanus sat that they could assist them if required, but not so close that they would block anyone else's view of the orator's endless fable.

Pavo watched Shapur's reactions to the poetry. His teeth and eyes shone in the sconce-light of the hall every time he laughed or cheered along with the others. But every so often, he noticed how the King of Kings glanced at some of his charges, as if gauging their reactions. In his opening address over a moon past, Shapur had talked of strange things – of what a man should do when he finds his right arm is hopelessly infected. Cut it off, of course! Some interpreted this as a thinly-disguised threat to some of his nobles whom he viewed as potential usurpers.

At long, long last, the orator's recital ended, and he bowed and accepted praise from every direction, prostrated himself fully on the dais steps, before backing away with exaggerated humility into the shadows.

'And now,' said one of the advisors, the flute music falling silent, 'we return to the matter… of the great friendship.'

Pavo scarcely even registered the comment. This was how they had termed the talks between the Roman embassy and Shapur on that first night. Then, Pavo had felt a great spike of tension and hope. A true friendship between Rome and Persia would be a monumental thing. Instead, Ambassador Sporacius had been allowed merely to introduce himself and lie prone on the steps, before a band of acrobats was brought in and began leaping, spinning and jigging the rest of the night away. Every night since, the discussions had proceeded infinitesimally, like the painfully gradual erosion of sea cliffs. Pavo was certain that Shapur's beard had grown a foot in the time they had been here.

To utter silence, Ambassador Sporacius stood, prostrated himself on the steps, then rose again. 'Six years ago,' he began, 'the then-King of Persia agreed to a peace between our two great empires. But a border was never defined. Yet was it not the *Gods* of our two lands who first sent the Euphrates cascading down from the north? A *natural* boundary that river has been for many centuries. This is the key to the peace, King of Kings. We must formalise the border agreement.'

Shapur's advisors whispered in his ears. The Shahanshah nodded slowly at each one's input. He lazily drummed his ringed fingers on the arm of the throne before responding. 'I understand Rome's anxiety to clarify our border arrangements. For I hear you have suffered a terrible defeat in your faraway lands. The Goths, they destroyed the eagles, did they not? Before roving across your lands, burning, looting, taking it all as their own?'

In unison, Pavo and Sura bristled.

Sporacius, skilled in controlling his reactions, merely bowed his head in agreement. 'It was a lesson hard-learned, Majesty. Indeed, the Goths dealt us a severe blow. But since, we have tamed them, found an agreement.'

Shapur's beard lifted as he grinned broadly. 'Agreement? With the wild men of the woods and hills? It must have been strange, to endure such disgrace.'

The Persian Satraps and nobles rose in a low chorus of amusement. Shapur basked in the moment.

'Yet that is how it had to be, Majesty,' Sporacius replied. 'For true darkness lies to the north.'

Shapur's smile faded, so too did the laughter.

'A darkness that stretches above your realm too, like a cloud,' Sporacius continued. He stepped to one side and gestured to the Roman table. 'General Stilicho.'

Stilicho rose and strode onto the floor as if he owned this hall. But, as decorum demanded, he sank to the floor before the King of Kings as Sporacius had done. When he rose, he clasped his hands behind his back and began strolling slowly in a wide circle. 'Seven years ago, we Romans thought of Persia as the only true threat. Likewise, Rome was a bane for you. Now, we know that we each need the other realm as an ally. We can survive only if we strike peace. For we both know of the strange race that rides the northern steppe like a rolling thunder. The Huns are numberless, peerless in their way of war, lethal... inexorable. It was they who drove the Goths into Roman lands. Soon, they will press upon our imperial river borders themselves. Soon too, they will pour south through the Caspian Gates and into *your* northern satrapies.'

Shapur shuffled on his throne.

Stilicho paused, noticing the Persian ruler's discomfort. 'It has happened already, hasn't it?' There was not a jot of triumph in his tone.

Shapur said nothing.

'I will not play games with false questions. We received news of the Hun invasion here,' Stilicho confessed. 'You sent a strong force to meet them.'

Shapur's continued silence was as good as a confirmation.

'A strong force indeed – a wing of your mighty *Savaran*… ' Stilicho continued. 'But how many of them came back?'

Shapur tapped his hand on the throne arm in irritation as the audience whispered the answer. Finally, he slapped his hand on the arm. 'The Huns tricked and slaughtered my force. Three of my cousins died to their cursed blades and arrows. Does it please you to hear me admit that?'

'Not at all, Majesty,' Stilicho said firmly. 'I pray it was swift for them. Just as I pray that we do not ignore the Hun threat.'

'The Huns butchered my men but then they turned around and roved northwards again, back through the Caspian Gates,' Shapur railed. 'They are gone. What is your point, Roman?'

Stilicho spread his hands, like a man showing he bore no weapons. 'They chase the fertile grazing grounds that come and go with summer and winter, to keep their immense herds strong. They may be gone for now, but they *will* return as the seasons guide them.'

A blaring discontent rose around the hall. The military men standing by the throne hissed and moved jerkily, clearly telling their ruler to ignore Stilicho. But Stilicho went on, undaunted.

'Should the Huns come in their full number – something neither Persia nor Rome has yet had to deal with… then your northern regions will fall. Next, they will pour south to Ctesiphon itself.' Animated now, he stabbed a finger to the arched windows and the starry night sky beyond. Sentries walked the city walls, the battlements mere pin-pricks of torchlight. 'This is my first visit to your royal city, Majesty, and when

I set eyes upon your mighty walls, I was in awe. But when the Huns come, fine walls will not stop them. You will need every man you have to face the north, and no distractions on your borders with Rome. These overtures of formal peace might save your realm...'

The babble exploded into hot shouts of outrage and a few of concern too. Pavo and Sura shared a glance, both impressed by Stilicho's poise and presence in this cauldron of foreign dignitaries.

'Peace, Majesty,' Stilicho reiterated above the clamour, 'it is the only way.'

Pavo saw Shapur's eyes glaze over, as if he was lost within himself, blessedly detached from the nay-saying of his courtiers. When he looked up again, it was at Stilicho, and his lips seemed to be on the verge of agreement. Until...

'But the terms of peace must be chosen carefully,' Sporacius added, stepping over beside Stilicho. 'As it stands, you lay claim to the lion's share of Armenia. It would only be right that the balance is redressed.'

Stilicho recoiled from the ambassador and then whispered frantically in his ear. The battle of wills between the two was still in progress, apparently.

Shapur stared stormily at the ambassador. 'You come here in a position of weakness and ask that I yield entire countries to you?'

'Agreement must come in a form that leaves our empire and yours equal, balanced,' Sporacius reasoned. 'To avoid future disgruntlement.'

A long silence passed, ending when Shapur slapped both hands on the arms of his throne. 'Pah!' he cried. 'Enough of this drivel for tonight. Bring in the wrestlers.'

With a clap of some courtier's hands, the flute music rose again along with a thick clamour of debate and laughter. A troop of seven men in loincloths, dripping with oil, barged Sporacius and Stilicho back off the floor and set about mangling each other.

Stilicho and Sporacius slumped down again at the Roman table. Then something happened that had not occurred in all their days here: Stilicho cast a look over his shoulder and beckoned Pavo and Sura. Pavo and Sura shared a look, then edgily approached. Pavo furtively eyed Ripanus as he sat quietly opposite him. The trierarchus was busy examining his fingernails. He had been little more than a shadow since their arrival in the city. Silent... but ever-present.

A glugging of liquid sounded, snapping Pavo from his thoughts. 'Drink, Urbicus, you deserve it,' Stilicho said, filling a copper cup to the brim with wine and shoving it to Pavo. 'You too, Mucianus,' he added, filling another for Sura. Sura's face lit up like a child who has seen snow for the first time, and he took one deep, long draught that half-emptied his cup, plonking it down again with a relieved sigh.

Pavo took a mouthful of his and in truth it was like an elixir, hot and musky, like a forgotten dream. He looked over to Stilicho, who was wringing his hands through his thick curls. 'You were so close,' he offered.

Stilicho looked up, eyes red-rimmed with weariness. 'Eh? Aye,' he sighed. 'They said to me these negotiations would be easy because "Persians do not lie".' He lowered his voice so only the ambassadorial party would hear. 'And they don't... but by Jove, they love to procrastinate!'

All around the table masked low chuckles, except Sporacius, whose back was turned to watch the wrestlers. Yet Stilicho's humour was fleeting, his face souring as he glared at Sporacius' back. 'I fear these negotiations will drag on for many months more. Years even. It took us this full month just to tease them into hearing our proposal in full... and then...' he said no more, catching the angry words on his tongue behind a wall of teeth.

Sporacius twisted his head to peer back over his shoulder. 'We were tasked with securing a strong deal,' he snapped. 'Not biting the first scrap that was thrown to the floor.'

Stilicho's teeth ground audibly.

Sporacius sighed and turned around in full to face Stilicho. He placed a hand on the general's broad shoulders. 'You spoke well,' he said in a far more sympathetic voice, 'but you have much to learn.'

Stilicho smiled tightly – anger caged behind his lips – then filled his cup again and Pavo's too.

Pavo took another deep gulp of wine, feeling his body soften and his mind slow. Such a long time since he had last shared wine or beer with his Claudia comrades. He thought of them once more, longing to believe that they were being treated as heroes should. *To be back home,* he thought, *home in sweet Thracia with my legion. An impossible dream.* He stared into the surface of his wine for a time, and the notion of dreams made him think of the crone and that odd eagle dream that had peppered his nights here. A great war lay on the empire's horizon, and for once, Pavo would be absent. But then a thought struck him: what if this – right here and now – was the first sparks of it all? What if the two eagles represented Rome and Persia? If these talks failed, might it trigger outright aggression between the two superpowers? He thought of Izodora's warning about the potential saboteur within the ambassadorial party. His mind began to spin and twist until he finished his wine and found himself staring into the bottom of the empty cup. A hand stretched out to tilt the urn and fill it again. He looked up to thank Stilicho... but saw that it was not Stilicho holding the urn.

Ripanus smiled. 'Drink. As General Stilicho says: you've earned it.'

Pavo returned the smile, taking a sip.

Ripanus' eyes never left him. 'I never saw it in you... Urbicus.'

'I don't understand?' Pavo said.

'All the way from Thracia on my ship, you two were quiet as mice,' Ripanus flicked a finger from Pavo, to Sura and back again. 'But on the way here when we were ambushed, you were like lions.'

Pavo took another sip of his wine.

'Leaders of men,' Ripanus added with a glint in his eye. He chapped the table twice absently and leaned forward a fraction. 'Forgive me for I have forgotten, but... what regiments did we pick you up from?'

Pavo stared into the man's pit-like eyes. He felt his heart pounding, but drew on the lessons of his years in the military to let the silence swell. Sometimes it was best to say nothing, to test the other's confidence.

At last, Ripanus blinked. His top lip twitched and he leaned back. 'Ah, I remember now,' he wagged a finger at Sura, 'The Thracian coastal watch, wasn't it?' he grinned.

Pavo tilted his head forward a fraction in feigned respect. 'Sign of a good officer if he can remember the names of soldiers, sir. Sign of an even better one if he knows their backgrounds.' He stood, patting Sura on the shoulder. 'Come, Mucianus, we should take our places at the side of the hall again.'

As they rose and left, Ripanus' eyes tracked their every step.

Chapter 4
January 383 AD
Thracia

The Claudia men moved through a dense mantle of fog, eastwards along an old countryside track. The air was thick with a musty petrichor and the late morning sun was but a pale silvery smudge. There was no singing, no proud and clattering march. Instead they went like thieves, spears held ready, shields clutched tightly.

Libo cycled mentally over their impromptu briefing – brought to them at dawn by a man who had staggered into their camp, his body blistered and weeping with recent burns. He was a Roman, and had fled the town of Deultum near the *Pontus Euxinus*. He told of some dispute between the Roman Governor and a Gothic Reiks named Ingolf – a belligerent chieftain Libo recalled from the Dionysopolis battle and the peace talks. The Roman Governor was lord of Deultum before the peace but Reiks Ingolf now claimed he was entitled to oversee it as his tribal *haim*, in light of the treaty. The Goths had seized the governor and his staff, and now they were holding them hostage, demanding that Ingolf's case be heard. The wretch had died moments after delivering the news.

'I knew it was only a matter of time,' Opis grumbled, face and helm beaded with moisture from the fog.

'We give them farms and don't even ask them to pay taxes and how do they repay us?' Datus agreed, his jug-ears hot with anger.

'What does Reiks Ingolf call himself now,' Indus asked. 'The Burner, isn't it?'

'He was always an arsehole,' Pulcher mused, eyeing his speartip. 'Perhaps it's time we ripped him a new one.'

Libo, leading, cast a look back over his shoulder. 'Think of the peace, and compare it to how it was before. Think of all we and our fallen comrades did to bring the war to an end. No matter what happens today, the peace *must* remain.'

Pulcher and Opis muttered in grudging agreement. Zeno, moving near Libo's side, was oddly silent. He had expected the tribunus to be the one to call for calm and perspective, but the man was gazing into the thick mist with a distant stare. 'That's what we're here today to do, sir, aye? To uphold the peace. To show that the war is indeed over.' He hesitated before adding. 'To show that your father, like so many others, did not die in vain.'

This snapped Zeno from his trance. For a moment he looked boyish, timid, eyes searching Libo's face. 'Peace is a golden thing. But how... how does one learn to live with it – the knowledge that those who killed one's closest walk free?'

Libo's eyes narrowed, confused.

'They will pay, Centurion,' Zeno continued, staring ahead. 'They may think they have escaped punishment but they *will* pay.'

They? Libo wondered. *Ingolf and his men?* He searched for the right way to phrase a reply, when a smell hit him. Like a hound, he tilted his head a little and sniffed the air. A salty tang. More, somewhere beyond the shroud of fog he heard the squabble of gulls and the distant wash of waves curling onto a shore. 'That's the sound of the sea,' he whispered to Zeno and to the men behind, the message being relayed down the small column. 'We don't want to get too close to the coast – this fog is our friend.'

He peeled left, heading north off of the countryside track, leading the legion across a heath of pitted, awkward ground and then onto a fen of grass and shallow pools. The mantle of fog thickened as they went. After a time, a shape emerged from the grey. A town. Thick, squat walls, from which jutted the bare poles where once purple imperial banners had fluttered. The stonework was in the early stages of disrepair, listing in places, the mortar sprouting with weeds. A glow of fire rose from within.

Silently, the small legionary band halted, crouching in the grass.

'This is it?' Zeno asked.

'Aye, Deultum,' Pulcher whispered.

'What happened to this place?' Zeno asked.

Rectus, sagging between them, muttered absently: 'The war...'

Libo's good eye scanned the dilapidated town. 'I once bathed in the hot springs in there and drank wine with fellow veterans.'

Pulcher eyed Libo askance. 'You once bathed?'

Libo scowled at him.

They edged closer to see outlines of men patrolling the mist-dampened walls. Gothic spearmen, tall, fair and vigilant. The walkway above the city's southern gatehouse was thickly patrolled and the gates lay closed. But from beyond, terrible sounds rose. Screaming. Along with the crackling of flames.

Zeno glanced over his one hundred and sixty seven charges, then at the well-guarded defences, then at his men once more. His eyes did not shine with confidence.

Libo already knew they had not the numbers to intimidate the Goths or to break into the town. He thought back over his years serving under Pavo, and remembered how his previous tribunus had handled situations like this with nerves of steel. He glanced up at the dense bank of fog hanging over the town. 'Sir, I have a plan,' he said at last, his stomach knotting and twisting like rope.

The small hatch in the city gate creaked open and the silhouetted Gothic sentry beckoned the six unarmoured Romans in while keeping them at spearpoint. Libo, Pulcher and Opis entered first, Betto, Trypho, and Datus following. They found themselves ringed by a dozen more red-vested, long-haired spearmen, each with their lances held like the first. While three of the tribesmen searched them for weapons, the one who had let them in leaned out of the hatch gate to scan the countryside.

'We are alone,' Libo lied. 'Here simply to sort out this dispute.'

The Goth scowled distrustfully at Libo and shouted something in the Gothic tongue to a man up on the gatehouse. The man shouted back down in an amalgam of Greek and Gothic. 'The heath is deserted... as far as I can see.'

'Rouse another score of Chosen Archers from the guardhouse, just in case,' the first replied.

A troop of red-vested tribal bowmen flitted out from one of the gatehouse towers and took their places at the merlons along the southern wall.

The Goth turned back to them then looked them up and down. 'Ingolf will be delighted to see you,' he said in a mocking twang. The troop of Goths marched Libo and his small party through the streets. Houses that had during the war lost their roofs to fires and neglect had been repaired with Gothic-style thatching. Tribal families sat around near the open doors to what had once been Roman homes, watching with suspicious eyes as the small group of imperial men passed them. Nearby a Gothic woman suckled a baby, holding the tot a little closer to her person as if afraid the six Romans might snatch it away.

Libo eyed the great city bathhouse, at first fondly recalling the ribald jokes and camaraderie he had enjoyed whilst sitting in the natural pools inside, then sighing when he saw the six domes of the roof, broken and caved in like the skulls one sometimes passed on a long-forgotten battlefield.

All thoughts vanished, however, when they rounded the bathhouse and came to the odeum, a rising amphitheatre of red-speckled marble, packed with an audience of Goths, drinking, eating and cheering. Their attentions were on the huge pyre which roared on the theatre's floor. At the odeum's open end, an arc of standing spectators watched the blaze likewise.

'To think that great orators would once have preached here to a rapt audience,' Betto grumbled. 'The plays of Terentius. The verse of Ovidius.'

Libo shot the young legionary a *shut-the-fuck-up* look as the escorting Gothic spearmen edged through the circle of spectators. Once inside the watching throng, his gaze fell upon the guts of the fire and the telltale black shape of a charred body in there, curled up like a man trying to shelter from the elements, encased in glowing mail and a Roman helm. Atop a wooden stage erected around the fire's edge, a yellow-toothed old vulture of a Goth stared at the blackened corpse, his single, long and silver chin braid gently swinging in the fire-wind, his moulded breastplate shining in the uplight. 'Burn, Roman dog,' he growled as he watched.

'That'll be Ingolf the Burner then?' Datus surmised glibly, and a little too loudly.

Libo was about to cast another sour look – this time at Datus – when Ingolf suddenly tore his gaze from the fire and began to stride to and fro, wagging a finger high in the air to draw the attention of the watching masses.

'Rome may have thought us weak when we agreed the great peace – guttering like a dying candle,' he lectured. 'But the fires of my kin, my ancestors, burn brighter and stronger than ever. We will *not* be denied that which we are entitled to. Lands in the north of Thracia, Emperor Theodosius' council granted us. What is this town, but a defensible, well-placed settlement in those very lands? And what is this,' he shot a hand towards the half-dozen men standing at the back of the stage, their faces shining with fear and sweat from the closeness of the fire and the Gothic guards' spearpoints pressing against their backs, 'but an embodiment of Theodosius' insincerity? A Roman administrator, who still lays claim to the overlordship of this town!' he almost spat the words towards the pear-shaped, hairless and somewhat gormless man in white imperial dress.

The crowd exploded with booing.

'And these five?' he gestured towards the five others wearing Roman mail and helms. 'Are they not the ghost of a garrison that long-ago ceded this town? Yet still they cling to their "right" to govern and guard.'

'Listen to us, Reiks Ingolf,' one of the Roman sentries up there said. 'Our families and many friends remain here, thus we like you have a great desire to see this place safe and well.'

Ingolf recoiled a little, and the Roman soldier went on: 'You and your forces are most welcome here, but it can only work if we live in accord. Peace,' the soldier pleaded. 'Peace!'

For a moment, it seemed as if the man's pleas had been heard, but then the pear-shaped governor butted-in. 'Aye, peace. Kneel before me, Reiks Ingolf, say it can be so.'

Ingolf jolted in dry amusement, then spread his arms wide. 'If I kneel before you, if I crown you as true Governor of Deultum... then we will have peace?'

The governor seemed taken aback for a breath, then suddenly very confident, realising his one line of rhetoric had worked. Libo and his small party watched, astonished like the ring of Gothic onlookers as Reiks Ingolf – fierce and famous and with all the odds in his favour – lowered himself to one knee. 'Deultum is yours... '

Libo noticed how one of the Gothic spearmen near the fire was poking into the flames with his spear, rummaging, drawing something out...

Ingolf rose, taking and slipping on lead-lined blacksmith's gloves, then opening his palms to accept the glowing thing hanging from the end of the spearman's lance. He raised the red-hot Roman helmet like a crown above the governor's hairless head. 'And now I place upon your head your rightful crown...'

The governor tried to back away, only to feel speartips against his back. 'No, wait, no... *no, no, n-*'

The final 'no' changed into a horrible, wet scream as Ingolf carefully planted the helm on the governor's head, pressing down once for a snug fit, then backing away. Black smoke billowed from the helmet's rim and the governor staggered madly, blood and melting flesh pattering on his robed shoulders and all around him as he grabbed at the helm's cheekguards only to horribly burn his fingers and palms. His scream went on and on and on until eventually he stopped and stood, swaying. A terrible, renewed stink of burnt flesh crawled across the odeum.

Ingolf, with the smile of a man seeing an old friend returning from a long absence, strode up and thrust out a boot, driving his heel into the governor's gut and sending him flailing into the fire.

The fire whooshed and the Gothic onlookers exploded with joy. As the glee faded, the men escorting Libo and his party called up to the stage. 'Romans, Reiks Ingolf. Here to sort everything out.'

Every single member of the crowd, including Ingolf, turned to look at Libo and his party.

Ingolf adopted that joyous look again. 'We can never have enough firewood. Bring them up!'

The crowds jostled and cheered, spitting and swearing as Libo's party were guided up onto the stage. Suddenly, Libo's bright plan felt decidedly less bright.

'Ambassadors?' Ingolf cooed, strolling around them, examining them like nags. 'I usually find they burn the best. Not inured to pain like soldiers, you see.'

The crowds exploded with laughter.

Libo felt his guts turn to water, seeing the man nearest the fire trying to fish out the glowing mail vest of the charred body in there. For a moment he imagined the pain of that heavy vest, hotter than the sun and pressing against his torso. He imagined his flesh melting away like fat, exposing white ribs and gaping black clefts in between. The lingering stink of the dead governor's melted scalp and the burning and popping of his roasting-alive body in the blaze just now only spiced the imagined terror. But despite it all, he knew that fear itself was the greatest danger. Tribunus Pavo had once told him that, on the cusp of a battle they seemed destined to lose. Fear here and now would rob him of his wits – his only remaining weapon. He let the terror dance within him, but sucked in a full breath and rose above it all.

'I am no ambassador,' he said, his voice full and confident. 'I am a soldier, a legionary – a man of the XI Claudia.'

The laughter and heckling faded into a babble of disdain, some mocking the claim. 'The legions of these parts are no more,' one sneered.

'I beg to differ. Outside, an entire legion awaits,' he lied skilfully. 'We approached under the blanket of fog.'

Ingolf's confident demeanour ebbed now.

'You mean you didn't send patrols out to watch over "your" lands?' Libo said calmly. 'How remiss.'

Ingolf rumbled with low laughter. 'Yet you walked into my town. Now you stand on the edge of my fire. Look at you, a soldier with not a scrap of iron on you... perhaps I can fix that.'

The Gothic spearman at the edge of the great fire had now dragged the glowing scale shirt off of the body in there.

Libo affected a deep sigh. 'If I do not return to my legion by noon, then they will unleash all manner of misery upon you.'

The babble changed again, becoming fraught and tense as many heads squinted up into the fog blanket, struggling to find the weak glow of the sun and ascertain the time. Ingolf afforded just a quick glance upwards, his face hardening. Shouts sounded from men who had heard Libo's threat. Spearmen and chosen archers appeared from their billets around the city and sped out towards the walls.

'Those are good and loyal soldiers you have there,' Libo commented. 'But they won't even *see* the first wave of attack, not in this fog. Have you seen what damage a catapult can wreak upon walls even as thick as these? And when one of those stones sails high over the walls and ploughs into the town,' he stopped and blew air through his lips.

The mothers watching clutched their children. Boys who had been playing on the rubble of a broken fountain now paid attention. Libo noticed Ingolf's gaze stretching across the town to a villa on a small hill. It was well guarded by elite Gothic soldiers in golden cloaks.

'They sail high and far, and they will make pulp of your best guards... and your loved ones,' Libo said, guessing that Ingolf's woman and maybe his children lived in there. 'After the storm of rocks, the legion will fall upon this place like a pack. How many soldiers do you have here?' he asked, switching his head around to total the small groups of men rushing to the walls. 'Six hundred perhaps? A strong force, but you know that is not enough.'

'I have defeated legions with the same number of men in the past,' Ingolf said, but his tone was defensive now.

'In the field? Very impressive. Here, in the tight streets, it would be very different. Every soul in this place would – in the eyes of the legion –

be an enemy.'

The crowd now rose in a new clamour of appeal to their leader. 'Reiks Ingolf, you said this town was our capital, that we would be safe!'

Ingolf's head swung to the suckling mother, his face ashen.

'I was there at the cliffs of Dionysopolis,' Libo said quietly.

Ingolf turned slowly back towards him.

'I remember you in the fray,' Libo continued. 'You fought well. But these children and mothers were not there. They have no place in battle. Do not bring it upon them.'

'You said you would keep the Romans in check, lead us to a glorious future!' another of Ingolf's people bellowed, every so often shooting a look back towards the walls and then up to the foggy sky and the faint glow of the sun – nearly overhead.

'Call your legion off,' Ingolf croaked quietly, all hubris now gone.

'Why should I?' Libo answered.

Ingolf looked up at him. 'Tell me what I must do to avoid this day being painted red.'

Libo sucked in a breath through his rotten teeth, folding his arms. He thought of Munderic and the murder of the Roman lad. Munderic had never been called to trial and that fact still rankled with Libo. The same could not be allowed to happen again. 'Two Romans lie charred and dead in those flames. I daresay the fat governor will not be missed, but you have commited a crime. Surrender yourself, and your people will be left to live their lives of peace. Refuse, and...' he gestured towards the sky and the noon position of the sun's glow.

'Don't make me surrender in front of them.'

Libo hesitated long enough to make Ingolf squirm, then nodded. 'Tell them you've convinced me to call off the attack, and that you're coming for talks with Emperor Theodosius. Tell them that, regardless of the outcome, they are to live at peace with the Roman enclave here. Do this and know that your loved ones and your people will go unharmed.'

'Will I be spared?'

Libo for once answered honestly. 'I cannot answer that. But you will be tried fairly.'

Ingolf nodded solemnly, then turned to address his people. Words short and guttural in a pure Gothic tongue. With that, he descended from the fireside stage, accompanied by Libo and his men. The Goths of Deultum wept and lamented as the six legionaries escorted him towards the city gates, but also saluted and heaped praise upon him for saving them from the legionary threat outside.

Libo led his small group back outside into the thick folds of fog and soon, Deultum melted into the grey haze behind them. They walked through the fen for a time, before the rest of the small Claudian band appeared around them. Zeno looked Ingolf up and down then turned to Libo. 'You did it. you prized the pearl from the shell.'

Libo shrugged, snorted and scratched behind his ear.

Reiks Ingolf jerked from one direction to the next, expecting to see an entire legion out here. Realisation dawned like a rising flame. 'You, you lied to me,' he rasped towards Libo.

Libo stared at him firmly. 'I lied, yes, but only to have a chance of preserving the peace. It is as I said: Face trial, knowing that you have saved your people and still have a chance of returning to them. Emperor Theodosius and his sacred council will hear your case.'

Defeated and dejected, Ingolf trudged along with the Claudians, watched closely by a tent party of eight. They emerged from the oppressive fog and onto the *Via Pontica*. The dark sea was flecked with white peaks and the sky, studded with shrieking gulls and cormorants, seemed especially bruised.

'While we're trekking down to Constantinople, who will watch the patrol route?' Libo asked Zeno.

'Ah, well there's been a change of plan,' Zeno replied. 'We'll take Reiks ingolf only part of the way to the capital. There is a fortified island, not far from here. We can deposit him in the gaol there. Even better,' he grinned, 'I received word just days ago from Primus Pilus Crassus – that our reinforcements were ready, and I instructed him and them to rendezvous with us there.'

Libo's face lifted in a smile. The sea air suddenly felt fresh and invigorating. The peace had been upheld in the most challenging of circumstances. Zeno had stepped into Pavo's boots admirably… and now the many empty Claudian ranks were to be replenished.

They came to a low, shingle cove near the coastal edge of the road. A liburnian waited there, the stern beached. A crew of sailors sat around the spar and on the rail, but jumped to attention when they saw the Claudians coming, throwing down a boarding plank and waving them forward.

'What is this?' Ingolf growled, halting halfway up the gangplank and resisting the shoves of the eight watching him.

'A temporary stop for you. You'll be fed and given a bed,' Libo assured him. 'Soon, another ship will come to take you to the capital.'

Once all were aboard, a handful of the crew stood at the stern and used poles to shove against the bay. With a grinding of timbers on shingle and shale, then a splash of oars plunging into foaming waters, the small galley bobbed away from the shoreline.

Libo stood with Pulcher and Rectus at the rail, each man's weathered and scarred face pinched against the strong sea wind, jaws working on well-earned meals of bread smeared with salty fat. The liburnian looked to be heading out into deeper waters, but then banked round and drew towards a small, rocky hump, less than a mile from the coast. It was a desolate looking isle with no shore – just sheer rocks, black and wet. The higher parts were streaked with gull droppings, gravel, shale and tracts of pale, wind-beaten grass. At the top of the island's hill sat a squat lighthouse painted white and topped with an old statue of Apollo. A wind wall ran along the island summit from one end of the lighthouse to the rugged eastern shore. They tacked round to the south of the isle, where the wind fell away. A small and dilapidated timber wharf and jetty sprouted from the shiny black rocks here, and a bull of an officer waited there, pewter eyes bright with enthusiasm and a cleft chin the size of an anvil. He wore a blue cloak, a vest of scale and a golden helm sporting a blocky noseguard, and rested the palm of one hand on the top of a thick, worn staff.

'Sir,' the waiting officer saluted Zeno as the liburnian docked and the Claudians disembarked onto the wharf to the sound of crashing, cold waves and moaning wind.

'Primus Pilus Crassus,' Zeno returned the salute, then turned to the Claudians. 'Come, I will show you to the barracks.'

'What is this place?' Pulcher muttered as they marched along the shale track around the isle's southern edge.

As he spoke, something shuddered in the nearby bushes, something grey and wet, slithering. All the legionaries' heads switched round to see the snake vanish from sight. Here and there across the wet rock they noticed other asps.

'Grey water snakes,' Rectus muttered. 'Watch your legs around here. A bite from one of them is not fatal but it will hurt like fire.'

'That's why they call this place Snake Island,' Crassus explained.

'Lovely,' Libo remarked as he walked with his Claudians into the barrack interior. It was a good-sized fort with strong walls that cut out the buffeting sea wind entirely. The square towers on each corner and the array of barrack blocks and storehouses dated the place – it was clearly an old fort. But then he saw something that swept such trivial detail aside: legionaries, emerging from the barrack houses in perfect lines, forming a parade front either side of and behind Libo and his band. Three sides of a square, gleaming with mail and intercisa helms. Two entire cohorts, nearly one thousand men. With a crunch of gravel, Zeno padded across to the praetorium building at the open end of this square of soldiers and swivelled on his heel to face the Claudians in the centre.

'Present *shields,*' he boomed.

With a rustle of iron and wood, the reinforcements swung their screens front to reveal the ruby and gold blazons. Claudian shields. There was even a knot of a dozen *equites* riders – again draped in gold and ruby.

Pulcher erupted with laughter first. 'Am I dreaming?'

Opis beamed as he swept his eyes around the reinforcements. 'By all the Gods. Were only Pavo and Sura alive to see this.'

Rectus was less enthusiastic. 'Where exactly did Emperor Theodosius find one thousand legionaries?'

'I will answer your questions in just a moment,' Zeno addressed them. 'But first: Primus Pilus, if you will?'

Crassus' ears perked up and that big anvil-jaw wrinkle in another grin. He slapped a hand down on Reiks Ingolf's left shoulder, then shoved him forward, out into the space before Zeno, turning the Gothic

Reiks to face Libo's Claudians.

Libo's face was still half-bent in delight at the array of reinforcements, when Ingolf shuddered. Crassus, behind the man, wrapped his spatha blade around Ingolf's neck and skillfully drew it sideways. A red line hung on the reiks' neck for a moment. The craggy reiks stared at Libo, confused, before a violent sheet of blood gushed from his slit throat and he crumpled in a heap.

Libo's heart fell into his boots. His good eye swung from the dead reiks to the grinning Crassus to Zeno. 'Why? If his people find out he was killed without a trial...'

But Zeno simply stared at the dead man.

Realisation descended like a cold, damp cloak. Libo took a few steps forward, past Ingolf's corpse and Crassus' bloody blade, closer to Zeno. 'It was him?' he said quietly. 'Ingolf killed your father?'

Zeno looked up from the corpse. 'No. I had him killed simply to destabilise this peace.'

Libo recoiled. 'What?'

Zeno cocked his head to one side, as if amused. 'My efforts at Munderic's settlement and today and every other day until now have been convincing, I presume?' he said. 'You must understand that I had to win your confidence, so much that you would let me lead you here onto this island prison.' As he spoke, the mast of the liburnian – visible above the fort walls, shrank, as the vessel sailed away.

Now Libo took a step backwards. 'Sir, what is this?'

'You honestly don't see the resemblance, do you?' Zeno asked, bemused. 'My father died during the war. He was slashed with a poisoned blade, and driven by the agony of it to batter his head against a rock and dash out his brains.' He slipped a ring from his purse onto his finger, working it into place. The single, staring eye emblem upon it glared at Libo and at the small band of men he had led in here. 'My father was Vitalianus, *Optio Speculatorum*, devoted servant of Emperor Gratian.' Silence, then Zeno continued. 'Tribunus Pavo wielded that blade. He is dead now. But you and your men are not. You helped him in everything he did. So now... all of you will pay.'

Some of Libo's men backed towards the fort gates, but they swung shut. Crassus swished one hand, and with a clatter of wood and steel, the three-sided cage of 'reinforcements' levelled their spears and the parade formation became a cage.

Libo stared at Zeno, heart pounding.

'Emperor Gratian sent these men to me with one express command,' Zeno said, face dark with malice. 'To make you suffer for as long as possible. Emperor Theodosius will continue to receive my reports about the patrol route, and some of my men here will carry out those patrols – in Claudian colours too. Nobody will know you are here, nobody will care. Years from now, perhaps someone will find your bones.'

Chapter 5
January 383 AD
Constantinople

The midday sky over Constantinople was a dome of angry grey. Snow tumbled down, lying in a thin layer upon the gilt domes and towering columns of the Imperial Palace hill. Sentries shuffled and stamped, blowing into their hands, most enviously casting eyes at the giant Chalke hall and the promise of heat glowing from its galleries of windows, tormented by the jabber of merry voices sailing from within.

Inside, the jovial clamour was deafening. The copper sconces affixed to the marble pillars cast ribbons of warm light and shadow across the montage of krakens and satyrs painted on the high arched ceiling. A sweet haze of myrrh smoke drifted above the feasting table. Officers both military and civilian, clergymen, magnates and foreign guests sat there, carving through huge platters of baked eel stuffed with spinach and fried carrots, marinated goose livers, fowl on beds of imported rice, yoghurt, heaps of freshly-baked flatbreads and urn after urn of wine. At the sides of the hall too, benches were set out and yet more notables stuffed food and poured wine down their throats. Up on the mezzanine too scores more drank and chattered, red-faced and sanguine about the peace and this opportunity to celebrate for once instead of coming here to discuss war, loss and famine.

One drunk official staggered across the tessellated floor, bashing into shoulders and apologising in a muted slur. Over it all, fistula pipes whistled in high and haunting tones, lyres twanged and timpani drums rumbled and faded like a gentle, rhythmic wind. For a time, it seemed as if even a clap of thunder would not be heard over the din. But Themistius the 'great' orator was louder than thunder.

'*Rrromans!*' he wailed dramatically as he emerged from behind a curtain and onto a balcony high up on the great hall's southern end. He was fatter than ever, wearing a thick cement of pale lead powder on his cheeks, his hefty body draped in a thin *pallium* embroidered with silver thread and decorated with gold leaf. His oily, thin curls of hair were scraped-forward and plastered to his temples like stiff wings. 'Has our empire ever known greater stewardship than in these last few years? Has one man ever possessed such skills? The steady hand of an admiral, the mind of a general, the heart of a lion!'

He shot out both hands towards the far end of the hall. All heads turned to the dais there and the grand table upon it, and all eyes gazed up at the tall, white-robed Emperor Theodosius seated at the centre. He wore a diadem studded with emerald, pearl and sapphire, the gems sparkling like his wide almond eyes, calm and aptly imperious.

A low thunder of acclaim was answer enough.

'Today, our emperor has made a monumental and golden decision. Mighty Theodosius, the *true* God's will here on mortal soil...' at this, Themistius glanced over to an adjacent, private balcony. Gregory, Bishop of Constantinople, and two clergymen – all of them in white robes and white of hair – sat there like fat nesting pigeons. The bishop discreetly nodded towards Themistius in agreement, like a teacher validating a student's progress '...has chosen to generously share his station, to grant another the title of Augustus of the East, to rule alongside him.'

Themistius lifted one arm towards the silver silk drape at the rear of the balcony. First, a woman emerged, bedecked in a golden headdress. Flacilla, Theodosius' wife, young and pretty. A low mumble of confusion arose around the crowd, before they realised that another had emerged from behind the drape with her. But because this other was not yet in his sixth summer, none on the hall floor could see him until he stepped up onto a small wooden bench, helped by his mother, to peek over the balustrade. Arcadius was draped in a purple gown, fastened on the right breast with a gold *fibula*, and he wore a diadem like Theodosius. Every speck of his imperial livery was majestic, yet every part of his face was that of a child who understood little about what was happening.

'Arcadius will be his father's deputy, learning from him every day. One day he will take up the mantle of empire on his own... though let that day be far, far from now,' Themistius said with a rather contrived sob, casting one hand over his face like a mourner unable to look at a dying loved one. But the orator swiftly got over his staged grief to stand proud again. 'But at least then we will have a dynasty, no debate over the succession.' He thrust one fist in the air. 'We will know lasting strength! Stability!'

'Strength! Stability!' the crowds boomed.

Themistius let the echoing cries fade, then gestured across the masses as they supped on wine. 'Already the young Arcadius learns from his father. Was the cowing of the Goths not our emperor's greatest lesson of all? Do we not all reap the fruits of that lesson? Does the grape pressed in times of peace not taste so much sweeter than that stamped upon during war? Does the banquet of victory not fill the belly more completely than the scraps of defeat?'

The rowdy and merry crowd agreed with a low, baritone rumble, a sea of cups rising to toast the orator. The timpani drums thundered in appreciation.

But with the dramatic skywards swish of one hand, as if he was addressing an invisible deity, Themistius brought them all to complete silence again. 'When the Gothic chiefs, beaten and broken, begged wise Theodosius for mercy...' his voice rose to a shrill, mawkish squeak, his raised fist and blubbery face shaking with emotion... 'mercy our emperor gave to the barbarian. And to his subjects, he gave peace. Philanthropy has prevailed over destruction!' he boomed. 'We chose not to fill Thracia with corpses... but with farmers. Not with tombs... but with living men. The barbarians – once fond of axe and sword, are already transforming their weapons into hoes and sickles. The Empire has pre-*vailed*.' Themistius spread his flabby arms like wings, leant against the balustrade and half-bowed towards the imperial dais at the far end of the hall. 'All hail Emperor Theodosius!'

'*All hail Emperor Theodosius!*' the crowds chanted as one.

As Emperor Theodosius basked in the adulation, Consul Saturninus, by his side, shrank in his seat. The bare lies that had poured from Themistius' mouth stung his ears like wasps. Peace had not been won, it had been agreed – by two sides broken and exhausted. On that final day of battle at the cliffs of Dionysopolis, both Goth *and* Roman had been on their knees. More, Emperor Theodosius had not even been present at the battle nor the peace talks that had followed. Saturninus tucked his shoulder-length dark hair behind his ears and traced the silver rivets in his black leather breastplate, recalling the ferocious fight – the stink of blood and earth, the discordant song of dying men, the horrid feeling of rivulets of blood running down his face. But, like sunlight burning off a chill mist, memories of the subsequent talks rose up to chase away the battle images. The pale white tent, the sound of voices exchanging ideas and concessions, of reason, of dialectic. He felt no crumb of offence or jealousy that few remembered his part in the battle or as leader of those crucial talks. That was not Saturninus' way. After all he had witnessed throughout the war, peace was reward enough. A stable and safe Eastern Empire. Was that not what he and every other man here had fought for throughout the war? More, Theodosius had not ignored his part in affairs: shortly after the war had ended, the emperor had promoted him from his military post to this consulship, the highest of civilian stations in the East. No more battle, no more blood. He swirled his wine cup, staring at the reflection of his narrow features, wan and delicate – almost feminine – and saw a hint of a smile there. The first time in years he had seen such a look on his face.

'Next time, maybe the fat windbag can describe the state of the lands we've gifted to the Goths?' a gruff voice cut through his reverie.

Bacurius One-hand sat on the far side of Emperor Theodosius. He was Saturninus' military equivalent: Master of the Palace Cavalry and *Comes Domesticorum,* Theodosius' highest general and most senior of his companions. He was leaning back on his seat, his stump arm – the hand lost in battle with the Goths – folded across his good one like a man unconvinced. His short crop of thin brown hair glistened with sweat, droplets of which ran down his malevolent face, following the course of the three thick, pink scar welts that ran from forehead to chin, leaving his top lip bent upwards at one side in a ferocious sneer. Bacurius claimed he had acquired the face-wound while fighting a bear that had annoyed him. Few dared to question him. 'The whole of middle and northern Thracia – once a Roman land through and through – is now a massive blind-spot,' Bacurius moaned. He held up the index finger of his good hand. 'Just one legion – and I use the term loosely, for the Claudia are but a rag-tag of one hundred or so men – has skirted the southern edge of that Gothic region in the three months since the war's end. The tribes are supposed to be settling down to farm, but from what reports the Claudia have sent back, I hear that they're building forts, gathering bigger horse herds, training new spearmen and archers.'

'So they might,' Emperor Theodosius said calmly. 'It may not sit well with you, but we *need* the Goths to be strong. They can muster forty thousand fighting men, all oathbound to me. At a time when the Eastern Empire has but three intact legions and a patchwork of others, we have secured an entire army of *foederati.* Anyone who might have once considered attacking our realm might now think again...'

Saturninus followed Theodosius' gaze as it drifted to the tessellated map on the far wall and moved from region to region: first to the north, above the Gothic settlements, across the Danubius and into the land where the Huns seemed to be gathering in huge numbers; then to the east, where the Sassanids held sway; and finally to the Western Roman Empire...

'Mah,' Bacurius muttered. 'When did the Claudia last send back a detailed report anyway? And how much gold have we paid the Goths to preserve this peace in the short time it has lasted? I stopped a bireme up at the Neorion Docks just before it set off. The ship wasn't on any schedule that I was aware of. Turns out they were sailing north, to Tomis. Tomis – once an imperial stronghold on the coast, now garrisoned by Goths. The ship carried a cargo of two hundred golden torques. The torques were to be given to the Gothic Reiks in charge of Tomis so he could distribute them to his men. And for the score or so original Roman sentries still serving there? Nothing.' He chopped his missing hand through the air decisively. 'Upon their return, the sailors even reported that the Goths had stripped those Roman sentries of their armour and weapons.'

Theodosius maintained that aloof, tranquil expression. 'The garrison of Tomis is loyal to the empire, and that is what matters. They will keep those lands at peace and bring the farming network back together.'

Saturninus could almost mouth Bacurius next words before the one-handed general stammered them. 'To whose benefit? They are under no obligation to pay tax nor deliver grain to the imperial silos!' A few nearby heard the gruff words, and glanced awkwardly up at the raised imperial table.

'Magister Militum, I remind you of your position as my general and advisor... not my opponent. Look around you, tell me this is not a better state of affairs than when last we gathered in this hall during the throes of war.'

'I look around and I see too many damned barbarians in here,' Bacurius said. He flicked his stump towards the near end of the main table down on the floor, pointing at a tall, gaunt and heavy-browed man in lozenge patterned breeches and a green Gothic tunic, sporting long amber hair tied in a tail, and a moustache neatly waxed and groomed. 'Modares, *Magister Militum* of the scrappy remains of the Thracian legions... Goth,' he spat. Next, he jabbed his stump at an older officer this time in Roman robes and a fine silver cloak, his face puffy and threaded with crimson veins. 'Richomeres, Magister Militum of the Orient... looks like a Roman, but he's a Frank.'

Bacurius now pointed out a man of some thirty summers with a predacious glare. His hair was cropped in the old Roman style and he wore a Roman tunic lavished with arrow stripes on the shoulders. 'Reiks Fravitta... *Goth!*'

At this, Saturninus exploded with laughter. 'He couldn't be more Roman if he tried. He cut off his hair, abandoned his tribal garb. He has even changed his name to Faustius!' A flash of the cliff battle again struck across Saturninus' mind. Back then Fravitta, as he was known, had sported a long dark mane and a trident beard. Yet it was he who had called for truce and he who had represented the many Gothic factions at the subsequent peace talks.

Bacurius leaned forward, looking across Emperor Theodosius and at Saturninus like an angry crow peering at another who has out-squawked him. 'So he dresses like a Roman now, but he rides back and forth to and from the Gothic region, to mix and plot with the new... *haims,*' he spat the Gothic word like a pip.

'Or to keep open the communications between our emperor and the various reiks up there,' Saturninus countered. 'He is the bridge between our peoples.'

Bacurius shuffled in his chair, his crow-head flicking around for another example. He eyed the line of stony-faced guards standing behind the emperor. Twelve of them, each armed and armoured in bronze and carrying a blood-red shield and tall spear. None of them wore helms, each had a bare scalp, the hair scraped away in a daily ritual. Each too sported a dark ink stigma on his wrist of a Christian *Chi-Rho.* These were the Emperor's Inquisitors, a hand-picked knot of soldiers tasked with guarding Theodosius, but also with enforcing – usually violently – the suppression of the old ways of worship. Ancient shrines and schools of philosophy had been forced to close, some replaced by Christian temples.

Bacurius spotted two, conspicuous for their pale eyebrows and fairer skin. He lowered his voice. 'I know you lost some of these fierce bastards at the end of the war, but did you have to replace them with *Goths?*'

'We lost much during the war,' Theodosius replied. 'Whole legions, precious wings of palace cavalry. Countless officers of every station. I had to fill the gaps in my *sacrum consistorium,* and I did so with great care. I seek to promote the best men, regardless of their origins. Take my newly-formed regiment – the Thervingi.' He pointed to the open shutters on the mezzanine just to the left of the imperial dais. Beyond the shutters, a pair of legionaries strolled along the snowy walkway out there. They wore green Gothic breeches and tunics, with iron Roman vests hugging their torsos, and long, fair tails of hair hanging to their waists. Each carried a pale blue shield emblazoned with a haunting, staring face flanked by two leaping golden wolves. 'An entire legion, raised from the Gothic peoples – from the Thervingi tribesmen, no less. And they are *auxilia palatina* – palace troops. A unit like that is not easy to raise and train, yet Tribunus Eriulf has done just that, and in record time too.'

The three watched as Eriulf appeared out there to speak to the two sentries. He was their commander and the pair hung on his every word. Built like an athlete and tall as a turret, Eriulf wore his golden hair in a spiked knot at the crown, stiffened and held in place with pine resin. His body was encased in a steel cuirass over a white tunic and Roman boots.

'Eriulf is a Goth,' Theodosius continued. 'Do you dispute *his* place by my side?'

Bacurius muttered something inaudible. It was a sound edged with acquiescence. He had been there at the Battle for Thessalonica, seen Eriulf's heroics first hand and had been saved by them too.

Saturninus smiled gently as he watched Eriulf at work, holding the gazes of the two freezing Thervingi sentries out there as a father might with twin sons, reinvigorating them with stirring words. The pair visibly stood taller, before saluting Eriulf and striding from view, off around the snowy outer walkway. Saturninus felt a warm sense of satisfaction too, comfortable that Bacurius' gripes about the Goths were nothing but the cantankerous groans of a wine-soaked mind. The snow grew thicker out there, and the wind began to drive it in wild whooshes... yet Eriulf remained outside, standing in profile, utterly still, facing the icy bombardment and gazing into the throat of the wintry storm. The man was an enigma: with his high rank he could be sitting here, next to the emperor, feasting and drinking. Instead, he seemed content to suffer out there in the cold. Saturninus noticed something else: Eriulf was not *completely* still, for his lips moved. It was almost indiscernible at this distance, but yes... he was speaking to someone. Yet there was nobody else out there. *We all have our ghosts,* Saturninus thought.

With perfect timing and a whoosh of winter wind, the hall's main doors groaned open. Saturninus almost jumped out of his skin. His head snapped round towards the entrance as the many sconces roared in protest, the flames bending with the wind. The pair of bronze-jacketed Lancearii legionaries guarding the doors showed a knot of men in. They wore a dusting of snow on their shoulders and hair. The lead man, strong-shouldered, strode with a confidence that drew almost every eye in the hall, his pale-brown cloak swishing in his wake.

'Maximus,' Bacurius slapped the table and rumbled with fond laughter. 'Now there's a true Roman General!'

Saturninus watched the man approach. Like Emperor Theodosius, he was a native of Hispania. He wore his short dark hair combed immaculately onto his forehead. His face was flat and wide, his eyes like tarry pools, his nose and chin prominent and his lips set in a thin line. He snapped his fingers and the three men with him peeled away to take places at the tables, while he strode assuredly up the steps to the imperial table. He sank to one knee charmingly. '*Domine*,' he said with a bow of the head.

'Rise, *Comes Britanniarum*,' Theodosius said softly.

'I apologise for my tardiness,' Maximus said as he stood again. 'Never once in my last two months here have I been late to your dining table.' All those near the imperial table were listening in with half-smiles, like an audience gathered to listen to an entertainer and waiting for the first laugh. 'But today I opened my door to find a snow drift blocking my way. The damned thing fell in on me, tumbled into my boots and soaked my feet through. They say I am a mighty commander of the regiments of Britannia, that I can rip an oak from the ground with my bare hands and summon thunder across that distant northern isle. But wet socks?' he grinned. 'No, that is my weakness.'

The crowds exploded in laughter.

Maximus climbed up onto the imperial dais. 'Excuse me, Consul' he said pleasantly, before squeezing in between Saturninus and the emperor and sinking to his haunches there to speak with Theodosius. Occasionally he would break off to crane his neck to look up at and shout greetings to familiar faces up on the mezzanine. Saturninus eyed him furtively. The man had been in Constantinople for two months, merely a visitor, yet he seemed more at home in the city than Saturninus had ever felt, anywhere. Such ease, such grace, such charm.

But Saturninus prided himself on riding high above jealousy. In truth he liked Maximus. Years ago in the West, the visiting general had served Theodosius' father, and some said that he had championed Theodosius' raising to the Eastern throne. He and the Eastern Emperor were right now like brothers, heads close as they hurriedly shared thoughts and memories. Few could elicit such affable manners from the often aloof and sombre Theodosius, and those who tried too hard were usually subject to his occasional bursts of temper – glares of fire and thunderous tirades. He listened in to one of Maximus' stories about a blind man who had beaten him at archery outside Londinium. The tale was jaunty, funny and self-deprecating. Yes, Saturninus thought, who could dislike this brilliant general?

But there was one thing that he had struggled to understand: Gratian, Emperor of the West, had turned every screw to undermine Theodosius' reign here in the East. So why... why had Theodosius invited this western general – one of Gratian's best – to his capital? Theodosius told Saturninus, his consul, everything. But on this matter, he knew nothing. One day, Maximus had simply arrived. It had only been during a whispered meeting in the depths of last night that he had come to understand it all.

After some time, Maximus rose and left the imperial table to mix with the many others around the hall. Saturninus shifted his chair back to where it had been and leaned towards Theodosius. 'Domine, I do not wish to tarnish this feast. But something concerns me.'

Theodosius, sinking his teeth into a pheasant leg, nodded for him to continue.

'In Persia, we still cannot be certain of Shapur's intentions. In the north, we have yet to see if the Goths will truly settle as we hope. Finally, there is this matter of Maximus. If we follow through with what we talked of last night...' he sighed and shuffled in his chair. 'Put simply, I fear that you juggle too many swords.

Theodosius dabbed at his lips with a handkerchief, then took a sip of watered wine. 'Too many swords, Consul?' he mused, then slowly shook his head. 'No, just enough.'

Saturninus shuffled a few times in his seat. His mind drifted back to his memories and that white parley tent on the battle-stained Dionysopolis cliffs. His mind's eye swung around the weary collection of Roman officers and Gothic nobles who had watched on as he and Reiks Faustius had thrashed out the terms. Then he remembered the Claudian Tribunus standing near the back.

'Have we heard anything from Persia?' he said.

Theodosius applauded a troupe of dancers onto the floor, letting Saturninus' question go unanswered for an uncomfortable spell. 'The discussions crawl along,' he replied at last. 'Ambassador Sporacius is well-used to such talks. He knew it would be like this. Stilicho is a fine prospect, but too fiery for my liking. I hope he has learned well from Sporacius' patient methods in his time there, for I have decided to recall him.'

'You are breaking off the talks?' Saturninus gasped.

'No, I just want Stilicho back here. My messengers in the imperial stables have a sealed scroll with orders to that effect. They're just waiting for this damned blizzard to ease so they can take ship.'

Saturninus planted one elbow on the arm of the seat and rested his chin on his palm, in a way that let him cover his mouth with his fingers as he spoke. 'I will be glad of Stilicho's return. But what of the escort legionaries with them?'

'Of all our problems, Consul, the fate of a handful of lowly legionaries is near the bottom of the stack.'

'They are not all lowly legionaries, Domine,' he said in little more than a whisper. 'I owe it to Pavo to bring him back.'

Theodosius stopped applauding, the smile draining from his face. 'The ex-Claudia Tribunus? The man you attached to the peace embassy... without my permission?'

Saturninus felt as though he were fifteen, his skin burning under Theodosius' glare.

'When I found out, I was irate,' the emperor said. 'I even considered stripping you of your consulship.' He paused for a long breath and his mood settled. 'But then I realised you had solved a problem for me. Gratian thinks Pavo is dead, and as long as he languishes out in Persia, he is as good as dead. But if he was to be subsequently found in my realm? No, that would not do at all. Gratian's Western Armies are vast, and ours are thin, scattered and in disarray. Thus, while the threat of Gratian looms, Pavo cannot return,' Theodosius said with a stony finality.

Saturninus felt the skin on the back of his neck prickling. He had learned how to persuade Theodosius – when to pander and when to provoke – but this was tricky indeed. Gratian was young and in a prime position of power on the Western Throne. All this meant a lifetime of exile for Pavo. His eyes drifted around the hall as he sought his next words. His gaze rose up towards the balcony and the lead-painted Themistius, bragging endlessly to Lady Flacilla. Beside her, the young, shy and purple-robed Arcadius was busying himself playing with the hems of his robes. 'Domine, with respect, you have just nominated young Arcadius as your heir – *without* consulting Gratian. When he finds out, he will be incensed – far more than he would about the harbouring of a mere legionary officer.'

'Oh yes, he will be furious,' Theodosius answered calmly. 'But contesting this kind of imperial and very public ceremony must be dealt with in the proper way. Even Gratian knows he will have to send an array of envoys and messengers to me and me to him before he can even think about using my son's new station as a *casus belli*.' The emperor half-smiled. 'And all that to-ing and fro-ing will cast up such a cloud of distraction, don't you think?'

Confused, Saturninus watched as Theodosius raised a hand, bidding farewell to a group of men. Maximus, Saturninus realised. They departed into the snowy storm to a chorus of farewell cheers.

'May your journey back to the West be safe,' cried one Eastern officer.

'And the wine and beer of Britannia sweet,' added another.

'And the women wanton!' slavered a third.

'He's leaving... *now?*' Saturninus said, eyeing the angry, driving blizzard outside.

'All is in hand, Consul,' Theodosius said with a languorous purr.

A few moments after the door had closed behind Maximus, the matter began to fade from his mind. Until Theodosius whispered quietly: 'Now, that matter we discussed last night...'

The hairs on the back of Saturninus' neck stood proud. 'Which matter, Domine?'

Theodosius stared at him and it was answer enough. He had barely believed the emperor's words that last eve. He had assumed that too much wine had been consumed.

'Do it,' Theodosius said quietly, passing a short, thin leather case to Saturninus underneath the table. 'Go after him... and do it.'

Saturninus' heart pounded – in a way it had never done even during his battle years. He felt the weight of the leather case, the weight of its import infinitely heavier. 'Are you sure?' he whispered, looking into his drink so any onlookers would not realise he was talking to the emperor.

'Do not make me speak the words explicitly, Consul. Remember, I must not be linked to, to... to what is about to happen. Now go.'

Saturninus slid the case inside his robes, took a few long breaths, then stood, his legs suddenly leaden. He edged towards the hall's slave door, trying to be light-footed but feeling clumsy and conspicuous. A few men greeted and saluted him, and he tried as best as he could to look jovial and carefree like them. He used the groan of the opening slave door to disguise his great gasp of relief. Outside, the snow stung him like sling bullets, and a frozen Thervingi sentry standing watch there chattered some frozen words of salute, throwing up a blue hand. Saturninus pulled a fold of his cloak over his face to shield himself from the blizzard, and padded his way through the whiteness. He noticed the prints of Maximus' retinue in the snow, headed along the main way, probably already halfway to the land gates. He couldn't be seen following the westerner in open view. His mind worked over things, and he realised there was another way, another chance to catch Maximus.

Coming down to the base of the palace hill, he passed through the gilded *Milion* arches which gave him a brief blink of respite from the winter winds before he hurried on across a paved ward. Ahead, a heavy barred gate was set in a low wall. His eyes slid one way then the other as he looked around. Nobody watching – indeed the wintry streets were bare. He withdrew a thick iron key from his robe and turned the lock. The gate moaned as it opened and he stepped inside.

He descended from the wintry squall into the dank, quiet stony staircase that wound down and into the depths underneath Constantinople. Upon a small table at the foot of the stairs rested six torches and beside it a flint lighting hook hung from the wall on a piece of twine. Taking a torch, he struck it alight, stared along the endless tunnel, then sped along through its blackness in a bubble of orange and a dance of shadows, thinking only of reaching the far end. The tunnel was intended as a private passageway for the emperor, should he ever need to pass through the city unmolested. Today, it was Saturninus' only chance of catching Maximus.

As he went, he felt the leather case Theodosius had given him chafing on his side. He clutched his Chi-Rho necklace and asked himself: was it right to do that which his emperor had bid him? Was it truly *God's* will? Such a high and terrible price…

The echo of his footsteps began to thin. Too late for deliberations, for he was already at the end of the tunnel, he realised – deep underneath the land walls and at the foot of a rising stairwell. He climbed the steps with the lithe movements of a dancer, blowing out the torch when he heard the sounds of chatter above. He came to a second grille gate. The stonework of the Golden Gatehouse guard room beyond was uplit by the warm glow of a brazier. He crept closer to the gate. There was just a single sentry in there. And then… *Maximus!* He fell to a crouch, peeling back to hide within the shadows of the tunnel steps, watching.

'Why so glum, Legionary?' Maximus asked the sentry as he drew on a thick woollen cloak, oiled so it would not absorb melting snow, then pulled on bearskin gloves. 'It could be worse: you are posted in here for the day with a fire crackling away to keep you warm; my men and I have to travel out into the freezing snow and across the countryside.'

The Western General's men stood around him, similarly tying and clasping on thick cloaks and woollen scarves. Saturninus felt his heart pound. There was no way he could do what Theodosius had asked – even if he wanted to. He had to get the westerner alone. For a moment, he felt a wash of relief. But it was short-lived.

'Bring the horses,' Maximus said.

As a group, Maximus' retinue strode off through an inner corridor that led to the gatehouse stables.

Just Maximus and the sentry.

The brazier beside the sentry guttered at that moment. Maximus looked at the dying fire then laughed once and flicked a finger towards the storerooms. 'Go,' he said to the sentry, 'get more wood, keep the brazier lit and stay warm.' He flashed the man a grin. 'I will be safe in the interim... and I promise I won't let any barbarian hordes in.'

With a chuckle, the sentry left too.

Maximus was alone. Back turned to the gate grille. 'Come on,' he called down the corridor leading to the stables. 'We need to set off now if we're to reach the first waystation by nightfall.' But his men remained out of sight down there.

Saturninus felt sick. There were no excuses now. He closed his eyes, clasped his Chi-Rho necklace... then slipped forward, slotting the key into the grille gate, turning it expertly so as not to make a sound. The gate swung open noiselessly too. He crept up on Maximus' back like a cat, drawing out the leather case, opening it and...

Like an acrobat, Maximus swivelled on the ball of one foot to face him.

Everything fell silent apart from the brazier which crackled and spat its last. Saturninus felt the cold prick of Maximus' iron blade under his chin. 'Consul,' he said calmly.

Saturninus' eyes rolled downwards, past Maximus' blade, to the thing from the case that he now held against the westerner's belly.

Maximus' eyebrows arched. He took the scroll from Saturninus' hand. It was unmarked, but he weighed it as if it were made of gold. 'Is this what I think it is? The thing you, Emperor Theodosius and I talked of last night?'

'Nobody must know of its origin,' Saturninus said.

Maximus grinned widely, sheathing his blade. 'I understand,' he said, tucking it away.

Footsteps rose from the stable corridor. Saturninus shrank back towards the secret passageway.

'Farewell, Consul,' Maximus said. 'Perhaps next time we meet, a great cloud will have lifted from the sky.'

'God willing,' Saturninus said. As he slipped into the passageway again and closed the grille gate, he watched Maximus and his men leave, braving the wild snow outside the city. It was done – the first stone had been thrown. What in all heaven and earth would become of it?

But then he realised that at least something good might arise from it. A promise given some time ago could at last be honoured. He set off at once for the palace ward and to the imperial messenger stables.

Chapter 6
January 383 AD
The Raetian Forests, Northern Italia

Emperor Gratian's grand camp was a sea of darkened tents, encrusted with frost that glittered in the moonlight. All was silent apart from the droning snores of sleeping legionaries, along with the occasional eruption of splattering flatulence. One tent glowed gently, a bubble of soft – almost apologetic – light. Within, uplit by the glow of a candle, three men talked in hushed tones.

'The legions crushed the Bucinobantes rebels in the woods today,' said the youngest of the three, an augur named Ulixes. 'The prominence of the old Jovian banners on his front ranks cannot be a coincidence. Nor the tridents of Neptune. We can speak to him, show him what this means: that the old Gods *cannot* be abandoned.'

'Yet equally, Ulixes, he will argue that he has won past victories with his Christian symbols on the shields of his front ranks,' replied a balding pontiff, finishing with a sigh. 'When did he last visit the Temple of Jupiter to pay homage to the Capitoline Triad? Has he ever given sacrifice? He is blind to the old Gods and deaf to us. We must face facts: Emperor Gratian has refused the title of *Pontifex Maximus*. As a child I watched emperors take the ancient robes, proud and honoured to be highest of all priests. Gratian spits on those traditions. He means to stamp out our ancient ways in favour of the Christ-God.'

The third man, a *curio*, sat at the edge of the tent, having said nothing so far. But now he clasped his hands together as if in meditation,

snoring and the occasional belch or yawn felt comforting in a strange way – normal things, a typical night in camp. There was even the comical sight of one tent, lit from within, the shadow play of the lone and furiously masturbating legionary occupant unwittingly projected onto the goat-leather. A few of Gratian's Alani chuckled at this, and when one grinned at him as if to share the joke, Ulixes nervously laughed in reply.

'Come on,' Ulixes whispered to the pontiff, 'straighten up. It was just a misunderstanding. We can assure the emperor that it was the curio's plan. We will have another chance. Remember – we are *not* alone.'

Gratian led them on to the camp's northern edge, near where the battle had taken place earlier that day. The forest was an army of shadows, but the few bars of moonlight sparkled on the frost-coated, slashed-open bodies strewn out there – Bucinobantes tribesmen, cut open by Gratian's legions, bombarded by javelins and arrows, then blown to pieces by his catapults. It was next to the end of the line of giant timber war machines that the Western Emperor stopped. He swung round, smiling brightly. He lifted one hand to the catapult's cup and patted the rim. 'Come on then, hop in,' he said jauntily. 'Who's first?'

Ulixes' body clenched as if the cold hand of a giant had seized him, pressing everything inside his belly down towards his rectum. 'What?'

Gratian laughed breezily. 'You want me to give sacrifice? You want to talk *about* the Gods, no? Well we can do better than that.' he flicked a finger towards the pontiff who still clung like a child to Ulixes' side. The Alani pair tore the pontiff away, bundled him over towards the catapult, hoisted him up and dropped him in the cup. There, he wailed and whimpered, scrabbling and flailing like an oversized spider in a bucket.

Gratian extended his arms wide. 'We can send you to speak *with* the Gods.'

Three more Alani wound the torsion handles either side of the catapult. The groan of straining ropes and bending timber just disguised the splatter of the pontiff's bowels loosening. 'Wait... no...*wait!*' he warbled as one Alani clutched the peg holding the stone thrower at bay... then grinned and pulled the peg free.

With a violent buck and a whirr, the catapult arm swept upwards, casting the pontiff into the forest at a great speed, a shower of his own wet shit spraying along with him. His scream was horrible – not like that of a person. Somewhere deep in the woods, it ended with a thwack of flesh pounding upon the trunk of a tree. All fell silent.

'What the curio said about my wife,' Gratian said quietly, looking off into the woods. 'It was true, all of it. Sadly, we were ill-matched.'

Ulixes' mind spun. *Were?*

He saw then what Gratian was looking at out there: a body hanging from a rope tied to the branches of an elm tree. A woman's body. Constantia.

'You see, augur, she was slow in bearing me heirs. Eventually, my physicians declared her barren.'

Ulixes slowly closed his eyes.

'She kicked and struggled for a long time,' a lighter voice added. Ulixes opened his eyes again to see a flame-haired woman stride from behind one of the catapults to circle Gratian slowly, the hems of her silver stola trailing behind her, her shoulders wrapped in wolf-fur. She moved like a vixen, her full and lustful face set in an unnerving grin. Laeta was older than Gratian, glowing with experience and reeking of rose and cinnamon oil… and ambition. Ulixes cursed her inwardly. Laeta – supposedly a mere court attendant – had been there when Constantia's attendant had passed on the watch details. The plotters' fates had been sealed from that moment on.

A violent groan of ropes being drawn tight scattered his dreadful spiral of thoughts: the two Alani were working the catapult's torsion handle, winching the cup back down again. 'You next,' Gratian said calmly, clicking his tongue.

Ulixes' legs seemed to be made of reeds, and he felt a hot wash of urine spilling down his thighs. But briefly, through the dark shroud of fear, he realised that he was dead no matter what he did. *No matter what.* His fingers traced against the hilt of the curio's dagger, hidden under a fold of his robe since that final moment in the tent.

'Come on,' Gratian beckoned as if calling a dog. Laeta laughed at this, settling down on a nearby stool to watch.

Ulixes stepped forward, shaking violently. Just a step away from the catapult, he pulled the dagger free and slashed it up towards Gratian's throat. The gleaming steel was but a hand's width from the emperor's unprotected flesh... and then a second blade flashed downwards, cutting cleanly through his bicep. The arm and the dagger dropped harmlessly to the ground. Ulixes gasped and fell away, engulfed by a white fire of pain, clutching the stump uselessly as blood pulsed from the wound. He fell to his knees by a low-burning camp fire and gawped up at the demonic figure striding towards him – a scowling Galatian Frank in Roman scale, sporting molten gold eyes and crowned with a hideous copper-coloured wig with two long braids. This demon's sword was still wet with Ulixes' blood as he swept it back across his shoulders and with one mighty strike, swooshed it through the augur's neck.

Ulixes' final memories were of whirling chaos as his head spun through the air, bounced then rolled into the nearby fire. The flames licked at his skin and eyes, and had he any lungs with which to scream, he would have screamed until they burst.

'Well watched, Comes Arbogastes,' Gratian clapped slowly. 'I saw you shadowing us as we moved towards the edge of the camp.'

The tribal general quarter-bowed respectfully, cleaning his sword and replacing it in his scabbard. An attendant came scurrying over to hand the officer his helm – a fine iron piece, topped with a golden plume. Gratian watched as he buckled it on. Arbogastes – nephew of Richomeres – was fiercely loyal... to gold and riches.

'And your ears,' he gestured magnanimously towards Laeta as always, 'are like a bat's.'

Her reply came in the form of a sultry and seductive smile – a flash of white teeth and a rolling back of her shoulders, accentuating the fullness of her breasts.

The crunch of running feet brought all eyes towards the heart of the camp. A giant loped towards the catapults, two legionaries running with him. Strands of thin, brown hair hung across his fire-scarred face. He wore just a tunic, thrown on in haste having been woken hastily. He carried a drawn sword. 'Domine – trouble?' Merobaudes panted, then halted, eyes taking in the scene: the smouldering head, the decapitated body and amputated arm, not to mention the pontiff-shit dripping from the catapult cup. When he did look up and meet Gratian's eye, there was a hardness in there. 'I came as soon as I heard the catapult ropes working,' he said. 'I thought the Bucinobantes had rallied for a night strike on our camp.'

Gratian stared back with a venomous mien. Laeta had listened and watched keenly, even following the suspects around for some time. Not once had any of them mentioned Merobaudes' name. *But that does not mean you had no part in it,* he growled inwardly. *You live in hope that my whelp half-brother Valentinian will rise to the Western throne in my place. Remember, you great oaf, I only tolerate you as master of my armies because of the many other irksome generals who support you. And those many become fewer with every passing moon...* 'Good of you to join us, Magister Militum,' he said saltily, adjusting his diadem. 'Had it not been for Arbogastes, I would right now be thrashing on the ground with a knife in my throat.'

'Had you not asked me to step aside from my old role as your protector, then it would have been I and not Arbogastes who saved you tonight.'

Gratian smiled at this. A hateful smile, for Merobaudes was confoundingly noble, so much so that he was inclined to believe the big man's claim. 'Back to my tent,' he said, swishing a hand and striding back into the heart of the camp. There, another ring of Alani stood watch. Nearby, more men trudged to and fro, caked in dirt to their knees as they brushed down the emperor's silver stallion and dug a fresh latrine pit. Most of them were moustachioed or bearded or sported the long red or brown hair that told of their tribal past. Gratian caught the eye of Lanzo, Tribunus of these Heruli. Once the Heruli had been his chosen regiment, but they had let him down. He had toyed with the notion of exterminating them. Emperors past had wiped out disobedient regiments entirely. He reached into his silk purse and felt the small token in there – a roundel of silver marked with the scythe of Saturn. *You don't know how lucky you are,* he thought as he glowered at Lanzo, *to be crawling around in mud and shit.*

He stopped by the entrance to his pavilion, beckoned Arbogastes inside but barred Merobaudes with a hand, looking the giant up and down. 'Oh, you can return to your slumber, Magister Militum.'

Merobaudes glared down at Gratian, then flashed an equally fiery look at Arbogastes – peering out triumphantly from within – before swinging away and stomping off. Gratian entered the tent, pouring himself a cup of wine then sinking back onto a chair draped with furs for warmth and comfort.

'The conspirators have been dealt with?' said the slight figure seated at the far side of the tent, almost apologetically. Ambrosius, Bishop of Mediolanum, leaned forward a little, the brazier casting his delicate face in a gentle uplight. His thin nutbrown hair was swept back across his scalp and he sported a close-cut beard. His clasped hands rested within the wide sleeves of his loam-coloured robe.

'I sent them on a final journey, shall we say,' Gratian chuckled to himself. His face fell gravely serious for a moment and he gestured towards the small Christian shrine set up at the end of the tent, with prayer scrolls and sweet oils laid out. 'I will, of course, pray tonight. A wealth of penitence. That will suffice, yes?'

The bishop smiled and relaxed back into his chair. By now Comes Arbogastes and the Alani Tribunus had assembled before him. Laeta lay on her side along a silk-padded couch, still wearing that teasing grin. Gratian felt a swelling in his loins. He snapped his fingers to clear his head and jog his memory. 'We had business to attend to before the conspiring priests were brought to my attention.'

'The East,' Arbogastes reminded him.

'Ah yes, some goings-on in Constantinople, you last reported. Riders and wagons arriving. Some kind of summit?'

'A ceremony, Domine,' Arbogastes replied. 'Theodosius again defies you. He has crowned his son as his heir.'

Each word felt like a droplet of poison that blazed through Gratian's veins. 'He has chosen his Caesar... *without* consulting me? Without seeking the permission of his master?' he said through clenched teeth, his head twisted a little to one side as if daring Arbogastes to repeat the news. 'He means to form a dynasty?'

'It is true,' Arbogastes sighed. 'It seems the threat of your many legions only spurs him to new heights of impudence. I have already formed a consular group and arranged their means of travel to Constantinople. Theodosius will answer for his actions. All they need is your say-so and they will set off.'

'Yes yes, send them,' Gratian said with a dismissive swish of one hand, then drained his wine then held it out to one side expectantly until a slave scurried over and handed him a fresh cup. He chuckled once. 'But the real solution is even simpler. I will form a dynasty of my own.' He turned a lustful look upon Laeta, who mirrored it with one of her own. 'I intend to marry again in the spring. The ceremony will be at Treverorum. Send word to the Western cities so my best men have time to travel to my capital. Oh, and do be sure to invite Lady Justina and my young stepbrother Valentinian from Mediolanum. It would only be fitting that my "Co-Ruler",' he said this with a comic wobble of his head and a pawky look, 'and his mother attend.' Arbogastes laughed obediently. 'Do make it clear that the invite is not optional, and that I wish for them to stay afterwards... indefinitely.' He swirled his cup. 'I am beginning to find it most convenient to have troublesome people close to hand.'

Arbogastes smirked at this. 'It will be done, Domine.' He scratched under his wig, then cleared his throat. 'There was something else. Our spies who witnessed Arcadius' coronation were on the road for a time after that – observing how things were panning out in Thracia. Over the weeks following the ceremony, they saw the many visitors disperse back to their provincial bases – some sailing across the Aegean, others to Aegyptus, most to the Macedonian cities. But there was one party who sped westwards. Hooded men, so they could not tell who they were or what their purpose was – but they were no ordinary travellers, going by their garb and steeds. They took the Via Militaris. All the way here.'

'Here?'

'Into the West, Domine.'

Gratian's eyes narrowed. 'Where exactly?'

'They tracked them for a while along the *Via Julia*, but then they vanished, somewhere near the crossroads – where the highways splay out like the fingers of a hand. They could have gone south to Italia, due west into the heart of Gaul, north to Britannia. Anywhere.'

Gratian's gaze drifted across the interior of his tent as he sank into a deep well of thought, finding no answers. 'Put a missive out to all of the waystations to be vigilant. Be sure that any more sightings are reported to me immediately.'

'I have already seen to both of these things, Domine,' Arbogastes quarter-bowed.

'Now, aside from Theodosius' impudence, what else can you tell me about Thracia? The Goths are settling?' *Like thorns in Theodosius' flesh, with any luck,* he added inwardly.

'They have established towns, repopulated broken imperial cities and spread out across the countryside to sow that long-untended soil,' Arbogastes answered.

'How dull,' Gratian chuckled. 'Nothing more?' Then his eyes lit up. 'Zeno! Crassus and the two cohorts I sent East should have met with him now. Has he-'

Arbogastes' shark grin and slow nodding stopped Gratian. 'The Claudians are on the old island fort. It is happening. Slowly, one-by-one, the soldiers who fought alongside Pavo will be...' he tilted his head one way then the other, 'retired.'

Gratian's gaze grew distant. 'Not too fast. I want them to live in misery for a year – more, even. Perhaps I will travel east to watch the last of them perish.'

A lingering silence hung like a smoke in the tent. Finally, the lustful look in Gratian's eyes faded. 'Anything else from Thracia?'

'Nothing,' he said. 'Well, there was just this oddity.' He rummaged in his leather bag and presented a golden band. A beautiful thing.

Gratian realised it was a torque. A ceremonial piece, the likes of which he would award to a brave soldier.

'One of our Speculatores concealed back in Thracia goes under the guise of a harbour worker. He was in a tavern one night, near the Dionysopolis cliffs. He overheard fishermen talking about a great find, then saw one of them flashing this. The Speculator waited outside in the darkness until the fisherman left, followed him home, cut his throat and took the piece. It appears to be one of the ones you awarded last year during the final push against the Goths.'

Gratian lunged up from his seat and snatched it from Arbogastes' hands, staring at the inscriptions on the gold. 'I placed it around the neck of that wretch, Pavo,' he laughed. The laughter was rich and full at first as he remembered his frantic swordfight with Pavo on the edge of those cliffs, then the sweet sight of the damned legionary falling to his death. But then the laughter tapered off. He had left his agents behind in Thracia to find... 'His body. What about his body?'

Arbogastes shook his head. 'The fishermen found the torque in the waters, so surely he must have drowned. Especially after that fall.'

'How does a corpse prize a torque from its neck?' Gratian said in a clipped tone.

'Maybe sharks pulled his flesh apart and the torque was all that remains? Maybe the fishermen robbed it from his body and decided not to mention that part,' Bishop Ambrosius mused.

'I want... to see... his corpse,' Gratian said flatly.

'Wherever it is, it would by now have long rotted beyond recognition,' Laeta added lazily from the couch.

It was a most unsatisfying truth. Gratian longed to have someone to blame for this. Perhaps the Speculator posted at Dionysopolis would burn for it. A fisherman had found more of Pavo than that useless agent.

'Shall I continue, Domine?' Arbogastes interrupted his thoughts. 'There is also news from the Persian front.'

Gratian blinked. 'Ah yes. How goes Theodosius' embassy to the King of Kings?'

Arbogastes spoke through a cage of teeth in a tone tight with frustration. 'The ambush failed. The embassy made it across the Euphrates and into Persian lands.'

Gratian clicked his tongue. 'That is a shame, a damned shame. You made all the necessary arrangements for the ambush, I presume?' he said, toying with the fang-ring on his finger, glancing up to check that Arbogastes understood the potential punishment had he failed in his preparations. Scores of men had been ordered to put on this ring, nick their own neck veins and bleed out in shame before him.

'I did everything, Domine. I swear to you.'

Gratian held up a pacifying hand. 'I trust you, Arbogastes. That is why I have elevated you above that great oaf, Merobaudes. That is why I have placed you in command of my Speculatores. My previous Optio Speculatorum made a hash of things and ended up smashing his own brains out on a rock at Dionysopolis. I know you will do better.'

'I will, Domine,' Arbogastes said. 'The ambush may have failed, but my best Speculator is embedded in the ambassadorial party and will foil the talks. Shapur will reject the overtures and Persia will return to an aggressive stance against Theodosius and the Eastern Empire.'

Gratian gazed into his wine and sucked in a deep, refreshing breath through his nostrils. It was perfect. The East had to be kept weak, dependant. His to control and to save from time to time. He noticed a faint wrinkle on Arbogastes' brow, partly-hidden by the copper-coloured wig. 'There is more?'

'I'm not sure. In his coded messages about the failed ambush, my Speculator reported something strange.'

Gratian stopped swirling his wine. 'Did he?'

'The rag-tag of legionaries gathered up to escort the ambassador and officers, they were chosen for their unsuitability. Deserters, physically-unfit types. Yet he said there were two amongst them who stood out. Two who fought like lions against the ambushers, apparently.'

'There is always a shiny coin amongst a sack load of dull ones, I suppose,' Gratian mused idly, sipping at his wine again. He swirled the cup, smacking his lips together.

'They speak with Thracian accents,' Arbogastes added reluctantly, 'and… and one of the ambassadorial galleys set off from the site of the Dionysopolis battle.'

Gratian frowned, looked at the torque, then Arbogastes, then at the torque again. His heart pulsed. The missing corpse. Surely… surely not? 'Oh come on now,' he laughed. 'You said it yourself – Pavo is dead.' He glanced at Ambrosius, then Laeta then Arbogastes, looking for assurance from each. Arbogastes smiled unconvincingly. Ambrosius raised his eyebrows as if entertaining the alternative possibilities. Laeta chewed on her bottom lip, a look dripping with dark suggestion.

He felt a throbbing in his ears. Blood, pounding. He saw in his mind's eye the thing that had plagued his dreams before he had thrown Pavo to his death. The thing he had not seen since. But now it was back. Neither human nor beast – just a great, swaying demon of pure shadow, its boots squelching as it drew towards him, its death-stink horrific, the sword hanging from its dark hand gleaming. At first it had been a distant blotch, swaying far across a great moor. Now it was close, so close. Its rattling breaths sent a deep chill through him. Its face was pure shadow yet in that spot of blackness he saw a thousand faces, of enemies old and current. Pavo and many, many others. *No... I vanquished you, and I...I have been repentant for everything I have done.*

Regardless, he felt his lips moving, beginning to whisper the Prayer of Penitence.

'O Almighty God, merciful Father,

I confess to you all my sins and iniquities,

with which I have ever offended you....'

'Domine?' Arbogastes said.

It was as if he had been wrenched from deep underwater. Suddenly the tent was quiet and still again, the sounds and sights of his nightmares gone. Gratian shook his head to clear his mind. 'The two legionaries out there, whoever they are... have them killed.'

Arbogastes nodded. 'It will be done. I will inform our Speculator within the embassy party.'

Meanwhile, in the north...

A ferocious westerly wind battered at the galley, the gold and white sails puffing like the chest of a giant, the timbers groaning in protest. The ship cut a brave path across the grey, angry peaks and soon, from the haze of spume and winter gloom a great white wall of cliffs emerged, topped with a carpet of lush green grass. Maximus stared at Britannia's rugged coastline, the freezing gale casting his short hair to one side. This cold, damp island had seemed like a prison of sorts when first he had been assigned to govern the province. Now... now he realised there were no bars around this coastline. Indeed, there were no limits at all anymore. He closed his eyes and recalled for the thousandth time the words on the scroll Saturninus had given him.

The galley followed the cliffs until they at last descended towards the bay of Dubris. Two towering, octagonal lighthouses stood like sentinels on the bluffs either side of this inlet, keeping watch over the fine harbour complex on the waterline. Here, the sails were hoisted and the crew skilfully guided the ship into the lee of the harbour. Maximus stepped down onto the wharf and was immediately surrounded by a retinue of elite black-armoured legionaries who cast him stiff-armed salutes.

'Your forward message arrived some time ago, Comes,' said the centurion. 'Your council is gathered and waiting.'

Maximus took a deep breath then, wordlessly, he led them in a trek through the grand marble arch on the wharf, then up through the market district and to the palace of Dubris' governor, Celer. As the returning *Comes Britanniarum*, this place was his to requisition.

Inside and blessedly out of the sea wind, the clatter of their boots echoed through the fire-warmed marble corridors until they came to a hall, painted with beautiful frescoes of springtime and scenes of the old Gods. In the centre of the room stood a half-circle of officers and officials. Britannia's ruling elite. Andragathius, known to most as simply 'Dragathius', was his towering and trusted cavalry commander. The expert horseman shot him a typically evil half-grin of welcome through curtains of prematurely grey hair, his shoulders encased in iron. Celer, the hunched old governor, was flanked by a dozen others in similar civilian dress. There were augurs and pontiffs from this island and a score more who had fled here from Gaul. All stared at Maximus, waiting on him to speak.

When he did speak, his lips barely moved, and there was a flintiness in his eyes. 'We have consent… from the East.'

The gathered ones whispered and murmured in excitement. Governor Celer edged forward, carrying a package.

Maximus stared at the package, then nodded gently. 'Let it begin.'

Celer smiled coldly, unwrapped the package and lifted out the purple cloak within. Carefully, the governor stepped around behind Maximus and draped the cloak upon his shoulders, fastening it with a golden fibula on his right breast.

Celer stepped back and said quietly. 'Hail Maximus, True Augustus of the West.'

Maximus felt a thrill of fire rise through him.

Dragathius threw up one of his ironclad arms, every other man in the gathering copying the gesture.

'*Hail Maximus!*' they boomed in unison.

Chapter 7
February 383 AD
Ctesiphon

Thunder rolled across the heavens and lightning ripped the sky in half. The two huge eagles broke from their circles and swooped towards one another. The white bird's talons extended first, each claw the size of a spatha. But the dark bird thrust its wings down powerfully, propelling it up out of the white one's path. As it sped over the white bird's back, the dark eagle's talons streaked through feathers and into flesh and the white eagle screamed.

Pavo, staring up at the great battle in the sky, a light spray of blood from above settling on his face. The crone, by his side, watched on too, her ancient visage also stained red.

'You show me a fresh war between Roman and Goth?' he asked.

She sighed, shaking her head.

'So it must be Persia and Rome,' he concluded. 'These talks, they are in danger of collapsing and if they do then-'

She held up a hand, demanding his silence. 'The war will happen far, far from here, Pavo.'

'Then I will not be part of it. I am condemned to remain at this sweltering edge of the world.'

A single tear rolled down the crone's face, almost disguised by the runnels of blood. 'I only wish that were true, Pavo,' she said, 'but men cannot escape their destiny. You will be part of this war and it will be dire.'

'You're wrong,' he said defiantly. 'For once, you're wr-'

His words faded when he felt a great whoosh of moving air above him. He looked up, seeing the two giant eagles grappling, entangled, plummeting towards him like an onager stone. No time to move, no hope...

He woke with a burst of breath and a defensive swipe of both hands. Eventually, his eyes adjusted to the pale stonework of the Persian palace cellar billet. His racing heart slowed and he wiped at his sleep-blurred eyes. On the bunk to the right of his, Clodus and Porcus were locked in discussion.

'Boiled thrush... mixed with cabbage,' Clodus said, sniffing the air.

Porcus lifted one leg and with a powerful *quack* released a new wave of stink into the room. Both began sniffing again. 'Definitely a touch of saffron in there.'

Pavo stared in utter horror.

A hand slapped down on his shoulder from behind, coming from the bunk on the other side of his. 'Come on, Pa... er Urbicus,' Sura grumbled. 'We're on duty. I was going to wake you but I could see you were having one of your dreams. Thrashing like a trout, you were.'

'Here's an idea,' Pavo said, turning to face Sura then swinging his legs from the bunk. 'Next time, just wake me. Especially if that pair are going to have an imperial farting competition right next to my bed.'

'A lasting finish to that one,' said Clodus lovingly, 'just a hint of burnt turnips and spoiled onions.'

Pavo, holding his breath, threw on his tunic and pulled on his boots, then buckled his belt.

The pair trudged up the stairs towards the feasting hall in silence. Nearly three months of this, they had endured. Day after day of directionless talks. Stilicho and Sporacius had been close to clinching at least a basis of agreement on several occasions, only for the rivalry between the two to spoil things – Stilicho's frankness at odds with Sporacius' more circuitous rhetoric. The Persian King of Kings seemed endlessly entertained by the Roman pair, enjoying their power-struggle and their frustrations.

Pavo entered the hall and took his place as usual by a pillar near the Roman table. At once, and as always, he kept Ripanus in the corner of his eye. The man was a poor fit. A ship's captain in the middle of Persia – why? Indeed, Stilicho had let slip that Ripanus was not supposed to have accompanied them inland. He was due to have dropped the ambassadorial party at Antioch then taken his ship back out to sea. But he had *asked* to join the party to help watch and protect them. Who would ask for this?

He noticed something else then: Shapur – sipping on wine chilled with ice brought down from the Zagros Mountains and munching through a fat goose leg stuffed with dates and herbs – made some signal with his eyes which his advisors read and they in turn gestured towards the Roman ambassadorial table. The hubbub of instruments and chatter faded – the time for talks arrived.

Tonight, Stilicho rose to speak first, falling prone before Shapur's throne. 'Permit me, Majesty, to take an alternative tack in our discussions,' Stilicho said as he rose. 'Perhaps it might be most conducive to a firm outcome, were we to first specify the desired result, then work towards it?'

Shapur stopped chewing on a goose leg and mopped at the grease on his beard – clearly not expecting to have to speak for some time, so used was he to Ambassador Sporacius' more meandering approach. He glanced either side of his peacock throne to his advisors, who all made gestures of agreement. 'Very well.'

Stilicho cleared his throat and began: 'You seem unimpressed with the notion of reorganising the territories of Armenia to give half to Rome while keeping half for yourself. But think of it another way. The Hun threat – which we both agree is very real – will likely arrive once more through the Caspian Gates, north of Armenia. If you insist upon retaining the majority of that land, then you and your armies will bear the brunt of the Hunnic assault. Your mighty cities will burn, Persian corpses will be thrown in great heaps by those vile horsemen. Is it not shrewder to have the forces of Rome there too, alongside your regiments? Will we not stand a better chance of repelling the Huns... together?'

The hall remained silent. Shapur's eyes grew wide, like a sleepy man trying to stay awake. Pavo saw the sparkle of realisation in there. Stilicho was no silk-tongued negotiator, but he was wise, particularly in the field of strategy.

'You make a strong argument, General,' Shapur said softly. 'Rome's military assistance in guarding the north in exchange for a few tracts of Armenian soil and barren mountains? Hmm. What guarantees could you give that you would not try to encroach and expand?'

Stilicho paced to and fro in the centre of the floor. 'I would need to plan this with Emperor Theodosius, however that would be *our* problem to solve. But in principle, can we work towards that model and-'

'King of Kings,' Sporacius interrupted, rising, moving over to Shapur's throne dais and hastily prostrating himself. He stood again and moved behind Stilicho, placing his hands on the general's shoulders. 'Here stands a great military mind. But Stilicho is perhaps not privy to the realities of the Eastern Empire's shortages – particularly manpower in the legions. I would not like to predicate any outcome of these talks on a promise that could not be delivered.'

Stilicho twisted his head round to pin the ambassador with a gimlet stare.

'We *have* fresh numbers in theory,' Sporacius added quickly, 'but forty thousand recently-pacified Goths is not – I imagine – what you would wish to have on your doorstep.'

Shapur jostled once with a squeak of mirth, then began shaking with a low, long bellyful of laughter. 'No, not at all... not at all,' he agreed, then lifted the goose leg and began chewing upon it again. An advisor clapped his hands and the infernal dancers and wrestlers came trouping out once more – closing off the talks for another hour at least.

Stilicho visibly slumped where he stood as the dancers pranced and sprang around him, before he trudged back to the Roman table. There, he and Sporacius shared heated words, fists being thumped on the table and tight lips moving, the exchange mercifully drowned out by the commotion of entertainment. Pavo watched the pair and tried to lip-read, but to no avail. He found himself willing Stilicho to win the debate. It was only after a time that he realised something.

Ripanus was gone.

It was like a sudden cold shower of rain. He flicked his gaze around the room. Nowhere to be seen in here. He glanced over to Sura, but he was staring intently at the gyrating buttocks of a female Persian dancer. He looked over his shoulder to the hall doors and the two prowling griffin statues. Out there the corridors were striped with torchlight and shadow, but he was sure he saw something moving – the trailing swish of a cloak, vanishing into some side-passage.

'Mucianus,' Pavo hissed across the room at Sura. '*Mucianus!*' But his friend was utterly spellbound by the Persian dancer's bottom. Pavo knew he should not leave his post, but in this chaos of feasting and dancing, nobody would notice. It could be explained away as following Ripanus to protect him. Convinced by his own argument, he peeled away from his post and left the hall. The eyes of the two ironclad pushtigban guards standing watch by the griffin statues slid inside the eye-slits of their masks as they watched him go, and indeed they did not try to stop him. He followed the main passageway until he came to the spur corridor where he thought he had seen the movement and the trailing cloak. Nothing down this unlit corridor, except more passageways and stairs at the end. He set off along it, the noise from the feasting hall falling into a muffled din behind him. He took turns here and there, trying to remember each so he could find his way back. The White Palace was, by night, decidedly black. Some corridors sported torches but others were lit by just smouldering saucers of scented resin or nothing at all. The further he went, the more the music and singing from the feasting hall faded. More and more until eventually, he could hear nothing but the singing of crickets from the gardens down below any time he came past an arched window.

Sure he was lost and had certainly lost the trail of Ripanus, he halted at one window, leaning on the sill and gazing out over the sprawling wonder of Ctesiphon. A sea of torches and glorious architecture, the moonlight making shadows of palm thickets and a silvery ribbon of the River Tigris. Despite such beauty, he felt a great sadness. Never had he felt so pointless, so alone, so lost – chasing some half-mystery when there was none to be found. He closed his eyes and thought of home, of the vital, pulsing life he had once known in Thracia. He recalled a breakneck horse ride across the plains, Felicia hugging his back, the iron-cold wind in his hair, the promise of youth and greatness swelling his heart. Everything about the memory was gone now – dead or changed irrevocably.

When he opened his eyes, they were blurred with tears. He almost missed the strange movement down on the ground, two floors below the window. Beside a slave's entrance, an undistinguished man stood by a horse, waiting. He was dimly lit by the guttering light of a torch mounted on a stone post nearby. Another man crept toward him from behind. *Ripanus!* Pavo mouthed, recognising the bow-legged gait. Ripanus seemed set to pounce upon the unsuspecting rider until, with a slight start, the horseman turned and the pair quietly greeted each other. Ripanus gave the man something. A scroll. The meeting lasted no more than a few breaths before Ripanus sank back into the palace via the slave door. The horseman mounted his steed and heeled it into a canter off towards the bridge and the city's western side. Pavo saw the telltale outlines of heavy water skins hanging from the saddle. A man headed west and prepared for a long journey…

The mystery was very real. Plagued with dark thoughts, Pavo paced to and fro by the window. It was the dull, distant sound of footsteps that stopped him. Distant, but coming closer, someone padding along the corridor below, then pacing up the stone stairs to this level. Ripanus? Struck with fright, he set off back whence he had come. Left, then right, then… was it right again? The directions he had tried to remember fell apart like a kicked-over stack of shields, but the footsteps behind him were there – telling him he was headed in the right direction if Ripanus was coming back this way too. He came to the end of one passageway and found the next one extending left and right. Hearing the soft thump of footsteps behind him, he felt his pulse quicken: which way to go? Peering left, he spotted a bulbous urn, chased with silver and taller than a man. He scuttled along that way and crouched behind it. Ripanus would either emerge in his wake, turn left and pass by this urn or go down the right-hand route and then he could follow. But no matter how hard he strained to hear, there was nothing but silence. No footsteps now. Treacherously, the slow, steady *thump-thump* of his heartbeat replaced the absent noise. His eyes raked the darkness at the end of the corridor from which he had expected to see Ripanus emerge. Nothing. Or was the man crouching in those shadows staring back at him? His mind began to mould the darkness there into wicked faces.

He rose, carefully and slowly, backing away from the urn and on down the left-hand route while keeping his eyes on those shadows. He flicked a glance over his shoulder, seeing a reassuring arch of night sky and faint orange city light at the end of this hall. Back, back, back he went. When he felt his heel touch the wall under the window, he halted, exhaling in relief. Ripanus had not emerged from the shadowy corridor. It had all been in his mind. The man had probably taken another passageway and he'd missed the change of direction. With a wry chuckle, he turned towards the window, began to draw in a breath of fresh night air… and froze. The blood in his veins turned to ice as he beheld the shadow filling the window arch, crouched like a killer ready to leap in at him.

And then it pounced.

Pavo threw up his fists to fight, only just checking out of a powerful hook when he recognised her dusky features in the dimness. 'Izodora?'

She pressed a finger to his lips. *He's following you,* she mouthed.

So are you, evidently, he mouthed back.

'Come, I know my way around this place,' she whispered, taking his hand. She led him up onto the window sill and out onto the balcony that ran along the palace's upper floor. They ducked as they passed other windows where pushtigban guards stood watch, then climbed through another into a small chamber, filled with bright gowns and scarfs. Pavo stared at the apparel, then almost leapt from his skin when he saw an army of men facing him, only to realise it was a crescent of tall, polished bronze mirrors and the men were reflections of himself. 'It's Shapur's dressing room,' she explained. She guided him into a tight stairwell at the back end of the room, and he followed her down the spiral flights. At last they emerged in the cool, stony cellar – a long, wide and torchlit corridor leading to the billet chamber. This area was brightly lit, and palace cooks and slaves passed by every so often as they walked along. Through the billet-room doorway, ahead, he caught a glimpse of the escort legionaries in there bantering and playing a game of 'bandits' on a coloured board they had bought at the royal market. From the adjacent main stairs, he heard the spreading babble of the attendees in the upper floor leaving the feasting hall – the talks and entertainment over for another night. After creeping around in the silent darkness of the upper floors, the familiarity of all this set him at ease.

He slowed, placing a hand on her shoulder, turning her to face him. 'Why are you here?'

'I come here every few moons to report to Shapur's council. It is not the first time I have returned since I brought you here.'

'But you weren't reporting to the council tonight,' Pavo said. 'You were climbing around the palace's outer walls like a spider. Why?'

'Because Ripanus is not who he claims to be. The last time I came here a few weeks ago, I witnessed him passing a message to the horseman. I heard them talking and arranging to meet again tonight. This time I returned, set on listening in to the full exchange. But then I saw you floundering around past windows like a blind man. I knew that if you caught him doing whatever he is doing then it would not end well for you.'

'So you're telling me you've saved me a third time?'

'More or less.'

'And what now? You leave for the desert once more?'

'Not quite,' she said, disguising a gulp.

'Izodora?' He took her hand, forgetting himself for a moment as he recognised the sharp look of anguish in her eyes.

'Three weeks ago, our camp was attacked by mountain raiders,' she said with some difficulty. 'The eighty Maratocupreni who saved you at that desert village number just nineteen now. Our time as a force... even as a people, is over. I need to inform the Shahanshah's council of this.'

He sighed, folding his arms around her, affording her the privacy to sob. 'You live on and thus so will the Maratocupreni. Think of all the lives you have saved: none will ever forget you or your kin. They will tell their children and their children's children about you.'

She looked into his eyes then – hers wet with tears. He saw in her gaze that same hopelessness he had felt during that moment of weakness by the upper floor window. The affinity only made him hold her closer. When a tear escaped her eyes, he caught it with the edge of his thumb and wiped it tenderly away. Now her sadness changed into a gentle smile... and the sight was like a glowing taper touching his heart. Such effortless beauty, such a need he felt to protect her. At that moment, he almost remembered what it was like to share such moments with another. Their heads moved a little closer. Her eyelids slid down just a fraction then, giving her a sultry look, and she moved her lips towards his. But, as if someone had doused that glowing taper, Pavo recalled his final moments with Felicia and with Runa the Goth. He turned his head briskly away. Izodora drew away from him, the misty look turning sour.

An awkward silence reigned. Then...

'Mithras' arse! What's going on here?'

Both jerked apart to see Sura, descending the main stairs to the cellar corridor, one side of his face red with the handprint shape of a recent slap.

'Ah, sorry, am I interrupting?' he said, mimicking a backwards walk up the stairs again.

'Interrupting? Interrupting what?' Pavo laughed, waving him down. 'Did you see Ripanus tonight?'

Sura bit his bottom lip. 'To be honest, I didn't see much tonight, apart from the most juicy, round arse.' He tenderly touched the red side of his face. 'I tried to speak to her with what little Parsi I've picked up...' he started with spread hands of innocence.

'...and?'

'And it turns out I called her a delicious cow,' he finished, crestfallen. But his head shot up again, eyes narrow. 'Anyway, at least I remained at my post. I had to cover for you when Stilicho asked where you'd gone.'

'Ripanus slipped from the hall,' Pavo cut in with a sharp whisper. 'I followed him. He's been passing messages to a rider.'

Sura's expression turned grave. 'I told you.'

'Have you seen him? Did he return to the hall for the end of the feast?'

Sura's brow crumpled. 'No, no he wasn't there.'

With a rapid clatter of hobnails, another figure came rattling down the stairs. Stilicho, dishevelled, face wrought with worry.

'General?' Pavo said.

'Urbicus, Mucianus... where is he?' Stilicho snapped, flashing Izodora a glance then a courteous nod of greeting.

'Ripanus? We don't know?'

Stilicho frowned. 'What? No, not the sailor. Ambassador Sporacius. He returned to his chambers, I to mine. I was undressing when I heard his door click. I went to see why he was stepping out, what he needed. His room was empty. He was nowhere to be seen.'

Pavo's heart thudded as he began to piece it all together. 'Sir. Sporacius is in grave danger. Ripanus... I think he was behind the ambush in the desert.'

Now Stilicho's face pinched in a mix of fury and horror. 'What?'

'That ambush was no coincidence,' Izodora agreed.

'He wants to sabotage these talks,' Pavo explained.

Sura's eyes darted. 'What better way to sabotage a negotiation...'

'Than by killing the lead negotiator,' Stilicho finished for him.

Pavo's mind raced as he looked along the cellar corridor. 'Sir, why did you come down *here* in particular?'

'Because the only other times he's left his room at night is to come for a walk in the gardens.' Stilicho jabbed a finger upwards to the ground floor and the grand doorway leading out into that terraced treasure box of blooms, orchards and hedgerows. 'But he's not out there, as I said. So I thought he must be down here... but he's not,' he shrugged in desperation, looking both ways down the corridor then pulling off his felt cap and wrenching at his thick brown curls, muttering frantically to himself.

'Sir?' a voice said apologetically.

All turned to see Porcus the escort legionary, leaning out from the billet room.

'I heard you mention Trierarchus Ripanus? I saw him, just a short while ago.'

'Where?' Stilicho demanded.

The legionary tipped his head in the direction of the cellar corridor's far end. 'He went that way.'

All gazed along the brick passageway. At the far end, poorly lit, was a heavy wooden door, the frame thick with dust. The handle too – apart from the recent spots where fingers had pulled upon it.

'If Ripanus crept down there, then I fear that's where we'll find Sporacius too,' Pavo whispered.

Izodora let out a low moan of woe. 'I hope, may the Gods of the Desert will it, *not.*'

'Why?' Pavo said. 'What's wrong? What's down there?'

She eyed them all, then turned to him last. 'In Roman lands, you might call it Hades.'

If the upper floor corridors had been gloomy, this dank, chilly stairwell was blacker than night.

'How can we be going *down*wards? I thought our billet chamber was in the cellar?' Sura whispered.

'It is. This is the *lower* cellar,' Izodora hissed over her shoulder, leading the small party by feeling her way along the stairwell walls. 'Shapur, like Kings past, uses this place to deal with his enemies... slowly.'

Pavo and Sura each shot a look at the spot in the darkness where the other's face was.

When Izodora suddenly halted, Pavo bumped into her back, Sura into his and Stilicho into Sura's.

Pavo reached out to feel the same thing she had: a wall of bricks. A dead end.

'These stairs were bricked up years ago,' she said. But then, with a low rumble of moving stone and a grunt, she pulled one free, and from beyond the wall a dim yellow glow of light shone. Piece by piece, she withdrew the bricks until there was a gap big enough to crawl through.

'Ripanus came this way?' Pavo asked.

She nodded to the recently-disturbed dust on the remaining few stairs beyond the hole. 'Looks like it.'

'Could he have dragged Sporacius through too?'

'At the moment, I'm not sure exactly what he can and cannot do,' Izodora said. 'Now come.' She beckoned them through one by one and they crouched at the bottom of the stairs. A network of brick tunnels spread out here. The two largest ones diverged like a Y.

'You and Su... Mucianus, go right,' Pavo suggested to Izodora, then turned to Stilicho. 'Sir, we can go left.'

The two pairs separated. Pavo and Stilicho kicked off their boots to move without a sound. Soon enough they heard plenty of noise. It was a low, gentle moan, tapering every so often into a wet cough and shriek. The pair saw an opening in the right wall of the tunnel ahead, above waist height – like some kind of viewing gallery. They fell to their haunches and crept along under the opening then halted, both signalling that they were ready to risk a look over into the recessed chamber beyond. Both men rose and then froze when they saw the source of the noise, each wishing they had not looked.

A man was suspended near the ceiling by his ankles and wrists like an awning, spread-eagled, facing the floor. From a bed of soil on the floor rose green and sturdy shoots of cane. Pavo cocked his head a little to one side.

'Bamboo,' Stilicho whispered. 'Brought from the distant east by traders.' He groaned and recoiled, realising what was happening. 'See the grating?'

Pavo followed his gaze to the iron grating on the chamber ceiling. He didn't understand the significance, until a gentle breeze of fresh night air wafted across him from the direction of the grating. Now he understood.

'The sunlight shines down here in daytime, and the bamboo grows speedily towards it. A few finger-widths per day.'

Pavo stared hard at the sharp tips of the many canes, and saw that some had pierced the man's belly, and now rested deep inside him. Others stretched out like killer's fingers towards his neck and face, and would pierce his throat and eyes within a few more days of growth.

The wretch's moaning struck up again as, with a sucking sound, he strained to lift his belly off of the cane tips. He enjoyed a few instants of relative relief, before the moan became strained and shaky once more and, with a wet squelch, he sagged in exhaustion, the tips plunging into him again. His cries bounced off the tunnel walls around Pavo and Stilicho and off down the passageway in both directions.

'We've got to do something,' Pavo hissed.

But Stilicho merely placed a finger over his lips and gestured to the rear of the chamber and its doorway, where a Persian guard now stood, face pinched, eyes sweeping the torture chamber as if suspecting he had heard something. *We can't be caught down here.* Stilicho mouthed.

Reluctantly, the two crept silently on along the tunnel. They passed filthy, barred chambers where men hung by their wrists or lay shivering, naked and starved. After a while they reached a stretch that seemed endless – no cells or recesses and no sign of guards.

'He's down here somewhere, sir,' Pavo whispered. 'He's been plotting against us all this time. I don't know who he is, but he's not Ripanus.' Silence. Pavo halted and turned back to Stilicho. 'More, I think he might be a Specu-'

But Pavo's words fell away as Stilicho lunged for him and pinned him to the wall with his forearm, bringing a dagger in his other hand to Pavo's neck. Panic flared in Pavo's heart.

'And what about you?' Stilicho hissed. 'Urbicus? And that unhinged friend of yours, Mucianus? I find it strange how both of you stammer when you say each other's names. You're no legionary grunts. I saw it at the desert ambush.'

Pavo felt the blade break the skin of his neck, felt his fake identity fall away like a dropped cloak. Of all people, Stilicho had been the one to fear all along. How had he known? Too late now. It was over. 'I am Numerius Vitellius Pavo,' he spat, his final words defiant. 'Tribunus of the XI Claudia.'

Stilicho's face changed then. He released Pavo, pulled the knife back and slammed it into the tunnel floor, the tip wedging between two stones. He fell back to sit against the tunnel wall, wringing his hands through his hair. 'I saw it even before the ambush… in your eyes. Eyes of a veteran. Eyes that have seen too much. The *Claudia*, you say? By the Gods, they went through it all during the Gothic War, did they not? And you are their leader?'

'Aye, and the lunatic is Sura, my primus pilus.' Pavo said as he slumped down next to him, heart still pumping. 'So now you know. I am in exile. Emperor Gratian wanted me dead and right now he believes I died at Dionysopolis.'

'Wanted you dead – why?'

'Because,' Pavo shrugged, searching in futility for a euphemism, 'I tried to assassinate him.'

Even in the poor light, Stilicho's face paled.

'He is responsible for the worst throes of the Gothic War,' Pavo explained. 'He had good men murdered, sent proud legions marching to certain death. Worst of all, he withheld his Western armies when the East desperately needed them – all in the name of power.'

Stilicho wiped his face with both hands, suddenly looking haunted and haggard. 'Emperor Theodosius can barely bring himself to speak his name. I thought it was just rivalry at first, but then I heard rumours – suggestions more than anything.' He worked his dagger free of the stones and sheathed it. 'I know Theodosius is not perfect: he raised me to his sacrum consistorium because I am a good general, aye, but more so because I have Vandal blood in my veins. He knows I can never challenge for his throne. All emperors have their flaws, their jealousies. But Gratian, a murderer? Plotting *against* the East?'

'I suspect Ripanus is one of his agents,' Pavo replied flatly, 'a Speculator, sent here to foil this mission.'

Stilicho rose, offering Pavo a hand. 'If he is, he won't leave this cellar alive.'

The two went on until the long tunnel opened out into a strange, gloomy place: a large circular chamber with a dank, green pond dominating the floor, illuminated by moonlight through another grating on the high ceiling. A narrow culvert entered the chamber from one end, feeding the pond. Algae and slime coated the walls and water dripped into the pond with a rhythmic *plink-plonk*. A stale, musty odour hung in the air.

Pavo and Stilicho stared up and down the place, confused, then both jolted when two figures emerged from an opening at the far side of the pond. 'Sura, Izodora,' Pavo hissed, recognising them in the gloom.

'We found nothing but poor, shackled wretches lying in their own waste.

'Us too,' Pavo replied.

'This is a dead end,' Stilicho said. 'There are just these two routes we took to get here.'

Pavo looked around, seeing that there was no other way onwards. But there was a wide balcony of some sorts near the chamber ceiling, overlooking the pond. 'He must have climbed up there,' he said.

'*With* Sporacius?' Sura replied from the pond's far side. 'Ripanus looks strong, but not strong enough to carry a man up there.'

The mystery felt like a rolling ball of snow, growing and tumbling out of control. Then the most apologetic whimper echoed through the oval chamber. All eyes switched to the culvert. From there, a strange shape drifted into view, carried on the merest of currents. Pavo stared at the thing. A half log canoe. Strapped inside with thick ropes across his ankles, waist, chest and forehead… was Ambassador Sporacius. His face was bright red and streaked with sweat, his lips stained with what looked like milk and honey. So tight and strong were his bonds he could not move anything but his eyes, which rolled madly round, seeing Stilicho and Pavo, then Izodora and Sura. 'Help… *help* me!' he cried. With his next breath, he vomited a milky gloop of honey and milk mixed together. It cascaded over his face and chest.

Instinctively, Pavo splashed into the opaque water of the pond, wading towards the ambassador. Sura ran in from the opposite side. The pair yanked at the ropes but they were thick as ship-rigging. 'Give me your dagger,' Pavo called back to Stilicho. Stilicho reached for his belt and the hilt of the dagger there, only for a new voice to still them all.

'Oh, I wouldn't do that if I were you…'

Ripanus waded out from the shadows underneath the viewing balcony where he had been hiding like a wraith.

'Numerius Vitellius Pavo. Decimus Lunius Sura?' he said with a winter grin as he waded out into the water.

All of Pavo's fears crawled across his shoulders like icy insects. 'There are four of us and one of you, *Speculator,*' he spat.

'Oh, I am not alone,' Ripanus grinned. From the viewing balcony, a quartet of dark-skinned, bearded Persian archers rose, bows nocked and trained upon them. Behind them, Shahanshah Shapur swayed into view, being carried on a rush litter-throne by four servants, his face wide with a broad anticipatory grin, a low laughter toppling from his lips. They set him down near the edge of the balcony to watch, while his advisors and a knot of pushtigban splayed out either side the royal chair, aping his laughter.

Ripanus, staring at Pavo, held up his right hand. A classic prelude to an archer's signal. When the hand chopped down, the bows would loose. Ripanus held his hand like that for a short time, prolonging the wait for death... then reached up with his left to unbuckle the leather bracer there. The piece splashed into the water, revealing the black ink Chi-Rho stigma on his bare wrist.

'I am no Speculator,' he said calmly. 'I am an Inquisitor.'

Pavo recoiled. 'But... you're *not* Ripanus,' he countered.

'No,' he agreed immediately. 'A Speculator cut the throat of the real Ripanus, back on the shores near Dionysopolis. I saw him commit the murder, then followed him and watched him make his way through the dock gates announcing himself as the dead man, come to take ship to Persia...and he nearly did, until I staved his head in with a rock and took on the role myself. From the things on his person I could ascertain only one thing: that he was to rendezvous with another of his kind on this Persian mission.' He patted the head end of the canoe.

'Sporacius,' Pavo said in a low growl.

The ambassador's red, vomit-covered face shuddered, trying to shake his restrained head in denial. He issued a strangled, gargling cry through all the filthy fluids clogging his throat. 'Don't listen to him!'

'This creature here is a Speculator,' Ripanus wrenched Sporacius' collar down, revealing the single staring eye motif inked on his chest. 'It was *he* who arranged the ambush, sent you legionaries into the desert village, and saw to it that he was well clear of the scene before the bandits struck. Here in Ctesiphon, it was *he* who waylaid General Stilicho's incisive efforts to secure peace with the noble King of Kings,' he paused to turn and genuflect towards the balcony.

Now Pavo realised what he had seen from the upper floors. The shadowy horseman. 'You were sending messages to Emperor Theodosius.'

'Aye,' Ripanus said. 'All while Sporacius was sending messages back to Gratian's court. I followed him tonight when he tried to do so again – another 'walk in the gardens'. I did not plan him any harm, yet. However, it turns out that Mighty Shapur also had his suspicions that Sporacius was not exactly "driven" in his efforts to negotiate a peace. Thus...' he gestured to the canoe.

'And it is feeding time again, I believe,' Shapur said with a contented sigh.

Taking their cue, a pair of Persian attendants threw rope ladders from the balcony and climbed down. Each carried a haircloth pack on their back. They splashed into the waters and brought out bulging leather bags fitted with reed spouts. Both forced these spouts into Sporacius' mouth, then squeezed hard on the bags. Sporacius convulsed, the fresh milk and honey bubbling and streaming from his nostrils as they piped in every last droplet. He gasped frantically for air when they withdrew, then vomited again, this time the vomit was streaked with blood.

'It takes most men over half a moon to die on "the boats",' Ripanus explained.

Sporacius wailed and shuddered uselessly, pleading his innocence. Soon enough, his pleas turned to threats. 'I... I'll see you flayed in Gratian's underground chamber for this... you worm,' he roared, his mask falling at last. 'And you, Tribunus Pavo. You will suffer the hardest and longest of deaths.'

Ripanus' eyes rolled up to meet Pavo's. 'I trust you have no quibble with his fate? Emperor Theodosius gave me remit to deal with any who might spoil these talks as I should see fit. The Shahanshah, as you can see, is quite content with matters. Besides, the archers would shoot you down should you even think of trying to free this mutt.'

Pavo looked up to see Shapur's face streaked with tears of joy, issuing flat bleats of laughter at Ambassador Sporacius' hopeless struggles. He nodded once and stepped back from the canoe, Sura doing likewise.

'What now?' Pavo said.

'Stilicho is to return to Constantinople,' Ripanus said, holding up a scroll bearing Theodosius' seal – cracked. 'I will lead the rest of the talks.' He tossed the scroll to Stilicho.

Pavo and Sura both gazed at the rolled document in Stilicho's hands, both at once achingly-sad at the thought of their distant home. Pavo felt a second scroll hit him in the chest. His hands shot up to catch it before it fell into the pool. He gazed at it, turning the cylinder in his hands, his eyes settling on the intact blue wax seal. A *different* seal. 'From Saturninus?'

'Aye,' said Ripanus. 'I wasn't permitted to read it.'

Pavo cracked the wax disc and unfurled the scroll, he and Sura then read the text. Once, twice, and again. Both stared, wide-eyed.

Emperor Theodosius believes that as long as Gratian rules the West, you must remain in exile. I have rarely defied my emperor, but on this matter I must. For Gratian's rule is about to be challenged, and for that challenge to be successful, men like you, Pavo, must be there when it happens...

Pavo shared a pale-faced look with Sura. Their time as outcasts was over. More, the crone's dream made sense now: the two eagles were not Rome and the Goths or Rome and Persia... they were both Rome in different guises. A great war was brewing from within the empire itself, and he and Sura *would* be part of it.

Meanwhile, in Britannia...

'Mag-nus Maxi-mus! Mag-nus Maxi-mus! Mag-nus Maxi-mus!'

The chant soared above the white cliffs on Britannia's southeastern shores. The hinterland, green and sweeping elsewhere, was silver here – arrayed with a host of ironclad legions, drawn from the island-province's main military fortresses, from the rugged valley-lands in the west and even from the great wall in the north. The Victores – his lone Auxilium Palatinum legion, girt in iron and clutching golden shields emblazoned with white, prancing deer – were like an iron sea. Beside them stood his two *comitatenses* legions, roving and well-equipped field units: the Primani, carrying amber banners blazoned with black boars; the Secundani with white shields splashed with golden eagles. There were older legions who now served as his border and coastal guards: The VI Victrix, the II Britannica. The foreign units too: the Tigrisienses – a dark-skinned eastern archer regiment first posted here generations ago. Cohort upon cohort of auxiliaries: the Lingona, the Batavorum, the Tungororum, the Frixagorum and many more, all raising and lowering their spears and banners in time with the chant. Thousands of wagons and pack mules waited nearby.

Down by Dubris' docks, the *Classis Britannica* bobbed: hundreds and hundreds of galleys – liburnians, biremes, triremes, three huge quinqueremes and a majestic hexareme.

Maximus stood atop an ancient boulder near the edge of the chalky bluffs, his armour as white as the cliffs, his hands clasped behind his back as he stared out across the channel. The waters were grey and white-flecked as usual, the gulls screaming. In the distance, the grey haze masked the line where the sea met the pillowy-white sky, but Maximus knew that not far beyond lay the coastline of Gaul. The sea wind whipped and toyed with his hair, the salty air stinging his skin. Many thoughts rose and fell in his mind. Past lessons, fears for the future, Surging pride... and raw, human terror.

The rock under his feet began to shiver and a great rumble rose. He edged his head to one side, looking back over his shoulder to see Dragathius leading Britannia's *Scholae Palatinae*, the island's two huge, elite palace cavalry schools. The *Sarmaturum* – Sarmatian riders long-ago settled on these lands – rode with golden vests and flowing long hair – and the *Dalmatarum* – iron-scaled Roman horsemen originally raised in Dalmatia. Their tall bronze *draco* standards moaned as the sea wind passed through the dragon-head mouths, and the bright ribbons on the tails danced madly.

'Domine,' Dragathius thundered as he rode up next to Maximus, lifting his spear in salute.

The title still felt false to Maximus, but he hid his reactions well.

Dragathius swept his spear across the serried army. 'Two thousand crack cavalrymen. Fifteen thousand footsoldiers and archers. A fleet unmatched. It is time,' he held his fist near his heart and shook it, grinning maniacally, 'it is *time.*'

An *explorator* approached up the hill path from Dubris. The scout rider was wet with sea spray and blue with the cold. 'Domine. The watch over at the port of Caletum are with us,' he said, pointing across the waves. 'When we land there, we will meet no opposition.'

Maximus stared out to sea again, his eyes shifting eastwards along the coast of Gaul. 'We're not going to Caletum...'

'Domine?' Dragathius said.

'We don't know for certain that those men over in Caletum won't go running to Gratian and telling him everything. So we keep our enemy guessing, throw him crumbs to lead him onto a false trail, while we strike right at the heart of his territory.'

Dragathius stared for a moment, then let a long, low laugh escape, before throwing his head back and roaring with delight into the sky.

Maximus drew his spatha and turned to face his army. The chanting fell silent, the only sound that of the gulls and the skirling breeze. He held the blade aloft, the sea wind catching his cloak and casting it eastwards like a banner. 'Don your packs and weapons and take ship. When next you set foot upon soil, it will be in an ancient land... a land that suffers the rule of a tyrant. And the tyrant will fall. *That* is our prize. *That*... is our destiny!'

The army of Britannia thrust their spears, swords and banners aloft and exploded with a roar that rolled across the sky like thunder.

Part 2

The Call of War

Chapter 8
Late February 383 AD
Roman Syria

The march from Persia back into the empire was as cruel as the journey there had been. The unchanging horizon of flat, golden land and pastel-blue sky made it feel as if they were treading on the spot, and the sun poured its burning anger upon them hour after hour. The glare prickled on Pavo's face as he marched, and even when he dipped his head to escape the brightness, the pale dust underfoot reflected the heat and the blinding light up at him anyway. But he endured these hardships of the desert gladly. Sores on his ankles, aching shoulders and a parched mouth were a small price to pay for this chance to return home. Home... and a chance to press on to the West for justice and revenge.

Stilicho led the way. Pavo, Sura, Clodus and Porcus marched behind wearing their helms and carrying shields and spears – their armour packed away on the camels of Izodora and Darik who headed up the two small screens of Maratocupreni on the left and the right of the small knot of marching men.

'You realise I'm a bad liar?' Stilicho said, falling back to walk with Pavo and Sura. 'I'm supposed to arrive back in Constantinople, greet Emperor Theodosius and tell him you two are still back in Ctesiphon?'

Pavo unrolled the scroll and for the thousandth time scanned Saturninus' directions. *Emperor Theodosius must remain unaware of your return. Meet me on the Neorion wharf, at midnight on the Kalends of April.* Just over a month from now, he thought. 'Ripanus pledged to say nothing about our departure from Persia,' Pavo tried to reassure the general. 'More, we will be gone from your side before you enter the city proper. Anyway, the Eastern legions will no doubt be gathering near Constantinople, preparing to march west and help this Maximus. Saturninus will take care of integrating us into the ranks – maybe even into the Claudia. We will be two soldier-faces amongst many thousands.'

Stilicho held out his palms as if weighing invisible goods. 'Look, do what you must. I won't betray your position to the emperor. Had you asked that of me before we went through that palace dungeon together, I might not have been so amenable.' He smiled a tired smile and added: 'And I have to say, your life would have been far less complicated if you had just chosen to stay in Ctesiphon as Theodosius wants you to.'

'Stay in Ctesiphon?' Sura nearly choked. 'Balls to that. Nearly four months. Didn't get proper-drunk once. Never even saw a bare tit.' He spat into the dust and peered ahead to the gold and blue bands of the western horizon with a flinty look. Oddly, the perfect line between land and sky seemed smudged now. 'It's time to go home. Time to put things right.'

Pavo felt the weight of his spatha against his hip – like a missing limb reattached, so reassuring after the months of standing around Ctesiphon's halls unarmed. He grabbed and flexed his fingers on the hilt. 'I know nothing of this islander, Maximus, but if he is an enemy of Gratian, then he is my friend. The Army of the East and the Army of Britannia will unite and crush the bastard on the Western throne.'

The gentle brush of a camel's leathery footpads sounded beside them, the rider latching onto their conversation. 'I wondered what put such a bounce in your step on this long trek. Now I know,' Izodora asked with a tune of disdain. 'You rush home again… enticed by the prospect of war? War with your own people?'

Pavo squinted up at her – beautiful even with that terrible sneer on her face. They had not been alone since Ripanus had given Pavo the scroll, so he understood her reaction. But she was wrong. 'You think war impels me to return?'

She eyed him for a time before replying. 'I don't know, Pavo. I find it hard to understand a man like you. Even when you remove your iron jacket, still you wear armour.'

'Justice, Izodora. I march for justice. If war is the price then I will pay it.'

Izodora snorted and steered her camel back to the screening wing.

Pavo stared ahead, annoyed. He barely noticed that the smudged horizon ahead had now swollen into an odd loam-coloured cloud. They walked until they sighted a small oasis in the distance. It was no more than a thicket of palms and a small watering hole with a dozen wicker and hide domed shelters dotted around it – erected by travellers and left behind for others to use. The sandy-coloured cloud beyond had grown even more, Pavo noticed, and he was sure he could feel the oddest of things out here on this barren, arid plain: a breeze?

'Right, I'm famously good-looking,' Sura interrupted his train of thought. 'No hint of a question about it. But him,' he said, flicking a derisive finger out towards Darik, leading the camel screen on the right, 'he's *ridiculously* handsome.'

Just then, Darik chose to sweep the horizon with a devastating gaze, his chin turning like a sculpted block in a stonemason's workshop, his teeth whiter than snow, arrayed in a dashing smile – bright against his dark face. His shiny dark mane licked out in the strange and strengthening breeze like an emperor's banner, dancing across his mighty shoulders.

Sura's envy nearly stoked a chuckle from Pavo, until he saw Izodora, returning Darik's smile from the opposite camel screen. There was a definite ease and warmth between the pair. He felt a needling sensation rise in his chest. Now he laughed, bitterly. *I'm cold as stone when she tries to talk to me, then jealous when he is playful with her,* he berated himself inwardly. He thought again of that lost moment in the cellar. The kiss that never happened. Her in his embrace. But then he remembered again the awful moments he had spent holding the slain bodies of Felicia and Runa in his arms. *If you care for her, then you'll stay away from her,* he hissed inwardly to himself.

As they neared the oasis, Pavo saw the limp leaves of the palms there begin to flap. At the same time, a light puff of pale dust blew up across the travellers' faces.

'We should hurry,' Izodora said, riding in from the left and waving them on.

Sura coughed, crunching at the blown sand between his teeth and spitting it out. 'What's the rush? We're almost at this shelter,' he said breezily. 'Though that dirty cloud ahead reminds me of something.'

'Me too,' agreed Pavo, suddenly alert.

At just that moment, the palms at the oasis suddenly bent sharply over towards them as if bowing, the fronds blown flat. Bulging, roiling breaths of lifted sand barrelled across the oasis and towards them. 'The last time the Claudia marched across this desert,' Sura realised. 'The sandsto-'

With a *whump* and then a neverending roar, the sand cloud battered Pavo and Sura like a dragon's breath, swallowing them up. The sun, a glaring orb a moment ago, was now like a pale moon, hidden behind the thick sheets of the sandstorm.

'Get into the huts,' Darik bawled, swishing his mighty arms to shepherd Stilicho and the sand-blinded legionaries towards the shelters.

'Move!' Izodora shrieked.

Eyes stinging and full of sand grains, nostrils, ears and mouth too, Pavo staggered on towards the sound of the voices. He couldn't see a thing. A moment later, his toe stubbed on something, a hand shoved the small of his back, he cracked his forehead on something solid them fell into a bubble of still, sandless respite. Untying his helmet and coughing violently, he uncorked his water skin and splashed the contents across his face and eyes. Panting, he finally re-opened his eyes and saw that he was in one of the cupola shelters, alone, the flap tied shut with a leather cord. The storm raged across the small domes, rising in high-pitched wails as if the desert djinns the Maratocupreni always talked of circled out there. He heard the muffled, muted noises of the others safely within the nearby shelters – including Sura, Porcus and Clodus crying out: 'Sand in my hair, in my mouth... in my arse!'

The storm raged on and on, and Pavo hugged his knees to his chest. An hour passed and he felt a rising agitation. An hour *lost*. Another two hours passed and the storm only grew stronger. Tired and thirsty, his agitation gave over to exhaustion. He lay down on his side, determined to only let his body relax. It was still daytime and it would be unforgivable for a soldier to sleep while the sun shone. He felt his muscles relax, the heat inside the shelter just right, the pillow of sand upon which his head rested perfectly shaped. Just a short rest. No sleeping. No sleeping…

He thought he could still hear the screeching desert gale, but it was in fact the cries of the two giant eagles in the sky of the dream world. They struck and swooped at one another, sometimes crashing together and spinning through the sky in one great feathery ball for a time before breaking apart, even more torn and red. The rain of their blood was now constant, pooling on the dark ground around him. For an age, he could not avert his gaze from the great contest in the sky. But then, from the corner of his eye, he noticed the red-streaked figure of the crone beside him.

'You were right,' he said softly. 'My destiny is war, again. I will do whatever it takes to get there, to see justice done.'

'Ah, destiny – that golden lure!' she laughed – a sound like crackling parchment.

Annoyed, he turned to her, only to see that the laughter was not reflected in her worn-out, drawn face. As she turned her ancient head towards him, her milky eyes grew hooded.

'Sometimes a man can be so transfixed by where he is headed, that he becomes blind to the journey,' she said quietly, '… and to the creatures that lurk in the shadows along the way.'

A terrible chill crept up his back. 'Creatures… where?'

She leaned close to him, her eyes suddenly wide, her lips peeling back to reveal her clenched, age-worn teeth, through which she whispered: 'Everywhere.'

He jolted upright, waking in a panic, hearing the susurrating taunts of the storm again along with the tortured groans of the cupola tent frame. The hide walls were bulging inwards and rippling, like claws outside trying to tear their way in. *It's just the storm*, Pavo assured himself, taking a full breath... when, suddenly, something batted – hard – against the tent's hide entrance flap. Something, demanding entry. Pavo's blood ran cold. There it was again. *Slap-slap-slap.* He grabbed his spatha and held it up towards the sound.

'Let me in,' Izodora's voice barely carried above the storm. *Slap-slap-slap* went her palm against the tent flap again. *'Let me in!'* The words were like knives, sharpened with twin meaning. This shelter was small. No distractions, nowhere to hide from the tension between them. 'Pavo!' she yelled, shaking him to his senses. At once, he felt a great worry for her out there. He crawled over and hurriedly untied the flap tether. With a surge of storm wind like a giant's sneeze, she bowled inside in a puff of sand, gagging. He hurriedly laced up the flap again. 'What are you doing?'

She tipped up his levelled sword like a mother adjusting her son's apparel and he felt a flush of embarrassment that he had still been holding it defensively. 'I was sheltering with Darik. He said you cracked your head on the cane frame of the tent. I was worried that you might be badly injured. The longer this storm went on I imagined you lying in here alone with blood trickling out of your ears.'

Pavo sat cross-legged, facing her, then pushed a finger into one ear and wiggled it, pulling it free with a puff of golden particles. 'No, just sand in there.'

She fell back from her haunches to sit cross-legged, harrumphing, resting her forearms on her knees. 'What took you so long to open the tent?'

'I...' he began, automatically picking up his helmet and toying with the chinstrap as if considering putting it back on.

'We have been on the road for days, and you have scarcely spoken to me. Talk to me, Pavo,' she said, pushing the helmet from his hands. 'Like the first time we spoke, all those years ago.'

'A lot has happened since then.'

'You have become a walking callus, for one thing,' she muttered, recoiling with a scowl. 'A stubborn mule in armour, braying about war.'

He looked at his empty hands then sighed, letting them fall limp.

'All those years ago, you told me about your childhood village,' he said quietly. 'About the Roman attack on your people.'

Her scowl faded. She ran her palms over her bare arms, gulping.

'If you had one chance to find the officer who ordered the massacre, the man who had the choice to speak those words or hold them back, is there anything you would not do to take that chance?'

Her eyes turned glassy. A slight rise and fall of her head was answer enough.

'Gratian, the one who tore apart my homeland and sent my loved ones and comrades to their graves, has been like an iron beast – mighty, invincible, untouchable. Now? Now a colossus of equal size ascends.' He thought of the two eagles in the dream. 'The Master of Britannia. Gratian's time to answer for his crimes has come. And I *must* be there.'

Izodora stared into the space between them for a time. 'It was not my place to judge you. Your choices are yours alone,' she said, her mood softer now. She listened to the gale outside for a moment, hearing the sand rattle against the hide furiously. 'Darik believes that this storm will be over before nightfall. We can resume the journey for an hour or two before the light fades, if General Stilicho wishes. We will reach Antioch soon and you can take ship to Constantinople.'

The words roused him and saddened him at once: destiny beckoned, ever closer; but he also realised that he and Izodora would be parted again soon – probably for the last time. 'What will you do?'

'I have to find a new home, a new purpose. As of yet I'm undecided on what that might be.'

Pavo unconsciously edged a little closer to her, untying his purse from his belt. 'You could take a home in Antioch or somewhere else in Roman Syria.' He dropped three thick gold coins into her hand. 'That should secure you a good house in the city's high wards. And if you grow bored, camel messengers are always in demand.'

She eyed the coins. 'Perhaps a villa and some camel work will be right for me. I don't know yet.' She tossed the coins back at him. 'But I *do* know that I can earn my own coin.'

Pavo caught the coins and dropped them back in his purse. 'I know you could,' he said, eyeing his fingernails. 'I just wanted to make things easier for you.' He reached out and placed a hand on one of hers, squeezing. 'I...I just...'

When he looked back up, Izodora was leaning in towards him, lips full, that sultry look in her eyes again.

He placed a hand on her shoulder to halt her. '...I can't.'

She challenged this with a slight tilt of the head and narrowed eyes. 'Why?' Suddenly, her eyes grew wide as she stumbled upon what she thought was the answer. 'You have a *wife* back in Thracia?' she raged like the storm outside.

He shook his head, staring into the dusty floor of the shelter. 'There were two women who could have been my wife. I loved them both, but my lips are poisoned. Both of them died in my arms.'

Now Izodora's hand took Pavo's and squeezed. 'I am sorry,' she said quietly. 'Loss is a ruthless beast. Once it rides into your life, it never leaves. Memories of those gone, and of how they were taken... they never grow less painful.' She stopped and shook her head, wiping away the beginnings of tears, then forced a smile onto her face. 'Perhaps that is why the storm put us together like this? Because we both understand.'

Pavo nodded. 'Both afraid of love,' he said absently.

'Love?'

Pavo's head shot up. He realised he was blazing with embarrassment. 'I don't mean I love y-'

She pulled a mock-affronted look, sitting upright and proper.

'But I don't mean that I don't like you,' he stammered. 'I do, I just...'

She threw her head back and laughed. 'I like you too. All too soon we will be gone from each other's side, probably forever. What harm is there in comforting each other in these last moments together?'

Pavo realised there was no danger here. Her words were persuasive, and her voice felt like silk brushing against his ears. He leaned towards her, suddenly eager to taste her lips. But a thought halted him. 'What about Darik?'

She leaned back. 'Darik?'

Pavo let his eyelids droop a fraction, giving him a look of hood-eyed superiority. 'Darik, the unfeasibly perfect specimen of manliness who rides with you. I see the way you look at one another.'

'He means everything to me,' she admitted.

'I knew it,' Pavo muttered, leaning back from her, feigning nonchalance.

'He is my brother, you idiot,' she purred. 'Family means everything to the Maratocupreni.'

'Ah,' Pavo stammered, 'your brother. Then-'

She grabbed him by the back of the neck and pulled his face towards hers. Their lips met and – apart from a few stubborn grains of sand – the sensation was soft and glorious, a sensual, passionate joining that lasted until both needed to part for air. They both stared at one another for a tense moment, before jolting into life, tearing off their clothes and coming together again. The storm grabbed and shook the tent frame wildly, and the leather walls bulged and flapped madly as they fell into a passionate tangle. In one frantic moment she sat astride and rode him as if he was a wild horse. Pavo ran his callused hands up and down her smooth, dusky contours, before throwing her onto her back and taking control as they rose to a shuddering climax together.

Sweating, panting, dazed, he slid to her side, drawing his cloak over them both and taking her hands in his. They stared into each other's eyes for a time in the warm comfort of the makeshift bed. The storm howled on, growing soporific, and Pavo watched as her eyelids began to droop towards sleep. 'I will never forget you,' he whispered quietly.

Suddenly, Izodora's eyes pinged open. 'No, you won't,' she said matter-of-factly. 'Because I know what I'm going to do next.'

Under a hot midday sun, they passed through a rocky valley and entered Antioch via its famous Iron Gate, watched by the gleaming, steel-clad and no-doubt stewing X Frentensis legionaries standing vigil on the gatehouse roof. Inside, the city's mountainous, dusty wards and tightly-packed streets were a welcome novelty after twenty two days of desert trekking, and the members of the party dispersed to take rest and nourishment. Darik set about bartering with a local merchant, asking for coins, fresh clothes, boots and provisions for the Maratocupreni in exchange for their remaining camels.

Pavo watched from the shade of a tavern awning, saddened to see the end of the Maratocupreni as a people. The nineteen whom Darik and Izodora commanded would now go their separate ways. Most had spoken of spending their camel money on houses in the city or buying farming land further down the River Orontes. But not Izodora, Pavo thought, a warm, soft sensation rising within his chest… swiftly followed by a twist of deep concern in his guts.

'Why is that big, handsome arsehole coming back to Constantinople too?' Sura grumped, edging over from the tavern bar with two cups of wine.

Pavo did a double-take at the cups, judging that they would be better described as buckets. He took his and gulped, enjoying the fierce tang and alcoholic punch of it. 'So that when we take ship and land back at Constantinople, Thracia will be twice as handsome,' he replied, giving Sura raised eyebrows.

Sura snorted in derision, then smirked to himself – clearly pleased at the insinuation. He lifted his cup to his lips and nearly dislocated his jaw so deeply did he drink. 'But *she's* definitely coming?'

Pavo nodded.

'And you're *not* happy about that?' Sura continued.

Pavo gave him one sorrowful look and it was well-read by his oldest friend. Sura clasped a hand on his shoulder and squeezed. 'I understand. The past has been cruel. But she will be safe.'

'As long as she doesn't stick with me.'

'Like she "wasn't with you" last night? Or every other night since the sandstorm?'

'Stilicho has reassured me that, when we get back to Constantinople, she and Darik will both be welcomed and looked after in the city. We, meanwhile,' he said, patting the scroll-shaped lump inside his tunic, 'have a campaign to join.'

'Stilicho has told you this?' Sura said, intrigued. 'Where is the Eastern Army mustering? When do they set off to join this Maximus?'

Pavo shrugged. 'Stilicho knows nothing. This scroll is all we have to go on, and all it confirms that Magnus Maximus is invading Gratian's lands. The war for the West is about to begin.'

Both of them, thinking of tomorrow's sea voyage, gazed down the city's descending wards to the glittering green waters of the River Orontes, where galleys and fishing fleets dotted the river. Dozens more galleys lay docked at the foot of the island acropolis in a serried stripe, masts standing proud, crewmen tirelessly buzzing over the decks to scrub and repair their vessels, knots of legionaries and dignitaries trooping onto and off of boats as they set out to reinforce or negotiate somewhere else in the Roman world. One moored ship was conspicuous for its condition: the sail – very grubby white – was down and a pair of oily-looking men crudely sewed what looked like the thousandth odd-coloured patch into the great sheet. The timbers were bleached almost white as if the thing had been found adrift at sea. Some craggy old captain swaggered around the decks, jabbing his cane into the backs of the boys who were on their knees sweating, rubbing the decks with sheets of shark skin to smooth the ragged timbers.

'That thing looks like it would sink in a pond,' Sura chuckled. 'No doubt that'll be our boat.'

'Don't,' Pavo said, clutching his belly at the mere thought of his chronic seasickness. They edged over to a free bench to sit. A bald, drunk man with a huge boil on his nose lay slumped at the far end, snoring. 'Actually, I don't care. Put me on a raft. Just get me back to Thracia before the Eastern Army sets off to join Maximus.'

Sura called over a tavern worker carrying a large serving pot of mashed olives. The man ladled two dollops of the salty mixture onto plates and gave them each a small loaf of bread. The pair began to eat.

Sura, chewing, looked up. 'Back to Thracia to see Libo, the filthy, one-eyed bastard,' he said fondly, taking another huge gulp of wine.

'Rectus, who'd saw your leg off to cure a stubbed toe,' Pavo said with a jolt of mirth.

'Pulcher, uglier than a Hun's arse,' Sura upped the stakes. Just then the bald drunk with the boil on his nose stirred, muttered some inebriated nonsense to himself and passed out again. Pavo and Sura chuckled at this, then returned to their conversation.

'Opis,' Pavo mused, seeing in his mind's eye the Claudia aquilifer marching with the legion standard held high, 'always clutching his shaft.'

'Indus and Durio, a proper pair of idiots,' Sura grinned.

'Just like us, once,' Pavo shot back. He drained his wine cup, feeling the punchy drink swim through his veins, softening his sore shoulders and easing his aching legs. The bread and olive mash filled him to contentment, promising tonight's sleep would be sound, and that he would be ready for the voyage tomorrow.

'For the Claudia,' Sura said, raising his cup.

'For the Claudia,' Pavo grinned, raising and clacking his cup to Sura's.

The tavern workers grabbed the drunk at the end of Pavo and Sura's bench by the shoulders and hauled him out, tossing him onto the street. He swore and slurred as he rolled through the dust, before staggering away. He staggered just far enough, over into the shadows behind piled bales of hay. There, as if rejuvenated, Hirrus fell to his haunches, his eyes suddenly alert, his boil-nose wrinkling as he smiled. Playing the drunk was so easy, and sometimes the best way to hide was to hide in plain sight.

He took his staring eye ring from his purse and slid it onto his finger again. He had heard nothing from Ambassador Sporacius for over twenty days. Too long. Something had changed out there in the Persian capital. When he had heard about General Stilicho's imminent arrival in Antioch, his interest had been piqued. Gratian had put out an order to have the two strange legionaries in the escort party offed. A shrewd command, given everything he had just heard. Claudians... the very two Gratian had been seeking last year in Thracia.

He watched the two drink more and more under the tavern awning. Eventually dusk came. He realised how easy it would be now to walk up behind the one called Pavo and plunge a dagger into his spine, then one flick of the wrist to tear it free and slash the throat of the one named Sura. But Hirrus' designs crumbled when the dusky-skinned desert warrior woman joined them, pretending she was not watching over them when she actually was. An unfeasibly chiselled nomad came with her, sitting by the legionary pair's side, sharpening his curved sword, eyes bright and watchful.

Not here, not now, the Speculator realised. So his eyes drifted down to the river – now but a pale stripe in the moonlight – and the galleys docked there. Hirrus' lips quirked at one edge, and he withdrew into the night.

Meanwhile, in Germania...

The Classis Britannica slipped upriver quietly, concealed within a bank of mist, scores upon scores of galleys lying low in the water thanks to the throngs of armed legions on board. Maximus crouched like a crow upon the prow of the lead hexareme, watching, listening. Just the gentle lapping of oars and the cool whisper of the passing fog, the drumming of woodpeckers in the Germanian forests on the eastern bank and on the western side... nothing. Deeper and deeper into Gratian's realm they went, closer and closer to his seat of power at Augusta Treverorum. *Get as close as we can unseen, Domine,* Dragathius had advised him, *get the tip of your knife right up to his heart before you thrust it in for the kill.*

It felt odd not to have Dragathius by his side right now, but it had to be that way.

'Domine,' a voice whispered from the mist-cloaked spar of the galley.

Maximus saw it too. A dim shadow of movement within the fog on the western bank-road. He peered at the spot. The mist seemed impenetrable for a time until he heard a shush of leather and iron and, at last, he saw the shadows for what they were. Legionaries on the march. He spotted the swirling blue and gold of their shields. *The Defensores,* he mouthed. One of Gratian's river watch detachments, patrolling the riverside road. If just one man amongst that unit spotted the fleet and took heel towards Augusta Treverorum, or even to the nearest waystation, then his edge of surprise would be gone.

The Defensores centurion leading the party paled and slowed as his eyes fell upon the huge fleet crawling through the mist. Maximus dipped his head like a bird about to take flight, pinning the man with his glare. The centurion cast a hand in the air and croaked some order to halt, then to call a rearguard horse scout forth. But the ground began to rumble around the western banks, and the centurion shot looks in every direction. The mist was unforthcoming... until – with a scream of battle horses and an explosion of throaty cries, the mighty Sarmaturum riders burst through the grey veil at a charge, spears levelled. Dragathius, leading them, shrieked, his long grey hair flailing madly behind him. The Defensores could only stumble backwards, with no hope of running from this charge. An instant later, the Dalmaturum riders surged into view behind the patrol, bawling and roaring likewise.

Maximus watched as his two formidable cavalry schools sliced through the patrol like scissors. The Defensores' cries were mercifully brief, and the sounds of battle ebbed. Now the mist was thickened by the steam puffing up from their ripped-open bodies. Dragathius circled on his mount then trotted along the banks in time with the fleet, saluting the legions on board, pumping his fist in the air with a wide, white grin – at odds with his blood-sprayed face. The armies of Britannia roared back in adulation. Maximus saluted him too, rising from his crow-poise to stand tall. Another river watch unit swept away, another mile deeper into enemy lands.

'Gratian's armies fall like stacked boards,' said the bearded tribunus of his Victores, standing near him on the decks near the prow.

Maximus looked down at the man. 'Do you know how many eagles Gratian can call upon?'

The Victores man lost his confidence. 'I have heard… but surely that cannot be true. Ghost units. Half-rank legions, no doubt.'

Maximus shook his head slowly, then replied in a low voice so only the tribunus would hear. 'His legions are replete, there are no ragged or ghost units like those in the East. Mighty as our armies are, he has enough men to pulverise us.'

The Victores man seemed caught on the horns of not offending his emperor and saying the obvious thing.

'So why, if he has so many soldiers, do we sail right up to his eyrie?' Maximus asked the question for him. 'Because there are other means of thwarting a foe with greater manpower.' He cast his mind over the details in the scroll Saturninus had given him, then beckoned to a young *explorator* behind the tribunus. 'Grumio, come.'

The explorator – wearing green trousers, tunic and cloak and a leather breastplate – hurried over, and Maximus drew from within his armour a small scroll. 'Take this. Take it far ahead, on along our intended route.'

'To whom, Domine?' asked the explorator, his pale, freckled face wrinkling in confusion.

Maximus gazed that way, as if seeing far through the mist. 'To our big friend.'

Grumio's frown deepened for a moment, then his face slackened as he understood. 'It will be done, Domine.'

Chapter 9
March 383 AD
Snake Island

A buccina horn keened through the darkness. Libo woke with a jolt, eyes peeling wide open, chest pumping with snatched breaths. At once, he felt the hundreds of cuts and bruises on his body flare into life like flames. But for a moment there was nothing but darkness inside the island barracks. Had he dreamt the sound of the horn? Were there still a few hours of precious, dark respite before…

His thoughts crumbled to ashes as he heard the rattling of a staff on the brickwork of the walls, the stamping of boots.

'Up, you bastards, *up!*' Crassus screamed somewhere in the blackness. Libo heard the whoosh of the staff then the crack of it striking flesh. Young Datus cried out from that direction, the sound shaking the barracks. All around Libo, dozens of Crassus' armed legionaries spilled around the waking Claudia men, shoving at them threatening them with their spears.

'Get up,' Libo yelled, scrambling from his bunk and pulling Farus from the adjacent bed then turning towards Trypho's bed too to help him. But like one of the island snakes, Crassus' staff struck through the blackness and whacked across Libo's wrists. He yelled out too, stumbling back as Crassus then drew his whip and began lashing Trypho where he lay, curled up in a defensive ball.

'When I say get up, I mean *get up!*' Crassus snarled.

Libo made a lunge for the whip, only for a spear haft to shoot out like a barricade, and the tip of another to press against his neck. 'Sir,' Libo snapped. 'It is not yet dawn. The horn sounded just a breath ago. At least give us time to rise. The younger lads – they have not yet experienced an emergency pre-dawn call.'

Like a nightmare emerging from the dark, Crassus stepped over nose-to-nose with Libo, his blocky face lit by the barest sliver of torchlight shining through a slit window. 'Oh, they haven't experienced *anything* yet.'

With that, he swished away, his armed men draining away with him, a pair remaining behind to shoo the Claudians – only half-dressed – outside like cattle.

'Do as he says,' Libo, Pulcher and the more senior legionaries whispered to the others as they filed outside. Each of them knew that their only hope of escape from this island prison was to wait, watch, find a weakness, and plan. Yet two months had passed and they had found no flaw: the island was too small for anyone to hide out without being easily found; the wharf lay empty apart from the occasional and irregular visit of the liburnian that had brought them here; and the sea between here and the mainland was laced with a murderous current.

They filed out onto the barrack parade ground. A crackling torch and the moonlight revealed the sorry state of the Claudian veterans: Big Pulcher stood with an awkward gait, his shoulder as black as ink, bruised from a beating two days ago. Opis' face was marbled with bruising down one side, teeth missing. Betto sported a wheezing cough from a strike to the chest that had snapped two of his ribs. Even poor Rectus, lame as he was, had been beaten and mocked for his afflictions, for needing a cane or the saddle of Balbina the mule to get around.

Worse than all of this by far were the empty spots in the ranks. One legionary from Pulcher's cohort had been beheaded for disobeying a direct order – an order to stand when his leg was broken. Three more had been hung from the fort walls for stealing food – when in fact they were starving and all they had done was scrape out the remains of the near-empty bowls of Crassus' legionaries. Two had been charged with striking an officer. Yet Libo had been there and witnessed what had really happened: they had merely raised their hands like shields when

Crassus had been beating them, and one man's hand brushed his face. Without hesitation, both were marched to the archery training posts and shot with dozens of arrows. Seventeen more had been summarily executed like this. Slowly but surely they were being killed off, the brutal treatment being masqueraded as some kind of legionary remedial training.

When a grubby man shuffled along their lines and shoved a cup of thin barley porridge into each Claudian's hand, Libo swallowed the lot in one untasting gulp. That and a similarly basic evening meal was all they were given each day.

'Horse food,' Pulcher growled.

'Eat it. Stay strong for when we get our chance,' Libo whispered to him, then swigged down the small cup of brackish water that came with the meal.

A crunch of shale sounded from somewhere up above the compound walls. Libo squinted to see Tribunus Zeno descending from the lighthouse towards the barracks. Crassus marched up and down the front of the ragged Claudians, while his armed soldiers stood behind, spears trained upon their backs. 'Today, it promises to be a harder drill than ever. Up and down the island slope you willl go. Any who lags or falls...' he stopped and sucked air through his teeth, patting his staff against his palm.

'Not all of you will endure the drill, however,' Zeno announced, pacing in through the gates of the barrack compound. 'For I'll be taking one of the replete cohorts,' he said, gesturing towards one block of the armed ones. 'And I need a group of this lot too,' he flicked a derisive finger at the ragged Claudians. 'Trouble on the mainland. Goths who need to be put in their place. I won't be giving you swords or armour, but I'll need you for scouting.'

Libo, Pulcher, Rectus and Opis all shared a look. *A chance?* Libo wondered, now spotting the liburnian's mast standing proud beyond the walls. 'Take my First Cohort, sir,' Libo volunteered. His mind was already whizzing through the possibilities that might open up once they got off this damned island even for a short time. Even if one man could escape, or simply get word to someone they could trust?

Zeno stepped over close to Libo. 'No,' he said triumphantly, then looked beyond Libo's shoulder. 'You, Trypho, isn't it?'

Libo's blood ran cold. 'Sir, if you want help dealing with the Goths, then take me and my cohort. We are old hands at this.'

'Come on,' Zeno beckoned Trypho, ignoring Libo.

Trypho – still striped red on his bare back from the whip and walking gingerly – led his Third Cohort out before the rest. Just sixty four of them now – none older than twenty years. Trypho's second in command, Optio Datus, shuffled awkwardly by his side. The armed cohort Zeno had selected trooped forward too.

Zeno stepped away from the ragged Claudians and led his contingent to the gates.

Libo watched the young men – like sons, some of them – of the Third Cohort drain outside, and it was a terrible sensation – as if he had just taken his heart from his chest and allowed it to go walking in the wild.

'Shame,' Crassus crowed as the sun finally rose and split the darkness. 'I was looking forward to breaking that big-eared optio's ankles today on the slopes. Means the rest of you will just have to work all the harder.'

Libo watched as the liburnian mast began to sway and then shrink. He inwardly recited prayers to Mithras – for the soldier-god to see the young lads safe... and maybe even Trypho or Datus could engineer an escape or organise the passing of a message to someone on the mainland?

'Seems I don't have everyone's attention,' Crassus said.

Libo blinked and turned towards the big primus pilus just as the man's whip came licking down for his face. The strike stung like fire, and hot, wet stripes of running blood shot across his forehead and cheek.

Crassus stared at Libo, his anvil jaw locked in an anticipatory smirk. 'You want to hit me back, don't you?'

Libo stared through him, into the distance.

Crassus chuckled and stepped back, as if opening the way to the gates and the training slope outside. 'Move!' he bawled.

Libo turned towards the gates, leading the remnant Claudians, tasting blood as he went. Outside, he saw the liburnian, now nearly across at the mainland shore, the young men of the Third Cohort on board and looking back, faces pale.

'Up the hill!' Crassus wailed, and so began the brutal and pointless hill-training. Up and down they went, to the shale brow near the lighthouse then back to the wharf area. Crassus' whip cracked in the air and occasionally slapped down on men's bare backs. A dozen of the armed ones lined the slope's edge, watching for any signs of retaliation. The slope was loose and steep, with sections of damp rock, crumbly shale or loose earth. The first seven ascents were strong – even from the injured or weary men. By the thirteenth they were wheezing, staggering, some looping arms across each other's shoulders for support. By the twenty-first climb, the toes of Libo's boots slipped and scraped, his head pounding, his mouth dry. Despite the fresh bite in the morning air, his back ran with sweat and his thighs burned. When he reached the shale brow at the top this time, a chill northerly blast of sea wind hit him, casting his tangled hair back. It was glorious. He sank to one knee, gasping... only for a wet *hiss!* To snap him to his attentions. A grey water snake sat there, body coiled, head raised, grey neck and belly shining, mouth open and fangs proud.

'Easy,' Libo whispered, keeping his good eye on the snake's piercing stare. 'Easy...' The snake's agitated, stiff posture slowly changed as it lowered its head again. A moment later, a splash sounded from one of the rock pools nearby. Intrigued, the snake slithered off to investigate. Libo half-smiled. It was quite something that these glistening serpents were more likeable than the reptiles in officers' uniforms who had brought the Claudians here. Once again his thoughts turned to escape: from the vantage point of the shale brow, he swept his gaze out over the all-surrounding sea. The fishing town of Apollonia Pontica and the bays either side of it lay tantalisingly close, but it would take a Herculean swimmer to cross that sound without drowning.

'Had enough, Centurion Libo?' roared Crassus, now sitting the exercise out down on the stripe of flat ground near the wharf, waving his staff like a sword. 'I did not say you could stop. You saw what happened to the last of your men who were disobedient. Everyone else, fall out.

Centurion Libo – you will continue until I say you can stop. Is that clear?'

Shaking with fatigue, Libo turned to descend, then climbed the slope again. Over and over, each time at the base of the hill he glowered defiantly at Crassus.

There was one moment of humourous relief: as Libo reached the base of the hill again, Rectus' old mule, Balbina, ambled over and began nosing at Crassus' hand in search of attention, but it all ended sharply when the primus pilus cracked the poor old beast across the muzzle with his staff. Balbina backed away, braying wildly, muzzle bleeding, while Rectus hobbled over to tend to the frightened creature. Libo dug down into his thinning reserves of restraint, and turned to ascend the hill once more. An hour passed, and Libo knew he was on the verge of collapse.

'You bore me, Libo,' Crassus sighed. 'Fall out.'

But Libo descended the hill again and turned around to climb once more. 'I will decide when I am finished.'

Crassus' eyes widened and his face rose in excitement. 'Ah, the grunt talks back to an officer?' he said, hefting his staff like a club-bearer eyeing up a strike.

Libo halted halfway up and swung to scowl down at Crassus. 'I am the Chief Centurion of the First Cohort,' he said, then added internally: *you fucking worm.*

Crassus cricked his neck one way and then the other. 'Let me guess: you think you are some kind of hero because you fought at Dionysopolis? Me? I think you could corner any old dog and it would snap and growl with false courage.'

Libo wondered at just that moment what it would be like to streak down to the base of the slope, to grab Crassus by the neck and crush his windpipe.

But the vision was only half-formed when horns blew from the fort walls. 'The ship returns,' a sentry called from one of the fort towers.

All attentions turned to the sea and the liburnian approaching under oar. Shouts came from the decks and they were not friendly. Libo's ears perked up as he heard braying and snarling.

'Gothic prisoners?' Pulcher guessed.

The question was answered by the stumbling debarkation of Trypho, Datus and the youngsters of the Third Cohort. They were shoved and prodded over the gangplank like thieves by the armed ones who then made a square around them, holding them in a teeth of spears on the wharfside.

'They said that during the war the Claudians were deserters,' announced Zeno, striding from the ship and around the Third Cohort. 'That they fled from the city of Thessalonica when Emperor Gratian was camped there. Well I was never sure if that was true... until today.'

'What happened?' Libo stammered.

'I sent this rabble to attack a train of Goths. They refused to fight. Cowards!'

'Sir, it was not like that,' Trypho tried to explain. 'They were not Gothic warriors. It was a farming caravan. And even if they were why should we attack the-'

Smack! Crassus' knuckles raked across Trypho's face, breaking his nose. 'Tribunus Zeno was speaking,' he rumbled.

'They refused to fight. They cowered in the face of battle,' Zeno exclaimed with a tune of delight. 'Remind me – how do we punish cowards? There was a routine, common in the legions of the ages past. One man in ten would pay the ultimate price for his unit's cowardice.'

Libo's heart froze. 'No...'

Zeno smiled, lending him a horrible, saurine look, then hissed the word like a snake: 'I sentence the Third Cohort to *decimatio...*'

'Sir, I beg of you,' Libo said, all defiance gone from his heart now. All he could think of was the young men – many of whom would never even have read of the punishment.

But Zeno simply watched, smiling, beckoning one of his legionaries over. The man carried a small sack of what looked like coins. 'Sixty four men,' Zeno explained, taking the sack and walking over to Datus, 'and sixty four tokens. Seven tokens are black, the rest are white. Take one.'

Datus frowned, then warily dipped his hand into the bag. He drew out a small white disc.

'Well done,' Zeno sneered.

He moved past three more who also drew white pieces, then came to

Trypho. Trypho, nose spread across his bloodied face, drew a black piece. He stared at it, his hand shaking. 'What… what does it mean, sir?'

Zeno leaned down a little like a teacher talking to a pupil. 'It means… you die.'

Trypho's chest rose and fell in panic as two of Zeno's soldiers dragged him back from the rest. Soon, seven of the Third Cohort stood like that, isolated, confused.

'The best part of all,' Zeno explained, 'is that the condemned are despatched without the honour of a sword to the neck or an arrow through the heart. No, you will die like vermin… clubbed to death by your own fellow legionaries.'

'No!' Libo roared.

Zeno's head snapped round, a finger shooting up as if to pin Libo and the rest. 'Hold them back,' he snarled. The armed ones surged for Libo and the veterans of the First and Second Cohorts, spears levelled at neck height, shields together like a barrier. They drove them back towards the fort wall, caging them there. One spear tip hovered right at Libo's jugular.

'One move and you're dead,' said the spearman.

'Just give us an excuse,' rasped another.

Libo stared up to the sky as he heard Zeno explain to the young men of the Third Cohort who had drawn white tokens that they had to be the ones to bash in the heads and chests of their friends, while Crassus moved around them, giving each a fire-hardened club or a large rock. First, Farus refused, dropping his rock. With a slash of Zeno's sword, the young legionary's head leapt from his shoulders. Next, the lad beside Farus turned to throw his rock at Zeno. The rock never even left his hand, for three of the armed ones' spears ripped through him.

'Do it,' Trypho snarled, demanding his legionaries sacrifice him to save themselves.

'Never,' Datus cried.

'Come on!' Crassus bellowed, gripping one of the Third Cohort men's clubs like a father showing a child how to hold a weapon, then swinging the club round, striking a condemned one beside Trypho in the temple. The stricken one staggered, confused, before blood rolled from his eyes and nose and he collapsed, moaning. 'And again,' Crassus sighed, guiding the young legionary's club round and down on top of the fallen one's skull. The lad's head collapsed in a pile of mush.

Zeno watched with a rictus smile, striding to and fro. 'That is how it was for my father, and that is how it shall be for you…' he purred as one-by-one, the men of the Third Cohort were driven at spearpoint or guided by Crassus to bludgeon their friends to death. At the last, Datus still clutched his rock, standing before Trypho.

'Please, do it,' Trypho begged his friend.

'I cannot.'

'You will,' Zeno advised, 'or you and every one of you lucky white-token holders will be speared down here and now.'

Datus turned a sickly shade of white. Trypho nodded slowly, tears streaking his face, and mouthed: *Do it, Brother…*

With a horrible cry, Datus raised the rock and brought it crashing down on his friend's skull.

Libo closed his eyes and wept.

Chapter 10
Late March 383 AD
Antioch

Under a blistering spring sun, Pavo and Sura walked to the Orontes River wharf and halted, both unconsciously planting their hands on their hips and sighing in perfect unison.

'Mithras' hairy testicles,' Sura muttered. 'General Stilicho gets to sail in that thing,' he flung out a hand towards the *Oceanus*, a pristine trireme, the purple sail emblazoned with a golden Chi-Rho, the deck lined with a century of fresh Syrian legionaries and the aft shielded from the sun by a purple awning within the shade of which waited a cushioned bench and a feast-laden table. Then he twisted his head towards the rickety old ship before them with the bleached timbers and the patchwork sail. This was the *Corvus* – the very craft he had just a few days ago joked would likely be theirs. 'And we get to sail on this glorified raft.'

Musa, the *Corvus'* craggy captain heard this and leaned over the rail. 'You impudent shit. This ship has sailed from here to Hispania a thousand times!'

'Yes,' Sura agreed, 'I can tell.'

Both sensed a presence behind them, and saw a shadow cast from that direction: Darik. 'I've seen discarded shoes in the desert that looked more sound than this thing.'

Pavo turned to Darik. 'You're not fond of sea travel? You get the sickness too?'

Darik shrugged. 'Oh no, I love it,' he replied, drawing out his polished dagger and using it like a mirror to observe chiselled reflection. 'I'm not affected by the rock and sway of a ship.'

'Of course you're not,' Pavo muttered to himself.

'Back in Thracia, I was once in charge of a fishing boat,' Sura began. 'We fished off the coast, you see.'

Pavo could guess where this was going. Darik was lost in his own reflection, licking the tip of his index finger and smoothing back the long, shiny dark locks at his temples.

'I'd spend most days at the top of the mast, watching for the telltale splash of fish shoals. Salmon and lamprey – lovely roasted over a shoreside fire. The Eagle of the High Seas, they called me – could see a catch from miles away. I must have led them to hundreds of catches. I'm pretty sure I made them more than enough to pay for the hole in their boat when they ran over a reef.'

Darik squinted, jarred from his preening by a flaw in the tale. 'Hold on, surely you with the eyes of a sparrow-'

'Eagle,' Sura corrected him, but Darik barely noticed.

'-must have seen the reef?'

'I was distracted.'

'By what?' Darik laughed.

'Sirens,' Sura said quietly.

'What?' Darik scoffed.

Pavo interrupted, having heard this story and Sura's confession before. 'He saw a pair of women frolicking topless in the nearby shallows.'

Darik stared at Sura, then exploded with laughter. 'The Sparrow of the Seas? The *Simpleton* of the seas, I'd say.'

Sura spluttered then wagged a finger. 'Now hold on…'

'Are we ready? Everyone else is,' Izodora's voice cut through their jabber. Pavo turned to her, captivated by her confident stride and easy beauty, the leather pteruges of her armoured kilt fluttering like her dark tail of hair in the warm breeze. He was struck with awe and desire in that one look. Only when she drew closer did he notice the smudge of recent tears in the kohl stripes under her eyes. The parting words between her and the last few Maratocupreni had been tough, evidently.

He glanced up at the trireme, seeing the crew there untying the ropes, ready to set sail down the Orontes towards the coast.

Nearby, General Stilicho approached the *Oceanus*. Pavo watched him stride up the gangplank of that more magnificent vessel. The general had mentioned only fleetingly the matter which they had first discussed in the underground tunnels of Shapur's palace, but Pavo sensed that he could trust this rising figure. As if Stilicho sensed Pavo's eyes on him, he halted halfway up the gangplank, swung towards Pavo and the small group with an ebullient grin. 'What are you waiting for? Let's go – across the ocean and back to the heart of the empire.'

Pavo and Sura saluted in reply, then boarded the *Corvus* and helped untether the craft from the river wharf. As the two-vessel fleet slipped downriver under the midday sun, a pleasant breeze combed across the *Corvus'* decks and through Pavo's sweat-matted hair – long and untended in his five months of exile – cooling his scalp. River sailing was not so bad, he thought, for there was none of the constant rolling, pitching and yawing one endured on the open seas, nor the endless groans of weary timbers. He thunked his helmet down on the deck and leaned with his elbows on the ship's rail near the prow, taking everything in as the grubby crew of oarsmen guided the ship past the palm-lined Orontes' banks, through the high, golden valleys, specked with shrubs. Deer and rodents sped across the valleyside on the left banks, compelled somewhat by the brown bear lumbering along behind them in search of a meal. On the right, Goats trudged slowly through the afternoon heat, munching on tufts of green, the tinkling of their bells soothing and gentle, while herdsmen watched on from the shaded comfort of ancient caves cut into sheer golden bluffs of the valley. Waterfalls toppled into the river every so often, sending a pleasant, cooling mist across the Corvus' decks.

Behind him he heard Sura – beset by a jealousy of Darik and feeling a need to assert his prowess in all matters everything – reciting his many adventures of the past to Clodus, Porcus and the crew. Some of the yarns, Pavo realised, were beyond even the realms of myth. Every time Sura reached his grand climactic sentence, Darik would explode with ever-louder bursts of laughter.

Izodora approached the prow after a time and said nothing, simply resting her elbows on the rail beside Pavo and staring ahead with him.

'Will you miss your home?' Pavo asked, then thought of her tears on the dockside and realised the question was absurd.

But Izodora did not even look back. She breathed deeply through her nostrils. 'The desert was never my home. Nor the lands near the Euphrates, nor the crescent vale where my people once lived. Not even that village of my childhood, on the edge of Roman lands.' She rubbed her fingers together as though testing the quality of herbs, then traced her index finger down her breastbone as if stroking her heart. 'Home is not a place, it is a state of being. A closeness to those who matter.' She flicked her head over her shoulder. 'Darik... and...' she said no more, merely shooting Pavo a glance.

Pavo simply reached over and placed one hand on top of hers.

The River Orontes emerged from the golden valley to wend across a stretch of fertile green coastal plains, rich with grain meadows and palms. A mile or so ahead lay a broad white stripe of sand, and beyond, the *Mare Internum* sparkled like a God's silver-threaded cloak, the shades of water ranging from white to turquoise to cerulean to deep sapphire near the afternoon horizon. Stilicho's *Oceanus* slid out from the Orontes delta and into the sea first, and the rickety *Corvus* followed a short while later. With a hum of ropes speeding through metal rings and a thunderous puff of linen, the sails of both vessels were unfurled and caught the steady sea wind, bulging like the chests of confident brawlers. A light, cooling spume floated across the decks as the ship rolled over the gentle waves.

Pavo turned to look up at the sky – pure blue apart from a few high wisps of white – then back at the rugged and sun-washed Syrian coast. Hundreds of small, lateen-sailed fishing vessels tacked up and down the shore. Men stood on rafts, taking turns to dive into the water, their hands and bodies stained purple with the precious dye of *murex* sea snails. A trio of war galleys moved south along the coast under power of oar – taking a garrison down to Judea, probably. Another pair of galleys was coming downriver too in their wake. The lead vessel's bronze beak shone majestically in the late afternoon sun, the white sail tumbling down from the spar, revealing a golden trident blazon. He closed his eyes and waited on the sea sickness to creep up on him but, mercifully, it did not arise. Perhaps it was the steady waters, or maybe he had at last mastered that wicked affliction.

A few hours later, the sun dipped towards the sea, a blazing copper eye of fire casting a final glare over the ocean, the waters smooth and shining like metal. When the light began to fade, Pavo, Sura, Darik and Izodora sat in a small circle near the mast while old Captain Musa stood over a brazier and cauldron, directing two younger members of his crew in the preparation of an evening meal for all. Hearing the clank of ladles and the chatter about which spices to use, Pavo felt a hollow ache of hunger in his belly. The stay in Antioch had almost been what Sura had hoped the time in Ctesiphon might be like: food, wine, long sleeps and – for once – a sense of safety. Indeed, this short few hours since leaving Antioch until now was the longest they had gone without food in a good number of days. *Food*, he thought again of the exotic tavern-fare in Antioch. *Spiced lamb wrapped in wine-soaked vine leaves, Chickpeas fried in garlic, fresh pistachios, creamy yoghurt and sweet, thick honey…*

A deep, echoing rumble startled Pavo from his thoughts. He clasped his belly, sure he was to blame, then noticed that Izodora's face had darkened a fraction in embarrassment. He grinned at her and she looked away coyly.

At last Captain Musa came waddling over. All four twisted towards him in anticipation.

'Delicious lentil and mutton stew,' he announced. 'Is what we were *going* to have. Until that fool over there burnt the meat at the bottom of the pot.' He cast a sour look at one of the young helpers. 'Tastes like bitter ashes now. So,' with a haggard grin, he plonked a disc of hardtack into each of their hands. Not just any old hardtack – this was the most dessicated, horrid looking biscuit Pavo had ever seen.

Musa waddled away again, humming to himself. Sura stared at the hardtack, his belly groaning too now and sounding much like one of Izodora's erstwhile camels. 'It looks like the sole of a bloody trader's sandal.'

'So much for the hardy Roman legionary, eh?' Darik laughed. 'In the desert, we had to learn how to dig for roots of dead plants to chew upon the flesh for just a speck of nourishment. We had to lick the dew from the rocks in the morning to keep our thirst at bay. We do not turn our noses up at food of any sort.' Righteously, he closed his eyes and sank his teeth into the biscuit. The teeth never even made a dent, not even when his jaw trembled with the force of his bite. His eyes peeled open and he set the biscuit down with a sigh. 'Perhaps we need something to distract us from our hunger?' He twisted away from the small circle and rummaged in the few leather bags the crew had brought aboard for him and Izodora. When he turned back to them he was holding a harp. Like a father caressing a newborn son, he cradled the instrument in his arms, one ear turned to the strings, and let his fingers dance delicately between them. The notes were quick and light at first, rising like silvery sparrows into the inky, star-strewn sky above the ship, then they turned slow and melancholy like heavy raindrops.

'Aaand he's magnificent on the harp,' Sura said, 'naturally.'

When Darik began to sing a low verse in some haunting desert dialect, Pavo could not understand the words, but the meaning was clear. Izodora might have shut out her feelings about the land she had left behind, but for Darik the sense of loss was strong.

The song was nourishing in a strange way, and a distraction indeed – for the growling in his belly ceased – albeit with the aid of a shared skin of wine. The crew operated shifts of sleeping and keeping the *Corvus* on course, while Musa endlessly circled the decks, humming and muttering to himself, offering occasional words of encouragement to the crew – some of whom were superstitious about night-sailing. Pavo, drowsy and relaxed, suddenly found Izodora shuffling up beside him, her warmth welcome in the rapidly cooling night air. They sat together for a time, until his eyelids began to droop. One moment he would be looking off beyond the ship's right-hand rail – at the inky sky and the distant black outline of the province of Cilicia. The next, he would see the flashes of some garbled memory, hear the songs of the march in Thracia, feel the sting of snow in the Haemus Mountains. One last time he tried to force his eyes open. This time, Izodora was asleep, her head resting on his shoulder. Darik too, on his back and still hugging his harp. Sura as well, although he was writhing and grinning, muttering some dream-conversation to himself: 'Bigger than a ship's mast, you say? Well yes, I suppose it is. You want to climb it, you say? Well, go on then...'

Pavo chuckled and turned his head a little to kiss Izodora's forehead. As he did so, the slightest blink of white caught his eye. Confused, he carefully lowered Izodora to the deck so as not to wake her, covered her to the shoulders with his cloak, then rose and stepped towards the aft. He wiped his sleepy eyes a few times, looking at the spot somewhere far beyond the *Corvus*' white churn where he had seen the light. It had not been a winking star, he was sure – it had been too low down – at sea level.

'Cannot sleep, Legionary?' Musa said quietly, ambling up beside him.

'I... I just saw a speck of light back there.'

He folded his bottom lip and frowned. 'Odd. Perhaps it's a fishing ship from Cilicia?'

'At night?'

Musa cocked an eyebrow in agreement, then he jostled with laughter, raised both hands and wriggled the fingers at Pavo. 'Maybe it's sea deeemons!'

Pavo batted the aft rail playfully and shook his head, laughing as he wandered back to the sleeping group. Mercifully he slept without dreaming and woke up in the same position he had lay down in – on his side, sheltering Izodora.

The next day passed slowly, the highlight being Musa's spearing of a bluefin tuna. Ravenous, they roasted and ate nearly a quarter of the giant fish around midday, then put in to the imperial port-town Corycus to take on more fresh supplies. Pavo and Sura donned their legionary helms and vests – a measure which seemed to quicken the pace of the supply workers. That second night, Pavo and Izodora once more lay together. He had meant to remove his boots and mail shirt but he did not want to break up the embrace. The thick drapes of another restful and deep sleep dropped across him. His body relaxed, his mind emptied. And then... a gentle croak. The most innocuous of noises to most men – but not to the ears of a soldier. Pavo's eyes blinked open. He sat up, confused. There was old Musa, standing near the side rail staring out to sea, illuminated by the pale light of a sickle moon, making that odd croaking noise. Odd though it was, at least for once the old dog was not pacing fretfully around his boat. Pavo was about to lie back down when the captain turned towards him, mouth ajar, still croaking, and now Pavo saw why: four arrow shafts jutted from the man's chest, and his pale tunic was blotched red.

He heard a *whizz* of more arrows. A breath later and crewmen fell from the spar and thumped onto the decks, jagged stars of crimson splashing underneath their broken, arrow-pricked bodies.

Then something visceral, something beyond the senses, drew Pavo's stunned gaze towards the blackness just off one side of the ship. Darkness, nothingness, just a hiss of water, then… a full trident sail bulged from the blackness, a great bronze beak glinting just underneath, lunging towards the *Corvus* at great speed. One of the two galleys that had slipped down the Orontes behind them. Braced on the prow like a hunting hawk was a man. The bald drunk from the tavern, his boil-nose bent over a smile. His knuckles were white as he held the oncoming ship's prow rail for purchase, and on one finger he wore a ring – a single, staring eye.

Speculatores! Pavo cried inwardly, frozen. *How?*

There was a hiatus of a single, thudding heartbeat, before…

Smash!

The Speculator ship's bronze ram cleaved into the *Corvus'* side. The *Corvus* jolted crazily as if it had been seized by Neptune's hand. The ramming ship harrowed on through the timbers and towards Pavo in a fury of splinters and foaming water and a noise that reminded him of huge city gates being smashed down by besiegers.

He had time only to roll away from the deadly bronze beak – and to pull the waking Izodora with him – before the lethal edge carved through the spot he had been lying. He saw Sura and Darik rise in fright in the trice before the attacking ship obscured them, thundering on to completely halve the *Corvus* and cut on into the sea beyond. For another moment, the *Corvus'* two halves drifted apart tranquilly and it seemed as if this crazed assault was over, yet it was but a trick of the Gods, for the aft end under Pavo's feet moaned terribly, and the settling water around it suddenly began to boil. The aft end listed hopelessly, like a whale turning from a surface swim into a dive. Crates and tools began skittering and sliding down the deck towards the inky sea.

'Pavo,' Izodora croaked, her voice betraying deep terror, 'I... I can't swim.'

'Hold onto the rail!' he cried, shoving her towards it. As Pavo scrambled over in her wake, the corpses of the arrow-studded crewmen toppled and skidded past them, down the steep decks. Pavo reached out to grab the hand of one living rower, only to miss the falling man and find himself falling too. One moment he was weightless, the next, he felt the hard punch of his body hitting the water's surface. A trice later and he was engulfed in a freezing netherworld, the cold shocking him to his core, blocking out all sound bar the rushing of bubbles and muted screams from above. Brine stabbed like needles up his nostrils and even seeped in through his tightly-shut lips. He felt the terrible sensation of the snatched quarter-breath in his lungs growing quickly stale. He flailed and thrashed, turning madly, seeing nothing but a storm of rising bubbles and pure blackness in every direction he looked. *Which way up?* There was a flash of star and moonlight and he kicked his legs in this direction. But instead of rising, he sank further and further away from the faint light. Suddenly, he was struck with fright as he remembered that he had lain down to sleep with his mail shirt on and that it would pull him down all the way to the sea bed like an anchor. Panic spiked through him, causing him to jerk and thrash like a rabbit caught in a trap, the action only drawing the snare tighter. He remembered divers' tales of finding shipwrecks with armoured skeletons standing on deck as if expecting their vessel to one day rise again. Now that would be him, lost and forgotten in a cold watery grave – just as Gratian had believed ever since the cliffs of Dionysopolis. The injustice spurred him into a frenzy. He contorted and heaved at the heavy garment, tugging it over his head, scraping his skin, snagging on his hair then catching fast on the collar of his tunic. His head began to throb with fatigue and the breath in his lungs now stung like fire. The urge to gulp in air rose like a raging flame inside him. He strained and jerked at the snagged mail until, at last, the tunic collar ripped away and the mail shirt came free. Dropping the armour and consigning it to a cold grave, he felt the sensation of rising slowly. He stared upwards, seeing the faint light of the night sky grow dim as his mind and body began to fade.

He was barely conscious when he surfaced, pale-faced, eyes closed, floating on his back. For a moment, he felt nothing of the air, heard none of the shouts and capitulating timbers. Then he exploded with a surge of water and vomit. His arms jerked out, flailing to grab onto something, anything. Nothing but water within arm's-reach.

'What happened?' Porcus gasped, spitting and thrashing nearby. 'I woke up underwater. Clodus is down there, his leg was caught in a loop of rope. I saw him sinking then he vanished into the black depths.'

Pavo could not bring a single word to his lips to comfort the poor legionary. Just then, as if the Gods had decided to grant them both a merciful death, a mighty groan sounded from above. He glanced up just as the *Corvus'* mast toppled like a felled tree from the fore-portion of the halved ship – now all-but submerged. The thing came down like a giant's club towards his and Porcus' skull. Pavo had the strength only for one kick against the water, and it was just enough to surge clear. The mast slapped onto the surface, crushing poor Porcus' head, sending stinging bullets of water into Pavo's eyes and a fresh tide of brine up his nose and into his mouth. The fore portion of the ship sank in a boiling mass of bubbles and foam.

Then... calm.

He threw a weary arm over the floating mast, eyes trying to make sense of the night. The ship which had rammed them was skilfully cutting on towards the *Oceanus* – a good mile ahead. The smashed *Corvus* was gone. Flotsam bobbed here and there, but the ship was no more.

'Sura...' he croaked into the night. 'Izodora? Darik!'

Silence sailed over the gentle lapping of waters. Such tranquility seemed like an affront to the chaos of moments ago. 'Anyone!' he cried. A terrible, cold hand pulled downwards on his heart and he began to shiver. 'No...*no!*'

The sea seemed like a sheet of black silk for an age – an age that was probably only a dozen heartbeats long – until Pavo spotted a tiny flurry of bubbles rising to the surface. His eyes widened, he sucked in a full breath and plunged underwater towards the source of the bubbles. Deep blue quickly became impenetrable blackness. He surged down as best he could, this time fighting the buoyancy of his breath. Nothing... nobody. He was alone. A great sickness crept over him and he wondered momentarily if it would be best to expel the air in his lungs and let the inevitable happen. But then he saw it.

A weak ray of moonlight somehow managed to penetrate this far down into the water, drawing his eyes to a rising bubble, and the one below it, then to the face of Darik, sinking, fast, into the gloom. The Maratocupreni's eyes were wide with terror, his mouth agape, his hands reaching upwards. But the anchor chain twisted around his waist was determined to pull him to the sea bed. Pavo swam down after him, kicking madly. He felt the water grow sharply colder, felt this clean breath grow dirty, saw the gap between his and Darik's outstretched hands shorten oh-so slowly. But with a downwards kick of both legs he grabbed the Maratocupreni's fingers, then seized his forearm. He levered his body round and kicked at the anchor chain – like a cat savaging a mouse with its back legs – shoving the chain off of Darik's person. He grabbed the desert man's limp body and kicked with what little he had left. Up, up... nearly. Then – sweet air. Another explosion of splashing water and gasping for breath. He hooked Darik's arms over the mast, untying and using his belt to rope the big man's wrists to the timber. He slapped and shoved at Darik's back until water exploded from his mouth. As Darik gasped and retched, Pavo stared all around. Nobody else. Was this it?

A short distance away, the water's surface churned white, and he saw a pale creature thrashing towards him.

'Sura?' Pavo cried. '*Sura!*'

Sura uttered some garbled moan of greeting.

Pavo's eyes swung madly over the bleak scraps of wreckage behind Sura. 'Izodora. What about Izo-'

'You saved her, you got her to the rail' Sura gasped, his breath steadying, flicking his head backwards as he swam. 'See?'

Pavo followed the line of rope trailing from Sura's shoulder. The other end was tied to a ragged chunk of flotsam – a few timbers from the ship's edge and a section of the rail. Izodora still clung to this as he had told her to, her chest heaving as she threw up stomachfuls of seawater. Despite the wretchedness of it all – the cold and the confusion – the sight of her and Sura too was like hot wine in his veins. He lunged away from the mast and splashed over to grab the rail section, easing Sura's burden. He and Izodora clasped hands then shared a frantic and relieved kiss, before he kicked his way back to bring the two 'liferafts' together, each of them clinging to the sides of the flotsam – enough to keep their shoulders and heads above the waves.

With Darik semi-conscious and Izodora tending to him, Pavo and Sura watched in silence as the ramming ship and the other that had left Antioch in tow went at the *Oceanus,* one attacking each side of the vessel. They saw blinking lights on the decks of Stilicho's boat, then the speeding flames of fire arrows rising. It was a blur of light and motion but the next thing they saw was the attacking trident sail erupting in a tower of flame, sapping the Speculator ship's speed. The *Oceanus* sped skilfully out of the ramming line of the second ship, before coming round in a tight arc to draw alongside that boat. Iron glittered and the distant yell of fighting men echoed across the dark sea. They watched as Stilicho's galley drew away again and stormed the now sail-less ramming ship in the same way.

'You… you saved me?' Darik gasped, coming fully round, squinting at Pavo. 'The last thing I saw was your face. And you saved my sister.' He reached over to slap a wet hand on Pavo's sodden shoulder. 'Thank you. I am indebted to you. I swear an oath to you that I will repay that debt. I am beholden to you. The Maratocupreni never break an oath.'

As the big man gasped and spluttered the oath over and over, the dim glow of torchlight from the distant boats began to fade, leaving just the eldritch silver light of the moon and the stars and the cold, black sea.

'What's happening, where did they go?' Izodora said through chattering teeth.

'I'd say Stilicho thrashed those bastards who put us in here.'

'So he'll come back this way to look for us?'

'Perhaps,' Pavo said, knowing the truth would not help. In the darkness of night, the *Oceanus* would have little hope of finding the wrecked fragments of the *Corvus*, let alone the few survivors. Worse, he realised as he felt the push of the currents on his body, they were being carried away from land... out to sea.

'What do we do until then?' Sura asked. 'Are these few shreds of woods all we have?'

Darik spat the last of the water from his lungs. 'Be thankful for the wood. In Persia, they have a saying: a drowning man would grab even a snake.'

'So we wait?' Izodora asked. 'Wait for Stilicho to come back?'

Pavo was about to answer, when he heard a gentle splash of water somewhere around them. Thoughts of what might be below them, circling unseen, prickled like needles in his mind. He had seen what the creatures there could do to men.

'Aye, we wait,' he replied. *And pray,* he added inwardly.

Chapter 11
Early April 383 AD
Gaul

In the four weeks following Gratian's marriage to Laeta, Treverorum echoed with the sound of flutes, drums and cheering. Every day, the great arena quivered with the thunder of applause at the games and races. Gradually, the wine stopped flowing and the feast fires dulled. The foreign guests and dignitaries filtered back to their far flung governorships and kingdoms and the citizens of the Western capital returned to normal daily life. But the games were not done.

Out in the countryside, three slaves stood in a line, shaking. Wearing just loincloths, they hugged their arms to their bodies in the damp Gallic breeze, staring at the spruce woods in the north.

Magister Militum Merobaudes sat astride his bay stallion, head dipped, long straggly hair hanging like weeds on the breast of his iron cuirass. He could feel the slaves' fear. The notion danced through his mind again: to set them free. But a score of Alani stood behind the slaves, not so inclined to disobey their master's orders: and so these three slaves would die today, in a way no man deserved to die.

The clopping of hooves sounded. Merobaudes turned to look back in the direction of Treverorum. A wagon rose into view over the brow of a hill, and swayed towards him.

Merobaudes recognised the vehicle and his heart sank. 'Lad, I told you to stay in the city!' he shouted.

But the wagon door swung open and the thirteen year old who

stepped out was with every passing day making a mockery of the term 'lad'. Valentinian was tall and broad in the shoulder, square-jawed and with a look of studious determination, dark brown curls framing his pale face, a white circlet on his brow. His silver vest and pale blue leather pteruges and cloak shone brightly.

He strode over to Merobaudes' side and looked up at the giant general while gesturing towards the three slaves. 'If my stepbrother insists on keeping me in his capital, then I will do as I please while I am here.' He noticed the slaves and shot Merobaudes a look, appalled. 'You promised me you would not let my stepbrother do this anymore. You said you were escorting him to meet with some religious procession.'

'I told you what I needed to tell you – to keep you safe from him,' Merobaudes replied, shooting a furtive look at the Alani – all of whom were listening in.

Valentinian leaned a little closer so only Merobaudes would hear. 'Let the slaves run,' he said. 'Once before I did this. I *defied* him. You can do so too, and if he questions you, you may say it was my command.'

Merobaudes gazed down at the lad, a soft feather stroking his heart as he remembered all they had been through, all the years he had sheltered and guided the boy through the nest of knives that was the Western Imperial court. What a tragedy it was for a golden-hearted lad like this to be born with the blood of emperors past in his veins. 'I could, but then all we have done would be for nothing,' he said sadly. 'Your stepbrother has killed men on grounds of treachery when they merely laughed at the wrong time at his jokes.'

'He will not harm me while you have the core of the army and the majority of the generals on your side,' Valentinian countered.

'My closest allies in the Western Army have had a habit of vanishing in these last few years. The majority is no longer mine to command. Your stepbrother seeks to tilt the balance. I am striving to prevent that. Do not work against me.'

Valentinian shook with indignation, staring into the spruce forest ahead. Suddenly, he fell still. Merobaudes recognised the look – a silvery mist glittering in his dark eyes. 'Look!' Valentinian said loud enough so the Alani would hear, pointing to the sky above the woods. 'Did you see? A signal arrow.'

The Alani straightened, their attentions – having been on the quarreling general and boy-Caesar – now suddenly snapped round to the trees.

'Aye,' the Alani Tribunus half said, half coughed. 'A signal to...' he fell quiet, hoping the young Valentinian would fill in the detail he had clearly missed.

'to call you to the eastern treeline.'

Merobaudes masked a smile, proud of the boy's authority and poise.

'Go!' Valentinian bawled at the tribal guard.

The twenty Alani burst into a run, speeding towards the woods. Merobaudes watched them go, laughing despite himself. 'By the Gods, lad – your father's blood runs strong in your veins.'

But Valentinian was barely listening and was already pacing towards the three slaves. 'You are free. Go, run to the south.' They stared at him, agape. 'This offer is no cruel chase like the ones my stepbrother enjoys in those woods. This is real and you have but moments. Go!'

But the three looked anxiously up at Merobaudes, afraid of passing the giant Frank.

Merobaudes growled, caught on the horns of dilemma. He spat into the ground and swiped a hand as if swatting a wasp. 'You heard the boy. Run!'

The three backed away to the south, towards a green highland region of winding paths and high tracks in which one could easily hide.

'He will be angry,' said Valentinian, 'but I do not care.'

Merobaudes lifted a ring from his purse and began toying with it. He had not dared to show this to anyone, but Valentinian needed to know.

The boy had spotted it already, and his eyes were wide, fixed on the embossed imperial seal upon it. 'You are not supposed to have that. I thought he made you give it to Arbogastes, his new favourite?'

'I did,' Merobaudes smiled wryly, 'but not before I had a craftsman make me a copy.'

'Why?'

Merobaudes sighed. 'I did not want to involve you... but you have a habit of involving yourself.'

'Tell me, my shield.'

Merobaudes shot looks around them. Nothing but deserted countryside. 'I expect all will know soon enough, but-' he halted when he saw the three slaves rising over the brow of a hill, coming back towards them. he sat tall in his saddle. 'What are you doing?'

The question was answered by the rising shapes of ten more horsemen in black leather armour behind the trio. Comes Arbogastes, on the central steed, walked his beast forward, his spatha drawn and pointed down and towards the slaves, his honey-gold eyes widened under the brow shadow of his braided copper-coloured wig. 'What's this? Runaways?' he laughed.

Merobaudes bristled in his saddle. Arbogastes had been gone from the capital for over a month – off gathering reports from the Gallic legions. 'What are you doing here?'

'What a warm welcome home,' Arbogastes smiled coldly.

'Back early,' Merobaudes rumbled. 'Why? So you can crawl deeper inside the emperor's arse?'

Arbogastes rocked with laughter. 'A man doused in resin should not strike flint, Merobaudes. Have you not spent the last eight years grovelling and flattering him?'

Merobaudes again thought of the terrible fire wounds on his body and the many other scars he had endured, all the indignities, the strategic toadying and flattery of Gratian, all so Valentinian would come to no harm. 'I would not expect you to understand. Your mind is like a dried-up tarn – shallow and empty.'

'What do you know of me?' Arbogastes seethed, now lifting his sword a little to point it towards Merobaudes. The nine riders with him also placed hands on their sword hilts. Merobaudes – without guards of his own – did likewise, instinctively moving his horse between Valentinian and Arbogastes' men.

Regardless, Valentinian stepped alongside Merobaudes and clasped a hand to his own weapon hilt. 'I know that you murdered your own father for gold,' Valentinian replied in lieu of Merobaudes.

The words seemed to hit Arbogastes like a volley of sling bullets. He kicked his horse forward a few strides.

But Merobaudes again moved to shield the boy, and now Arbogates slowed. 'The truth angers you? They say you left your mother in slavery while you came into the imperial courts to seek your fortune,' the big Frank said, walking right up to Arbogastes. 'With the fortunes you have accumulated since, how many times could you have bought her freedom? Do you even know if she still lives?'

Arbogastes' left cheek twitched. 'You don't realise how close the end is, do you? The days of your hold over the emperor are almost over. Perhaps I should deal with matters for him here and now. You... the boy...'

The air seemed to crackle with tension, the horses on both sides nickering and spluttering, pawing at the ground as if sensing it too. Then...

'*Haaaaa!*'

The joyous scream exploded from within the woods.

All heads snapped round just as a figure burst into view from the trees. It was a strange thing – a creature with the head of a hare and the naked body of a man – flailing through the undergrowth, brakes of fern shuddering in its wake. From within the animal mask a most inhuman wail sounded – an antithesis to the joyous cry from moments before. Just as the masked slave leapt over a fallen spruce, the treeline a short way behind him shivered and exploded again. This time Laeta sped from the forest depths on a white mare. She wore a silver cloak, her flame-hair dancing madly behind her as she sat proud on the saddle and nocked an Alani bow, winked and shot. The arrow hummed through the air and ripped across the slave's shoulder. A cloud of red burst into the air. 'Haaaaa!' Laeta cried again. The masked slave kept running – a hopeless flight towards the three lined up next to Merobaudes who were to be the next 'animals' for the hunt.

'Haaa!' a deeper cry sounded. This time Gratian burst from the trees, lay flat in his saddle and drew a sword. With his left arm he hugged his silver stallion's neck and allowed his body to sag right on the saddle, holding the sword out straight, speeding up on the back of the masked slave. The emperor's face widened in anticipation as he drew his sword arm back and hacked across the fleeing man's hamstrings. The wretch went down like a puppet whose twines had been cut. The tall grass obscured much of his thrashing and, mercifully, Merobaudes saw little of what happened next, when the Alani footsoldiers emerged from the woods. Gratian waved away their confused questions about the fictional signal arrow, simply demanding a spear from one of them, then driving it down seven times into the spot where the fallen man lay as if spearing for fish. Laeta circled the scene at a canter, drinking in the sight of the slave's brutal end.

Chest heaving, breath clouding in the air, Gratian stabbed the spear into the ground, took Laeta's hand and kissed it. Next, the newlyweds walked their mounts over to the gathered men.

'Stepbrother,' Gratian cooed coldly when he noticed Valentinian there. 'I did not think the hunt was to your taste?'

'It isn't,' Valentinian replied stonily.

Gratian smirked. 'You should be careful, riding into the region where a hunting party roams. Flying arrows, speeding horses.'

'Anything could happen,' Laeta added softly.

Valentinian said nothing, and refused to look at her, keeping his eyes on his stepbrother.

Gratian's head flicked towards the other newcomer since he had sped off on the hunt. 'Arbogastes,' he smiled. 'How do things stand with my Gallic legions and riders?'

'I have some interesting reports on that front, Domine. I first wanted to check that all was well out here with you.' He shot Merobaudes a sly look as he said this.

'All is well, as you can see,' Gratian replied.

Just then, Laeta leaned in towards Gratian and whispered something in his ear. Gratian rocked a little in his saddle as if laughing at some remembered joke. He eyed the three surviving slaves, then kept his gaze on them as he addressed his Alani guards. 'Take dry tinder and lay it around the edges of the woods. Make an unbroken loop of kindling.' He turned his gaze on the three remaining slaves, who shook madly now. 'You three, I seem to have dropped my purse in those trees somewhere.

Somewhere near the centre. Go, fetch it for me.' He wagged a rebuking finger and added with an ill-fitting tune of playfulness. 'And don't you dare come back out until you've found it.'

'Domine,' Merobaudes contested. 'There is no need for this. If you burn these woods you will have to ride further out to the elm forest whenever you next wish to ramble... or hunt.'

'Move,' Gratian hissed to the slaves.

But they were rooted to the spot with fear.

'Your emperor gave you a command,' Laeta roared like a tigress. 'Now mo-'

Trampling hooves halted her furious cry. A rider from Treverorum galloped with a flailing white feathers tied to the tip of his skywards-pointing spear. A messenger.

'Domine,' the man called out. His face was bright, the news clearly good. 'One of Arbogastes men awaits you in your palace hall, and he says he brings word from the East – relayed here at great haste. He would tell me nothing other than that it is news that will warm your heart!'

Gratian sat up proud in the saddle and cocked his head to one side. As if the slaves no longer mattered, he swished a hand towards the western track that led back to his capital.

Gratian led his entourage down the gentle slope into the Mosa River valley. They followed the river path past a run of ruddy sandstone bluffs and onto the Treverorum road. The city's beetling grey walls and huge eastern gatehouse had the look of a mighty tombstone, streaked with patches of pale lichen and dampness. Gratian swished up a hand and someone in one of the many dark arched windows on the gatehouse's flanking turrets called out. A few more shouts followed and with the clanking of chains, the portcullis slowly rose like a rictus being prized open. They made their way through the market day crowds and straight into the imperial palace grounds – a patchwork of spring blooms and fountains. When they came to the arched doors of the grand hall, two Alani standing guard there opened the doors to admit Gratian, Laeta and Arbogastes before swiftly making an X of their spears, halting Merobaudes and Valentinian. Gratian heard and ignored their gasps of protest, then the boom of the doors swinging shut to cut off the noise.

The grand hall was streaked with the pale smoke of scented oil burners. The recently-polished tesselated floor and forest of porphyry columns glinted in the light that shone down in grey bars from the high windows. Striding across the hall, Gratian pulled off one glove and held it out for a body slave to take away. 'The news?' he called over to the tall man waiting at the far end of the hall, back turned. 'Give me my good news,' he repeated.

The man swung round on his heel and instantly fell to one knee, locks of his brow-length silver hair falling across his face. 'Domine,' he said in a sibilant whisper to his emperor. 'Domina,' he added, bowing again to Laeta. 'Optio Speculatorum,' he added, dipping his head a third time towards Arbogastes.

Gratian peered down his nose at the man, recognising his sharp, crow-like features. It was Vulso, a Speculator he had several years ago sent to the river fortress of Cusum – a gateway on the Danubius watching traffic passing from East to West and vice versa... and a relay point for Speculator messages from the East. His heart surged with anticipation.

Arbogastes realised what this meant too. 'The Persian talks...'

'Yes,' the Speculator replied.

'They are in ruins?' Gratian asked excitedly. Laeta listened intently, her face cat-like.

Vulso's expression sagged and he steepled his fingers in trepidation, glancing at Gratian's notorious fang ring. 'Not quite.'

Gratian recoiled, shooting his hands out wide in exasperation, throwing a tailored look of shock at Arbogastes then back at the Speculator. 'I was told to expect good news. What is Sporacius *doing* out there?'

The Speculator winced. 'Sporacius has... fallen silent.'

Gratian's mind spun. 'Dead?' he said quietly as the body slave now began unbuckling his green Alani cloak.

'By now, maybe,' Vulso replied. 'It seems that the Shahanshah put him on "the boats".'

Gratian's eyes darted, then he jolted with laughter. 'Shapur killed Sporacius? He put the lead envoy from Theodosius' ambassadorial party to death? Then Sporacius has done his job: there can now surely be no settlement between Shapur and Theodosius!'

The Speculator winced again. 'The talks continue.'

'What, how?'

'Another within the ambassadorial party has taken over and continues the negotiations.'

Gratian shoved away the body slave who was making a hash of unbuckling his cloak then took to striding across the floor and back. 'How did you come by this news?'

'This is where the good part begins, Domine,' Vulso said with an unctuous grin. 'You had suspicions about two of Sporacius' escort legionaries. Hirrus, my colleague stationed in Antioch, witnessed General Stilicho return there from the Persian talks.'

As he paced to and fro, Gratian thought of Hirrus – the bald, stocky agent with the unsightly boil on his nose whom he had assigned to that faraway place.

'More, Stilicho had the odd pair in tow. He tracked them, heard them talking in an Antiochan tavern. He was astonished to hear their names...'

Gratian halted and swivelled his head towards the man like a crow spotting a worm. 'Pavo. Pavo *is* alive.'

The Speculator nodded slowly, his grin widening with every repetition. 'And his Primus Pilus, Sura. They took ship from Antioch and set off towards Constantinople with Stilicho.'

'What?' Gratian felt the cold, wet hands of that awful moor creature from his dreams reach slowly for his neck, as if measuring him up for the kill. 'Hirrus let them *go?*'

Vulso shook his head slowly, enjoying the moment. 'He halved their ship near Corycus, in the dead of night.'

Gratian's fears slid away like melting snow from a tiled roof.

'He even saw Pavo on the decks, said the beak of his galley almost sliced him in two. And what the boat started, the seas finished. Pavo's ship sank in moments. Unfortunately Hirrus could not send General Stilicho to the sea bed too. It seems he sailed with a strong crew of marines, and his galley was fast and-'

'Did Hirrus see them die?' Gratian said with a clipped tone.

'Domine?'

'Did he see Pavo *die?*' he raged now.

Vulso jolted. 'No. Hirrus stressed that it was night and it was chaos. But, Majesty, those waters are treacherous, the currents strong – pulling man or boat far out into the deep. If any of them survived the impact of the ram, they will have drowned… if the sharks did not get to them first.'

Gratian slammed the heels of his hands down onto the edges of a water font, staring into the rippling surface. He heard the wet rattling laughter of the moor creature, imagined it in there, staring back at him with its thousand pairs of eyes, felt its fingers flexing on his throat. 'I paid my penance,' he growled through gritted teeth.

'O Almighty God, merciful Father,

I confess to you all my sins and iniquities…' he began.

'Domine?' Arbogastes asked tentatively. 'Our agent is right: they cheated death at Dionysopolis, but not this time. The news *is* golden.'

Gratian looked up, dazed.

'And the Persian talks,' Laeta interjected, her rose and cinnamon scent wafting as she leaned closer to him. 'Yes we failed to spoil them this time, but in any case they will rumble on for an eternity – we will have another opportunity.'

Gratian, still dazed, stared at his new wife and then at his head agent. 'Can you hear it?' he said.

'What?' Laeta replied.

Gratian swung round and grabbed her by the shoulders. 'It… it has a thousand faces. It smells of death.'

Arbogastes gulped and tried to intervene. 'Domine, it has been a long day.'

Gratian grabbed his sword hilt and part-drew the blade, turning now on Arbogastes. 'It thinks it can frighten me... it thinks it can harm me.'

'Domine,' Arbogastes pleaded, 'perhaps you need to rest?'

The sound of rushing footsteps sounded from outside. Gratian's eyes crawled up towards the hall doors. 'It's coming. Can you hear it?'

Arbogastes' face paled as he did hear it this time. Just as he twisted to the doors, he heard garbled words outside, then the doors blew open. A wall sentry barrelled inside, gasping for air. The Alani sentries followed him in, watching his step. But he slid to his knees before Gratian. 'News, Domine,' he panted.

As the strangeness of moments ago was sucked away, Gratian suddenly became aware of the others who had poured into the hall with the man: Merobaudes and Valentinian; Lanzo and his Heruli – covered in stable filth. Slaves and palace staff too.

'I have already been updated on the Persian situation,' Gratian snapped, suddenly certain that the man was about to blurt out a repeat of the Speculator reports – more than he wanted those now in the hall to hear.

But the wall sentry's face wrinkled in confusion. 'Persia? No, Domine. This is news much closer to home. Riders arrived at the gates not long after you returned from the hunt... they bring reports of a fleet moving up the River Rhenus.'

The words were like boxer's blows swishing but missing, the strange wind of each strike unsettling. 'The Rhenus?' Gratian said.

'A fleet?' Arbogastes added.

'A huge fleet,' the sentry confirmed.

Gratian's head spun. The Rhenus was the mighty barrier between the empire and the wilds of Germania. 'The Franks have no fleet, nor the Vandals or the Saxons or the Alemanni. Fishing ships and a few raiding crafts, yes, but a fleet? No.'

'*Roman* galleys, Domine,' the sentry said with a note of despair.

Gratian's heart pounded. 'I don't understand. My *Classis Germanica* is moored near the Rhenus' upmost stretches is it not?'

'It is not our fleet,' Merobaudes surmised.

'It is the *Classis Britannica,*' the sentry confirmed. 'It is Maximus, Domine. He has gathered the island armies and sails them into the continent. He is not content with his rocky, damp home. He comes to conquer all the West for himself.'

Gratian's eyes darted across the hundreds now in the hall, all staring at him. He saw their mouths open and close as they rose in a clamour of gossip, yet all he could hear was the slow, rasping breaths of that dark moor creature.

'This audience is not helpful,' Laeta hissed in Arbogastes' ear.

The Optio Speculatorum blinked, taking the prompt. 'Out!' he roared, his jagged tones cutting through the wretched noise.

Gratian stared blankly into space for a time, the tesselated floor shivering under his soles as the crowds were driven from the hall.

'We should visit the war room, Domine,' one voice advised as the clamour abated.

'Yes… yes,' Gratian muttered.

Valentinian followed behind Merobaudes, watching his stepbrother's erratic and furious strides, Laeta and Arbogastes flanking the emperor.

'Maximus?' Gratian spat. 'I appointed him to his station. I *gave* him Britannia. Now he turns upon me? Well, he will find a high station in my realm. I will cut off his head and mount it upon a pole atop this palace!' he roared as he booted the door at the end of the corridor open. A flurry of dust danced through the shafts of light that fell from the room's windows and onto the wide cherry wood table. Arbogastes hurriedly stretched out the scroll that lay at one side, stabbing his dagger into one end and placing a small marble bust on the other to keep it unfurled.

Valentinian's eyes combed over the map.

'Where are the Western armies?' Gratian demanded.

Without a word, Valentinian opened a small box and picked out figurines of imperial soldiers. He placed one figurine in Africa and another in Italia. 'The legions of my lands are positioned here… and here.'

Gratian glowered at Valentinian. 'You have no place in my war room, whelp,' he hissed.

Valentinian gestured to the pieces he had just set down. 'If this Maximus comes to storm across the West and take it all for himself I, as Caesar of the West, stand to lose my lands should he succeed.' He saw Gratian's top lip quiver with distaste as it always did whenever he used his title.

As if to distract Gratian, Merobaudes swaggered over to the table's edge, eyeing the handful of figurines still in the box. 'More importantly, where are the rest of the Western legions?'

Hesitantly, Arbogastes lifted some out and placed four legionary figurines and two cavalry pieces in southern Hispania and just one legionary piece in Gaul.

'What are you doing?' Gratian snapped, gesturing at the pieces in Hispania. 'What is this?'

'That, domine, is the Celtae, the Petulantes, the XIII Augusta and the I Noricorum, and,' he gulped sheepishly, 'the horsemen of the Armatura and Gentiles.'

'I know what they *represent*, but why have you placed them there?'

'Because,' Arbogastes croaked, 'because that is where they are.'

Gratian's face crumpled in disgust. 'The legions of Gaul are in Hispania? My best legions and my two elite cavalry schools... in *Hispania?* Why? Of all the empire's lands, it is the most stable.'

Arbogastes shuffled and scratched: 'I did not think to bother you with it at first, Domine, but that was the news I had for you regarding the legions of Gaul. It seems that rebellion stains the province of Hispania Gallaecia,' he explained, shifting the various figurines more precisely to Hispania's northwestern corner. 'It sprouted from nothing in the last few months. It was only minor bouts of insurgency at first, but reports suggested it could boil out of control.'

Gratian's eyes rolled round to Arbogastes. 'You sent the spine of my armies away... without even consulting me?'

Arbogastes paled. 'That is the most confounding thing, Domine. I didn't.'

Gratian recoiled, then laughed absurdly. 'Well they didn't go of their own accord.'

'No, but the commanders there claimed they were given an order stamped with the imperial seal.'

Silence reigned.

Valentinian tried as best as he could to control the shivers racing up and down his spine as he realised what had happened. But he could not suppress a glance up at Merobaudes, a look of pride and awe. *The seal ring!* Merobaudes simply stared at the map table, emotionless.

A bang scattered Valentinian's thoughts as Gratian slapped his palms on the map table and slumped over it. 'More than half of my army is in Hispania.' He stabbed an index finger into the area of Gaul again and again, as if underlining each word. 'So bring them *back*.'

'It is not as simple as that, Domine,' Arbogastes explained. 'The messenger I spoke to said the commanders expected it only to be a short tour – a show of force to put the rebels back in their place. But they have become entangled there. Hispania Gallaecia is notoriously hilly and rugged, and the rebels have used that to their advantage, blocking valleys and bursting riverbanks to stunt our legions' movement. Thus, our forces have neither ended the dissent nor are they able to easily return to Gaul.'

Gratian's teeth ground like rocks as he glared at the region.

Laeta rested her palms on one of Gratian's shoulders, and her chin on her knuckles, looking over the map with him. 'Hispania Gallaecia? That is the land of Maximus' birth is it not?' she said softly. 'Where still he owns estates and the people there hold him in high esteem?'

Gratian's eyes glinted like polished steel. 'The bastard will pay dearly for this.'

Arbogastes, reading a new scroll brought to him by a just-arrived second messenger, explained: 'He brings nearly fifteen thousand men... plus the riders of Britannia.'

Gratian looked up. 'The Sarmaturum?'

'And the Dalmaturum,' Arbogastes answered.

A silence hung over them all.

Gratian flicked a finger towards the two pieces Valentinian had placed on the board. 'Stepbrother – send for the legions in Italia and

Africa. Summon them at haste.'

Still glowing with awe at Merobaudes, that his big protector was at last moving against Gratian, Valentinian hesitated to respond. *You knew Maximus was coming, my shield, didn't you? You and I will ally with him?* It was a golden moment of realisation. He did not notice Laeta watching him.

Arbogastes replied before either Merobaudes or Valentinian could. 'It will be done, Domine. More, the few regiments still here in Gaul should be able to come to your call within days,' he added quickly.

Gratian nodded slowly, studying the map, the distance to the River Rhenus and the distances between Treverorum and his various forces. 'How soon can the legions in Hispania be recalled?'

'It is a matter of *if* they can even fight their way clear of that land before the summer comes and goes, Domine,' Arbogastes replied with a shake of the head.

'You will need every legion, every cohort, every vexillatio you have,' Laeta remarked with the lazy air of a casual observer. 'You should gather your... agents, as well, from far and wide.'

'I will call on the city garrisons, the river marines, even,' Arbogastes said quickly, eager to solve the problem before Merobaudes or Laeta could. 'Remember you have two cohorts stationed out in Thracia,' he paused to choose his next words carefully '*reforming* the XI Claudia – the traitor-legion.'

Merobaudes and Valentinian looked up at this. Neither said anything, yet Valentinian could not help but think of the brave men of the ruby shield who had dragged peace from the flames of war, and of Pavo, their leader.

'The Claudia?' Gratian spat. 'That ragged eastern legion is an insignificance now. 'Pavo is dead, drowned in the Mare internum.'

The words hit Valentinian like a hammer. *No!*

But Gratian carried on: 'Yes, bring those two cohorts back.'

'What of the Claudia men, Domine?' Arbogastes asked. 'Do we consider them... reformed?'

'I don't care about them, just-' he started, but Laeta pressed her lips to his ears. His eyes darted as she whispered something to him and eventually he jostled with a single humourless laugh, then brought something from his purse – a coin-sized token of some sort. 'I'm finished with the Claudia. Send word to Tribunus Zeno to bring my two cohorts back. And...' he tossed the strange token to Arbogastes.

Merobaudes' eyes narrowed. Valentinian looked up at the giant, equally perplexed and suspicious.

Arbogastes seemed confused for a moment too, but blinked when he recognised the token. 'Ah, yes,' he said, a smile rising across his face. 'I will despatch a messenger at once.'

Chapter 12
Early April 383 AD
Mare Internum

The warring eagles above shrieked and flapped madly, and the rain of blood was driving now, soaking Pavo and the crone as they stood in the black dream world, unable to escape the gory deluge. Indeed, Pavo felt the blood settle in pools around him, splashing at his ankles. Rising, rising...

'It has begun,' the crone said.

'You sound sad,' Pavo replied, his voice heavy with tiredness. 'Why? This Maximus seeks to topple a cruel tyrant. Gratian wears a mask of piousness and youthful innocence, but you know of the things he has done.'

'I know the things he has done and the things he will do. I know the paths of sons not yet born, the taste of bread not yet baked, the feel of silk not yet woven. Look up again, what do you see?'

Pavo felt the pooled blood rise past his knees. So much of it! He looked up, shielding his weary eyes from the teeming crimson rain. The two great birds continued to rake and slice at each other, and both were striped in grievous wounds. 'I see two rival claimants to the imperial purple, locked in battle.'

'But which is which?'

Pavo frowned. It was odd how the scars and blood of their fight had coated both birds so completely. At first they were starkly different – one white and one dark. Now, both were a sullen shade of red. 'I can't tell.'

'No… and for the first time I can remember… nor can I.'

'As long as the right one wins, what does it matter?' he said, feeling the swell of spilled blood around them rise to his chest. A moment later and it came to his shoulders. Soon, he found himself sweeping his hands in broad strokes to stay afloat in this blood ocean. He twisted this way and that to find the crone, to save her too from the rising swell, but she was gone.

'What does it mean?' he cried into the dream ether. Yet the blood sea rose and rose, and soon he felt his strength fading, his paddling limbs growing weak and his mind clouding over with a strange fog. The fatigue soon morphed into a numbness, then a deep, heavy weariness. His paddling arms began to slow, then stop, and he felt himself fall below the surface, sinking into the blood, dropping into a dream within a dream.

'Wake up, Pavo,' the crone's voice whispered to him in that dark void.

'I need to rest, to let go…' he croaked in reply.

'WAKE UP!'

'WAKE UP!' Sura roared.

With a gasp of half-air, half-brine, Pavo grasped out for something to hold onto. His palms slapped against water, and his legs kicked out at nothingness below. Deafened by a screaming gale and almost blinded by drilling bullets of rain, he saw not the calm teal and blue of sea and sky that they had endured for these last nine days, but a manic range of sharp, jagged and almost black waves and a furious grey sky, veined with lightning. He thrashed his arms to turn around. Sea, everywhere. No sign of the fragments of flotsam that had kept them alive. 'Sura?' he spluttered, realising that in his sleep he had drifted away from his comrades.

Suddenly, the deep began to roil and swell around him. He heard a cacophonous roar from behind and turned to see a wall of water like polished black stone, the churning peaks like snow on a high and jagged winter mountain. The colossal wave rose, swallowing up the water underneath him, pulling it and him down as it grew and grew.

He heard his own cry, felt his body being dragged up and round and spun in every direction as the massive wave crashed down like teeth over him. Gone was the roar of the waves and scream of the gale. Now brine filled his head and again he felt that savage battle of wills – to breathe and drown or to resist and suffocate.

Amidst this chaos, it was a thorn of lightning that lit the dark sea and showed him salvation some way away – the mast and the kicking legs of the three bodies clinging to it. He pumped his legs with what little strength remained in them, surging up, up and bursting clear of the surface nearby.

'Pavo,' Izodora cried over the screaming winds, her hair plastered across her face as she reached across the mast and out to him, grabbing him with a shaking hand and drawing him back to the fragment of timber. 'I woke to Sura's shouting and saw you were gone.'

'You were muttering to yourself,' Sura cried over the storm, offering another hand. 'Your arms slipped off the mast and you were gone, drifting.'

Darik added his hands to the mix, clasping Pavo's arm also. 'I swore an oath to you, to save your life as you saved mine when the ship was halved. Don't go dying without giving me the chance to repay that debt.'

The four stayed together like that, hands clasped and arms linked over the mast as the sea thrashed and tossed them to the heavens then dropped them back down into valleys before casting down more monumental waves upon them. It was exhausting, and the mast was becoming waterlogged and gradually losing its buoyancy.

Nine days, Pavo estimated. Nine days they had endured the sea with just one salvaged skin of drinking water between them. It was a wretched existence, eight days of blistering sun followed by this storm, and they could now think only of closing their eyes and succumbing to exhaustion. He knew death was close. All four turned their heads to the heavens every so often, opening their mouths and catching a few drops of fresh rainwater before sometimes gulping tossed sea spray and gagging. The moments in between the giant waves required a few kicks of their exhausted legs to avoid being smothered by rolling banks of water. He realised now that it was quite possibly the Kalends of April, or maybe that day had already passed. His meeting with Satuirninus would never happen. The chance of justice in the West was gone. He turned to the night sky and cried out: 'Where are you, Mithras? We gave you our hearts, our oaths. We need you now!'

The Gods did not answer, but the storm eased at dawn. The sea settled back down into a gentle plain and golden shafts of sunlight pricked the clouds. Pavo stared across the tranquil ocean, realising he had again been asleep, but he felt in his hands Izodora, Darik and Sura's palms, clasping him as tightly as he held them. He poked out his tongue to wet his lips, but it was dry too, and his lips felt rough like a crocodile's skin. He saw that the others' lips were blistered and shrivelled, and all were badly burnt from the constant exposure to the sun – fair-skinned Sura worst of all. The drinking skin made its way around them for the final time. Pavo forwent his turn, giving the last of it to Izodora. All four watched the empty skin float away, none daring to say what they were all thinking.

Pavo raked the horizon with his gaze. In every direction, just sea and sky. He felt a deep, heavy sense of despair in his breast, like a weight trying to pull him away from the mast and down into the inevitable.

'Tell me of your home,' Izodora said.

The words snapped him from his spiralling thoughts. He saw from the look on her face that she had read him like a scroll. It was a trick he had seen mothers use to distract upset children.

'You grew up in Constantinople, didn't you?' she added.

'In the slums. Well, they were not slums to me. Every lane was an adventure waiting to happen. Every forum a new world. The city sits on a peninsula, and it is wrapped in magnificent walls.'

'As I will soon see for myself,' she said with a weary smile. Nobody was cruel enough to voice their doubts over the likelihood of this.

Despite the nothingness all around them and the endless licking and lapping of waves, Pavo reflected her smile as best he could and continued: 'I used to stare up at the walls, wondering what it would be like to be a sentry, watching ships sailing in from foreign lands, staying vigilant for the approach of enemy war fleets.' The words toppled from his parched mouth like a water from a fountain. It was easy to talk of the simple and innocent days of his youth.

Sura decided to contribute too. 'But of course, Adrianople was where all the excitement happened. Back when I was just a boy, I used to follow the patrols out into the countryside. I noticed things before they did – warned them about nearby bandits and enemy raids. They said I had an uncanny awareness. All-seeing like a god. It was as if I had a third eye square in the centre of my forehead. The Cyclops of Adrianople, they used to call m-'

'Enough!' Darik slapped the water with the palm of his hand.

Sura stared at him, his blistered mouth still open.

'You make more noise than a pig with wind! I've suffered your... *nonsense* all the way from Ctesiphon. I thought you might run dry of preposterous stories by the time we got on the boat, but no. Even now when our ship has been ripped in half, leaving us adrift with nothing, no water, no food, no hope – *still* you spout your useless tales.'

Sura's shocked look faded. He closed his mouth and the playful sparkle in his eyes faded for a moment. Silence reigned and finally he replied. 'When I joined the legions I was given a shield. They said I should paint it brightly, and that it would protect me. Aye, it has stopped plenty enemy swords and axes. Yet in that time I have watched a thousand brothers die. To live with those kind of memories... a man needs a different kind of shield.'

Darik's rage – stoked by heat and helplessness – faded. 'I am sorry,' he said quietly. 'I forgot myself for a time. I forgot who you were too. Finish your story. What was it? The Cicada of Adrianople?'

Sura stared at him stonily for a time, then quirked his lips at one edge and returned to the tale. 'The *Cyclops* of Adrianople. God-like awareness. They said I could detect trouble from miles away. Most of the soldiers actually admitted they wanted to *be* me, to have my gift. But omniscience, I explained to them, was not something a man could teach.'

On and on Sura went, not even noticing when the others' faces lit up, staring past his shoulder.

'Omniscient, you say?' Darik asked.

'Oh, that barely even covers it.'

'Wouldn't miss a thing?' Izodora said.

'Not a thing.'

'Not even something *that* big,' Pavo croaked.

Sura frowned, then flicked his head left and right in confusion when a shadow crawled over him from behind.

'By the Gods, what happened here?' a voice said in Greek from above and behind Sura.

To Pavo, the gnarled, hoary old fisherman up on the craft looked like Neptune himself. 'Rough seas,' he croaked in reply, helping Izodora and Darik clamber aboard the round, flat-bottomed vessel. 'Where are we?'

'A morning's row south of Side,' the old fellow said, bemused as he watched Izodora then Darik then Sura collapsing onto the decks of his boat, groaning. 'And that's where we're headed back to.'

Pavo clambered aboard the boat last, his body suddenly feeling like a massive burden of rocks – having spent days bobbing in the water. His legs shook and he slumped to his knees, then slid onto his front like the others, landing atop a rough net that reeked of fish, muttering words of gratitude then sliding into a deep, dark sleep.

A riot of tinging bells, squabbling seabirds and babbling market-goers brought Pavo round. He groaned, his head aching as if it had been struck with a hammer. They were coming in to Side harbour, he realised. The terraced crescent of harbourside houses, painted bright white, shone like a mouth of perfect teeth in the sun, the doors and windows shaded by bright drapes of gold, purple, crimson and blue, all fluttering in the hot sea wind. The ship clunked gently against the long timber wharf. As he stepped from the fishing boat, Pavo took a gold solidus from his purse and placed it in the fisherman's hands. The man stared at the coin, aghast at such generosity. But Pavo refused to take it back. 'You saved our lives. There is no price I can put on that, but I hope this will buy you what you need to live well.'

In a blur, he led the others from the wharf and to the nearest tavern, bringing out a silver *miliarense* to buy them all rooms and food and, as Sura put it 'enough water to drown a horse in'.

Pavo and Izodora shared a white-painted room. Days passed, spent in the comfort of a soft bed dressed in fresh linen. Such a simple thing as a pillow was glorious, and the cool shade of the room soothed their burnt and battered bodies. A bar of sunlight shone through the balcony door, calmed by the thin emerald drape hanging there. Each day the gentle patch of light would amble across the bed, soft, slow and tenderly warming. They woke only to gulp on the fresh water the tavern keeper brought to them every few hours, and then to eat like gannets every night – roasted mullet, baked perch, yoghurt and honey and charred discs of freshly-baked flatbread.

On the fourth day, Pavo rose, refreshed, his body still bruised but feeling less battered, and most definitely fully-hydrated. While Izodora still slept, he drew a sheet around his waist and walked slowly out onto the room's balcony. The sun-warmed tiles out there felt insanely luxurious on the pads of his toes, and the balmy wind stroked his skin like a lover's fingertips as he gazed over Side and the blue waters that had so nearly claimed them.

Later that morning the group met up and enjoyed a tavern breakfast of salty bacon, eggs and thick hunks of bread. Around noon they bought new tunics, leather bags and provisions. In the afternoon, they set off to the north across the Anatolian interior. They joined the Ionian road and followed it through the high city of Hierapolis, past the chalky cascade of waterfalls and pools at Pamukkale – a place where old men from the empire over came to spend their final years. Here, Pavo spent another silver coin to buy passage on a carriage. The wagon sped north and as they passed through Ephesus, Smyrna and Troy, the chatter on the streets was the same: talk of great upheaval in the west, where the Lord of Britannia had declared war against Emperor Gratian. Pavo and Sura said nothing, but each felt it – the burning sense of destiny. Every place they passed through seemed more populous, louder, more stirred by the news. Yet it was on a quiet night, just after dusk, when they paid for a berth on a private ferry to cross the Propontis on the final approach to Constantinople.

After so long away and so many doubts about whether they would ever return, Pavo and Sura stared at the capital as if suspicious that it was a cruel illusion. The city had the look of a gold mine about it: streets veined with a molten glow of torch and firelight, domes and high monuments uplit like marble Gods. Pavo peered towards the distant land walls, seeing the long line of sentry lights there. The countryside beyond was black: if the Eastern legions were gathered out there for the march upon the West then they were cloaked by night. The thought turned his mind to the one legion that meant everything to him.

'Tonight we drink wine with the Claudia lads,' Pavo said. 'We're so close.'

'I can almost smell Libo from here… or it might be the sewers,' Sura said, his eyes glassy and his face wide with a fond smile.

'As soon as we've spoken to Saturninus, we can go to them,' Pavo sighed warmly.

The ferry drew round the great palace hill on the tip of the peninsula then slipped into the tapering inlet of the Golden Horn on the city's northern edge. The vessel docked at the Neorion Harbour. The stone-flagged wharf was a jumble of shadows broken up by the light of the torches held by the sentries patrolling the sea walls.

Pavo took a deep breath, all of Saturninus' warnings clanging like bells in his head.

Emperor Theodosius must remain unaware of your return…

'Follow me, heads down,' he said.

He disembarked first, leading the way to the sea gates. The sentries peered down at this unusual night arrival. With a groan of timber and clanking of chains, the sea gates parted and a small detachment of sentries filed out to meet the newcomers.

'There were no scheduled arrivals tonight,' a pug-nosed optio grunted at Pavo, then cast an evil look at the ferry captain, who stammered some half excuse before hurriedly shoving his boat away from the wharf.

Pavo tried to gauge the optio. Spoiling for trouble, certainly, but there was a dullness in his eyes – either hungover or tired. Easy to fool.

'Imperial business: Consul Saturninus sent us to the slave market at Chalcedon to pick him up two Persian slaves,' he said, holding up the scroll with Saturninus' seal on it and jabbing a lazy thumb over his shoulder towards Izodora, Darik and the far side of the Bosphorus Strait. He could almost feel the fiery glares of Izodora and Darik on his back – affronted at being referred to as slaves. The optio's lips arched in a half-sneer and he seemed slightly disappointed that he wouldn't get to use his sword tonight. 'Come with me.'

The optio and one of his men led them into the city. They passed the Neorion Barracks. For just a trice, Pavo saw the glorious red Claudian banner on the low turrets of the place. But he was mistaken – rather than a ruby bull it was a white eagle of some Macedonian unit.

'Where are the Claudia?' he asked the optio.

The optio held out his empty palms. 'That's what everyone is asking these days,' he laughed.

Confused, Pavo followed the man as he led them past the Severan Wall ruins at the foot of the the Second Hill, then up the broad, flagged and tavern-hemmed way that lined the slope of the Third Hill. Here, he was sure to keep his head down, just in case anyone recognised him.

'Are they with the other legions?' Pavo asked the optio as they went.

'Eh?' the man grunted.

'The Claudia. Are they gathering with the other legions for the war in the West.'

The man simply looked Pavo up and down and laughed. Before he could respond, he realised they were at Saturninus' estate up on the brow of the Third Hill. The optio left them with the two men standing guard there, who pushed open the iron gates and ushered them inside the garden area. Pavo spotted Saturninus – sitting on a veranda, one leg crossed over the other, deep in thought and sipping a cup of some herbal brew. When he looked up, Pavo grinned broadly. Saturninus' face, however, bent into a stunned gawp.

'Sir?' Pavo stammered as Saturninus threw down his cup and staggered down a short flight of marble steps towards them.

'How?' Saturninus whispered, touching Pavo's shoulders then Sura's as if trying to test whether this was a dream. 'I waited for you that night on the Kalends of the month. Stilicho arrived the next morning and said you died in the sea? Rammed by a Speculator galley?'

'We spent some time in the water, aye. But we're not done yet.'

The Consul's face grew pale as the moon and he glanced over to his two guards, then down the slopes of the Third Hill. 'Who else knows you are here?'

'Nobody,' Pavo replied, thinking of the ignorant optio and his men. None had recognised them. 'Yet. We have heard all kinds of rumours on the way here, sir. But you must tell me: the rebellion of Maximus in the West – is it true? Is this the challenge to Gratian you spoke of in the scroll?'

Saturninus nodded absently. 'Aye, *Magnus* Maximus as he calls himself now, has entered Gratian's territory.' He said this with a guilty tone, his eyes drifting down to the spring flowers around him.

'Sir, you know what Gratian has done in these last years. You know how many Romans, Goths – families of all backgrounds – have died because of him.'

Saturninus' eyes snapped back up like a whip. 'Oh I have no shred of doubt left that Gratian is a vile master.' He clutched his Chi-Rho necklace. 'But it turns my heart to ashes to think that this long-overdue rebellion might cause the biggest loss of life yet.'

'If he is overthrown, it will be worth it,' Pavo replied.

Saturninus stared into Pavo's eyes. 'Gratian has many more soldiers to call upon than Maximus. Maximus can field fifteen thousand men, but Gratian has twice that many. Maximus' only hope is the fact that Gratian's legions are scattered and ill-prepared. He has been in contact with Merobaudes to make this so.'

Pavo felt a thrill of hope. 'And Valentinian?'

'Aye, but both walk a dangerous path. Should Gratian find out what they have been doing...' he stopped and gave Pavo the gravest of looks.

Pavo understood, but refused to dwell on the possibility and turned his mind to the litany of questions the ignorant optio had not answered. 'When does the Eastern Army set off? Where are the legions of these parts gathering? When is the march?'

Saturninus gazed into his eyes. 'There is only so much I could say in my letter,' he sighed. 'The Eastern legions will not be supporting Maximus. He must fight this war alone.'

A response rose in Pavo's throat like a spout of fire. 'Why?'

'Emperor Theodosius does not wish to be part of this uprising. He cannot be seen to be supporting it.' he grabbed Pavo's shoulders again. 'And he cannot risk being seen to harbour Gratian's enemies. *You* cannot be *here.*'

Pavo shook free of Saturninus' grasp, disgusted by the news. 'Surely you must see this is no time for political posturing. The Tyrant of the West must be overthrown. Why deny Maximus our support?'

'That is why you are a soldier and I am a statesman, Pavo,' Saturninus said softly. 'Were I still a man of the legions then I would be asking him the very same question.'

Pavo paced to and fro, wiping a hand over his mouth as if he had tasted something foul. After a time, he swung back to Saturninus. 'Then tell me at least, where is my legion?'

'Far from here. They were tasked with policing the heart of Thracia – the region near the military road between the old Roman cities and the new Gothic *Haims*. They have been out there for months.'

'I heard rumours that they had been assigned a new tribunus? A… Western man?'

Saturninus's face sagged, and it told Pavo everything he needed to know. 'Zeno. I saw no cause to worry, at first. He seemed like a good man. There *are* good men in the West. But then my scouts recently intercepted messages passing to him from the court of Gratian. Messages marked with the staring eye. Zeno is…' his sentence trailed off as if he was trying to find an impossible euphemism.

'He *is* a Speculator,' Pavo finished for him, his breath sagging like sails on a suddenly calm sea. He turned away, pinching the top of his nose between thumb and forefinger. 'Just tell me where the Claudia are. Where exactly. They may be few in number but you know they are like no other legion. I can deal with this Zeno. I can have my men march west with me, we will join Maximus, help bring this to an end and-'

The rapping of hooves drowned out his final few words. A dark-cloaked explorator rode in, sliding from his saddle to land like a gymnast before his horse had even come to a halt. He straightened his felt cap to reveal a sweat-streaked face, jaw grey with stubble, and threw up an arm to salute Saturninus. 'More western messengers spill across our lands,' he explained between quick breaths. 'Gratian is recalling the few small garrisons and handfuls of advisors he left behind here in the East at the war's end.'

'And Zeno?' Pavo and Sura said in unison.

The explorator seemingly only just noticed the pair, Izodora and Darik now. 'Am I at liberty to speak?' he asked Saturninus.

'More so than ever,' Saturninus replied.

The explorator drew from his satchel a scroll with a broken wax seal. Pavo's blood chilled at the sight of it – a single, staring eye.

'I distracted one of the Western messengers at a waystation by buying him a heavy meal and a large jug of unwatered wine. When he went to the latrine, I searched his bags and found this scroll. It compels Zeno and the detachment of Western legionaries under his command to depart from the East and return to Gratian's side like the others. But... but, there was something different about this instruction. A printed symbol at the foot of the message.' He wetted his lips as if afraid to say any more, simply handing the scroll to Saturninus.

Saturninus' eyes scanned side to side as he read the text then grew wide as moons when they fell upon what looked like a dark circular marking near the foot.

'Sir?' Pavo asked.

'This scroll is but one of three copies,' the explorator said apologetically. 'The order will by now be well on its way to Zeno.'

'What does that mark mean?' Sura pressed.

Saturninus looked up. 'It is the scythe of Saturn... an order for extermination.'

Sura fell into a stunned silence.

Darik's face fell as if he had heard a desert demon whispering a curse.

Pavo shook as if he had been speared through the chest. Izodora clasped his shoulder like a bypasser offering support to a dizzy man. 'Where. Where are they?' he stammered.

'An island,' the explorator answered. 'I tracked the Western messenger to the coast north of Apollonia Pontica. But he boarded a boat and slipped out into the water in the blackness of night. I had no vessel and so I could not follow, but I saw him row out to a bleak, wind-beaten hump of rock.'

'How long ago?' Pavo said.

'Four days,' the explorator croaked. 'It… it might be too late already.'

Pavo stared at Sura, both lost.

'Sir, I ask of you two things,' Pavo said, turning to Saturninus. 'Grant my two friends here shelter,' he gestured to Izodora and Darik, then towards Saturninus' small private stable. 'And lend me two of your best horses.'

Chapter 13
May 383 AD
Snake Island

'It's alright, lad, you are strong enough,' Libo said, his good eye filled with tears, 'for this... for anything.'

Datus' eyes searched the centurion's face, his chest rising and falling rapidly. 'Will... will Mithras see me right. After it is done? Will I see Trypho again?'

Libo felt as if a huge invisible hand had grabbed his throat. It took him three tries to reply without sobbing. 'Aye, Mithras will see you right. Trypho will be there for you.' With that, he stepped back into the small ranks of the unarmed Claudians serried near the wharf on the southern edge of Snake Island, and stared into the blue spring sky – streaked with wispy clouds painted there by the fierce northerly wind.

'This,' Crassus bawled gleefully, striding purposefully to and fro in front of the Claudians with his staff tucked under his arm, 'is what happens to deserters.'

Libo could not bare to look, yet could not help but see either as, from the edge of his vision, one of Crassus' men approached Datus, holding a sack. The sack writhed and bulged – the score of grey water snakes in there frightened and angry. Tribunus Zeno stood, crow-like, on the shale ledge near the lighthouse, looking down on it all.

'Thought he could swim like a fish,' Crassus continued. 'Until he got halfway out into the currents and began thrashing like a demented trout. We *could* have let him drown, but we thought the rest of you could do with another example. The greatest deterrent to disobedience is to let a man *see* what will happen to him should he stray onto that path. Thus, this young man will not see his eighteenth summer. Desertion will *not* be tolerated.' He spoke every word as if this prison island was truly a legionary base and not a cruel torture camp. Two more of Crassus' men grabbed Datus by a shoulder each, and edged him towards the sack.

Libo's good eye tracked Datus' horrified steps. The youngster's legs and back were a mesh of not just scars and scabs like the others, but weeping, grievous wounds, inflicted in the month since the decimation of the Third Cohort. Ever since the moment he had brought the rock down upon his friend's head, Datus had been a shell, muttering to himself during the days, singing gently during the nights while others slept. Yesterday, when Crassus had been flicking his whip at their backs as they ran up and down the island slope, Datus had wandered aimlessly to one side, staring, calling his dead friend's name. Crassus had lashed him until white bone shone through the wounds. No wonder he had fled, maddened, during the night.

A hiss of angry snakes snapped Libo back to the horror of the present as the one with the sack opened it. The two holding Datus bundled him over before the mouth of the sack and halted there. Crassus grinned, eyes sweeping across Libo and his men. Libo bit down on his lower lip, knowing Crassus and the watching Zeno were just waiting for one of the Claudians to break ranks, knowing the armed legionaries – arrayed in a line behind the Claudians, spears trained on their backs – were just aching for the order to be given to strike down any mutineers.

Something had changed, he realised. Zeno and Crassus no longer seemed happy to gradually whittle away the original Claudians. They were itching to kill now. It had begun a handful of nights ago. Libo had been woken by the sound of voices from the wharf and had crept to the edge of the barrack house, peering through the narrow windows to watch the visitor climb the hill to the lighthouse. He had witnessed Zeno accepting a small bundle of scrolls from the messenger. In the days since, there had been a hasty cataloguing of supplies, stacking of arms and armour on wagons and discussions amongst Crassus, Zeno and his officers about 'moving out'. Indeed, the liburnian had docked here this morning and was already stacked with what looked like provisions for a long journey. Leaving the island did not sound like a bad thing, but Libo had a dreadful feeling that it would not be to a better place.

The snakes hissed again.

Libo felt the eyes of every true Claudian on him too, eager for the order to rebel. He had always envied his commanders, especially the leaders of the legions he had served under. Pavo more than all. It was a cordial envy, but often he had wished for the chance to be the decision-maker, the thinker, the leader. Now that he *was* the most senior of the true Claudians… he wished he could crawl back through time, back to his days as a recruit, before all of this sorry mess had begun… before this horrible choice had settled upon his shoulders. Surely a good commander would not let one of his own die like this – a stage-managed execution of a young man driven to despair? Yet surely only a fool of a commander would throw the lives of all of his men into the fire with one emotional outburst that could only end one way.

Forgive me, lad, Libo mouthed.

The two holding Datus bundled him into the bag then drew and knotted a cord to seal him in there. His screams were shrill – first yells of terror, then spikes of agony as the snakes attacked. The thrashing seemed endless, the screams growing ragged and terrible.

'Drown him,' Zeno called down calmly.

The trio around the sack hauled it over to the edge of the black rocks, swung it once and hurled it over the short drop into the sea. Libo closed his good eye, but the noises of thrashing water and Datus' final screams could not be blocked out so easily. When it was over, the silence hung like a damp shroud over them all.

A sixty-strong column of Gothic heavy horsemen ambled southwards along the Via Pontica, led by two of the most powerful Goths in the world. Eriulf wore Roman mail but kept his long blonde hair gathered atop his head in a topknot, the ends rising in a sprout of resin-stiffened spikes. He looked sideways at his odd-looking kinsman every so often. He had once admired Faustius – envied him, even. He had watched the man sit opposite the Roman, Saturninus, and engineer a strong peace settlement for the Goths. Back then, Faustius had looked every part the tribal warlord. Now, he was as Roman as could be, draped in a white tunic blazoned with purple shoulder stripes and embroidered discs on the hem and each bicep. His dark hair was short, the fringe carefully arranged on his forehead in an array of curls.

'How did the legions ever control this place?' Faustius said, snapping Eriulf from his thoughts.

Eriulf regarded the green, sun-soaked hills inland on the right edge of the road. Such vastness. Yet he knew – having surveyed the Roman maps – how small a portion of Thracia entire he could see from here. The sea puffed and sprayed a short way to the left of the road, and in some ways, it felt like a natural barrier, but then he remembered Theodosius and his council's careful talks and plans to watch those waters for incoming raiding ships from the north. 'They were never truly in control,' he replied. 'For a time, circumstance allowed them a notional command. Then,' he gestured over his shoulder, as if casting a pebble towards the far north, 'the Huns came.'

'But now our people are here, settled and at peace, the Hun threat from the north will be rebuffed,' Faustius replied firmly. 'Forty thousand Goths will do what the legions could not. We will *be* the armies of the Eastern Empire. Over time, we will be Goths no more – they will call us Romans. Just as they long ago learned to accept the men of Gaul as Romans too.'

'Is that your vision?' Eriulf scoffed. 'To stir our peoples' pasts into the Roman cauldron and to have our lore, our ancestry, our old ways, everything, blended away into nothing? To vanish into history? You might have rid yourself of your tribal trappings, Fravitta, but the rest of us have not.'

Faustius shot him a look that would put frost on a hot meal. 'My name is *Faustius*, and you would do well to remember that.'

Eriulf chuckled humourlessly, leaning back a little in his saddle. 'When did you decide to change your name: was it before or after Emperor Theodosius granted you Kabyle – the widest and most fertile estate in these lands – to establish your *haim*?'

'You have profited from him just as much,' Faustius snapped. 'He put that golden torque around your neck and raised you to lead his new palace legion. More, at least I rove between our new settlements and speak with our people. You spend most of your days in Constantinople with your regiment, toadying by Theodosius' side in the meetings of his sacred council.'

'And still I wear my heritage like a war-belt,' Eriulf replied in a proud burr. 'While you parade and prance in your Roman garb through the streets of Kabyle. Oh, if Fritigern could see you now he would turn his longsword upon himself.'

'Fritigern died in search of peace,' Faustius growled. '*I* saw it through.'

Both men fell silent for a time.

Eriulf broke the silence when a nagging thought arose in his head. 'I heard something recently. Apparently Reiks Ingolf has been deposed.'

Faustius snorted. 'Aye. The fool flouted the simple laws we were to obey, casting Roman officials onto a great fire as if he was still a rogue warlord in the woods north of the empire.'

'Where was he taken to?'

'I hoped you might know,' Faustius replied, slowing a little.

Now Eriulf slowed a fraction too. 'I assumed he had been arrested by your Kabyle guardsmen?'

Faustius' brow wrinkled. 'I heard he was taken by a legion – back to Constantinople, presumably. You are the one who dwells in the capital, so you must have seen or heard of his arrival there?'

Eriulf shook his head slowly. 'Ingolf's *Haim*, Deultum, is north of here, and there are no legions in these parts or for many miles to the south.'

Faustius clicked his fingers as if trying to beckon a memory back to the forefront of his mind. 'They said it was the Claudia legion,' he answered at last. 'They showed their numbers outside Deultum and forced Ingolf to surrender.'

Eriulf's head switched round. 'The Claudia? They are but a ragged band, and they've been out on patrol for months – keeping the peace, supposedly? And… and they numbered no more than one hundred or so. Ingolf had a strong warband at Deultum.'

Faustius shrugged. 'Ingolf was a danger to the peace. Now he is a danger no longer. As far as the people of the Gothic *Haims* are concerned, he is in the cells under the emperor's palace at Constantinople. I have spread the word across our kin. Any reiks who dares to threaten the peace will answer to me.' Haughtily, he heeled his mount into a gentle canter then slowed again at a position at the clear front of the column.

Eriulf mouthed oaths at his back. A few moments later, hooves clopped up from the column rear to fill the empty space by Eriulf's side. Alaric was just fourteen summers old, but already he had the build and poise of a man – well-learned having spent his childhood with the horde and around high-ranking Goths. His golden braids swished and swayed across his bronze breastplate, his bare arms muscular and milky-pale, his face set in a determined look.

'Did I hear right, Master?' Alaric said. 'Did he just dismiss the disappearance of Reiks Ingolf?'

His voice was too loud for Eriulf's comfort, and the tone too scathing. He shot the young warrior a stern look, but Alaric merely read this as confirmation. The young man hissed air through his teeth: 'Anything to keep in with his new Roman masters.'

In truth, there was no difference between his and young Alaric's views. It was just that the lad had yet to learn to harness his anger and mask his darkest feelings. Once again, Eriulf stared at Faustius' back. After the peace had been concluded, Eriulf had hoped that Faustius might be the key to the dream that his sister, Runa, had spawned. A dream that he now carried on in her name: a dream of Gothic supremacy, of a people rising to overthrow the empire from within… a dream of the worthy, of the Wodin-chosen… a dream of the Vesi.

Vesi, he mouthed, seeing in his mind's-eye the many members of the secretive sect within the Gothic populace. Most were carefully chosen – artisans, trackers, hardy warlords and the elite Gothic soldiers he had chosen to make up his Thervingi palace legion. Many of the more northerly *haims* were well-seeded with high-ranking men who had taken the Vesi oath. These settlements would serve as a fine core. Even better, young Alaric was well-placed as Eriulf's ears and eyes out here in the Gothic world while he was watching matters in Constantinople carefully. Eriulf himself had been the leader of the Vesi sect since Runa's death. Now, as one of Emperor Theodosius' chosen men, he had risen almost to the apex of Roman power. He was the man who could – when the time was right – draw the blade, slay the Roman ruler, issue the call to his followers from the *haim* settlements to throw off their guises and see in the rise of the Vesi. *I will do it for you, Sister,* he mouthed to Runa's spirit, *when the time is right.* He felt a cooling of the spring breeze and knew it was her reply.

They ambled on southwards for a time, and the afternoon grew hot, the tall golden grass nodding in the breeze and the cicadas humming incessantly. Soon, they would reach the southerly limits of the Gothic-controlled section of Thracia. There, he would ride back to Constantinople while Faustius – having performed this regular tour of the villages with him – would veer northwest back to his headquarters at the *Haim* of Kabyle.

But just a short while before they reached the crossroads where they were to part, a strange thing happened. The sea – a gem box of sparkling light – glinted a little more brightly just a short way off the coast. Eriulf squinted, but could see no more than a hump-island with a white lighthouse and a statue of Apollo atop it. He raised a hand to shield his eyes and saw more this time: armoured men on the southern edge of that bleak-looking isle. Standing in formation. Legionaries? It was not a huge surprise, for the nearby coastal town of Apollonia Pontica was still under full Roman jurisdiction. But why send so many legionaries out onto such a pointless bump of rock? He slowed a little as he tried to discern some detail. He saw that a small line of them wore no armour, but the rest were bedecked in silver vests and helms. More, they were facing a group of four. Three ironclad soldiers manhandling a slight one in nothing but his tunic. A cold stone settled in Eriulf's belly as he realised what he was witnessing at the same time as the slight one was bundled into a sack. The screams carried across the water from the island, as did the thick splash when the bag was tossed into the sea.

Beside him, Alaric laughed heartily. 'I thought the light was playing tricks on my eyes. First we hear of Roman armies sizing up to fight one another in the West. Now we see the shattered fragments of the army that remains in these parts… drowning one another?'

But Eriulf's attentions were snared by something else: the armoured ones on the islet carried ruby-red shields, bright and new. The designs were striking – golden mithraic stars and leaping bulls. For all the world it looked like… *the Claudia*?

That strange coolness tinged the spring breeze again. For a moment he remembered how it had been, before Runa died. She and Pavo had been lovers, he and Pavo like brothers. But Pavo was dead, and the ragged remains of the Claudia had become embroiled in some dark internal power struggle, it seemed. For a moment, he wondered how he should report this… then *if* he should report it at all. After all, these replete ranks of gleaming soldiers were surely not the old sparse band of Claudians who had lived with and led his people into the empire some four years ago, who had become friends. These ones were but a regiment of men, a symbol of empire.

'Come, Master,' Alaric beckoned Eriulf away from the scene as the Gothic column clopped onwards, 'leave them to kill one another. We have greater matters to consider.'

Pavo crouched low in the tall grass between the Via Pontica and the shore, struck with horror at what he had seen on Snake Island. Datus – one of the most earnest, hard-working young lads in the legion. A hero of Dionysopolis. Executed like the worst kind of deserter. He stared at the hulking brute with the drill-master's staff who had overseen the execution, and at the crow-like red-cloaked officer who watched on from a shale ledge near the lighthouse – Zeno, he realised. Tendrils of hatred tightened around his body, his fingers coiling into shaking fists. Consumed with fury, he nearly missed the scuff and scrape of horses' hooves on the road behind him.

He and Sura swung round, staying on their haunches within the tall grass, to see the line of Gothic horsemen ambling down the highway – bulky riders draped in thick leathers and iron, topknots swishing like the manes of their steeds. Both froze.

Pavo's eyes widened as he recognised Eriulf. The sight of the Gothic nobleman sparked a flurry of memories: his time with Runa and the adventures she, he and her brother had shared. When it was all over, when Runa had died, Eriulf and Pavo had called each other brothers.

The memories faded. What to do? On his and Sura's covert journey here from Constantinople – stealing through the Golden Gate with one of Saturninus' civic parties, then riding north up the coast road like shadows, hiding out at night in caves and woods – they had been sure not to cross paths with anyone who might report their presence to Emperor Theodosius. But Pavo knew – to his core – that it would be safe to show himself to Eriulf. He braced to stand up, rise above the tall grass, when he noticed how Eriulf had slowed, and the young Goth, Alaric, had slowed with him. Both horsemen were staring out at Snake Island. At the execution. A terrible sound poured from their direction then. Laughter. Cold, triumphant laughter.

Pavo remained on his haunches, staring, as Eriulf and Alaric moved off again at a walk with the rest of their cavalry, past their hiding spot in the grass and off to the south.

'Allies?' Sura spat into the ground. 'They saw what just happened on that island... and they were *laughing.*'

Pavo stared at the back of Eriulf. *You mock the death of a Claudian?* he mouthed towards the distant rider. *The legion who fought to save your people?*

'Pavo,' Sura hissed. 'I don't think it's over.'

Pavo back swung round to stare at the island. Now the officer with the staff was calling out another from the unarmoured ones. Even from this distance, Pavo recognised Libo's wild mop of hair as he stepped out. 'No...' Pavo croaked. Was this the extermination? A horrible death for every last one of his men? 'Mithras no. Not yet...'

Both watched, sure Libo was about to perish like Datus. But the staff-bearer barked something once more – a sound shapeless but vitriolic by the time it reached Pavo and Sura's ears. Libo turned to face the shale slope below the watching Zeno, then loped towards it, running uphill and back down. Up and down he went again, exhausted but unyielding, seven more times. Eventually, Zeno made some signal down to Crassus, who barked something which dispersed the armoured ones and the true Claudians back towards what looked like a barrack house. Datus was gone, but for now it seemed like the others would be spared.

'We made it in time,' Sura said, 'this extermination order – it hasn't happened yet.'

'It could happen at any moment, Sura. To Hades with the West and the rebellion of Maximus. This is all that matters right now: our brothers are out there – and in the hands of that Speculator bastard, Zeno. We have to get out there. That galley,' he said, pointing at the liburnian docked on the island's small wharf, 'that's the key.'

'We could swim out there, no problem,' Sura said, eyeing the channel between the coast and the island. 'The Kraken of Adrianople they used to call me...'

Pavo ignored the beginnings of the story. 'No, see how the water moves – the current is strong through that channel. If you didn't drown in the water then it would take you hours to swim across.' Next, he pointed to the lighthouse on the apex of the island and the legionaries strolling up there. 'The island is bare and that tower means they can see everything approaching – you'd be spotted straight away.'

'So we must cross at night,' Sura reasoned, turning towards the pebble bay near Apollonia Pontica. About half a mile south lay the telltale brown bumps of upturned fishing skiffs, stored just out of the tide's reach. 'Come on, we can move down the coast road towards those boats and wait on the darkness – I saw a fisherman's shack when we passed on the way here.'

But as Sura made to rise, Pavo caught his wrist, keeping him on his haunches.

'What is it?'

Pavo said nothing. The gentle spring breeze combed through the grassy hinterland as he looked behind them, north, west, south. Nothing. All the way here they had moved like shadows, he reassured himself again, careful to come off of the roads whenever travellers approached from either direction. They had made cold camp at night – foregoing a campfire and leaving no trace behind them. But all the way here, he had felt that strange presence, somewhere in their wake. The breeze danced through the grass again with a sussurating song, like the whispered words of a shade.

Sura sneezed – a sound like a horse being lanced from anus to mouth – and Pavo's heart almost leapt from his chest. 'Sura for fu-'

'Sorry,' Sura spluttered, then realised what was going on, looking down the road with Pavo. 'You think we're being followed? You *always* think we're being followed.'

Pavo shot Sura a vinegary look. 'Perhaps it's something to do with our many instances of being followed?'

'Look!' Sura insisted, stretching a hand southwards along the Via Pontica. 'Deserted.'

They crept out onto the road and moved south, finding the fisherman's shack as Sura had promised. It was big enough for the pair of them to sit and no more. The place was a good hideout, allowing them to watch through a slit in the shack door as the sun gradually set. They shared a lump of tasteless hardtack and tried not to salivate over the tantalising scent of roasting fish that wafted across them every so often from the taverns of Apollonia Pontica, then quietly discussed how they might approach and infiltrate the island. The first obstacle was the lasting indigo twilight – they could never hope to cross without being spotted until it was properly dark. Even when true night fell an hour later, a waxing gibbous moon and stars emerged, triumphantly casting a silvery glow across the sound. More, there was still hearthlight being cast across the waters from Apollonia Pontica here on the mainland as well as from the island itself – torches from the barrack house, the lighthouse tower and from the harbour too, where a watch of twenty stood guard around the liburnian. It would have to be darker still before they could make their way across to the island unseen. Hours more passed. The moonlit waters lapped quietly on the pebble shore as they waited and waited. The silence grew trancelike and soporific. As if to keep them awake and alert, a school of dolphins leapt from the waters some way out, their skin like quicksilver in the moonlight. Mackerel nearby, Pavo realised. The thought stirred a memory of youth, which in turn brought a great lump into his throat.

'What are you thinking about?' Sura asked, toying with a dried piece of net.

'My father taught me to fish when I was a boy,' Pavo replied quietly. 'Such a long time ago. Back then, I wanted for nothing. We *had* nothing. Simple, sweet happiness. I've often thought that… that one day I will set down my sword. Find another way to live. Izodora, she is…' his words tapered off with a fond sigh. He had almost had to draw his blade on her to convince her to agree to stay in Constantinople. In the end it was Darik who had assured her it was for the best. To the big man's credit, he even affirmed Pavo's lie – that this would be a swift and simple mission.

Sura smiled. 'When this is over. When we have freed our brothers. When we have faced Gratian and dealt him the justice he has escaped for too long… perhaps you and she can settle together.'

Pavo half-smiled. 'You make it sound so easy. Our legion is but a handful of men – trapped on an island of executioners. More, the breadth of the empire lies between us and Gratian. We have no weapons, no armour, no money, no men, no legion, no right to travel to the faraway lands upon which Maximus seeks to face him down.'

'One step at a time,' Sura encouraged him. 'And look – the first step beckons.'

Pavo looked out to sea, noticing that the sky was now inky black and, although the moon was high, clouds were now cutting across it and dulling its light. Moreover, the many lights from the taverns and houses of Apollonia Pontica had been doused and out on the hump of Snake Island the barrack building had fallen dark – leaving just the lighthouse and two harbour torches glowing.

Rising from their shack shelter, the pair crept down onto the beach, annoyed by the snapping of shale and grumble of shingle underfoot. But there was no sign or sound of the fishermen or any other nearby. As they took one of the skiffs and heaved it the right way up, Pavo stared across at the island, picking out the key locations he and Sura had discussed: the lighthouse on the apex, and on the southern edge, the dimly-lit wharf, the skeletal mast and rigging of the liburnian and the black outline of the barrack compound.

'So we row out to the island's northern end,' Sura muttered, reciting the plan.

'Aye,' Pavo agreed. 'See how it is darker on that rugged side of the isle? They won't expect boats to arrive from that seaward side. We'll have to scramble over wet rocks to get onto the island proper, but we can do that. We skirt round the isle's eastern edge and get inside that barrack house. We've stolen into forts before,' he said as they lowered the skiff into the shallows. 'We'll sneak in and find Libo first of all – establish exactly what is happening. After that, we find the armoury, arm our comrades.'

'But they'll be hugely outnumbered. Two cohorts versus our hundred or so.'

'Doesn't matter. All we need is enough men to storm the harbour watch and get aboard that liburnian. Once we get that boat away from the wharf, they're stranded and we're free.'

With a gentle splash, the skiff bobbed in the shallows. Pavo set one foot aboard, lifted an oar and handed the other one to Sura. The pair were braced to step aboard fully, when the grass behind the fisherman's shack rustled. Both swung towards the noise, oars held up like spears.

'Ha!' Darik barked with a wild grin as he lunged into view, landing in a warrior's crouch. His hands were empty, and he straightened up, laughing, resting his hands on his hips.

'Mithras' crotch!' Sura stammered, sagging in relief.

'You. It was *you* who tracked us all the way here,' Pavo realised.

'You promised Izodora this would be a swift mission,' Darik said. 'But I knew you were not telling the truth. I knew it was a *noble* lie, but a lie nonetheless. Besides, you saved my life back in the sea and I still owe you that debt.' He clasped a hand across his chest and part-bowed. 'I am a Maratocupreni, and we honour our debts. I will not leave your side until it is settled.'

'But you followed our every move to get here. How? We moved like *shadows,*' Pavo protested.

'You were like charging elephants!' Darik roared with laughter. 'Your horses left piles of shit that a blind man could have followed, all the way to where they are tethered about a mile back. You dropped crumbs of bread where you camped and one night,' his nose wrinkled, 'failed to dig a deep enough pit to empty your bowels into.'

'One night,' Sura spat, reddening. 'You make it sound as if it happened every night on the way here.'

'Keep your voices down,' Pavo hissed.

'What? Why?' Darik frowned.

'The Claudia are over on that island and-'

'I know, I know,' Darik scoffed. 'Set that pathetic skiff aside, this lot have promised us a proper ferry.'

From either side of the fisherman's hut, a pair of strangers in pristine Claudian armour emerged, faces stony, eyes trained on Pavo and Sura.

'See, I found some of your comrades. You could at least show some gratitu-' Darik started, before his body jolted forward, his eyes rolled in his head and he whumped face first onto the shore, unconscious. The legionary behind who had knocked him out with his spear haft edged forward, lance tip hovering towards Pavo, the other doing likewise with Sura. Pavo and Sura backstepped into the shallows, oars now held up fully like makeshift shields. Only when it was too late did Pavo sense the other two coming at them from the flanks. With a thick crack of a sword hilt whacking his temple, his mind burned bright white for an instant, then faded to complete blackness.

Zeno strolled around the table in the lighthouse command room, enjoying the heat of the low fire, periodically taking sips from his wine cup and gazing from the open window to the dark and silent barrack compound – an arrowshot away and below. It was his last night here, and he realised that he would miss the place. Despite the bleakness of the island it had felt like his own little empire.

'We've finalised the route plan, sir,' Crassus said, ambling in, 'the wagons and packs are ready too.'

Zeno smiled amiably and sipped his wine again, now gazing from the westwards-looking lighthouse window – off into the darkness in that direction. 'War looms in the West and Emperor Gratian calls on us personally, Crassus. We might be heroes. Saviours!'

Crassus grunted happily. 'Still one last thing to take care of though, sir.'

Zeno's smile rose. 'Oh I hadn't forgotten. Certainly not.' Gratian had initially tasked them with a slow and gradual disposal of these Claudian legionaries, one by one, supplanting each with one of his own western men and in time turning the Claudia – before now a bane to the West – into one of Gratian's greatest assets, an Eastern legion answering publically to Theodosius but entirely loyal to the master of the West. A fine plan, ruined by news of the invasion, he thought. Still, he mused, thinking of the dark print of the Scythe of Saturn – a tacit command for extermination – it meant that they could now pick whichever means they chose to dispose of the Claudians briskly.

'I really thought they'd lose their heads and attack us at the wharf today, I really did,' Crassus sighed. His mouth lifted at one end, his cleft chin swelling. 'We could have cut them down in a few heartbeats. So we're going to have to be a little less subtle, I reckon. How shall we do it? Archers – shoot them down at morning roll-call? Drowning – set them all free... but only if they can swim back to the mainland? We could take the liburnian out and club their heads in as they swim.'

'I have a better idea,' Zeno beamed, one eyebrow rising. 'The journey to Emperor Gratian's side will be long and tiresome. We have no pack mules to carry our tents and provisions. But we want to stay fresh, so we reach him in good condition – so we can impress him when we help to crush the invader.'

Crassus' evil smile faded, confused.

'We. Have. No. Mules.' Zeno repeated as if speaking to a dim-witted child.

Crassus' smirk returned as he understood at last. 'Ah, then I had best take a spare staff or two – to help drive on our "replacement mules", sir.'

Zeno took another swig of wine. 'We'll only use them to cross the rugged ground. They can haul our provisions over Mons Asticus – that highland region is a shortcut to the Via Militaris. Once that great road is in sight, we can... dispose of our mules.' He rested one hand on the small of his back and supped at his wine with the other, enjoying the sound of the sea foaming against the island's ragged shores. But then another sound joined it – the hissing of something being dragged. Zeno and Crassus turned to the command room door to see his sentries backing up the stairs. Three of his men posted on the mainland shore – and they were each dragging limp bodies.

'Sir,' one barked. 'Trouble on the shore. We spotted these three watching the island from the coast.' He pointed to the big, darker-skinned one. 'We found this one first, and when he saw our shields he greeted us as if we were friends. He said these other two were Claudians also, come to find their legion.

Zeno's left eyebrow rose like a gravestone being pushed up from below. 'Claudians?' He crouched beside the darker-haired, eagle-faced one, pulling the collar of the man's tunic down. 'No soldier tags. But he does have the scars of a veteran.' He checked the blonde one too. 'Bring them round,' he snapped.

The sentries vanished for a short time before returning with buckets of seawater. Two held up the dark-haired one by the shoulders and the other tossed the freezing water into his face.

The cold, heavy slap hit Pavo hard. Another briney punch. He gasped and spluttered as the bucketful of water sheeted down over him. For a moment he thought he was still adrift in the Mare Internum and that everything since – the rescue, the comfortable room in Side, the journey back to Constantinople – had been a dream. Then he saw the shapes and colours of the small room spinning before his eyes, and heard a throbbing inside his skull like the boom of a war drum. It took him moments to realise where he was and who the officer standing before him sipping wine was. Zeno the Speculator. Datus' murderer. He saw on the desk behind the officer a ring with a staring eye emblem… and a dagger. Within arm's reach.

'They say you are a Claudian,' Zeno spoke with a snake's look.

Pavo realised the man was testing him, and the dagger was deliberately close and on show. The fact Zeno was trained as a Speculator meant Pavo would likely lose his hand before it reached the weapon. 'I am... Urbicus of the First Century, First Cohort,' he lied, drawing the old pseudonym instead of the blade.

'I'm Mucianus,' Sura chimed in. 'We've been posted at the Neorion docks in Constantinople since last spring.'

'Missed the end of the war,' Pavo added, building the story.

'Nobody tells us anything,' Sura said. 'We heard only that you led the rest of the legion out on patrol months ago. We haven't been paid since last September and that Centurion Libo holds the records that say so. We came out from the city to see if we could find any trace of him… and you.'

Zeno's expression changed – from dark fascination to slight boredom. For the first time in a long time, Pavo thanked the Gods for his friend's silver tongue.

At that moment, Darik moaned, his head lolling, rising with difficulty. With eyes like slits he peered at Zeno and Crassus, then up at the sentries holding him.

'What about the Persian?' Crassus said.

'Persian?' Darik spat, bristling. 'I am a Maratocupreni!' he growled through caged teeth.

'And he's one of us too,' Pavo said quickly.

'Joined the Claudia from the eastern borders a few years back when Valens brought the desert legions to Thracia,' Sura confirmed with another pristine lie.

A look of suspicion passed over Zeno and Crassus' faces once more.

'Look, we're not deserters,' Pavo said in an overly-grovelling tone – knowing it would stop them thinking too hard. 'We just wanted our pay, and to be part of the Claudia again like good soldiers – to take every step they take.'

Crassus rumbled then erupted in deep laughter.

Zeno's eyebrow rose again. 'Oh, you will… you *certainly* will.'

Chapter 14
May 383 AD
Mons Asticus

Come dawn, Zeno, Crassus and their sentries marched Pavo, Sura and Darik down the island slope from the lighthouse towards the barrack compound, through a gentle hiss of early summer rain, a smell of musty earth and wet grass rising around them. Pavo blinked through the rain, seeing the thin line of his Claudians formed up nearby. As they drew closer, Pavo realised the danger he had put himself and all the others in. One salute, one mutter of his real name, and the extermination would happen here and now.

Big Pulcher looked up first, his pitted, greasy face contorted in displeasure at the rain and the presence of the armed soldiers ordered behind them. His eyes rolled upwards and fixed on the approaching party. It was a blank look... then his eyes widened like a falcon spotting unexpected movement. Rectus, labouring to stand with his cane, peered up too, his mouth peeling open. Libo stared hard, his face paling as if he was witnessing shades descending from the island summit. And he was, Pavo realised. For their own good, none of them knew that he and Sura still lived. Until now.

Opis rose a little on the balls of his feet, face widening with awe. Betto, Indus, Durio – one by one they rippled to stand taller like the stalks of a ripe wheat field lifted by a stiff wind.

Pavo met every man's eyes through a patina of tears, arriving at Libo last. All he could do was gesture with a tight expression and hope that it would be enough.

Libo frowned.

Beside him, Opis' mouth shaped to bawl out in greeting and his right arm tensed to salute.

Pavo shook his head almost indiscernibly – too much and Zeno might notice, too little and his comrades would not. On and on he tried to signal as they stepped down closer to the barrack area and then onto that strip of flat ground by the wharf.

But Opis bellowed as they approached, his saluting arm shooting upwards. 'Tribunus Pa-'

Libo's eyes widened like moons and he swung an elbow sideways into Opis' ribs.

Zeno halted. Pavo saw him cocking his head askance. Crassus and the sentries halted too and thus so did Sura, Pavo and Darik.

Opis shot Libo a foul look then recoiled a little in realisation. Turning back to Zeno's party, the Claudia's standard bearer spluttered a few times then composed himself to finish: 'Pa...have...*have!* Tribunus, it's good to *have* you back with us,' he saluted, but this time directing his salute clearly towards Zeno.

Zeno stepped forward to examine Opis as if he was a madman. With a derisive snort, he stepped away again and gestured to Pavo, Sura and Darik. 'Three more of your mutts from the docks of Constantinople came looking for you.' He called over his shoulder, commanding his sentries: 'Put them in line.'

The sentries thumped Pavo, Sura and Darik in the small of the back with their spear hafts, driving them like cattle into the Claudia ranks. Most men on the front line shifted to make space there for their rightful Tribunus, and it was only a few low and terse curse words from those in the know who corrected them, allowing these three 'lowly legionaries' to return to their normal position in the rear rank.

Pavo sensed the eyes of those in line with him sliding to stare at him. The rain had soaked him through now, but a heavier, wetter cloak of guilt pressed upon his shoulders. *I should never have gone into exile in Persia*, he realised, spotting the absence of Datus, Trypho the Cretan, Farus too. Spaces where others should have been. What had happened here? *Not as bad as what's about to come,* he realised.

Zeno stood, feet apart, facing them. 'Today we begin a journey. A long journey of many, many days. March in good time and I will have no reason to complain.'

A whisper of amazement floated around the Claudians.

'Things can only get better if we're to leave this island,' whispered Ancus, standing on Pavo's right, staring at the liburnian by the wharf.

'The eyes are quick to deceive, Ancus,' Betto said with a theatrical grumble. 'Where one might see a ligneous liferaft of liberation, others may perceive a Stygian ship of sorrow.'

Pavo shot Betto a look for his unhelpful comment, then whispered to him and the others. 'Keep quiet. Stay watchful. Things are... not as they seem.'

Ancus and Betto stared at him, faces paling. Pavo realised how rusty he was with his choice of words to men like these.

The Liburnian ferried most of the armed ones over to the mainland first, then came back for the Claudians, Crassus and a strong watch of his men. Libo led the Claudians aboard the Liburnian, Rectus getting on last, leading old Balbina the mule across the gangplank and rattling into place. A gentle swell in the sea caused the ship to rock slightly, and the mule brayed anxiously. Rectus petted her back, whispering to her.

Crassus' men split into two parties, arraying on either side of the Claudians. Crassus himself strode to and fro in front of them, patting his staff against his palm. 'Any questions?'

Libo stared through him. 'I'm sure you'll tell us all we need to know... sir.'

'Hmm,' Crassus said with a chuckle, 'you're learning.'

The ship rolled gently once more and Balbina brayed again in fright, drowning out Crassus' words.

Crassus' head shot up, his cleft jaw working. 'Though some are slower learners than others...' he strode over to Rectus and shoved him away from Balbina. 'In what part of my instructions did I permit you to bring pack animals aboard?'

Rectus flailed to steady himself, his bad leg buckling until he gripped the ship's seaward-facing rail. When he tried to step forwards again, two of Crassus' soldiers barred his way with raised spears.

Crassus paced around Balbina, eyeing the mule with disdain. 'This thing's a flea-ridden wreck.' He flicked his head to four more of his men. 'Drown it.'

Rectus' face turned sheet-white with shock. Pavo's ears burned as if he had misheard. But sure enough, the four stomped over and seized the shaking Balbina, hauling her up. The poor beast brayed and thrashed in fright as they roped her legs together.

'Sir!' Pavo snarled. 'Let the mule go back onto the wharf. She is old but she is a good aid for Rectus – the best medicus in Thracia.'

Crassus acted as if he had not heard, continuing to stare at the struggling animal as the four soldiers now hoisted her like a litter towards the seaward rail.

'Sir... *sir!*' Pavo rasped.

'Put her in the drink then we can be on our way,' Crassus purred.

Pavo felt himself shaking like those moments before battle, saw Sura, Libo and Pulcher twitch and pulse too, bending at their knees ever so slightly as if ready to pounce. Opis, Durio, Indus... all of them. Suddenly, Rectus shambled over in front of Libo and Pavo, wrapping his arms across their chests like a father embracing two sons. 'Let her go,' he whispered to them all, his voice choked with emotion, his tears spotting on their shoulders.

A great splash sounded. Pavo closed his eyes and tried to summon from the vaults of memory songs of the march and visions of better times to block out the poor mule's drowning screams. Mercifully, she went under within a few heartbeats. Rectus sagged against Libo and Pavo like a banner at the end of a storm.

As the liburnian peeled away from the dock, Libo and Pavo helped Rectus to turn around and face front, fearing Crassus would target the medicus next. They supported him, feeling him shake with grief and shock. Pavo noticed Crassus' strange expression: mouth slightly open, eyes scanning the Claudians – like a man who has heard an exotic bird call and waits still and silent for the next. When nobody stepped forward to avenge Rectus' animal companion, the primus pilus sagged and shrugged, then strode away to the ship's prow. They were definitely on borrowed time.

The voyage was swift, and they disembarked on the same bay he and Sura had been on the previous night. Zeno and the armed ones stood on the bay, formed up beside a mountain of leather packs, grain sacks, water bottles, tent leathers and bound tentpoles, watching as the true Claudians disembarked down the gangplank. Pavo wondered if it would happen here. His skin crawled every time one of Crassus' men strolled behind his back.

'The Via Militaris offers us the most direct route back to the West,' Zeno explained. 'We will cut across the open countryside towards that great highway. Lots of tough ground between here and there, as you will know. The heights of Mons Asticus pose quite the challenge for the marcher. Thus,' he proclaimed, 'our armoured men must not be over-burdened. You,' he swept a hand across the true Claudians, 'will carry these provisions and supplies.'

The hundred or so men stared at one another, then at the burden – a load that, even divided equally, would be far greater on each man's shoulders than one might expect even an ox to carry. Crassus stepped to and fro in front of the Claudians, his cleft chin jutting smugly, patting his staff against his free palm, almost begging one of them to complain. 'Well? You heard your Tribunus. Get to work – take up your burdens.'

A hot, clammy breeze blew pillowy clouds of light rain across them as they encircled the great stack of supplies. Libo directed the others in dividing up the burdens into individual loads. While binding rolled tent leathers together with a rope, he beckoned Pavo over to help as if he was indeed a mere ranker. In turn, Pavo beckoned Sura and Darik. Pavo noticed Zeno and Crassus watching as they worked, and so said nothing, simply helping Libo by bracing a compressed tent leather with his foot while Libo tied one rope, and Sura tied the other. When Zeno and Crassus finally averted their gaze, Pavo whispered. 'Forgive me, I did not know it had come to this.'

'Forgive you? We've been *mourning* you for the last seven months. What happened?'

Pulcher, Opis and Rectus, working nearby, twisted their heads a little to listen in.

'Gratian tried to kill me on the day of the peace talks. I fell from the cliffs, but I woke on a ship bound for Persia. It was Saturninus' doing – he realised that the Thracian countryside was still crawling with Gratian's Speculatores and thought I could hide out in Persia until they had dispersed. But Emperor Theodosius decided to turn my stay there into a more permanent exile, knowing it was too dangerous for him to be seen harbouring one of Gratian's most wanted men. Only Saturninus knows we're back.'

'What about you, sir?' Pulcher whispered to Sura. 'I saw you fall from the cliffs too – during battle.'

'The Cormorant of Adrianople,' Sura replied with a kink of one eyebrow. 'Can dive from the greatest heights and plunge to the deepest depths with incredible grace.'

Pulcher cocked one eyebrow. 'I see the fall didn't knock any sense into you.'

Sura gawped in mock-horror, then winked. Pulcher grinned back. Opis stifled a hearty laugh. Indus and Durio looked over, their eyes bright, hopeful. 'Tribunus Pavo and Primus Pilus Sura are back!' Ancus whispered to others. 'Everything will be well.'

Pavo, hearing their names spoken even in that hushed voice, picked up and tossed a pebble close to Ancus, who turned ashen-faced. 'My name is Urbicus, and this is Mucianus,' he hissed so all those close by would hear.

'Pavo, on that matter,' Libo whispered urgently. 'There's something you need to know: Zeno is not just any Speculator. He is... he is Vitalianus' son. He's doing this for revenge. If he finds out who you really are...'

'Vitalianus' son?' Pavo whispered. His skin crawled as, at just that moment, Zeno strolled past behind them, observing, listening. But he said nothing and walked on by. Their identities were still hidden.

'Hold on.' Pulcher said a moment later, face rising in mirth, looking at Sura. 'You said your new name is Mucianus. Muci...anus?'

'Aye aye, shut up. Pass the message on. Do *not* use our real names.'

'And I'm Darik,' Darik added, somewhat nonplussed by all this. He shot a look over his shoulder at the pairs of Crassus' men who circled the supply works. 'I... I genuinely thought these men were your Claudians.'

'They call themselves Claudians,' explained Libo. 'They wear Claudian colours... but they are not. They are soldiers of the West, led by agents of the Western Emperor.'

'And they murdered our comrades...' Pulcher said in a low drawl.

Pavo looked to each of them, wanting one of them to explain yet at the same time dreading confirmation of those gaps in the ranks.

'He ordered a decimatio,' Libo growled.

The word struck like a whip across Pavo's shoulders. And the knowledge that even worse – a full extermination – lay in wait struck again like a whip of fire.

'Trypho, Farus, Datus...' Opis whispered the long list of those killed, 'all gone.'

Each name was like a rusty nail being hammered into Pavo's chest.

'They've been killing us off, slowly but surely,' Libo confirmed.

'And what's this journey all about?' Durio asked.

Pavo flashed his gaze around the men. 'You don't know?'

Blank looks.

'Magnus Maximus has risen in the West, he is in Gaul with his legions.'

Libo's jaw slackened. 'Maximus? The Army of Britannia marches against Gratian?'

Pavo nodded carefully.

The men rustled and whispered in barely-contained excitement.

'Then we must be part of it,' Indus said, eyes wide with hope. 'After all Gratian has done – to our comrades, to our families, to our land.'

'Steady on, lad. There's just the small matter of getting these bastards off our backs,' Pulcher said glibly, then turned to Pavo. 'So what's the plan?'

Pavo thought again of the extermination order. It would do no good to share this with the men – it would likely frighten most of them. His mind tumbled over and over as he sought an alternative tack. Then he realised: there must be spare weapons in these supplies. Or there would be a place along the route where they could drop their burdens and make a break into the countryside. They might cross paths with one of the

Thracian legions who would see their plight and come to their aid. But, like a stone falling from his chest and into his guts, the sensation faded: there were no weapons in these supplies. The route from here into the Mons Asticus massif was rugged – not the kind of place where a man could run in any direction for any great length of time. And the Thracian legions? Saturninus had explained just how impoverished they were: what few men remained in those insufficient regiments were stretched as it was – garrisoning and patrolling the southern tracts of Thracia. He and the Claudians might spot a few lone exploratores riding along the Via Militaris at best. Finally, like a hobnailed boot stamping down on his hopes, his thoughts returned to the dreadful scythe symbol on Gratian's scroll.

When would it happen?

'We will find a way out of this, sir, won't we?' Indus pressed.

Pavo looked them all in the eye, then managed to twist his lips into something resembling a smile. 'Mithras will show us the way.'

They marched away from the coast throughout the rest of that day, and the true Claudians carried terrible burdens – more than six times the weight of a legionary pack. The leather straps of Pavo's burden bit into his shoulders, and every step felt like twin knives digging deeper as if rooting for lodged thorns. Sura, Libo and Pulcher wheezed with every pace, the loads too great even for these veterans to bear with a mask of tolerance. The younger legionaries were struggling badly: Ancus, Betto, Indus and Durio winced and groaned with every few strides, while Crassus jogged gleefully up and down the baggage line, braying at those who lagged behind, lashing the thighs of the laggards. Darik soldiered on manfully, taking the weight on his great shoulders without complaint for a time, but by the last hour of light he too was hunched and staggering.

Worst of all, nobody had seen to giving them water, so while

Crassus' men drank frequently from their water skins, the baggage-carrying Claudians merely turned their faces skywards and stuck out their tongues as they trekked – catching only a scant and insufficient drink from the continued puffs of fine rain. When Ancus asked for water, the reply came in the form of Crassus' cane across his face, breaking his front teeth.

On they went, and all the while, Pavo's mind stirred and stretched, seeking something, anything, that might pull his men from this cauldron. But still there was nothing – the terrain offered no means of escape and the armed ones marched like iron walls all around the true Claudians.

That night, they camped on the plains. Crassus distributed hard tack biscuits to the exhausted baggage carriers – dry as those ship's biscuits on the voyage across the sea... but again no water. There was a brook nearby, from which the armed ones drank deeply. But when Betto rose to try to approach it, a dozen of them barred his way, and Crassus stepped over, patting his staff against his palm. Thus, some of Pavo's men took to licking the moisture from leaves or catching what they could on their tongues again.

The next morning, Pavo woke from a deep sleep, stiff as a stone, with a head like thunder and a mouth like sand. His shoulders stung like fire and he pulled his tunic collar down to see that the baggage straps had rubbed the skin away, leaving a wet, unctuous mess of blood and fluids.

'Up!' Crassus bawled to the Claudians while his armed ones took their time, eating bowls of steaming porridge and drinking more deep draughts of cool water. The true Claudians groaned and winced as they lifted their burdens onto their backs once more. Pavo braced as Sura helped him to lift his into place. The straps settled down into the bloodied grooves in his shoulders like teeth chomping into a juicy cut of meat.

By noon, the summer rains eased. Puffs of vapour rose and swirled away from the green shrubs and grasses, vanishing into the cloudless blue sky. The Thracian sun came out in full, gleaming on the iron shells of the armed ones, and burning on the faces and necks of the Claudian baggage-carriers.

Pavo's ragged tunic was dark with sweat and stained with blood around the shoulders. Likewise, his ankles were rubbed raw. Every so often, he would stick his thumbs inside the pack-straps at chest height to take some of the weight in his wrists. It offered a few moments of blessed relief before his hands trembled and he had to return the full weight to his shoulders. It reminded him of that wretch suspended above the bamboo in the cellars of Ctesiphon. All the while his head pounded and his tongue grew swollen, robbed of fluids.

Marching beside him, Sura was nearly doubled-over with his burden, panting, his steps growing ragged. He glanced skywards, seeing that seven or more hours of light remained, and that the rising green sierra of Mons Asticus rose just a mile or so ahead. The hill paths would ruin some of these men, and Zeno and Crassus knew it. He even saw them conspiring, ahead, talking and pointing out the weakest of the Claudians. Pavo realised his thirst and fatigue had robbed him even of his ability to think and search for ways to escape this march. How long before Zeno and Crassus would give the order for the extermination to kill off those who did not collapse during the march?

Libo walked with Rectus, one arm around the poor medicus' back to give him what support he could. Both men carried colossal weights on their backs. Indus and Durio were pale-faced and flagging, hands frequently reaching down to their hips where normally water skins would hang. But still no water had been distributed to the baggage crew.

The rise into the mountains was even harsher than Pavo had expected. Grey tracks wound up into the range, through gradually sparser greenery. The tracks became broken up, causing boots to slide, tired ankles to wobble and burdens to seemingly double in weight. Worse, there were no more thickets or flanking hills to offer shade – just the unbroken molten stare of the sun on their faces and numb shoulders. The air became dry and unpleasant, thickened with the dust cast up by the marching boots of the armed ones ahead and behind. Worse, amidst this miasma of dust and the internal fog of fatigue, Pavo continuously saw spots flashing at the edges of his vision. But also… something else.

His head switched to the left. A grey rock there on the slopes. Something had moved.

'You saw it too?' Sura whispered.

'I... saw what?'

'We're being tracked,' Sura replied.

'By whom?' Pavo felt the last droplets of hope drain out of him as he realised the answer. 'More of Crassus' men are waiting somewhere up here. This is where it's going to happen.'

Sura stared uphill with him, eyeing the massif like a giant tombstone. 'We're not dead yet,' he grunted, hitching his huge burden and stepping onwards. 'Mithras is still with us.'

They ascended onto a high, winding track, the sheer mountainside rising on their left and a steep drop on the right, when a gasp of despair sounded behind Pavo. He twisted to see what was happening: Indus had sunk to one knee in exhaustion. Crassus' eyes lit up. He bounded back down the column. With an unmeasured swish of one arm, he brought his staff whacking across the backs of Indus' thighs. The Rhodian cried hoarsely, falling onto all fours.

'Up, *up!*' Crassus snarled.

When Durio tried to help his comrade to his feet, Crassus brought his staff slashing down across the young man's wrists. Now Durio fell to his knees in agony, clutching his wrists.

'Please. Give us water,' Betto begged. 'How long, sir, will you abuse the patience of your mules?'

Crassus' brow wrinkled in confusion as Betto's metaphor and ancient adapted quote floated somewhere high over his head. He answered with a brutish whip of his cane across Betto's thighs. Betto bit into his bottom lip, said nothing more, and kept going.

Ancus, nearby, began to slide his pack from his shoulders, swaying, his face grey and his lips tinged blue. With shaking hands he pulled one of many supply water skins from the netful of them he was carrying, pulled the cork out and staggered towards Indus and Durio. Crassus swung on his heel, before swishing his staff round to bat the skin away. 'Not for you,' he bawled as the drinking skin slapped onto the ground and the water pulsed free, seeping into the grey dust near the edge of the mountain path, turning it black and gloriously wet.

Ancus, staring at the spilled water, swayed. Suddenly, his eyes rolled in their sockets and his knees buckled. Like a pushed over broomstick, he toppled from the right edge of the path and plunged down the steep slope in a chaos of flailing limbs and puffs of golden dust. His body halted with a crack halfway down – folding over an outcrop. All stared down, all saw the legionary's neck sagging like cloth, and the vertebrae jutting from the top of his back.

'Pick up his burden,' Crassus said matter-of-factly to the Claudian legionaries nearest where Ancus had been marching. They stared back, dumbfounded. 'Unless you wish to join your friend?'

Quietly, the four men near Ancus' spot began to disassemble his dropped burden and heap it onto each other's packs. Pavo watched as the primus pilus strutted proudly back to Zeno's side.

'Forward!' Zeno bawled.

As they went on up the hill, Pavo slid back, swapping his pack for one of the overburdened ones. Returning to his marching spot, he noticed a small pebble rolling down the steep rise on the left hand of the mountain path. It bucked and bounced across in front of him and clattered on down the steep drop on their right. He looked up whence it had come: nothing there, but a strange swirl of dust, as if someone *had* been there a breath ago. A few moments later, he heard a sigh and a crunch. He looked back to see one of Ancus' tentmates lying, face down.

'Halt!' Libo shouted. 'Man down!'

Crassus and Zeno looked back, irked by the shout.

Rectus wheezed and staggered his way to the fallen man and knelt by his side. When he turned his fellow legionary over, the man's face stared through him and into eternity. Rectus pressed his fingers to his comrade's throat and waited, his shoulders eventually sagging in despair. 'He's dead. Dead from thirst and heat exhaustion.'

Zeno stared back down the column at the scene, then swished a hand onwards. 'Leave him. no time to waste.'

On they went, higher into the mountains.

Another groan sounded behind him, followed by the commotion of another body falling from the path and rolling away into the deep gullies by the side of the track. 'Keep moving!' Crassus bellowed.

As Zeno and Crassus talked, Pavo watched their lips. Slowly, he understood that the extermination order was almost upon them. It was too late. It was over.

'Sura,' he croaked.

Sura could barely turn his head, so exhausted was he.

'Sura, they're going to turn upon us, at the top of this mountain.'

Now Sura twisted to look at him, his eyes sunken and black-lined with exhaustion.

Worse, Pavo realised the other veterans nearest had heard and understood.

'What? What do we do?' Pulcher said, his voice trembling with weakness.

'What's the plan? When do we make a break for it?' Libo added.

Pavo again saw in their faces hope and, worse, trust. He knew there was no way out of this. They were on their knees, weaponless, isolated.

'Sir?' Indus pleaded, concerned by Pavo's non-reply.

But just then, they crunched up and onto a level path. A hot wind struck them from the east and they stared across the Mons Asticus summit. Some men gasped in relief at the level way, but Pavo did not, for ahead he saw the dip in the high, flat summit. A sheltered hollow of sorts, lined with caves and overhangs where once there had been mines. A single, old oak rose down there, like a lone worshipper to the sky above. The sunlight shone down upon the hollow, sparkling on the tarn and three brooks within, giving the depression the look of an open jewellery box.

Zeno stepped away from the head of the column and waved to the baggage men. 'Come, come,' he called, gesturing towards a gentle path into the hollow, down which a knot of fifty of his armed men were already filing. 'Set down your packs. Go down there to the tarn. Slake your thirst.'

Some of the younger Claudians who had not realised what was happening rumbled in relief. Pavo's heart turned to ashes. This lonely height would be their grave, like a Persian Tower of Silence.

'Tribunus, what do we do?' Pulcher asked again.

Pavo wanted to weep, but he bit back on his fears and emotions and met the eyes of his men. 'Do as he says. Set down your burdens. Descend into the hollow. But as soon as we're down there, we turn upon the fifty there. If we are quick, if we can get their shields and a few spears or swords, we can organise a fighting retreat. Perhaps a chance to slip away.' As he spoke, he hated himself for lying to them. But were they not soldiers? If they were to die then did they not deserve at least to die as soldiers, in the fray?

Indus, Durio and Betto issued low, youthful growls of hubris.

Pulcher, Rectus, Opis and Libo shared grey looks, reading Pavo's tone, understanding the noble lie.

'Come on!' Crassus shouted impatiently from the hollow's edge, waving them over. 'Aren't you thirsty?'

The Claudians set down their burdens and – with a chorus of groans and cracking joints – they filed forward onto the hollow path and down onto its floor. The fifty armed ones down there were already formed up in an arc at the hollow's far end, spears levelled. Worse, the rest of Crassus' men spilled around the rim of the hollow, like spectators at a bear-fighting pit – except armed to the teeth with bows and javelins. Zeno and Crassus halted halfway down the hollow path.

'You know by now that you were not brought here to drink,' Zeno said with a playful tune.

At the same time, the shudder of two hundred stretching bowstrings echoed around the hollow's edge, and many more of Crassus' men raised javelins. The fifty armed ones down in the hollow base crouched a little, facing Pavo and his men, ready to race in and rip apart whomever might survive that pregnant hail.

Pavo heard the younger ones croak and whisper in confusion, and the veterans sigh in resignation. But he felt all of them, to a man, gather close to him, shoulder-to-shoulder, back-to-back in one last defensive mass, but this time without shield or weapon.

'The archers will tear you apart. But there is a group of specialist bowmen,' Zeno explained, nodding towards three who held strange-looking arrows to their bows, the tips dripping with some dark, unctuous mix. 'Their sights are on you, Tribunus Pavo…'

Pavo's hackles stood on end at Zeno's use of his real name. His eyes rolled up to meet the Speculator's predacious glare.

'… and their arrows are coated with the same poison you used to kill my father. They will aim for your limbs so you do not die instantly. Instead you will have to suffer the same moments of torment my father did.'

Pavo held Zeno's glare. 'I turned your murderous father's poisoned sword upon him. My heart is clean.'

'Your heart will be crow-food in a few moments,' Zeno laughed. 'Anyway, you should be commended for your efforts,' he said, clapping cynically. 'Oh, you think I hadn't heard about the strange legionaries out in the Shahanshah's court? About Agent Sporacius' disappearance. And then you turn up, claiming to be forgotten Claudians... with a Persian in tow?'

Darik spat on the ground and pointed up at Zeno, his long dark hair cast across his face by the hot wind. 'I told you before, you son of a whore, I am a Maratocupreni. Remember that when my spirit comes for you.'

Zeno stared at Darik for a time, then laughed breezily. 'He understands,' he pointed at Darik while speaking to Pavo. 'It's over for you. You must have been desperate to be reunited with your men. And now you will be... forever.' His face fell like a flag on a windless day as he half-nodded to Crassus.

Crassus' face rose in the most bestial smile. 'Loose,' his command boomed around the bowl.

A great whoosh rose. Pavo stared at the great orb of blue sky above the hollow, waiting for death. But the archers up there had not shot their bows. They too seemed confused by the noise. It must only have been a trice, but it felt like an eternity... and then Zeno and Crassus' men jerked and shuddered as a storm of arrows hammered into their backs. Scores upon scores of them toppled forwards, silent or screaming, into the hollow, leaving red smears down the sides. A heartbeat later a storm of men rose up behind the rest of them like a tidal swell. Golden-haired warriors girt in iron and leather. They speared Zeno's men through, hacked at necks, barged shields away, grappled with others, falling in tumbling balls down into the hollow. At once, the hollow echoed with a riot of screams and crashing steel – Zeno's men hopelessly entangled in hand-to-hand combat with this huge band of newcomers.

Still huddled together in the eye of this storm, Pavo and the Claudians watched on, weaponless and stunned, as Zeno's legionaries were slaughtered. Living but torn-open men rolled around clutching belly wounds, trying to rope back in the filthy, dust-coated entrails that had spilled out. One shrieked, clutching at the huge cleft in his skull made by a longsword.

'Goths,' Sura stammered. 'It was they who were tracking us.'

'How?' Libo croaked.

'Why?' Pavo added.

Just then, the knot of Zeno's fifty – stationed on the floor and not yet caught up in the Gothic attack – rushed at them.

Pavo stared at the teeth of the fifty spears coming for them. No order to brace would save them from this. Then…*thrum…whack!* A fresh rain of Gothic arrows hammered into the backs of the fifty. More than half fell. Pavo stared at the ragged knot of them left, shocked, disordered.

'Charge!' he screamed to his Claudians.

They rushed the tattered remnant with the pent-up fury of all that had gone on in the months at Snake Island, shouting the names of the dead, pouncing upon the false ones like wolves, wrenching spears from their hands and ramming them into their chests. Pavo took the dropped intercisa fin helm of one and used it like a lethal glove, punching another in the face, the fin slicing deep into the man's cheekbone and stunning him, while Sura stabbed a stolen spatha up into the man's ribs. Both swung to face the next, only to see that the last of Zeno's men has been cut down. Within a few breaths, the hollow fell silent. Pavo and his Claudians twisted and turned, panting, sweating, swaying, trapped down here now by this ring of ferocious Goths.

But the Goths on the hollow floor and lining the sides rose from their battle poises and stood tall, turning their spears skywards to rest on them like walking poles, chests heaving from the effort of the sudden attack, all eyes on Pavo and his men. Likewise the Gothic archers let their bows fall slack. One of them – a young man in a noble's bronze armour with golden braids and a fierce, pale face, seemed hesitant to lower his bow. Alaric, Pavo recalled.

'What are you waiting for?' Libo rasped, arms outstretched to this one.

But two figures rose either side of Alaric, one placing a hand on the young one's bow to lower the weapon. 'No, Alaric,' Eriulf said. 'This is not why we came here.'

Eriulf stepped to the edge of the hollow with the second figure, a woman in hardened leather armour and an iron helm topped with a long, trailing plume.

Pavo could muster but a croak: 'Eriulf... Izodora?'

The pair gazed solemnly down upon the Claudians.

'I feared you had got yourself into a terrible mess,' Izodora replied. 'Darik and you are the only two people I have in my life now. I could not simply wait back in Constantinople. I had to do something. I spoke to Saturninus again, and he said there was nothing he could do, that no legions were available and even if they were, they could not be seen to march into the new Gothic region without prior agreement.'

'I, on the other hand,' said Eriulf, 'have the means to rouse my kinsmen from the *haims*.'

Eriulf and Izodora slid down into the hollow, thumping down in front of Pavo and Sura. Izodora embraced Darik, while Eriulf approached Pavo.

'I thought you were dead,' Eriulf said. 'After Dionysopolis-'

'I spotted you on the coast road,' Pavo cut in, taking a step back with one foot, like a man ready to fight. 'I saw you and your riders, gazing over at the forsaken island, watching as one of our brothers was beheaded. Watching... laughing...'

'Ah,' Eriulf said, his face sagging. 'Young Alaric laughed – but merely to show his mettle. I did not think it could be you on the isle,' he assured Pavo, also catching the eyes of Sura, Pulcher, Libo, Rectus, Opis and the others who had all been there four years ago on the forest plateau, who had all lived with his tribe for an entire summer before leading them in a breakneck flight from the Huns, across the Danubius and into the safety of the empire. 'But then I heard just recently from one of my men that they had some time ago crossed paths with a young Roman claiming to be a legionary. Datus was his name – he had briefly broken away from his patrol party just long enough to impart some story about he and his fellow legionaries being imprisoned. Soon after that, Izodora came to me and explained it all. I summoned Alaric's warband as quickly as I could.'

Alaric made some reticent gesture of greeting, sneering and tilting his head slightly backwards.

Pavo ignored him, staring at Eriulf.

'After you went missing at Dionysopolis,' Eriulf said quietly, 'everyone was sure you had fallen to Gratian's agents.'

'I fought him,' Pavo sighed. 'Soon after the peace talks I had Gratian but a swipe away from the end of my sword. But he won. I lost. I nearly lost…' he gestured around his men, 'everything. The bastards who marched us up here wore ruby shields, but they were not Claudians – they were Gratian's men. They brought us here to kill us all.'

Eriulf enveloped Pavo in a tight embrace. 'When the desert woman came to me for help, I felt great despair at the plight of you and your comrades,' he explained quietly in Pavo's ear. 'But then I heard Runa whisper to me, give me hope that I could put things right,' he added fondly, pulling back a little to let Pavo see his full smile, a wetness in his eyes, and patted his heart with one hand. 'She is with us both still, Brother… always.'

Pavo felt a great softening in his chest, and remembered just how passionate his and Runa's short time together had been. 'I owe you my life, Brother,' he replied.

'And me… again,' Izodora added.

He turned to her and the pair let their fingers weave together, then he took her in a full embrace, drinking in the scent of her hair, the softness of her cheek against his. 'These parts are troubled, Izodora. You did not come all the way from the eastern deserts for this,' he said.

'No, but I found you along the way, and I do not wish to lose you.' She seemed to be on the edge of saying something else, when her gaze darkened, looking past his shoulder.

Pavo turned to see a group of Alaric's men up at the top of the hollow path, bundling forward Zeno and Crassus. With a pair of stiff kicks, both were sent tumbling gracelessly down the slope, rolling over in a chaos of cloaks and dust onto the hollow floor before the Claudians.

Crassus scrambled to his feet first, looking hopefully around the Claudians, then with wide, frightened eyes at the Goths.

'It is not the Goths you should fear,' Pavo said calmly.

Footsteps thumped up behind Crassus. One of Pulcher's hands whacked down on his left shoulder, one of Libo's on his right. Suddenly, he was torn away from Pavo and bundled over to the edge of the tarn. 'Now hold on,' Crassus stammered. 'I'm a primus pilus. An officer. I will answer for any alleged crimes to the proper officia-'

His words were smashed from his mouth – along with a spray of teeth – by Pulcher's meaty first. Dazed, Crassus could barely resist as the two pushed him to his knees. Without a single word, Libo drew and spun his spatha expertly to hold it over the nape of Crassus' neck. The primus pilus regained his senses just in time to utter a half-appeal for mercy. 'Wait, wai-'

Slice.

His head dropped like a windfall apple, splashing into the tarn. His face spasmed, eyes and tongue bulging horribly as his head sank slowly into the tarn's dark depths. Crassus' body remained where it was, kneeling and slumped, blood pulsing from the neck stump like a grotesque fountain.

'For Datus, for Farus, for Ancus, for Trypho,' Libo and Pulcher recited these and the many other names quietly and in unison.

Pavo turned to the still-grounded figure of Tribunus Zeno. The man still lay on his back, propped on his elbows, his red cloak tangled around him. 'Now you might escape with killing that oaf, but you will let me leave here, unharmed, you hear?' he said, rising slowly.

'With two tent poles, we could fashion a cross,' Pavo said calmly. 'Up here, under the baking sun and with nothing but crows for company, you would have a long time to contemplate your choices in life as you edged agonisingly towards death.'

Zeno half-smiled then shook, the humour draining from him. 'You would not dare leave me like that. I would find a way out. You know I would.'

'Yes,' Pavo agreed, 'for you are a Speculator. Only a fool would leave such a creature alive.'

Zeno fell silent, realising he had talked himself into a pit.

'I will not kill you, Zeno,' Pavo said, calmly unfastening the Speculator's red officer's cloak. 'I have more important business to attend to.'

Pavo turned away, swishing the red cloak around his own blood-streaked shoulders, leaving Zeno where he stood, beckoning his Claudians up and out of the high hollow, Eriulf and Izodora in tow.

'Get back down here,' Zeno screamed after him. 'This is not finished!'

As Pavo emerged from the hollow and back into the warm wind of the Mons Asticus summit, he passed young Alaric. 'You itch to strike down another Roman? Well the one down there just called your mother a whore.'

As Pavo walked to the edge of the summit to gaze south over the hazy summer countryside of Thracia, he heard Alaric's bow draw tight, then hiss loose. A heartbeat later, the wet punch of an arrow plunging into an eye echoed from the hollow floor, and Zeno's protests ended, followed by the thump of a dead weight hitting the ground.

Awful family, Pavo mouthed.

'Where for you now, Tribunus Pavo?' Eriulf asked.

Pavo stooped by the corpse of one of Crassus' men, lifting the fin-helm from the man's head and placing it slowly on his own. The cape and helm both felt good… right.

'Now? Now we will drink from the brooks here until our bellies ache. After that?' he looked around the summit, seeing his Claudians stripping the fallen ones of their ringmail, belts, helms, weapons and shields. One brought him a spatha. He swished and sheathed the blade, and his gaze drifted to the silvery stripe of the Via Militaris, following the path of the great road as it faded towards the western horizon. He raised his voice. 'After that, the Claudia are going to march west… to war. To join Magnus Maximus. To bring Gratian's reign to an end.'

Over one hundred spear hafts thumped on the mountain summit then the sparkling tips were held high like saluting hands. 'For the Claudia!' the men boomed. Opis ripped the confiscated silver legionary eagle from one of the huge packs the men had been carrying. He held it high, the ruby bull banner catching the warm wind and rippling proudly.

Soon, Alaric left the mountain, leading his warband back towards Kabyle. The Claudians gulped hungrily at the hollow streams and began to prepare good food from the rations within the cruel burdens they had carried up here. Sura despatched two men back down the path to find and bury the bodies of the ones who had fallen on the climb up.

'This land may be at peace, but strange things are afoot,' Eriulf said.

Pavo took a slug of water from a freshly-filled skin, the sensation glorious on his parched lips. 'How so?'

'I hear rumours that Reiks Ingolf was arrested.'

The water now no longer tasted so sweet. Pavo glanced over at Libo, who had told him about Ingolf's murder at camp the previous night.

'Some say he was marched south to Constantinople or one of the other cities of southern Thracia. Yet I have not heard of any such prisoner. If he was in those parts, I would know.' Eriulf gazed across the hazy land, but Pavo could see his jaw working. 'They also said it was the Claudians who arrested him.'

'The head of the man who killed him lies at the bottom of that tarn,' Pavo said flatly, pointing over at Crassus' kneeling body. 'And he was no Claudian.'

Eriulf sighed, dipping his head. 'Once Izodora told me what was going on, I suspected that was the case.'

Pavo wondered if Eriulf might grow angry or sour, but he remained silent and staring into space. 'If you value the peace, friend, do not let Ingolf's fate be known. Word of a Roman murdering a Reiks would tear everything apart.'

Eriulf shrugged. 'Ingolf was not a good man,' he said. 'Now the definition of 'good' is a slippery beast, but Ingolf enjoyed burning people alive for nothing other than his entertainment. His death lifts a shadow from this world.'

'That's why I must lead my legion west to face Gratian,' Pavo said, casting a hand to the Via Militaris. 'His shadow is dark as ink.'

Eriulf rested one foot on a rock and sighed, gazing south at the military road while the two Thervingi legionaries he had brought here with him saddled and watered his horse. 'It is not as simple as that. The great road marks the point where things change – where the legions hold sway and there are no more *haims*. In Emperor Theodosius' eyes, you should not be in this part of the world, nor should the Claudia or any Eastern legion be travelling West.'

'Yet Theodosius hates Gratian,' Pavo cut in. 'Gratian murdered his father.'

'And that is why he has privately granted Magnus Maximus free reign to invade Gratian's territory. Maximus is a Westerner, and his assault on Gratian cannot be pinned on Theodosius, should it fail. But if the Claudia were to be witnessed marching to aid Maximus' rebel legions?' He shook his head. 'He will not let it happen. I have been privy to recent conversations in his sacred council. That highway will by now be studded with the eyes and ears of Theodosius. Let's just say... he will take no risks. You must forget the military road.'

'I'm not sure what you're trying to tell me, friend? How else can we reach the west and the army of Maximus?'

Eriulf turned his gaze from the Via Militaris and onto Pavo, the hot summer wind casting a loose lock from his topknot across his face. 'Go north instead, through the heart of the Gothic region all the way to the River Danubius. You need only avoid Reiks Faustius at Kabyle. He is overly-fond of his newfound Roman identity, and despite the agreement that there would be no more Gothic Kings, he acts as if he is Fritigern's true heir, riding back and forth to Constantinople to parley with Theodosius. So plan your route carefully. Once you reach the River Danubius, make for the town of Bononia. It is now a Gothic *Haim*. The tribal garrison there protects the imperial riverbanks, watching for Hunnic movement on the far side. I hear they also found a galley there. A small ship, but enough for your small band.'

Pavo's mind flashed with the two alternative routes west. Eriulf was right: the Via Militaris was direct but complicated in other ways. A trek through the Gothlands and onto a galley – a ship that could take them all the way upriver, through the Iron Gates, past the Alpes Mountains and right into the heart of the Western Empire – could be the answer.

'This Bononian garrison. They might not take too kindly to a rabble of legionaries turning up and asking for their boat.' He took off the tribal bracelet on his wrist – a thick leather band inlaid with polished stones of black and green, and marked by a hot iron with some Gothic symbols. 'But the Bononians will obey my orders more readily than they would those of Theodosius. Oh, and whatever you do, stay away from the town of Oescus, another riverbank *haim* a day's sail downriver from Bononia – governed now by Reiks Folcher.'

'Oescus? Why?' Pavo asked, taking the band.

Eriulf seemed caught on a few potential answers. Eventually, he just repeated the advice with a grave look in his eyes. 'Just... stay well clear of the place.'

Pavo half-smiled wryly. Eriulf knew those riverlands well – as well as Pavo had once known them when they had been in full imperial control. He snapped his hand shut over the bracelet and tucked it into his purse. 'I thank you, Brother. But this is not your battle; why do you help me like this?'

'Hmm,' he said, gazing past Pavo and into the distance. 'Runa tells me it is the right thing to do. I hope your soldier-god grants you victory... and that we will speak again, Brother,' he said as he turned away, beckoning the two Thervingi legionaries over with his horse, 'in the halls of Constantinople, with the Emperor of the West no more. Death to Gratian,' he finished in a tone that sent a chill through Pavo, vaulting onto his horse and heeling her away at a trot, the two Thervingi legionaries jogging alongside.

Pavo watched him go. There was always a strange charge in the air when he and Eriulf spoke – like the odd feeling that rises before a thunderstorm. The man had masked his grief for his sister Runa well, but it was there, as sharp and raw as ever, he realised.

Quarreling voices snapped him from his thoughts. Izodora and Darik squabbled nearby.

'Trouble?'

Darik shot him an exasperated look. 'You're going west, and I'm coming with you,' he said to Pavo. 'You pulled me from the waves and saved my life. I am indebted to you.'

Pavo cocked his head to one side. Surprised, but not disappointed.

'My "legion" numbers less than two centuries. We need every man we can get.'

'And that is the problem. She will not let me come.'

Pavo twisted to Izodora.

'You are a headstrong fool,' Izodora snapped at Darik, then turned to Pavo. 'I will not be separated from him again,' she said. 'He is my brother. The last link to my old life.'

Pavo raked his fingertips across the stubble of his unshaven jaw. 'You could travel west with us too,' he said, hesitantly, and instantly wishing he had not. Flashes of Felicia and Runa's last moments slapped him hard again.

'She cannot,' Darik averred.

Pavo expected Izodora to contend this. She and her brother were skilled warriors, and she was as headstrong as he. But instead, Izodora sighed, turning away from them both. No objections, no argument.

Confused, Pavo looked to Darik. The big desert warrior stepped closer and whispered. 'You don't understand… she *cannot* come.'

'Why?' Pavo said, at once secretly pleased that she would be safe from what lay ahead and guilty for it.

'Because… ' he stopped and shook his head. 'You must ask her.' With that, Darik left them alone.

'Izodora?' He said, approaching her back, reaching out with one hand. 'I do not doubt you. You can march, you can fight, he paused to shake his head in wonder, 'like a desert *djinn!* But you remember the things I told you. I fear for you, that my poisoned lips will curse you to the same fate as the few I have loved before. What awaits us in the West is unknown… deadly, and-'

She spun on her heels to face him, her cheeks wet with tears.

'Izodora, I did not mean to upset yo-'

She silenced him by planting her lips against his. She tasted sweet, her tears salty, and her billowing tail of hair stroked the side of his jaw. He was happy to forget everything for that moment and enjoy this intimacy. He scarcely noticed when she took one of his hands and placed the palm on her belly. He opened his eyes, their lips parting slowly.

'I *am* fearless. I *could* fight any battle, Pavo. But I will not endanger the life within me too.'

Pavo stared at her armoured midriff, then into her eyes. Memories of their tryst during the desert sandstorm, and the many others since, scudded across his thoughts.

She gulped and blinked away more tears. 'Take Darik. Go west. Do what you must do. But promise me you will keep my brother safe. And swear to me that *you* will return. Our child, *every* child, needs a father. For all you have told me about yourself, you know that is one of the greatest truths of this world.'

Part 3

Across the Empire

Chapter 15
June 383 AD
Northern Thracia

The summer sun blazed down on the golden plains and green hills of Thracia as the one hundred and twenty five men of the XI Claudia struck northwards, deep into the land of the Gothic *haims*. They went bedecked in iron and the ruby-red shields taken from Zeno and Crassus' men… and with the bull standard held high and proud. The men chattered as they marched, talking of good times. It was as if the past few months of brutality had never happened – a deliberate strategy and one familiar to all legionaries. Insects hummed and barley dust floated in the hot breeze, lending a faint nutty scent to the air, and the wall of the Haemus Mountains lay ahead, basking in the summer heat. But Pavo hardly took in any of the singing, the sights or the smells, for his mind was lost on other matters.

It had been six days since that moment atop Mons Asticus, but it felt as if his heart was still nailed to the rock up there, pulsing like a drum in response to Izodora's revelation. He was to be a father? It was exhilarating and terrifying. He had been an orphan, a slave boy and then a young man sorely needing guidance and example. Now he could make right for this child those things which had been wrong for him. Yet the mere thought of the realities: that harm might come to Izodora in the time he was away, or that she might perish from the strain of delivering the babe when the time came… or that he might fall on this journey west or the battle that lay at the end of the road, condemning the child to the same fatherless path he had walked.

He rose from his well of thoughts when he heard a short grunt of surprise from Sura. They were coming to a deep ravine, over which a timber bridge had recently been erected. Twin winks of sunlight betrayed a pair of Gothic spearmen over on the far bridgehead. A small watch station of sorts – and they had stumbled right up to it carelessly. Until now he had been ultra-careful, guiding his men well-wide of the few *haims* they had spotted on the horizon. He slowed the Claudia with a raised hand.

The two Goths over on the other side instantly bristled. Pavo heard his men do the same behind him, and felt his own hackles rise. From what Libo had told him about the lands overseen by Reiks Munderic and Ingolf, there were good reasons to be wary. More, no legion had ventured this far north into the new world of settled Goths since the peace. When one Goth shouted over his shoulder, a dozen more came running from a thatched longhouse nearby.

Pavo set down his spear and shield and stepped onto the bridge, alone. 'We are on imperial business, heading for the river.'

The Goths muttered amongst themselves, and some levelled their spears in threat. 'We were not told to expect a legion in these parts… *our* parts,' the lead Goth said. 'For these lands belong to Reiks Sigibert.'

Pavo held up Eriulf's bracelet. 'At ease. We're all on the same side here.'

The Gothic sentries peered at the bracelet. 'Reiks Eriulf sent you?' one said, his face brightening. 'Come, come,' he grinned now, waving them across. His comrades sagged, retracting their spears, their hateful looks morphing into easy smiles as they beckoned the legionaries towards the longhouse.

The longhouse was pleasantly shady inside, the air spiced with the scent of sweet woodsmoke and leather. Pavo noticed instantly the rows of beds laid out at one end – very similar to a legionary barrack arrangement. But the lead Goth ushered them over to a table near the other end. They drank barley beer with the Gothic watchmen, sharing stories – tactfully edited wherever they involved details of the war – and jokes. Pavo took small sips of his beer, enjoying the refreshment but knowing he had to keep a clear head in this much-changed land. Libo gave the Goths a hare he had caught that morning, which they roasted on the longhouse hearth and shared around. One Goth seemed intrigued by the legionary mess kit, and Libo's plate in particular.

'You Romans carry kitchens around on your backs?' he rumbled with laughter, supping at his beer. The other Goths laughed along with him.

With a complete lack of grace, Libo licked his plate clean of hare juice, then slid it back in his pack – 'clean'. Pulcher, Rectus and the Goths who noticed this winced in disgust.

Libo looked up sourly. 'Well it could be worse,' he shrugged. 'There was a cocky little shit in my old auxiliary cohort at Sardica. I was just a *Decanus* then – in charge of my eight tent-mates. Really worthless position – no extra coins and all the shit jobs, like getting the tent set up every night when we were out on the march and making sure the other seven in my group kept their armour and kit clean and in good condition. This cocky bastard, well he liked to minimise the work he had to put in, if you know what I mean. He'd shake the water clock to make his shift on Sardica's walls end early – that sort of thing.'

The Goths and legionaries rumbled in gentle laughter.

'Worse, he'd worked out a way to get around the mess kit inspection.' Libo jabbed a thumb towards his plate. 'He had *two* plates – one that was spotless and shining that he would present for inspection… and one that he actually ate off of.'

All were intrigued.

'He kept the clean one under his bunk in the barracks. So one morning I crept in while he was sleeping and left him a little surprise. An hour later, the horns blared for morning roll-call, everyone's leaping out of their beds. I come striding in shouting *ready for inspectiooon!*' Libo said, sitting bolt upright and sticking his chin and chest out. 'The cocky bastard drops down to his haunches and slips a hand under his cot – thinking nobody will notice – and pulls out his 'clean' plate. Except this time, it was loaded with a massive, steaming turd.'

Laughter exploded.

Rectus looked up from his beer, exaggerating a look of horror. 'It is even worse than it sounds. The smell lingered for weeks!'

The place erupted with hilarity again, before Opis kicked off another story. Next, the Gothic leader piped up with an overblown tale of his own, before a sentry topped that one. Unsurprisingly, Sura then produced one of his most preposterous stories ever… only for Darik to top it with a desert legend about a camel with two cocks. On and on the stories went, the fire crackling and the beer flowing.

They spent the night there without trouble, and Pavo woke from a deep and untroubled sleep, feeling refreshed and strong. As the legion ate wheat porridge and prepared to set off again he could feel the camaraderie between them – and an edge of excitement about the great journey ahead. Following their night of comfort and good food and drink, the fears about these Gothic lands seemed to have been tempered. But then one Gothic sentry spoiled it somewhat.

'You said you were going north to the Danubius, but you didn't say where on the river exactly?' he asked, resting his weight on his spear and ladelling some of the legionaries' leftover porridge into his own bowl.

Pavo hesitated. How much to say? Would it be more dangerous to seem overly reticent? But memories of last night's repartee eased his doubts. 'To Bononia,' he replied. With an artificially disinterested gaze off to the north, he added. 'The last galley on the river is moored there, I hear?'

The guard straightened up. 'Aye, aye it was.'

Pavo's head jerked round. 'Was?'

'I heard word just a few days ago. The galley was taken downriver.'

'Where?' Sura asked, listening in.

'To Oescus,' the Goth grinned, sure he was being helpful, then shovelling a spoonful of porridge into his mouth.

Pavo and Sura looked at one another, recalling Eriulf's advice.

Whatever you do, stay away from the town of Oescus…

'We were told to give Oescus and Reiks Folcher a wide berth,' Pavo asked the Goth just as the man was about to turn away.

The Goth twisted back and with the most harmless expression on his face, replied: 'Quite right. Trouble there, I've heard. Don't know much about it, don't care. But then again, I don't need a galley… and it sounds like you do.'

As the Claudians formed up for the march, Pulcher, Libo and Opis gathered around Pavo and Sura. Pulcher spoke first. 'Did he say this galley is now at Oescus?'

Pavo held up a hand. 'He did, and no, we're not going there.'

'But if the only galley is at Oescus,' Opis reasoned, 'and we *need* a galley if we're to have any hope of reaching the Western Empire to meet with this Maximus, then surely-'

'We're not going to Oescus,' Pavo repeated.

Libo hitched his crotch and scratched behind one ear. 'Then how do you propose we will travel to the West, sir?'

Pavo snatched in a few half-breaths and shot volcanic looks at all of them. 'I don't know yet, but I told you: we're *not* going to Oescus – and that's final!'

Two days later, as the light began to fade, the marching column emerged from a pine wood and slowed to a halt. Pavo stared across the plain ahead: a vast tract of wild grasslands and thickets of spruce and beech. And... a glow of torchlight illuminating the twilit horizon – a riverside town. He sighed in deep frustration. Libo, standing by his side, planted a hand on his shoulder. 'Welcome to Oescus,' he said with a tune of playful triumph.

Pavo rolled his eyes to his side and cast a gimlet stare at the chief centurion, then turned it upon the river town ahead. He had insisted for an entire day that they should continue on towards Bononia, certain that an alternative plan would emerge. Admitting he had been wrong and redirecting them to this place had been like swallowing acetum. So he took in a deep, long breath and shouted back to his men. 'Forward. We'd best approach before darkness falls.'

They set off towards the glow of the town. As they went, the winking reflections of the star and moonlight betrayed the great River Danubius, winding west to east just beyond the town, and the closer they drew the louder the sound of the river became – first a distant murmur, then a constant, bold rumble. Soon, they arrived before the pale hulk of Oescus, snug in the crook of the Danubius' southern banks and a small tributary waterway from which the town took its name. The walls, high and white with red bands at every storey, shone in the moonlight. The sections of the battlements that had been destroyed during the war or had crumbled during the years of neglect had been patched up admirably, if not particularly beautifully. Dark shapes of tall Gothic sentries lined those defences. Remembering the tense situation when they had approached the bridgehead watchhouse, Pavo took out the bracelet – like a key in these lands – and filled his lungs to call out to the garrison. But before he could utter a sound, he saw the glint of something silver whooshing through the air from the gatehouse and towards him. His body tensed to leap out of the way but he knew there was no time and then – *thud!*

The arrow quivered madly in the earth between his boots.

Pavo stared at it, then up at the gatehouse. The Claudian legionaries bristled with a clank of spears levelling and shields rising around Pavo.

'Stay back!' the sentry snarled in a sharp Gothic twang.

'Lower your bows!' Pavo raged. 'We're on the same side.'

'Are we?' the sentry rasped.

Just then, a second tall, dark figure raced up onto the battlements beside the shooter. Pavo could hear the hiss of their heated argument, before the second one waved his arms. 'Come inside!'

With a growl of rusty hinges, the gates below the shooter's spot on the walls peeled open, revealing the torchlit interior of Oescus.

'Sir?' Opis whispered. 'What do we do?'

'Smells like a trap,' Sura growled.

'This place reeks of danger even more than Deultum did,' Libo whispered. 'And the burning bodies there fairly reeked.'

Pavo eyed the figures up on the walls for a time. 'We can't back away now. We go in... but stay watchful.' He glanced to Opis and flicked his head in the direction of the city. Opis raised the ruby standard and the small band marched for the gates and passed under the great stone archway. The place still bore the ordered hallmarks and street plan of the legionary base it had once been, and the embellishments of the city it had morphed into. But now it was now a place in decay: the wide flagstoned avenues were cracked and sprouting through with grass and weeds; a high Temple of the Capitoline Triad stood not like a shining marvel but like a ragged tombstone, the architraves having been chiselled off crudely to be used in the wall repairs. The argent moon shone archly behind it as if to highlight the scars. The town had once been home to one hundred thousand Roman citizens, some said. Now, it looked as if it housed no more than a few thousand Goths – probably the warband who had been granted this estate in the peace agreement, along with their families.

Footsteps pattered down the stone steps of the gate tower, just behind the Claudians. Pavo turned to see a tall and bony Gothic noble with short golden hair slicked back with resin, his weak chin clean-shaven, wearing a red Roman cloak over his green tribal jerkin and trousers. The bowman who had shot at them walked behind the noble like a shadow, his snub-nose wrinkling as he regarded the Romans.

'Tribunus Pavo, of Legio XI Claudia Pia Fidelis,' Pavo greeted the noble, ignoring his menacing guard.

The nobleman eyed the Claudia standard up and down, cocking one eyebrow. 'The Claudia? I tangled with the ruby bulls once before,' he flicked his head towards the city's far end where the walls rose on the Danubius' banks. 'But over on the far side of the river. What are you doing here? We have seen nothing of the legions since the news of the peace spread.'

'You weren't at Dionysopolis?'

The noble's look grew stoic. 'We were in these parts at the time. We heard of the horde being pinned by the Dionysopolis cliffs and so we said goodbye to our women and young and set off with our warriors to join the fight. It was a dejected and unwelcome march – for we were tired of the war by then. But... we could not get to the battle in time, and then we met kinsmen spreading back across the countryside. They told us that there had been heavy fighting, but that it had ended with peace,' his face grew bright again. 'They persuaded us to set down our arms, return to our families and wait to see which part of the land we would be assigned as a *haim*.' He held out his hands and looked around. 'And here is our new home. We aim to watch it as well as the legions did.'

Pavo eyed the noble carefully, raking through his memories of that chat with Eriulf, trying to recall the name of the man in charge here. 'Reiks... Folcher?'

The noble looked confused for a moment, then started in realisation. 'Ah, no, I am no reiks. My name is Bedrich. Reiks Folcher is,' he stopped and shook his head. 'I will explain later. First, come with me. We use the old forum as our feasting area,' he said as he led the Claudians into the heart of the town – a huge forum across which lay the fallen statue of the Goddess Fortuna. Benches and tables were set out under the stars, and cooking fires blazed in the nooks of the broken goddess' body, boars turning on spits above the flames and pots of root stew bubbling away too. Pipes skirled in the night air as families ate and chatted, few noticing the Roman arrivals yet. 'You can eat there and take beer – we have wine, even – and there are many empty homes in which you and your men can sleep.'

Pavo glanced back over his shoulder and cocked an eyebrow to convey the offer. The men read the 'order' and gladly fell out, setting down their packs, shields and spears in a heap – but keeping their spathas on them – and taking the empty benches nearby. At this sudden din, the eating Goths realised they had visitors. The pipes and the chatter fell silent, every face stared, stunned. *Afraid,* Pavo thought. *Afraid of a small band of legionaries?*

'Come on now. Our allies are here to aid us. Bring them boar and drinks,' Bedrich called across the square. Slowly, the people made brief and minimal gestures of welcome, raising cups and nodding heads. The men tending the fires carved slices of boar meat onto a silver tray for the Claudians.

'You *are* here to aid us, I presume?' Bedrich said privately to Pavo. 'You've heard about the trouble in these parts?'

Pavo noticed the keen look in Bedrich's eyes, but decided not to pull on what was clearly a knotted twine. 'Not quite. You have a ship, I believe,' he replied curtly.

Bedrich's expression sagged a little. 'Ah, the *Justitia*?'

Pavo arched an eyebrow at the name of the vessel. Apt, he thought, for his journey to the West.

'She was quite a find. Moored upriver near Bononia in a low boathouse that was carpeted over with algae and reeds, with her mast down. Who would have thought it – an intact galley, hidden, forgotten! Reiks Folcher, requisitioned her from Bononia because he thought it might help us with our…troubles,' he let the word hang for a moment before adding, frustrated. 'Why do you ask?'

'She's the only imperial ship left on this stretch of the river. We need her.'

His face fell a little more. 'Ah, but Reiks Folcher made me swear that I would keep her for the defence of these walls.'

'Well perhaps I need to speak with Reiks Folcher.' Pavo glanced around, trying to locate which of the city's buildings the leader of this *haim* might have chosen as a residence. 'Where is he?'

Bedrich's expression collapsed completely now. 'Back before the war, when we dwelled upon the Danubius' northern banks, we used to say the river's currents were blessed with magic, that in the darkness, demons could glide over water like crawling mist. As a child, I believed this. When I grew into a man, I laughed at the thought. But now, after these last few moons, I'm not so sure.'

Pavo stared at him, jaded from the day's march and by the circuitous conversation. 'Can I speak to Reiks Folcher?' he repeated flatly.

Bedrich smiled one of those sad smiles that pull on the lips and make the eyes look old and lost. 'Come,' he said, beckoning him past the feasting area and on towards the river walls.

More puzzled than ever, Pavo followed him up the battlement steps and to the parapet, overlooking the dark and broad stripe of the Danubius. His gaze was drawn instantly to the two long-broken bridgeheads, one sprouting from the base of these walls, the other on the far banks, like hands stretching out, trying to reach one another over an impossible gap. A few piers stood midriver, stained green and as tumbledown as the Capitoline Temple. 'Constantine's bridge,' Pavo muttered. 'I've heard of it, but never did believe a stone bridge could weather the battering currents of this river.' He laughed once, dryly. 'Seems I was right.'

'For the best, Tribunus Pavo,' Bedrich said. 'Dark creatures roam on those far banks. An intact bridge would be a curse.'

Pavo's eyes narrowed on the far side of the Danubius: a wall of tall pines stood like the front ranks of an endless phalanx, the few gaps between thick with night shadow. 'The Huns? I would not disagree.' He chapped the top of the battlements and twisted to Bedrich. 'But you still have not answered my question: where is Reiks Folcher?'

Bedrich, face grave, simply pointed across the river again, like a tutor showing a pupil the obvious thing he had missed.

Pavo turned back to the far banks, straining to see. Blackness, pines, gorse. Close to losing his patience, he scanned again: shadowed boles, roots, more pines... and an X of stakes. Hanging on the stakes, upside-down and stripped of clothing, was a man – streaked with deep furrows of torture, the body glistening with blood and bodily fluids.

'Folcher?' Pavo whispered. 'The Huns did that to him?'

Bedrich gave a single, slow nod, eyes fixed on the body.

'What possessed him to cross the river?'

'That is what I was trying to tell you, Tribunus. He did *not* cross the river. They took him. It was during the night. He wished us all a good sleep then retired to the old governor's villa to rest. In the morning, he was gone... and come dawn we were greeted by the sight of that *thing* over there.'

'The Huns took him,' Pavo said. He wasn't sure if it was a question. His eyes darted around the walls and the river. 'But how did they cross a river like this? The bridge is gone. No man – and certainly no Hun – can swim across this river let alone tow a captive back. The *Justitia* remains moored here on this side, you say?'

'Aye,' Bedrich confirmed, pointing upriver to a low-roofed wooden wharf. In the moonlight, just the prow of the vessel was visible – a carving of the Goddess of Justice herself, distinctive by her blindfold and the scales of fairness she clutched to her chest.

'Then the Huns couldn't possibly have crossed,' Pavo reasoned.

'Couldn't they?' he whispered, extending one arm and uncoiling the index finger to point to a bank of roiling vapour upriver. 'In the darkness, demons glide across the water like crawling mist...'

Pavo stared at the creeping grey vapour, slinking and undulating its way across the flow with ease. For a moment, he felt a stark chill on his neck, then he pushed back from the battlements. 'The Huns walked across this water to capture your reiks?' he scoffed . 'Spare me!'

Bedrich held out his hands, at a loss. 'If there was a better explanation then I would be glad to hear it, Tribunus. But there is not, and Reiks Folcher is dead. Surely you now understand why I must honour my oath to him? I cannot grant you our one and only boat. It is our only means of countering *them* and whatever means they have of getting across the river.'

Used to dealing with solid tactical and strategic concerns, this felt to Pavo like trying to sculpt water. For a moment, he considered simply sequestering the galley by force, but then remembered the balance of his small band of Claudians versus the few thousand Gothic soldiers in this town. More importantly, he realised that such an act could destabilise the fragile peace. Already Reiks Ingolf's murder was a dangerous secret that might unpick those weak seams.

'Doubt it if you choose, but the Huns are getting across somehow,' a gruff voice snapped behind Pavo. He turned to see the angry, snub-nosed one who had shot at him, coming up the steps of the river battlement.

'Garamond, now is not the time,' Bedrich started.

But this Garamond was not for being interrupted. 'The night Folcher went missing, I saw a trio of them riding wild in the moonlight – over here, right outside the very gate where I stand watch. That's why I nearly shot your balls off tonight. For a moment I thought you were them.'

'Nearly shot my... so that wasn't a warning shot?'

Garamond shrugged. 'Maybe, maybe not. But aye, they've been crossing the river and roving out there, most nights for over a moon.' He glanced up at the night sky and growled. 'Don't believe me? Well, it is nearly time. Come with me, we can watch together...' he suggested to Pavo then glanced to Bedrich, 'if I have your permission?'

'Yes, yes,' Bedrich rolled his eyes and waved his hands, ushering the pair away.

'They're crossing every night?' Pavo asked, following Garamond back across the town to the land gate.

'They must be. We range far and wide along this side of the river on daytime patrol, and you know what these river plains are like – flat and wide – no place for a man to hide. We haven't seen a sign of the Huns during those patrols. Yet come night – almost every night – they ride outside our city.'

They flitted up the steps to the land walls and stared out across the flatlands. Nothing moved, bar a few shaking trees and quivering bushes where rodents darted. Owls hooted and bats rapped across the moon, but apart from that the only noise and signs of life came from behind Pavo, down in the feasting square. The jabber of Darik's voice rose and fell as he launched into story after story of his life in the desert, interleaved with Sura's manful if increasingly ridiculous attempts to better the easterner's tales. Time rolled past. Pavo felt his belly ache and began to fantasise about how glorious a foaming barley beer might taste to wash down a mouthful of warm, soft bread. He felt his eyelids growing heavy, and was about to tell Garamond he had had enough, when the sentry batted a hand across his chest. 'Look!' he hissed.

Pavo jolted wide awake. He stared out across the plain. There, picked out by a finger of cold moonlight, a horseman trotted, then four more, flanking him. Pavo blinked again and again, rubbing his eyes, not believing what he was seeing. The jaundiced skin, the strange, flat faces, the squat, stocky mounts, and the long, swishing black hair. The lead Hun – scalp shaved from his brow to his crown, the back and sides hanging in long, thin strands – held his bow aloft and loosed. The shaft hurtled across the night and smacked the battlement edge between Pavo and Garamond, sending both leaping back. With that, the Hun rider held his bow aloft like a trophy and cried out that horrible throaty sound they made. '*Whoop!*'

A score of Gothic wall sentries bustled over to see, some loosing arrows at the spot the five riders had been. But the Huns were gone, as if vanished into the blackness. The sentries muttered amongst themselves.

'Don't tell the people,' one hissed. 'Keep this to ourselves,' said another. But already, many down in the square were looking up, jabbering in tight and fearful voices. They had heard the Hun cry too.

Garamond turned to the people, waving his hands downwards. 'They are gone, we are safe. Bedrich assures us he can outsmart the steppe riders. We must have faith in him.'

'I'll leave you to your shift,' Pavo said to Garamond, backing away from the walls. Back at the feasting square, he walked through the clamour of shouts back and forth between the Gothic people and Garamond and the sentries on the walls. They were petrified of this threat, he realised as he slumped down beside Pulcher, Darik and Sura, taking one of Sura's unnecessary two cups of beer and draining half of it. The beer was cool, bitter and refreshing. He lifted a piece of bread and dunked it in the fatty juices of the boar plate they had all been eating from. It tasted as wonderful as he had imagined, but the moment was soured by the situation.

'So when are we getting the ship?' Darik asked. 'Not that I'm overly keen to get on a boat again.'

All nearby craned in to hear the news. 'We're not, and it's complicated,' Pavo explained. 'The Huns roam across the river overnight, it seems, and Bedrich isn't keen on relinquishing his only galley.'

'The Huns? Was that what that cry was from outside? But how?' Libo scoffed at the notion. 'They have no boats, and they don't swim.'

Just then, an old Gothic man at an adjacent table leaned closer. 'But I can assure you, they come. I saw them with my very own eyes three nights ago, circling, making that dreadful noise.' He looked Pavo up and down. 'I do not know who you are, Roman, but I know what *they* are.' He nodded furtively towards a Gothic woman sitting on her own, rocking back and forth, there but absent at the same time. 'Earlier this moon, her husband and three boys did not come home from a day of hunting. That night, we heard the Huns howling. The next morning we sent out a search party... and found her family nailed to a tree. Dozens more have gone missing and been found like this. It has made some of us wonder – has Wodin forsaken us by granting the Huns a way across the river... on the crawling mists, perhaps?' he halted, shuddering. 'I just pray to Wodin that Bedrich will protect us better than Folcher did,' he added before turning his back on the legionaries.

Pavo cradled his chin between thumb and forefinger, staring into the cooking fire nearest, the flames dancing like the riddle of the Huns.

Libo belched, then wiped the back of his hand across his mouth. 'So this Bedrich won't give us the ship because he thinks he needs it to stop the Huns crossing the river on... winged mist horses,' he shrugged and belched again, his good eye bulging with the effort.

Rectus wagged a finger. 'But if we find out how they are getting across, and we stop them...'

'Then that boat's ours,' Sura finished for him. 'And we'll be on our way west in time to join this Magnus Maximus.'

Pavo drummed his fingers on the table as – like that crawling mist on the river – an idea gradually took shape.

The following night was black as a demon's pit – with clouds crawling across the sky, blocking out the moon and stars, and once again a bank of mist creeping south across the river. Pavo's thighs ached and his body – clad in just tunic and cloak – felt cold through. Squatting by the reeds on the Danubius' southern riverbanks for over two hours had seen to that. But this stubborn wart of marshy land was the best vantage point he and his team of five chosen men could find outside the town – jutting proud of the banks, allowing them to see up and downriver, and hopefully to see what the Oescus sentries could not. Every so often his eyes slid from side to side, from the old broken bridge by Oescus to the slight narrowing of the waters here, a quarter-mile downriver. There were no other feasible crossing points, no ice bridges at this time of year, and every other section of the river for miles was as wide as an archer's best shot. He recalled what it had taken when he and his Claudians had once crossed the river without a boat – hours of shouting and splashing, casting ropes over to the far banks to establish a rail of sorts, then each man carefully using his shield as a float to paddle their way across with one hand, the other carefully holding the rope rail to prevent them being washed downriver to their deaths. But these Huns were crossing *with* their horses. Some said the Huns rarely washed, let alone learned how to swim. But there was no doubt about it: they had gotten across and returned to the northern side with Reiks Folcher as prisoner, he mused, eyeing the shadowy spot on the northern banks where the Goth's body was still on display, decaying slowly. They must have cobbled together rafts, he realised. Or perhaps seized a ship of their own.

'This country, so different from home,' Darik muttered, crouching behind him. 'Perhaps it is rotting reeds or something, but these parts in particular smell so bad – like the most appalling funghi mixed with terrible cheese.'

Pavo was about to reply, when he noticed Libo, crouched beside Darik, hitching and rearranging his loincloth every few moments. Every time he did, Sura, perched on his other side, would gulp for air, seal his lips and pinch his nose for a few moments to avoid the horrific wafts coming from Libo's undercarriage. Pavo and the veteran Claudians had become inured to the centurion's hygeine habits – or lack of them – but poor Darik was only just learning of such joys.

'There are some words I should perhaps teach you, said Betto, voice shrill thanks to his pinched nose. 'Graveolent, being one.'

Darik frowned.

It means 'stinking', Sura mouthed in explanation so the oblivious Libo wouldn't see.

'Sir!' Durio hissed with the urgency of a man who had just spotted a snake in his bed. Pavo's head snapped round, as did the heads of the others. 'My socks are wet,' he complained.

Pavo gave him a gimlet stare. 'The Eastern Empire lies in a fragile peace with the Gothic tribes. The Western Empire is about to be shaken by a great civil war. We *need* to be there when it happens. Yet here we hide, while Hun 'spirits' ride around us... but worst of all you have wet socks.'

'But, but I can feel a chill coming on and... and,' Durio began, then fell silent, seeing the scowls of the others. Eventually, his head lolled forward in shame and he wiped snot from his nose.

'Wet socks indeed,' Sura muttered. 'I'll tell you a story about wet socks that'll turn your stomach. It was in a brothel where-' he stopped. All looked at the primus pilus, surprised by his sudden silence. Normally a herd of stampeding elephants could not stop Sura in full flow with one of his tales. Pavo saw it first – Sura's grin melting downwards like fat sliding in a hot pan, and his eyes growing wide like moons. *They're here,* he mouthed.

Pavo frowned, head switching up and downriver. Nothing, just the rolling mist on the water and the dark woods on the far banks. Sura grabbed the back of his head and twisted it to look behind them. Here on *this* side of the river, swaying slowly on the backs of stocky steppe horses, rode the five Huns they had seen the night before. *How?* Pavo mouthed. *How had they crossed unseen?* They were but a rock's throw away from the crouched legionaries, apparently headed towards Oescus again, pointing, muttering amongst themselves. They wore layers of animal skins the same colour as their chestnut mounts, and goat wool capes. From their belts hung lassos, expertly-crafted asymmetric horse bows, quiverfuls of bone-tipped arrows and longswords.

'Remember, we're not out here to fight,' Pavo whispered to his men. 'We simply watch what they do and track them back to their crossing point. Once they're back over on the northern banks, we destroy whatever bridge or raft they are using.'

When the busy clouds parted, a wink of moonlight briefly illuminated the riding quintet. The lead rider's shaved crown and brow gleamed in that moment. Pavo's eyes slid down towards the man's face, and he felt a cold lance of horror pass through him. All Hun warriors looked strange to the Roman eye – flat-faced and sallow-skinned. Some wore long, trailing moustaches and some had strangely misshapen skulls, tall and elongated. More, they prided themselves on scarring their cheeks with three deep gouges on each, and shoving grit into the wounds as some kind of tribal rite of passage. But that man's visage was... inhuman. His eyes were like dark pits, his mouth like that of a trout, his expression horribly blank. But before Pavo could be sure he had not been mistaken, the sky swallowed up the moonlight again.

'Now, the Huns are ugly bastards,' Sura whispered, saying what they were all thinking, 'but *that* one was horrific.'

'How did they get across?' Darik hissed. 'They are not even wet. We would have heard their horses braying in panic if they had crossed on a ship of any sort.'

Pavo's mind began to spin, sure there was some shape and sense to all of this. He tried to piece together what they knew and indeed, things did seem to fit in a certain order. He just needed to concentrate, to think, when…

Durio's head rolled back, mouth open, eyes closed. '*Tchoo!*'

As the sneeze rang out over the southern banks, the five Hun heads snapped round upon their position. Pavo suddenly felt like a man in a bear pit. Out here, no weapons or armour, no time for help to come. 'Oh shi-' Libo began, just as a Hun arrow whispered through the air towards him. Pavo sprang forth, shouldering the one-eyed centurion out of the way. The arrow splashed into the reedy shallows.

'Run!' Pavo cried.

'Spread out! They'll ruin us if we stay in a pack,' Sura roared.

The six Romans exploded like shards of a clay urn dropped onto a stone floor. In the blackness of night, Pavo flailed wildly through the rough riverside land, each stride landing in a deep rut or stubbing on a tussock. He heard arrows whizzing through the darkness, one humming past his ear. He stumbled to his knees over a moaning shape on the ground: Durio, ankle twisted.

'Get up!'

'I can't,' Durio moaned.

'Get up or you're dead,' Pavo snarled, looping an arm around the legionary's back and hoisting him onto his good leg, the pair then hobbling together as best they could like a three-legged dog.

'Head for the gates,' Libo cried from somewhere nearby.

'*Whoop!*' cried the Hun five.

Like a giant beast being woken by the sudden commotion, orange lights glowed into life on Oescus' walls. A jabber of confused voices rose as the Gothic sentries up there peered out to see what was happening. The town's land gates creaked open just a fraction and a smattering of Claudians spilled out, throwing each other armour and weapons, bracing, squinting into the darkness, shouting to their comrades. 'Run!' they cried.

Pavo realised just how distant the town and the safety behind the gates was, then heard the thunder of hooves rumbling up behind him and Durio. A moment later a rhythmic buzzing noise rose. Pavo glanced over his shoulder to see the lead Hun bearing down on them, a rope lasso whirling above his head. That inhuman face, the empty pit of a mouth and chasm-like eyes. The lasso whooshed out and Pavo knew he was done for. Too many times he had seen fellow legionaries seized around the neck by these Hun ropes, then plucked from their ranks with the crack of a breaking spine. The rope sailed down... but flopped harmlessly past him.

It was like a Gods-granted mercy and a flash of clear understanding all at once. Pavo shoved Durio to one side – clear of the oncoming Hun leader, then bowled clear himself in the other direction just as the Hun burst through the spot they had both been occupying. As he rolled onto his knees, he saw in the darkness how the Hun turned his mount back towards them... slowly, awkwardly. Not at all like the demon riders he had faced in the past – for they were creatures born in the saddle, spending their lives glued to their horses like centaurs.

The Hun leader came round for him, but this time Pavo stood his ground.

When a Goth on the walls sent a fire arrow into the night, aimed at another Hun rider, the bright missile streaked across the riverside plain, illuminating the Hun leader's face again in a strange light. Pavo stared into his hollow eyes. *The Huns did not cross the river,* he knew now for sure.

'*Whoop!*' the leader howled, bearing down on Pavo, drawing his bow at close range.

Pavo jinked just before he loosed, then launched himself at the Hun's midriff. The body blow nearly broke Pavo's shoulder, but also unhorsed the Hun leader and sent both flying then barrelling over and over through the grass. With a flurry of kicks and punches, Pavo wrestled the man into a solid hold, one arm around his neck from behind. Just then another Gothic fire arrow ripped across the night sky. Pavo grabbed the Hun leader's shaved crown and clawed at it. The entire skin of his scalp and face – hair and moustache too – sloughed away with no resistance, revealing a short mane of golden hair, slicked back with resin. The man staggered back from Pavo, staring at him, then at the walls of Oescus. The Goths on the walls stared in horror. The Claudians defending the gates too.

'Bedrich?' one Gothic guard stammered in disbelief.

'Aye, Bedrich, Warden of Oescus,' Pavo roared out into the night, holding the mask of a long-dead Hun's skin aloft, then tossing it away. 'He sheds his skin like a snake!' Pavo then thrust a boot into Bedrich's thorax, sending him tumbling through the grass. '*He* killed Reiks Folcher, *he* murdered your daughters and sons... '

Now the other four 'Hun' riders bolted, realising their game was over.

Sura, Darik, Libo, Betto and Durio came to back Pavo up as he stomped towards the backwards-scrabbling Bedrich, driving the pale-faced traitor towards the town he had been terrorising.

'You captured Folcher, your own reiks. You took the galley and sailed him across the river in the blackness of night and gave him to the Huns. Then you rode these plains at night to terrify your own people with a false danger and to compel them to accept you as their new leader. You murdered the innocents who looked to you for protection.'

The woman who had lost her husband and boys to these 'Hun' raids appeared on the walls, stared for a moment, taking in what Pavo had said, then screamed – a terrible sound that split the night – before falling to her knees, raking her nails down her face to leave scarlet trails, shrieking some awful tribal curse upon Bedrich.

Pulcher, Opis and Indus rushed out from the gate area to complete a circle around the Gothic traitor.

Garamond the sentry barged through, then halted, staring down his snub nose at the kneeling Bedrich. Other Gothic soldiers joined him.

Pavo stepped back, stooping to pick up Bedrich's dropped lasso and hooking it to his belt, then waving his fellow legionaries back too. 'Do what you will with him,' he said to Garamond

More Gothic sentries and townsfolk now came out to see what was going on, forming a thick ring where the legionaries had been a moment ago. Bedrich stared up at them all, face almost white as milk even in the orange torchlight as he heard the whispers spreading. 'He did it.' 'He killed Folcher.' 'He murdered your daughter.' 'Your brother died at his hand.' 'He nailed your sons to a tree.'

Garamond drew out his axe. 'Why?' he said, the word dripping with disdain.

Bedrich eyed the axe fearfully, then his face changed, warped with hate. 'We killed only those who threatened our veil of secrecy,' he rasped.

Pavo, walking away, now turned back, his flesh creeping when he saw the man's sudden change in demeanour. Now, his face was so shrivelled up with malice that he looked almost as horrific as the Hun skin mask.

'Folcher threatened to betray my kind to the Romans,' Bedrich ranted. 'And so did your brother, your daughter, your husband,' he went on, shooting accusatory fingers out at members of the circle surrounding him, spittle flying with his every word. 'That is why they had to die. None of them were worthy...'

Pavo felt a horrible sensation crawl through him. He had heard rhetoric like this once before, in the guts of the war and from the mouths of Goths. Garamond lined the edge of his axe up with Bedrich's forehead, and lifted the weapon back over his head.

'Wait,' Pavo said, pushing through the ring of Gothic onlookers, trying to reach Garamond.

But his words were drowned out by Bedrich's sibilant growl. 'None of them were *Vesi*...'

Pavo halted in his tracks, stunned.

'...and the *Vesi* will rise...' Bedrich boomed as Garamond drew his axe back above his head.

'Wait!' Pavo shouted now.

'...and the empire will burn!' Bedrich roared even louder. 'My master will see to it!'

Thunk! Garamond's axe swung down, breaking Bedrich's head like a thick flagstone. A pulse of black blood pumped from the awful wound, and Bedrich's eyes rolled in their sockets. With a strangely peaceful sigh, the traitor fell onto one side, where the contents of his skull – a slurry of broken-up brain and blood – slid out across the grass, steam rising from the mess.

Garamond's glower never left the corpse. With a low burr he said simply to his nearest fellow soldiers. 'I'd say we should show the Romans to the galley.'

'Aye,' the others rumbled in agreement, dispersing.

Pavo stared at the corpse, feeling the chill of a long-forgotten shade rising around him.

'Did I hear right?' Sura whispered.

'He was a Vesi,' Pavo answered, peering down at the corpse, Libo, Pulcher and Darik looking down with him. 'The Goths have no king. But the Vesi live... and they have a master?'

'We should set sail tonight,' Rectus advised, hobbling over with the aid of a stick. 'I make it that we'll need to keep moving this and just about every night if we're to reach the West before summer's out.'

Pavo looked upriver, seeing the Goths already at work in erecting the *Justitia's* masts. The strange events of tonight would have to be left behind for now... for the way to the West was open.

Chapter 16
July 383 AD
The River Danubius

The *Justitia* cut upriver thanks to a stiff wind and the relentless effort of the Claudians on the oars. The prow was a brightly-painted carving of the eponymous goddess, her blindfolded and austere visage pointing upriver. Betto, sitting on the spar, legs dangling, played the role of *hortator* by blowing a jaunty, rhythmic tune on a flute to guide the oarsmens' timing.

Pavo pulled on his oar for the thousandth time that day, feeling a fire in his palms and an ache in his bare shoulders – still scarred with the burden-wounds of Zeno. He looked around the deck nearby for some source of distraction, only for his eyes to fall upon the coil of rope and Hun-style noose on the end that he had taken from Bedrich. The riddle of the Vesi rose in his mind like smoke – shapeless, unruly, threatening. It had kept him awake last night and the night before. Garamond had assumed control of Oescus and seen to it that the galley was well-stocked with supplies for this journey. But just before they had set off, Pavo had questioned him about Bedrich's last words. Garamond had not been forthcoming about the Vesi or the 'master' Bedrich had spoken of. *It is tribal business, something I do not care for and nor should you,* he had said. *Now, do you want the ship or not?* Thus, they had set sail in the dead of night, leaving the mystery behind. Pavo's head throbbed at the thought of it all.

He tried to concentrate instead on rowing in time. Before and around him dozens of sweating, muscular and scarred backs contorted with a rhythmic dull grunting and the clean sound of oars slicing through water. As he did so, he noticed big Darik's bare, muscular back working away on the oar in front of him, his long dark hair wet with sweat and sticking to his dusky skin. The colour of his skin made him think of something else, something golden and good: Izodora shorn of her battle gear and kneeling like a mother by a crib, cradling a small bundle of blankets. In his mind's eye he heard a weak cry, saw a tiny hand reaching up to touch its mother's chin. The vision was mesmerising, different, gloriously terrifying – something that rode over his military confidence like a runaway battle horse. How would it feel? What would it mean?

The galley's mast creaked gently in the hot wind, shaking him from his thoughts. He glanced up at the ship's faded red sail. It was plain – perhaps for the best, he mused. This simple galley from the Classis Moesica could probably slip past most of the Gothic-garrisoned river towns without question. Indeed, they had passed three such small forts and *haim* towns already in their four days on the water; only one set of Goths had challenged them, sailing out to block their galley on a skiff, but Pavo had produced Eriulf's bracelet and the men had no quarrel with letting the *Justitia* on past. But – absurdly – he knew that when they crossed into the Western Empire where *Roman* eyes would be watching the river traffic, it might be different.

'Pavo, come, see,' Sura said, batting his shoulder.

'My shift isn't over yet,' Pavo grunted in reply.

'Your shift was over at noon,' Pulcher scoffed, his pitted face dripping with sweat as he worked the oar adjacent. Then he added with a wry grin, 'sir.'

Pavo glanced up at the sun again and saw that indeed it was well past noon. Indus stood at the end of the rower's bench, poised like a relay runner ready to take over. Pavo rose, shaking with fatigue, patting the young legionary on the back as he edged out and Indus shuffled in and sat in his place.

Rowing was a strange thing – always looking to the stern of the ship, seeing where you have been instead of where you are headed. So when Sura turned him towards the fore, he was struck dumb for a moment. What looked like two massive stony jaws lined the river sides. A colossal stone canyon of a scale that made the Danubius seem like a brook, the sides were steely grey and glittering in the sunlight, the tops carpeted in lush green. Over countless eons the river had worn this path through the lower tracts of the Carpates Mountains. Sura guided him towards the prow for a better look. Tiny imperial watchtowers atop either side of the river canyon stood proud but clearly unmanned and in early decay. Tucked into the base of the cliffs on the southern edge of the river, a small imperial wharf jutted, abandoned also. This section of the river defences had still to be reinstated.

'The Iron Gates, Brother,' Sura said quietly, staring ahead with him.

Behind them, Betto's mellifluous flute song faded away to nothing as he himself was caught up in the wonderment. 'Aristotle was right,' he said, leaning forward on the mast. 'Nature does nothing without purpose or in vain.'

'A few more days' sail and we will enter the West,' Sura said quietly to Pavo.

Waves of emotion crashed together inside Pavo. Overhead, two birds glided. They were merely herons, making *kaark* noises evey so often, but as Pavo squinted up at them, he thought of the eagle dream. The dark bird, the bright one. Both covered in blood. He felt a rising thrill of anticipation and dread, saw in his mind's eye a horrible collage of war-memories and experienced then a deep fear that he would never return home... never see Izodora again, never hold their baby. He gazed through the Iron Gates and felt a stark chill pass across his body.

'You're doing this for them,' Sura said quietly. 'Izodora and the child will never be safe while Gratian rules the West and undermines the East.'

'It is really happening, isn't it?' Pavo said.

'Aye, and it's the biggest thing we've ever done,' Sura replied, handing him a skinful of fresh drinking water.

'I have no business in the West,' Pavo said. 'I'm risking everything.'

'We all are,' Sura corrected him, 'and gladly.'

Pavo turned to his legionary crew, seeing those who were rowing snatching looks over their shoulders at the great cliffs, and those off-duty staring up at them too. Darik seemed entranced by the landmark, mouthing some desert oath as he drank in the sight. They all wore that same look of trepidation.

He felt a presence beside him then. A steadying hand of one who was now but a memory. *Speak to them*, whispered the shade of Tribunus Gallus.

He stepped up onto a bench. 'We have served together for many seasons, some of us for many years, iron comrades sworn to do as our emperor commands. Now, it goes beyond that. We step past the directives given to us by our Eastern Emperor and strike westwards for the good of the entire Roman world. I cannot assure you how this journey will go, if we will even reach this Magnus Maximus, nor even if he can indeed overthrow Gratian... nor if all of us will return to the East again.' A notion struck him like a hammer hitting a bell. 'In fact, the only thing I *can* guarantee you is that some of you will *not* come home.' The words seemed to breeze around the deck like an ill wind. The rhythm of the oars slowed. Pavo looked around the boat, meeting as many eyes as were turned to face him. 'See the old wharf a short way upriver? We will dock there soon. Should any of you choose to disembark and discontinue the voyage, no man will think ill of you. You have all proved yourselves as heroes many times over. Go, if you wish, back to your homes, your families.'

The oars slowed further. Many exchanged glances.

Durio stood up. 'My parents are dead, sir. The house I grew up in is now but ashes – razed during the war. The legion tent is my home now and you...' he swept his gaze around the decks, 'you glorious bastards are my family.'

Indus rose beside his friend. 'I have nobody but an arsehole of a father, a drunk who didn't even care when I left to join the legion. Now you lot are all drunks too...' light laughter rose, '...but the difference is that you care.'

Opis was carving at a piece of fruit with his knife, the Claudia banner resting in the crook of his arm. He simply shrugged. 'You'll have to pull that standard from my cold, dead hands, sir.'

One by one the Claudians spoke. It had never struck Pavo as much as at that moment just how deeply the war had affected them all, how tightly it had bonded them as a group.

Then... Betto stood up, balancing precariously on the spar, and began to play a new powerful flute song. As one, the oarsmen's bodies swelled up and writhed as they drew a fast and powerful stroke that sent the *Justitia* lurching forward. Some of those not on duty squeezed onto the rowing benches to add their strength to the cause.

Pavo felt his throat thicken as the ship surged on upriver past the abandoned wharf without stopping. He had asked so much of them before and never had they denied him. *To the end, brothers... to the end.*

'From now on, we are in enemy lands,' he continued, stepping down from the bench and striding up and down the deck. 'An enemy more cruel and far-seeing than any you might have faced during the Gothic War.' His voice echoed around the great canyon of the river cliffs, punctuated by the lapping of the oars. 'Until we make contact with Magnus Maximus and his invading army, we cannot be seen in our legionary guise.' He held up his military belt and tunic as he said this, dropping them into a sack where his helm, cloak and armour were already stowed. From another sack he took out a shabby brown garment – something that scarcely looked Roman, never mind military, and pulled it on over his sweaty torso. 'If anyone questions us, we are shipping textiles to Guntia. But we have no documents or seal-marked tablets to prove this... so try not to get questioned in the first place.'

As the legionaries not on the oars set about stowing their military gear like Pavo had, Sura sighed. 'So until we reach Maximus and his army, should we become... Urbicus and Mucianus again?' he mused.

'Makes sense,' Pavo replied.

Sura chewed the end of one fingernail absently, then wagged the finger like a businessman coming up with a great idea. 'Next time, remind me to choose a less ridiculous name. That Persian woman with the amazing round arse. She was spellbound by my stories that night. It was when I told her my name that it all started going downhill.'

Pavo nodded once with a sincere look. 'Very well. Next time, you can be Pupianus.'

They passed through the ancient stone canyon and soon glided into view of the bulwark of Cusum – a fortified harbour and effectively a gatehouse guarding river entry into the Western Empire. The fort's pale, stony walls glowed in the sunshine, and the wharf region was awash with telltale glimmers of steel. Gratian's soldiers. Not many of them, he thought, but all it would take was for one of them to see through the Claudians' disguise. A small but dangerous western fleet was moored there too – tasked with challenging passing ships. A tall brick turret rose at the riverside, and two legionaries up there stood by a pole from which hung a bronze buccina – a warning horn to be blown upon sighting any form of threat or unexpected ships.

Pavo, Sura and Libo buzzed around the decks of the *Justitia*, trying to look like busy trade crewmen, but all the time glancing at the impressive docks, fearing the blowing of that horn that would see the Cusum fleet put out to bar their way and the marine officers asking the questions they could not answer. Indeed, he noticed the purple-plumed *Navarchus* of the garrison fleet, standing on the Cusum harbour's wide stone steps that led down into the Danubius' waters. The man's eyes were on the *Justitia*, watching the ship glide by. Watching keenly. Suspiciously. The two on the tower were staring now as well.

Pavo averted his gaze. *Mithras, see us through. Mithras, show us the way,* he mouthed over and over, lifting and moving a wooden crate for no other reason than to look the way a river trader should.

Suddenly, angry shouts arose and the braying of donkeys too. Pavo shot a sideways look at the stony wharf. The *Navarchus* had become entangled in a blazing row with the captain of a supply vessel, who had let his drove of pack donkeys disembark and lumber around the wharf unchecked, blocking another flotilla from landing at the busy waterside. Even the pair of lookouts up on the turrets became engrossed by the argument, turning away from the river to watch. The horn never sounded, and the *Justitia* sailed on upriver, into the West, unchallenged. Libo managed to hold onto his caged and relieved laughter until they were safely past, but once he let it loose, every other man on board joined in. 'Donkeys,' Sura proclaimed, 'sent by Mithras in our moment of need!'

Pavo watched Cusum shrink into the horizon behind them –

relieved, but also surprised by the relatively small number of military personnel that had been there. A skeleton garrison, almost.

As they forged on upriver, Claudians who finished their shifts on the oars flopped down on the *Justitia's* decks to sleep under the shade of the sail, and those rested enough and with time to spare before their next stint of rowing took to fishing from the boat's edge. Every night, the catches of carp, salmon, trout and sturgeon were baked either on the move or – when Pavo saw that his men were close to exhaustion – at a mooring spot on the riverbanks, far from towns or cities, but sheltered and defensible enough to spend a night at. After a few days of sailing through Western territory, the river became somewhat clogged with other ships. Galleys and fishing skiffs, trade cogs and private vessels cutting up and downriver. The *Justitia* sailed along the northern edge of the Diocese of Pannonia, passing more river towns, fortresses and the cities of Mursa, Aquincum, Brigeto, the amber-trading capital at Carnuntum, then Vindobona and Lauriacum – each walled and bedecked with fluttering imperial banners. None of the small garrisons challenged them, thanks perhaps due to the heavy traffic of other vessels and the assumption that any ship sailing from the East would already have been questioned at Cusum. Pavo watched it all from the boat's edge, toying with a splinter of wood between his teeth: at each of the towns he noticed that – just like at Cusum – very small numbers of legionaries manned the walls. More interestingly, he spotted silvery flashes from the riverside and inland roads. Small legionary detachments and riders, all moving westwards.

The *Justitia* powered on, skirting the edge of Italia's border province of Raetia. When they approached the great fortress city of Castra Regina – another of Gratian's strongholds – he noticed that the river traffic here was thin and so this time, they stowed the sails and waited downriver until a trade fleet overtook them, then picked up the pace and sailed through as if they were part of that fleet.

Twenty five days passed before they reached the Danubius' upper tendrils, arriving at the Raetian trading city of Guntia, nestled on the banks of one of the many tributary waterways. Half of the city was splashed with golden sunshine and half lay in the shadow of a tall green mountain range. They loaded their sacks of weapons and armour onto their shoulders, then stepped down onto the wharf. The place was buzzing with gossip. Pavo was just about to edge closer to one group in an effort to hear what they were saying, when an overly-hirsute and stumpy hand slapped down on his shoulder.

'Trading papers,' the greasy homunculus snapped, holding out his other palm expectantly.

A harbourmaster, Pavo realised. These bastards lived to make life difficult for everyone else.

'Is there a problem?' the harbourmaster added.

Pavo glanced past the man's shoulder, seeing a trio of harbour sentries glaring around with menacing looks. Bored and clearly there to enforce this man's will. *Not now, not when we've come so far,* Pavo hissed inwardly. They had nothing, not even falsified documents. They didn't even have any sham goods they could show to prove they were traders.

'Do you want a ship?' Sura said calmly, appearing beside Pavo.

The greasy harbourmaster looked offended at the interruption. 'What?'

'The *Justitia*. Take her, she's yours.'

The man looked stunned. 'I... I'll confiscate her if you don't show me your trading documents.'

Sura sniffed nonchalantly. 'And then the ship will become imperial property. You'll get a pat on the head, and tomorrow you'll still be wearing the same sweat-stained tunic, standing in the baking sun all day long.'

The harbourmaster fizzed at this. But Sura leaned closer. 'The *Justitia* was an imperial trireme. Part of the *Classis Moesica*, pride of the East. Nobody knows that but us, and now you. Do you know how much money you could make if you were to sell her? Or how much you could earn were you to rig her out to trade downriver at the amber markets?'

Pavo watched as the man's irritable look faded and his eyes grew wider, his tongue darting out to lick his lips a few times.

'Or shall I call your grunts over?' Sura said quickly, looking up to the three sentries, raising a hand as if to hail them.

'No, hold on...' the harbourmaster laughed anxiously, grabbing Sura's hand and lowering it. 'I'm sure we can come to some arrangement.'

Within the hour, the harbourmaster strode, alone and somewhat stunned, up and down the decks of his new galley. More, the Claudia men were past the harbour checkpoints and moving through the wharf markets. Darik shook his head, chuckling, him and Pulcher exchanging disbelieving looks a few times before the big Maratocupreni spoke: 'I once criticised you for your bullshit,' he said to Sura, hastily adding, 'sir. But now I wonder: could you bottle it? For if you could then we could all become rich one hundred times over.'

Sura began some tale about a class he had once led in Adrianople where he had taught youngsters the art of persuasion. The Plato of Adrianople, they had apparently called him.

But Pavo hardly noticed. Instead he listened into the Guntian people all around them. Men chattered, children play-fought, talking about war. Women huddled by spice stalls, whispering, and Pavo heard a few choice words. 'Lord of Britannia... moving through northern Gaul... riders and legions... Emperor Gratian surprised, ill-prepared.' Knots of Western legionaries too stood huddled deep in discussion. Pavo watched one of them chop a hand into his palm then slice the hand around in a curve as if explaining what he would do in battle were he a general.

Suddenly the hubbub was sliced apart with a whinnying of horses. A *turma* of cavalry trotted through the wharf, the crowds of citizens parting like water before the prow of a ship. The silver-cloaked *Decurion* leading the thirty whistled then snapped at the gossiping legionaries: 'Get into line – or I'll whip you all the way to Augusta Treverorum.'

Instantly, the gossiping ones fell into shape, forming a small marching column. The mounted officer rode past them, waving them with a clipped, hasty tone. The group rode and marched off along the wharf promenade towards the gates and the highway skirting the city's landward side – a road stretching northwest.

'Gratian is pulling every soldier he has back to his capital in Gaul,' Sura said. 'Even the scraps of his city garrisons.'

Pavo realised that was what he had seen from the river – pockets of men being summoned back like claws retracting into a leopard's paw. Gratian – for so long an invincible and ominous creature – was scared. He felt a pulse of something almost foreign inside his chest. Hope, he realised. Belief that this might just be the beginning of Gratian's end. With a grinding of teeth, he snuffed out the fantasy. This would not be real until it was over. 'And so we must follow,' he growled to his men, looking northwest, 'into the bastard's lair.'

Chapter 17
July 383 AD
Augusta Treverorum

Valentinian crossed his arms on the sun-warmed limestone windowsill, resting his chin on them and gazing out over the wards of Augusta Treverorum. The distant hum of the sweltering countryside – stripes of green and gold – changed every so often, as winding ribbons of silver emerged from the haze of distance, converging on the city. Centuries and cohorts, bands of riders, all gathering, answering Gratian's call. As each one arrived and the army gradually took shape outside the city's western gates, the more dejected Valentinian felt. Another sound briefly lifted him from his despair – the sound of laughter and wooden swords clashing friskily down in the gardens a few floors below the sill. But then he spotted the source of the noise: on a small green ringed by a colourburst of flowers, Gratian was at play.

The Emperor of the West spun and leapt, expertly blocking and parrying as his Alani went through a combat drill with him. He wore just his pteruges and boots, a measure seemingly designed to impress Laeta, who watched from nearby under a white awning to protect her from the strong afternoon sun. Beside her sat a rather lobster-red and sweat-slicked Arbogastes and the round-shouldered and placid-looking Bishop Ambrosius. Officers stood and sat around nearby too, clapping Gratian's every move. None could watch and fail to be impressed, Valentinian conceded, for his stepbrother was physically honed and fast as a cat. The Alani were clever enough not to try to beat him at swordfighting, but it was clear even still that Gratian was a master with the weapon. Perfectly-timed, Gratian batted the sword from one Alani hand, then crouched to sweep the legs from another with a swipe of his foot, before rising to grab the hand of the third, bring the man round like a shield and use his sword to pin the fourth, the blade's tip hovering at the guardsman's neck. With a burst of laughter, Gratian let the one he was holding go, threw down his wooden weapon and stalked over to a nearby table where refreshments had been set out. 'Who will win the next bout?' Gratian asked Laeta, his nostrils flaring as he stooped to brazenly sniff her neck, inhaling her oil-scent of rose and cinnamon.

She smiled in a way Valentinian had only ever seen actors do, and replied: 'The strongest. I always back the strongest.'

Gratian laughed and swept his gaze around his watching men, who rose in flattering laughter like stalks of hay set alight by a passing torch. 'Strength? Listen!' he cried, cupping a hand to his ear. 'Do you hear the drum of boots and rustle of iron? That's the sound of my garrison soldiers pouring in towards this city from every corner of this land. Soon too the southern legions will be here, and the African riders. Tonight,' he purred dropping to one knee and lifting Laeta's lower leg to kiss her ankle, 'we will look out from these city walls over a sea of steel. Then… you will know what strength truly is.'

Laeta planted her bare foot on Gratian's chest and playfully shoved him away. Expertly, he rolled over once, grabbed his training sword and sprang to his feet, launching into a new combat session.

'Why do you watch his pompous games?' Merobaudes scolded.

Valentinian pulled back from the sill, turning to the giant general sitting at the table behind him. He was blowing on a cup of hot root brew to cool it down and for once dressed in a simple soldier's tunic instead of the usual case of steel armour. 'Because I am confused. People often tell me I am stronger than him. Yet I cannot brandish a sword like that.'

Merobaudes supped on his brew then one edge of his mouth rose in a wry smile. 'Better,' he corrected Valentinian. 'People say that you are *better* then him. Physical strength will come,' he added, cupping one of his scrawny biceps. 'As for skill? Aye, he is an expert swordsman, but you could be too. Perhaps we should see about training you.'

Valentinian laughed. 'He would not be pleased to see me grow strong like him.'

'I can organise private lessons.'

'But these walls have ears and eyes!' Valentinian countered.

'He can't keep you by his side forever,' Merobaudes grumbled.

'He can. He does! I am a prisoner,' Valentinian replied. 'He keeps me close for a reason. He has threatened to kill me once before – in the burning halls of Sirmium.'

Merobaudes pounded a fist on the table. 'Had I been there…'

'Tribunus Pavo was there. He saved me.'

Merobaudes grunted, dissatisfied. '*I* should have been there. I carried you from the flames once before, young master. I would do so again. I would burn for you.'

'And that would break my heart. I do not want you to suffer injury for me, my shield.' Valentinian stared at his midday meal of bread and mashed olives – untouched. Eating seemed pointless. 'But it seems inevitable. What lies ahead will be terrible. In the coming clash between my stepbrother and Maximus, countless men will fall or be broken. This is not what I dreamt of. When I helped Pavo win peace in the East, I dreamt of harmony here too. Of accord in every corner of the Roman world and beyond.'

'Sometimes a forest must burn to grow strong again,' Merobaudes said, staring into space.

'But this will be a massacre, Valentinian croaked. 'Maximus cannot win.'

Merobaudes looked up, a hangdog look on his big, fire-scarred face. 'Well thank you for those words of encouragements, young master.'

'You taught me to be direct, realistic,' Valentinian retorted.

'What makes you so sure Maximus cannot win? The core of your stepbrother's armies are still mired in faraway Hispania,' Merobaudes said with an arched eyebrow. Like a prosecutor presenting irrefutable evidence, he lifted out the forged seal ring that had sent those legions away.

'But garrison detachments stream to this place from every corner of Gaul. Worse, the legions of Italia are arriving here *today*. And the

Moorish cavalry are being shipped here in droves and will not be far behind. He will still have more than enough to repel this Maximus.'

Merobaudes set down his root brew. 'One day you will be a fine general, lad. What makes a good general? Many things. One is the tendency to mistrust everything. Even your own eyes and ears.'

Valentinian cocked his head to one side, picking at his bread.

'On that day of the slave-hunt in the woods, when your stepbrother was first informed of this invasion, you heard Arbogastes in the war room, bleating about summoning the Moors and the Italians, aye?' Merobaudes said.

'Yes. I saw the courier horsemen taking the summons off to the port of Massilia – they rode like lightning!'

'So you did *not* see the messengers I sent in advance.'

Valentinian sat tall, mouth falling agape.

'Remember, I have been in contact with Maximus for months, I knew your stepbrother would call upon the Moors and the Italian regiments when he heard of the invasion. Now the Moors are a fickle people, but they prefer you to your stepbrother, lad. The Italian legions too. You as their patron and I as your guardian have offered them a choice, a chance to usher in a new, righteous emperor – one whom you will eventually succeed. All they have to do… is stay where they are in faraway Italia and even more distant Africa.'

Merobaudes rose from the table and guided Valentinian over to the south-facing windows on the other side of the room. From here, the cool shade cast by the palace stretched over Treverorum's market wards, and the sun-baked southern countryside beyond seemed bare apart from two more small pockets of approaching garrison bands. 'Do you see the tiny flicker of colour out there?'

'The incoming garrison groups?'

'No – beyond.'

Valentinian squinted. 'I see nothing but heat. The land is bare and-' he stopped, noticing the pin-prick of dark brown. A lone man, riding.

'Aye, you see him now, don't you. I spotted him earlier. But I couldn't tell then who he was. Now I can. See his white-feathered spear? He's a messenger. One of those who was recently sent south by

Arbogastes.'

The rider grew as he neared, his polished brown leather cuirass gleaming like the hide of his sweating horse, his cape and the stallion's mane thrashing in his wake. The drum of hooves rose, before dropping away to nothing as he vanished from view, obscured by the city's eastern walls.

'What news does he bring, my shield?'

Merobaudes calmly returned to the table. 'Well I could risk a guess... but it is best to catch the bear before you sell his skin. Sit... eat.'

Valentinian did as he was told. He chewed carefully on his food, desperate to speak, to know more. Merobaudes drank the last of his brew and plonked the empty cup down with a contented sigh. Silence, then... the rising clop of hooves, this time from the garden-facing windows.

Shouting rose from down there. Both moved from the table and to the garden-facing window. The rider from before had ridden in through the garden gates, and was now slowing as he turned in a tight circle. Officers clustered around the man eagerly. The rider ignored them all, dismounted and sank to one knee before the bare-chested Gratian. They heard nothing of the man's news, but Gratian's reaction told them everything they needed to know. The Western Emperor dropped his wooden sword and took three clumsy steps backwards, then began wringing his hands through his hair. 'I have an empire to defend. I *need* my legions, my riders!' he spat to all around him.

Valentinian heard Merobaudes' low laughter and looked up at his guardian. The big man's fire-scarred face was bent in a smile – a rare thing. 'It seems our friends in Italia and Africa have chosen wisely,' Merobaudes whispered, cupping an arm around Valentinian's shoulder, hugging him like a father. 'Gratian will face Maximus with nothing more than what little he has here in Gaul. His days are almost up, young master. The golden dream can be real.'

Chapter 18
August 383 AD
Gaul

Swallows arrowed and darted across the cornflower-blue sky, and the sun-washed meadows of Gaul were green and splashed with colour: bluebells that seemed to hover above the pastures like an indigo mist, bright flurries of red and orange where butterflies danced, bursts of yellow broom and, far to the south, the hazy white flame of the snow-capped Alpes Mountains. Above the chirruping of birds and hum of insects rose a gentle shush of men walking through the grass.

Pavo, still clad in shabby trader clothes with his armour hidden in his pack, squinted as he gazed around the summer fields, taking deep and clean breaths of the honey-scented air, enjoying the gentle brush of grass on his shins, watching the butterflies dancing above the low green rise to their right... when suddenly the butterflies scattered. A strange sound arose from beyond: thunder.

'Down,' Sura hissed. As one, the band of Claudians fell prone, eyes glinting like jewels as they looked to the low green rise.

Pavo signalled silently to Sura, and the pair rose to creep low up the rise, falling to their bellies again near the top. The two watched the train of legionaries moving along the road there at full step – the source of the thunder. The sun dazzled on the iron coats and helms of this unit as they sped northwest along the Via Julia, headed into northern Gaul just like those men who had set off from Guntia.

'The III Julia Alpina,' Sura whispered, squinting at their ice-blue shields. 'Or a cohort's-worth of them at least.'

'The roads are still crawling with Gratian's men,' Pavo added, pointing to the seven dark outlines of imperial messengers, flat in their saddles and capes flailing madly as they sped in both directions along the road, calling out in salute as they passed the legionary train.

This had been their mode of travel since Guntia: staying near the roads but not so close that these Western legionary detachments and cavalry wings all heading towards Augusta Treverorum might scrutinise or challenge them. There had been a few close calls, once when Durio had gone to relieve his bladder and had been in mid-stream when a Western scout had galloped into view. Thankfully, Durio had taken one for the legion, throwing himself to the grass and into the puddle of his own urine before he was spotted. For five days, they had been moving like this near the roads, halting at brooks to drink deeply and camping in forests of elm and alder, eating caught deer roasted over a fire or bread smeared with bacon fat – a gift from the Goths of Oescus – from their ration packs, and one night pork sausages and cabbage bought from a friendly farmer, washed down with fresh milk. It was a strange existence, Pavo thought, like walking alongside a great predator, hoping it would not turn its head.

'Look, do you see it?' Sura whispered.

Pavo shaded his eyes from the sun and stared north with Sura – at the wide, glittering ribbon wending across the land, south to north. 'The River Rhenus,' he realised. The great natural barrier that part-shielded the Western Empire from the wilds of Germania just as the Danubius served as a border for the Eastern Empire. The marching III Julia Alpina men were now just a glinting line, moving north along the river's western banks.

Pavo mentally marked out the next section of an off-road route that ran parallel to the highway. 'We follow these units… and we find Gratian.' Soon, he thought, there would be no place to hide. *For Gratian… or for me.*

On the fifth day's march they walked upriver near the Rhenus road. In the quiet moments, Pavo thought about home. When they halted to take on water, he plucked buttercups and tried to imagine Izodora sitting in Saturninus' gardens, doing the same. She would be swollen with their child by now. He closed his eyes and tried to imagine that he was there with her, holding her, the tinkle of bells and squabble of gulls from the Golden Horn, the soft babble of Constantinople's busy wards rising around them. Then he imagined her sitting in the doorway of one of those tranquil farmsteads out in the Thracian fields – homes he had often envied as he had marched past. Aye, that would be the place for her and the babe to live, he thought. He remembered times past, comrades gone. Big Zosimus, prone to grow teary-eyed after a few jugs of barley beer or wine when he would start talking about his wife and girl. Pavo *thought* he had understood the big man back then. Now he truly did. 'Were this any other war, any other foe, I would not be here,' he whispered into the warm air. 'But I take every step here for you and for the little one in your womb. I will do what must be done to ensure that you are safe.'

'Now you understand why I had to come here with you?' said Darik quietly, overhearing the private words. The big man smiled that perfect, ivory smile of his.

'You mean what happened in the sea, your oath? You owe me nothing. I would have swum down into the depths for any of us,' Pavo responded.

'The sea? Ha! My oath stands good. The Maratocupreni never break an oath. I will save you one day as you saved me. But no, I meant something more important than that. I am with you now because of Izodora and the young one, when it comes. I know you were whispering about her and the babe. You, her, the child and I will share a bond of blood. Stronger than steel. Family means everything to the Maratocupreni. I was thinking that you and I will be like brothers,' he chuckled. 'Then I heard how you Claudians talk. You also call each other brothers.'

'Because we are,' Pavo said without pausing to consider the matter.

'And that's why I know I made the right choice to come,' Darik grinned again.

Later that day, they came to Noviomagus, a city perched on a high riverside spur – well-placed to watch the wild lands on the far side of the Rhenus. The heavily-fortified stronghold on the highest point of the spur bore numerous ancient scars, for this was oft the place the tribal federations concentrated their attacks in their attempts to break into the Western Empire's rich and fertile lands.

Pavo eyed the *vicus* – the sprawling shanty-ward spread out near the safe, western walls of the city – then glanced back at the men. They had used up all of the small delicacies the Oescus Goths had given them, and he noticed most eyeing the vicus bread stalls, wine wagons and soup-sellers' urns longingly. There were no sentries watching the vicus region, he realised, and his Claudians were all looking pretty convincingly non-military anyway in their shabby trader-garb. He clicked his fingers and whirled a hand overhead. 'Break into small groups, go and buy what you need, but keep out of trouble.'

A relieved sigh spread amongst them as they joined the general contraflow of people.

Pavo went with Sura, Libo and Darik. He noticed that there were definitely more people leaving the place than coming in. Women carried overly-crammed baskets of bread and men heaved sacks of flour, anxiously glancing to the northwestern horizons as they heaped them on wagons already stuffed with belongings and crewed by family members, ready to set off south or east. Others paid for what they wanted then scurried back into Noviomagus through its wide western gates. From within, he heard the clack of shutters being barred or nailed shut.

'War is coming!' a nearby flour seller cried gleefully. 'Fill up your larder now, before supplies run short.' One wine-seller stood atop the roof behind his stall: 'Come, come!' he cried. 'Buy *my* wine, aged under the sun in the vineyards north of Augusta Treverorum – in Emperor Gratian's very own estates! Buy all you can at my crazy prices – for soon those estates will be trampled by Magnus Maximus and this wine will be no more!'

Some of the agitated citizens snapped up amphorae of the wine-seller's produce. Libo too. But he took one gulp of it and spat it out, looking back over his shoulder bitterly. 'Gah – Emperor's estates, my arse; tastes like onion-sweat! If we weren't in such a rush I'd go back there and-'

'Waft your crotch at him?' Darik finished for him.

Libo shot him a sour look, then turned the glare on the shrinking sight of the wine-seller. 'Aye.'

By mid-afternoon, the Claudians were on their way again, trekking up the low, pleasant Rhenus valley. When they reached a break in the valley's western side, they peeled away from the great river and turned due west.

For the next three days, they saw not a sign of fleeing citizens, marching soldiers or speeding messengers. Everything had grown eerily quiet. So deserted was the land, that Pavo guided his men from their grassy route and onto the easier-going of the imperial road. They trekked for hours like this, with no sign of danger.

'I don't understand it. We should almost be there by now,' said Sura. 'At Augusta Treverorum and Maximus' siege lines. But the sky is blue and clear – no smoke, no sounds of strife in the air or-' his words tapered off as they crested a slight rise. He and Pavo halted, frozen by the sight ahead.

A river wound across the land ahead. The Mosa, he realised. A great grey city sprouted, nestled on the waterway's near and far banks. Augusta Treverorum. Gratian's capital. But the eastern gates lay open and the shadowy arched windows on the flanking gatetowers stared back at Pavo like a laughing skull.

'Sir... what is this?' The Claudians buzzed like this behind the pair. 'Where is Gratian's army? Where is Maximus and his?'

Pavo scanned the city and the green hummocks and meadows all around it. No sign of siege, no markings on the ground or blackened or broken stonework. Not even anything more than a token wall guard. A terrible sickness crept over him then. There was no invasion, no war against Gratian – just a steady, calm normality. Was this Gratian's plan? This is how it had happened to Gallus – lured West then trapped. A thousand cold pins stabbed at him. Suddenly he felt the flagstones underfoot shaking. *Horsemen!* 'We've got to get off the road,' he said.

'Sir?' Opis said, confused.

Pavo sucked in a full breath and rose into a roar. 'Get off the r-'

But the roar went unfinished as the rapping of hooves exploded behind them. Pavo twisted to see two turmae of steel-clad imperial riders speeding around a hillock and towards the tail of their small column. The lead rider threw up a hand to slow his horsemen. Panting, he straightened in the saddle and stared down at Pavo, regarding his shabby tunic and boots, then cast his eye over the other disguised Claudians. Vitally, his eye snagged on one silver wing of the legion standard that had slipped free of its leather covering.

Pavo's eyelids rolled shut. *Mithras, no.*

'You… you are soldiers,' he said. It was not a question, but an accusation.

Pavo felt a cold hand twist his gut as he mentally calculated the odds of survival should these riders work out who they really were. They were not good odds. 'We…' he started, fishing for some set of words that might explain everything.

'You are the tower garrisson from Noviomagus?' the cavalry officer snapped, finishing for him.

'The tower garrison?' Pavo croaked.

'Aye, I thought so. There is no excuse for your lateness,' the man snarled at him. 'Emperor Gratian called for you days ago.'

Pavo hid his confusion well, throwing up a hand in salute. 'I apologise, sir. We were delayed, but indeed that is no excuse. But we are here now yet there is no sign of our emperor's army?'

The man snorted derisively. 'Didn't you read the latest missive?' His face melted into a condescending smirk. 'You can't even read, can you?'

Pavo gulped and tried to look ashamed. 'No, sir,' he lied.

'Emperor Gratian has abandoned the capital and retreated further west,' the officer spat.

Pavo looked up, dangling a deliberately blank expression like a fisherman's hook.

The man shuffled in his saddle then gasped in exasperation. 'The usurper brought his fleet up the Rhenus to Colonia Agrippinensium. His army poured off of those boats there and has since been marching south through the highlands.' He stabbed a finger towards the hills north of Treverorum. 'Moving *this* way. The southern reinforcemernt legions and what remaining soldiers are present in Gaul are now to rendezvous with our emperor at the Round Fortress of Remorum,' he finished, casting a finger westwards, somewhere beyond Augusta Treverorum.

Pavo's eyes darted to further the impression that he was a dim-witted infantry officer who struggled even to remember names. 'Remorum… aye, sir.'

The horseman flared his nostrils in despair, then heeled his mount into a trot. 'Then get a move on!' he screamed at them, simultaneously waving his riders on ahead.

Pavo shouted for the Claudia to break into a full-step march, but as soon as the riders thundered off and out of sight behind and beyond Augusta Treverorum, he raised a hand and the legionaries slowed again. He turned to face them. 'You heard him. Magnus Maximus is somewhere north of here. Near enough that Gratian has abandoned his capital.'

'The rat is on the run,' Opis said in a low drawl, his eyes somewhere distant, his mind trawling over the cruel events of the past years.

'And it is time we met with the rat-catcher,' Pavo added. 'Move out.'

They moved with the speed the Western cavalryman had demanded, not on past Treverorum and to the west, but north, into the rolling hills and valleys of Belgica Prima – an interior province of Gaul – in search of the Army of Maximus. Yet the summer sky remained clear, stained neither by cloud nor pillars of cast-up dust – the telltale marker of a great army on the move. After a dozen scouting sorties ahead yielded no sightings of Maximus' invasion army, the zeal began to ebb.

'Not a thing,' Betto shrugged as he jogged back from his forward foray. 'Though I did descry two women washing in a stream,' he added, his eyes gazing lovingly at the memory.

'Descry?' Pulcher frowned.

Betto shrugged. 'Forgive me. My sesquipidalian tendencies oft obfuscate the import of my utterances. But as the great Horatius once said: when I labour to be brief, I become obscure.'

Pulcher's oily face curled up in an angry knot. 'What?'

'Saw!' Durio clicked his fingers. 'Descry means saw. He *saw* two women washing in a stream.' The young legionary's neck lengthened in excitement. 'Naked?'

'Cah!' Betto swiped a hand through the air. 'Such crude tastes. They were beautiful... and fully clothed.'

'One day you'll get to actually speak to a woman, Betto,' Indus chirped.

Betto looked up, angry. 'I've had many women-friends,' he snapped. 'Ladies of intellect and fine words with whom I have recited Vergilius, Sophocles, Homer. Every town and every waystation in which I have stayed houses a broken heart.'

'Hmm,' Pulcher mused as they trekked up the latest valley slope, 'I can imagine. Having to wash your cum-stained sheets after you'd left would be a heartbreaking task indeed.'

Betto was on the edge of exploding with some cerebral retort, when Pavo slashed a hand through the air for silence, his ears catching the scarcest whisper of something strange. Something wrong. All slowed and fell still like him.

Pavo suddenly saw the lie of the land for what it was. They had walked uphill, following a track that led between the horns of a col. The two peaks of the col loomed over them on each flank like triumphant giants. They had walked into a perfect killing ground.

As the men fell still, Pavo heard again what he thought he had heard just heartbeats ago. The slow groan and shudder of a bow extended. He let his eyes creep up towards the leftmost peak. Up there, an archer knelt, silhouetted by the sun. Within a breath he spotted the dozen others posted on the nooks and ledges near that first archer and more on the right-hand tor as well. They wore ringmail shirts and iron helms with noseguards and long, flowing red cloaks.

'Identify yourself, or you will be dead within three breaths,' a voice pealed from up there, echoing between the col peaks.

Pavo could not tell who had spoken, he knew only that he was staring death in the face. For a moment, he considered using his well-worn identity of Urbicus the rank and file legionary... but of which legion? Which legion had business here in these parts? A badly-bolted together story rose in his throat, but something strange happened just before it reached his tongue. He heard the scream of an eagle, and saw the giant bird swooping down to settle on the rightmost peak. He couldn't tell if it was the sunlight, but for all the world it looked white. Sucking in a breath, he stepped back towards the wagon, and drew out from one of the sacks a ruby-red shield, emblazoned with a golden Mithraic star. Holding it high like a trophy, he called out: 'I am Numerius Vitellius Pavo, Tribunus of Legio XI Claudia Pia Fidelis – a band of men who have travelled West to seek retribution and justice.' He lowered the shield and let it rest against the wagon, exposing his unarmoured torso to the many archers. 'Death to Gratian,' he finished.

'Death to Gratian,' the Claudians echoed without hesitation.

A heartbeat passed and the silhouetted archers maintained their aims on the Claudians, before the strange voice spoke again: 'Death to Gratian,' it echoed.

With a creak of wood and sinew, the archers relaxed their bows and stood tall, saluting, as a man strode into view up on the edge of the rightmost peak.

'Hail, Magnus Maximus!' the archers boomed as one.

Right where the eagle had been, Pavo realised. But the eagle was gone – nowhere to be seen. Had it even been there at all? The reflected sunlight blazed from Maximus' armour like a signal arrow – breastplate, helm and leather pure white – with a purple cloak fluttering gently in the high summer breeze. He peeled off his helm and clutched it underarm, revealing a wide, flat-boned face, framed by immaculately combed-forward black hair and a prominent nose and chin. His lips were thin and it was hard to gauge whether he was smiling or not. His eyes were equally unforthcoming – like black pools. He was a picture of self-assurance.

'The Claudia?' he said, now crouching on one knee to take a closer look at the ragged band down in his col trap. 'When I was in Constantinople, they said the Claudia were roving in mid-Thracia, along the notional boundaries between the old imperial and new Gothic settlements. They were to police that land, keep it free of troublemakers and bandits. But it seems that...' he cocked his head a little to one side, scanning the small Claudian party and their shabby garb, 'it seems that you instead robbed the bandits of their clothes. And is that,' he said, peering at Pavo's belt and the lasso coiled there, 'is that a Hun rope?'

'We dress like this only so we could safely make the journey here,' Pavo replied.

'My scouts spotted you at Treverorum,' said Maximus. 'They tracked you all the way here. Last night I was almost certain you were a detachment from Gratian's forces, sent here to find me. I nearly gave the order for my scouts to fall upon you while you slept,' he said with a cold glint in his eye.

Pavo held his gaze despite the blinding reflection of sunlight from his armour. 'That would have been foolish, for our watch was strong – always is. Your scouts would have died needlessly.'

Maximus stared at him for a moment, then threw his head back and laughed like thunder, the sound rising into the hazy blue sky. He swished a hand, beckoning them all through the col. 'Come, come,' he said.

Pavo felt a moment of hesitation... then the pull of destiny. 'Claudia, forward!'

Chapter 19
August 383 AD
The Camp of Maximus

Maximus descended from his high point and guided them towards the brow of the Col, walking with his hands clasped behind his back. A noise rose now, like the distant crashing of waves growing closer. Not waves… voices, the jabber of many thousands of voices and the clatter of great industry. As Pavo stepped onto the col brow, a great green bowl of land opened up beyond. Almost every single part of it was crammed with pale leather tents and fluttering standards, silvery-clad men polishing armour and weapons, archers shooting at practice targets, cavalrymen racing their steeds around a paddock, some brushing and tending to their horses.

Sura turned to Betto, agape. 'How the *fuck* did you not spot this?'

'I… but… the beauties in the stream were north of here,' Betto stammered.

'By all the Gods,' Pavo croaked. It was real. The invasion – until now just words, fantasy, fragile hope … it was all *real*. For so long it had felt like he alone had been on a quest to bring Gratian to justice. Now, he saw that there were real legions of men here to see it through.

'The Army of Britannia has long been overdue a mustering and a march like this,' Maximus said. 'You are impressed?'

'I haven't seen a Roman force like this since…' he fell silent.

'What happened at Adrianople was cruel indeed,' Maximus guessed.

Pavo looked sideways at Maximus. 'What happened happened. It is the man whose hand set up the pieces and arranged the disaster, who is cruel.'

'I have spoken with Emperor Theodosius. I know what went on,' Maximus explained. 'For too long men have cowered in fear of Gratian. None have had the means – or the *courage* – to stand up to him.'

'Oh there have been two who stood up to him,' Pavo corrected him briskly. 'My old commander, Gallus, defied him at every turn. Me too – I was but a trice from sending a plumbata into his chest.'

Maximus eyed him with an eyebrow raised – a mark of respect, Pavo assumed.

He led the Claudia into the huge camp, past ancient western legions. The VI Victrix men stood in serried ranks, going through a combat drill. A great *shush* of iron rippled from their massed lines as they quickly fell into battle poise, labarum standards raised high and Christian-marked shields swinging forward and swords positioned at the right edge of each, before returning to normal stance just as rapidly. Then there was the Tigrisienses – Syrian bowmen like the archers up on the col. Legio II Britannica cooked and ate and cleaned their kit under their silver hawk banners. The golden Victores stood to attention, listening to their Tribunus' address. They were clearly a palace legion, resplendent in a full regalia of ribbons, patterned tunics, jewelled helms and embroidered cloaks, each man holding spears that were painted in red and white hoops. Nearby the Primani and the Secundani were camped, elite Comitatenses field legions whose amber boar and white eagle standards stood tall as two men. There were also countless cohorts – self-contained legionary units of five or six hundred men, each trained to provide swift and flexible support to the main legions. Most strikingly of all were the camps of the famous horsemen of Britannia. The Sarmaturum paddock was marked out with a tall bronze draco standard, from which ribbons of sun-gold and blood-red wafted in the hot breeze. Every so often the wind would pass through the draco's mouth and the bronze beast's head would emit a low drone then a long, high and eerie wail. The golden-vested, long haired riders numbered in their thousands. The Dalmaturum too – more Roman in appearance than the Sarmaturum, with iron shirts and studded ridge helms, working on their tactics in a field marked out by four tall, pale blue banners blazoned with Pegasus the winged horse. Watching over all of this from a raised timber platform, crunching on an apple and studying every piece of horsemanship carefully, stood a tall, lithe officer with long grey hair, his shoulders exaggerated by a shell of iron. The man's intense interest in the cavalry faltered for just a moment as he swung his rather evil-looking face in the direction of Maximus and in particular, Pavo. He slowly raised one arm in salute to Maximus, and gave Pavo a slight nod of the head. 'Dragathius is the mind that controls the swarm of my cavalry wings.' Just then a young, freckle-faced man in explorator leathers rushed past on foot. 'And of all my scout riders, Grumio is the most nimble.' Just then, Grumio heard his name and stumbled as he ran. Maximus laughed. 'Usually!'

Near the cavalry tents, Maximus gestured to a patch of bare grass. 'Have your men set up camp here. Please, tell them to wash and dress in their soldier garb – your time in hiding is over.'

Pavo passed on the instruction, then followed on alone as Maximus beckoned him towards the heart of the vast camp. A square of tents had been erected to form a principia area. The Victores guardsmen standing either side of a break in the tent square saluted briskly and stepped aside as Maximus led Pavo into the square of grassy space inside. The air here was rich with the smoke of meat roasting on a spit somewhere out of sight. A large pavillion tent was erected in the centre of the enclosed area, flaps pinned open on each of the four sides to allow a breeze to pass through. Maximus walked inside and strolled around a circular table upon which a map was pinned out with polished stones. A slave discreetly poured him a cup of wine and was about to sneak off again when Maximus clicked his fingers and pointed at Pavo. The slave poured a second cup and sheepishly handed it to him.

Pavo took the water jug on the edge of the table and diluted the wine greatly – his appetite for merriness far less pressing than the dryness of his mouth. He gulped on the refreshing, cool mixture and studied the map too. 'Gratian has abandoned Treverorum,' he said.

'So I understand,' Maximus mused, 'but where has he gone?'

'We crossed paths with some of his riders. They thought we were

Gratian's soldiers and urged us towards Remorum – the Round Fortress.'

'Remorum?' Maximus said, stroking his chin, his dark eyes sliding across the map, westwards across the hills and valleys of this region, then over a great crescent plain beyond and the city at its far side. He tapped the spot. 'Some six days' fast march from here.'

'But Treverorum lies open and undefended,' Pavo replied, tapping the far-closer city just a day's march south, 'you could claim it tomorrow with just a single cohort.'

Maximus looked up, intrigued for a moment, before he shrugged the idea off. 'I did not mobilise the armies of my island to take an undefended city. I came here for Gratian. I will spare the people of Treverorum the sight of my forces appearing on the hills around their home. Instead, we will push on west in pursuit of our true quarry. My scouts tell me that Gratian has mustered less than half of what I have here. He hurries for Remorum because he needs more time – time for his reinforcements to arrive from afar. But running to Remorum will do him no good.' Maximus fell silent for a moment. His eyes grew hooded as he studied the map and Pavo could not read his expression. 'You see, I have a second army in the field.'

The hairs on Pavo's neck stood up.

'Aye,' Maximus said, eyes rolling up from the map to regard Pavo. 'Another four full legions have crossed the water from Britannia and are now marching down this way from Caletum. I will send a rider to them. Direct them towards Remorum too. They and we will be like pincers.'

Pavo felt something knot and twist in his mind. Something wasn't right. His eyes scanned the map again and again… then he realised what it was. 'That is impossible.'

Maximus pinned him with a hood-eyed look.

'They say the Classis Britannica lies docked in the upper Rhenus,' Pavo explained. 'Every single galley of that fleet. How could you have ferried another eight thousand or more men across the water?' Now he noticed a glint in Maximus' eyes. A cold wave of realisation passed over him. 'You're feeding me false information. You're testing me.'

Maximus set down his wine cup and clapped, slowly. 'Very good.'

'But why?'

Maximus guided him quietly towards the rear tent flap. As they emerged into the sunlight there, that tang of charred meat stung his nostrils again. Half-expecting to see a spitted deer turning over a fire, he stopped dead, staring instead at the black shape of a man tied to a post, smouldering. There were no features. The lips had been burnt away leaving a horrible death smile of clenched teeth.

'You are not the first to have flocked to my banner during my march across Gaul. A few of Gratian's garrison parties have come to me also. Some outlying road watchmen too. A pair came, just yesterday. Both men bent the knee before me, swearing to fight my cause.' He flicked a finger at the smoking corpse. 'I told this one about the phantom army coming from Caletum. He lapped the story up like a thirsty hound. Last night, he tried to steal away from camp. I had my archers seize him and bring him back to me. He burned like a torch.'

'Gratian's spy,' Pavo realised. 'But you said he came with another?'

'See the black rings under my eyes, Tribunus?'

Pavo noticed the slight pouchiness and discolouration.

'Lack of sleep. Understandable given what happened last night. The second one managed to creep into my tent. I woke to the sight of him standing over me, hunting knife hovering over my chest. I rolled clear just in time and my guards seized him.'

Pavo frowned, half-expecting that he had missed a second blackened corpse on the other side of the fire. Instead, he noticed the slight hump in the earth next to the ashes. Now he heard something too: a distant, muffled, angst-ridden moan – like a man begging for mercy from a distant room. But no, it was coming from underground. His flesh crept as he noticed the small reed pipe rising from the mound. An airhole, to prolong the assassin's demise. He heard the dull whump of the man down there banging his fists hopelessly on the timbers of whatever crate he had been buried in.

'Burying a man alive is a difficult thing to do, Tribunus,' Maximus said, lifting a small trinket from his purse – a necklace with a silver amulet hanging from it, emblazoned with a single, staring eye, 'even though he was... is... one of *them*.'

Pavo's stomach turned at the thought of such a demise – even for a

Speculator. Then his gut twisted sharply when he noticed something else: another dug hole on the far side of the fire. A second grave, as yet unfilled. A thousand cold fingers stroked his back as he realised this had probably been meant for him, had he failed Maximus' test.

'Rest easy, Tribunus,' Maximus said. 'You have won my trust. But tell me more about why you are here. Do you thirst for war?'

'I thirst only for justice. I am sick of war. I have no desire to fight fellow Romans, but if that is what it takes to get to Gratian, then that is what I will do.'

'There may be less Romans to fight than you think, Tribunus.'

Pavo rolled his eyes to the side. 'How so?'

'Our friends within Gratian's camp have been busy.'

Pavo's mind flashed with visions of the past. The few in Gratian's world who had risked their own lives to save him and his Claudians. 'Valentinian... Merobaudes?'

'Aye. The big Frank has stymied the arrival of Gratian's reinforcements. We will not have to face the armies of Africa, Italia and Hispania.'

A thrill of amazement passed across Pavo's skin – it was like scales slamming down, one side heavily outweighing the other. The thrill quickly soured as a dark realisation hit him. 'But that means it will be a slaughter.'

Maximus stroked his jaw and laughed darkly, gazing west with Pavo in the general direction of Remorum. 'So much bloodshed, when all we need is the death of one man,' he said, the words dripping with insinuation.

Pavo looked at the burnt and buried men, Gratian's agents, then saw the sly beginnings of a grin on Maximus' face. 'You've sent an assassin into his camp?'

'I am wont to fight fire with fire, Tribunus.'

'When did you send him?'

'This morning. Eborius is stealthy and shrewd. He should be at our enemy's side by now.'

Pavo's heart pounded. Would that not be golden? Gratian gone and not a single soldier hurt? But then a jealous, fiery monster thundered within him. *No, I have to be there. I want to see him die!* He realised he was shaking with emotion.

Maximus patted Pavo's shoulder. 'Go, rest and eat with your men. Polish your armour and hone your blades. Tomorrow, we will set off towards Remorum to chase our enemy down. Perhaps along the way, my man might return to me with golden news and it might not come to battle.'

Pavo nodded absently... he was about to turn away, when Maximus slapped his other hand on Pavo's free shoulder, pulling him closer – nose-to-nose – to burr through a cage of teeth: 'But if we must face him in the field, then I want to see your ruby red banner held high on my front lines... I want him to see the teeth of his past closing in on him.' A steely malice flashed in Maximus' eyes then. 'I want him to feel *sick* with fear.'

Pavo, stirred and somewhat unsettled by Maximus' demeanour, stood back and saluted. 'The Claudia will be there, sir.'

Maximus stared at him for a time, with a slight twist of displeasure. Pavo realised his mistake. 'The Claudia will be there... *Domine.*'

Chapter 20
August 383 AD
Remorum

In the violet light of dusk, disordered wagon caravans and knots of men and riders streaked across the vast Gallic plain towards Remorum, casting up puffing dust plumes in their wake as they converged upon the rectangular camp at the foot of the city's brown earth scarp mound. Here they joined the hotch-potch of Western units already gathered. As they made camp, many looked up towards the stony eyrie of the citadel itself. Gratian's voice echoed out through the windows of the basilica hall up there. Angry, impatient, exasperated.

'*This* is all I have to fight a war with?' he scoffed, waving a dismissive hand towards the window and the camp down below. A single legion, the III Julia Alpina, resided there, surrounded by satellites of those small and hastily-gathered detachments. In total, no more than seven thousand men. Legionaries, archers and slingers. Few horsemen apart from three turmae of scouts.

'It is,' Tribunus Lanzo said flatly, arrayed with the rest of Gratian's retinue before his makeshift throne in the gloomy hall. 'Though you could allow my Heruli to don steel again, and you would have another full palace legion to swell that camp.'

Gratian stared fire at the tribunus and his civilian garb. 'Perhaps,' he said through taut lips. *And I'll put you on the front line to face the invader, you mutt.* 'But one legion does not tilt what are looking like heavily unbalanced scales.' He swung his glare across the arc of officers standing with Lanzo, until his eyes snagged on Arbogastes. 'As it stands, I have barely half of his number to call upon. Were my southern legions here, amassed as one, I could stamp on the island usurper and be done with him. So tell me, Comes Arbogastes,' he drummed his fingers on the arms of his throne, then whacked his palms down, lurching forward in the seat, 'where... the... *FUCK* are they?'

Arbogastes' gummy lips peeled open but he could not speak. The braids of his copper-coloured wig trembled.

'Comes,' Gratian said softly, slouching back into the throne, toying with the fang ring on his finger, 'speak, or I will ask you to carve yourself a second mouth.'

'I have nothing to tell you, Domine,' Arbogastes croaked. 'I don't understand it. The core legions out in Hispania have been sparing in their missives. I *thought* they were on their way. I *thought* they were close... but it seems they are still not even clear of Hispania – snared and beset by the rebels in the Pyrenaei Mountain passes.'

Gratian balled his fingers into fists, chapping on the throne arms now. 'Then what of the Italian regiments and Moorish hordes? We fled from Augusta Treverorum because of their lateness. So where are they now?'

Arbogastes shuffled where he stood, sweating profusely. 'I... I once again had messengers sent to watch for them, to instruct them to come here instead of to your capital. I was confident that the Moors would have made shore and be on their way overland by now, and that the Italian regiments would have poured through the Alpes passes too – maybe even be here before us.'

'Well they are not here before us,' Gratian said slowly, like a teacher talking to a slow child, 'so when can I expect them?'

'I do not know, Domine. My scouts still have not made contact with either force.'

Gratian's gaze grew flinty. 'The invader is but a short march away from this place, and you do not even know *where* my reinforcements are?'

Arbogastes shrank on the spot.

'I drew back here because *you* advised me to. *You* said they would rendezvous with me here.'

Arbogastes' laboured breathing rang out around the hall.

'Perhaps I chose unwisely when I raised you above Merobaudes. I am sure he would have brought my legions to my side in good time to meet the threat of the invader.'

Merobaudes, a giant amongst the rest, straightened. 'I am always ready, Domine… to do that which is right.'

Arbogastes flashed him emerald looks of jealousy. 'Give me one more chance, Domine. Let me prove to you my worth.'

Gratian, tracing the fang point on his ring, shrugged. 'I'll give you one breath. Tell me what I should do now.'

Arbogastes straightened and cleared his throat. 'With the soldiers we have here at Remorum, we cannot be certain of holding the place, should the invader fall upon us here. But further west – just a short way – sits Parisiorum. A stoutly-walled city and a river island fortress.'

'You advise me to flee… again?' Gratian said.

'Parisiorum will afford more time for our reinforcements to rendezvous with us, Domine. More, should they not make it in time, the Sequana River fleet is moored there – a perfect means of retrea-' he halted, seeing Gratian's eyelids grow hooded with distaste for the half-uttered word. 'A means of a "further tactical withdrawal". For Maximus has no boats.'

All watching seemed to stiffen with tension, eyes looking pitifully upon Arbogastes as Gratian traced the tip of his fang ring. He moved the fang ring up and down his finger a few times… but finally replaced it. 'Very well, let us evade Maximus as best we can,' he said quietly. 'Take word to the regiments outside: we rise before first light and draw back to the west, to Parisiorum.' He sighed. 'So it shall be. Go, eat and rest for tomorrow's early departure.'

As the crowds departed, Gratian called after Merobaudes. 'Magister Militum.'

The big Frank halted, turning back to face the throne. 'Domine?'

'In times past I have doubted you,' Gratian said. 'Doubt is never a healthy state of mind. But now, now I am *certain* of your loyalties.'

Wordlessly, Merobaudes half-bowed, then melted away with the others.

Gratian let his eyes drift up to the balcony. Laeta was up there, having watched it all. He met Laeta's gaze and gave her a half-smile and the faintest of nods. She returned the gesture and peeled back from the balcony, into the shadows.

From the edges of the hall, Eborius had seen it all: the strangeness of Gratian's words, the spikes of rage, the unusual displays of mercy – from what he had heard, the Western Emperor rarely spared anyone after threatening them with his fang ring. Strangest of all were his words of apparent praise to Merobaudes. There was only one certainty here – all was not as it seemed. As he faded from the hall unseen, in the same way as he had melted into Gratian's column on the way here, he noticed the boy-Caesar Valentinian, trudging up a well of stone steps. Alone. Like a shadow, Eborius drifted up in his wake.

The roiling stormy skies seemed darker and angrier than ever, but the crimson rain had stopped and the blood sea had drained. Pavo stared at the fallen eagle, lying nearby on the dark ground. Its chest had been torn open by the other bird's talons. Coils of steam rose and blood wept from the wound and its chest rose and fell weakly, clinging on to life. The victorious bird came swooshing down in tightening circles to land beside the beaten one, its talons click-clacking on the dark ground as it approached the dying one. He saw now that there was no distinction between the two. In the beginning, one had been white as snow, the other black as night. Now, both were the colour of battle.

'I thought I was beginning to understand your visions,' Pavo said, the words addressed to the crone, hunched by his side. 'But this... what is this?'

She said nothing, but Pavo could see from the corner of his eye her ancient face drooping, her dry lips moving as if tasting a few alternative replies and disliking each. She sighed deeply, then said. 'You fought through everything to get here, Pavo. From one end of the world to the other. You know why you are here.'

'To bring Gratian to justice.'

'Justice?' she said with a jolt of disgust. 'Is that what you call the runnels of red on a sword?'

'What other way is there? If... when we defeat his armies, he has to die. Exile or imprisonment would be folly. A man like him has too many roots in too many places. Agents, allies, men bound to do his bidding for fear of their loved ones.' He gestured to the wounded, twitching bird and repeated. 'He simply has to die.'

She cocked her head to look up at him. 'Oh, so you know for certain that the dying eagle is Gratian, do you?'

A cold horror struck through Pavo. 'It must be. Tell me it is.'

She threw her old head back and laughed a horrible laugh, like the sound of an urn smashing in the dead of night. 'It is, Pavo, in one future. In another, it is not. Many paths, the route yet to be chosen.' She raised a crooked finger and pointed it at him like a spear. 'You and your iron comrades are the watchmen of such crossroads. What you choose to do in the coming days will determine the future.'

Pavo stared at the two eagles as the victorious one stomped around the dying one, shrieking, flaring its wings. 'There is no choice for me,' he said quietly. 'There is but one path: I have come to kill Gratian. Then I will return to the east, to Izodora... to our child.'

The crone stared into his eyes. 'That last vow is the only one from which good will come.'

Pavo stared back. 'And it will happen.'

The crone continued to stare at him. In the lower lids of her sightless eyes, moisture gathered, and then a single teardrop stole down one withered cheek.

'What, what is it?'

She took a time to respond. 'I see now a thousand futures. In one you are with your love and your child.'

'And in the rest?'

Her ancient head sagged. Without a further word, she turned her back on him and began to walk away into the dark.

'Wait, don't go...'

But she vanished into the blackness.

With a stark crunch, the victorious eagle bit down on the dying one's neck, twisting it sharply. The fallen eagle flopped, dead. The triumphant one shrieked madly at the black heavens, clacking round to face Pavo. The great creature's head dipped, its glare affixing on him. With a pulse of energy, the eagle leapt into flight, speeding towards him, the mighty talons swinging forth and opening, razor sharp, trained on his neck, ready to snap shut...

Clack! Pavo sat bolt upright in his bedding, torn from the dream, seeing not the eagle but the waking world: the tent and the near-blackness of night. His senses came back to him: it was the sixth morning on the march with Maximus' great army. It would all be over soon. But then... *Clack!* That noise from the dream again – the sound of talons snapping shut. *Clack!*

A toenail sped past his face and embedded itself in the goat leather of the tent. Pavo, holding up a hand to guard his eyes as they adjusted to the darkness, made out the shape of Sura sitting in the gloom at the other edge of the tent, mauling his toenails with a pair of rusty scissors, the blades chewing pathetically at a discoloured nail.

'Whoa!' Pavo snapped, voice and head thick with sleep. 'At least give me a chance to put my armour on.'

Sura's head swung round. 'You're awake! I thought about shaking you – you were having one of your twitching nightmares again, all speaking in tongues and moaning.' He tossed the scissors down.

'Anyway, Rectus is a cheeky bastard – he charged me a week's wine ration for those, said they were sharper than a spatha.' He flexed his toes and mangled nails. 'I just thought that after the victory there will be, you know, excited women only too happy to show their appreciation. Got to look my best.'

Pavo shuddered. 'Let's hope they have a thing for "boots on". Anyway, who said there will be a victory?' he asked as, uninvited, the crone's odd insinuations crept back into his thoughts.

'Well I didn't march across the world to lose,' Sura said, shooting him an 'are you mad?' look. 'And Remorum is just hours from here. This is it, Pavo – today is the day.'

A thrill of hope rose through Pavo, but then he realised the absurdity of the situation – there wasn't even a blink of morning light outside. 'Today? It's not even dawn yet – why are you up?' Pavo said, the thought of sinking back into his warm bedding for another few hours most appealing.

Sura stopped fidgeting and fell curiously quiet.

'Sura?'

He shrugged and gazed around the dark interior of the tent. 'I had a strange dream of my own.'

Pavo sat up a little. 'Tell me.'

'It was a dream of battle,' Sura said, his voice quiet. 'Not here. Not now. It was a time yet to come.'

Despite the gloom, Pavo could see his oldest friend's lips caging the next words. 'What was it. What did you see?'

Sura's lips parted a little, but he seemed unable to speak, and the most awful look of concern crossed his face.

Pavo sat up. 'Sura, you can tell me anyth-'

Just then, the low drum of a solitary set of hooves rose from the stillness outside, slowing to nothing to be replaced by the panting and spluttering of a horse. A hurried and badly-muted jabber of voices followed – from the direction of Maximus' principia. Pavo and Sura stared at one another. A moment of silence followed before a horn blared across the camp – the call for all legions to rise early.

Sura spoke at last. 'Something's happened.'

Pavo's eyes widened. 'A lone rider... urgent news,' he said. *Maximus' Assassin, Eborius?* he thought.

All around their tent, the silence was swept away by the low grunts of men, the swish of tent flaps being opened, the shuffling of feet and the rasp of flint hooks striking over kindling. Many of the voices whispered and muttered, confused about the unexpected pre-dawn muster.

Pavo sat up on his knees, stretched each arm in turn behind his back then rose to his feet, draining a cup of water resting on a stool between his and Sura's beds. All the time, Maximus' words echoed in his thoughts: *I am wont to fight fire with fire...* His heart pounded at the thought. Was it over without a single pair of Roman swords clashing? Was Maximus rousing them all to announce that the dark eagle was dead?

Regardless, he knew it would not do for a Roman officer to come stumbling out of his tent in nothing more than a loincloth. He drew on his soldier boots and pulled on his white military tunic, belting it around the waist. He helped Sura to buckle on his mail shirt, then Sura returned the favour. With a swish of his right arm, he slung his baldric strap over his left shoulder so the scabbarded spatha hung on his opposite hip. Next, he tossed his ruby-red officer's cloak around his back, pinning it just above his right shoulder with a bronze brooch, the hem settling around the backs of his knees. He scruffed at his bristly scalp – shorn of overgrown locks by Rectus yesterday at dusk. It was an old ritual, scraping away his hair when the prospect of battle loomed. It made him feel lean, spry. Finally, he slid on his finned helm, the cheekpieces cold against his skin as he knotted the soft leather cords under his chin. All the while, Sura's excited words from moments ago rang around in his head: *today is the day.*

With a deep breath, he moved to the tent flaps. It was with a murmur of afterthought that he picked up the loop of Hun rope on the way, tying it to his belt. He pulled back the tent flaps and he and Sura emerged into the dark hill camp – a tapestry of shadow and torchlight. Many breaths puffed in the night coolness, wheat porridge bubbled in pots, smoke rose in blue tendrils from new campfires, horses nickered and neighed as their handlers led them to and fro, spoons and knives clacked on plates as men dug into their wheat porridge, adding salt or honey – whichever was to their taste.

The pair of them gazed over this Claudia section of the camp: a broad square of leather tents, the legionary eagle standing proud. Guarding the standard, Opis and Pulcher cast dice along the ground in between mouthfuls of breakfast, mocking each other mercilessly as they each won and lost. Libo and Rectus supped on cups of some hot brew, speaking quietly, their eyes gazing into their distant and shared past. Old friends. True comrades. Each took it in turn to brush the coat of Ocella, a young mule granted to Rectus by Maximus the day before last. Betto, face uplit by the fire, sat cross legged atop a pile of sacks, playing his flute for a troop of younger legionaries, stopping every so often to narrate a little more of the Aeneid. Durio, and Indus ate with Darik, rocking with laughter at each of his tales – the stories given an extra edge of charm thanks to his occasional dropped or mispronounced word. Darik was still new to the legion, but the big Maratocupreni had bonded well with the others on the journey west. Pavo looked over the young men of the Third Cohort – still leaderless since the murder of Trypho and his optio Datus on the prison island. They needed an experienced figure to look up to. He sat down next to Darik.

'I'm going to ask something of you,'

'How do I groom my hair so perfectly?' he guessed, wrongly, albeit with a playful look in his eyes.

Pavo rocked with unexpected laughter. 'You are well-used to leading soldiers. Maybe not legionaries, but soldiers nonetheless.'

Darik's ludic expression faded. 'I did not seek to command the desert riders. It just happened.'

'That tends to be the way with the best leaders,' Pavo replied.

Darik shuffled a little. 'I think I know what you have in mind.'

'Today and in the days to come,' Pavo said quietly, 'these young lads will need a lion like you to lead them. They already respect you, and I've heard some of them calling you sir.'

Darik tilted his head one way then the other. 'I'll do this, for you and for them,' he said at last. 'So that makes me…?'

'Chief Centurion of the Third Cohort. Not to tarnish the promotion, but in all honesty there is nobody else even close to being ready right now.'

Darik smiled. 'Is the wage good?'

Pavo grinned. 'No, it's shit. I haven't been paid for over a year.'

Darik exploded with laughter as Pavo rose to leave him with his new charges.

The soldiers finished their meals, deconstructed their tents and began to gather in their marching positions along the wide avenues of the camp. About one hour before dawn, trumpets blared again. Three times. This brought a sudden silence across the place. Pavo knew this meant that Maximus was about to address his army – and his army treated him like a god – and explain the early call to rise. All heads turned like grass stalks touched by a gentle breeze towards the camp's western edge. There, a train of at least one hundred wagons was drawn up, each covered with leather sheets, tightly tied down – jealously guarding the contents. Maximus rose onto the driver's berth of one wagon, using it like a plinth. Little pomp or ceremony – something Pavo had come to understand could be a good measure of a man. It reminded him in ways of Stilicho and Saturninus... of Gallus. Yes, he wore striking white armour and the purple cloak of an emperor, but who would deny him that, given all he had risked? Most telling of all, despite Pavo being one head in a sea of many, Maximus picked him out with a firm look, read his hopeful expression, and gave the faintest shake of the head. *Nothing,* he mouthed.

Pavo sagged. So Eborius the assassin had been thwarted? That odd mix of emotions swirled within him: disappointment and... a glowing red flame of hateful glee, for if Gratian had not been killed, then his life remained to be taken in battle.

But another thought rose amidst all this, chasing the storm of emotions away. If Eborius had failed in his task, then why the early call to arms? What had changed?

'My legions,' Maximus boomed, his voice carrying across the dark hilltop. 'I woke you early because it seems our enemy too rises like this, for he is once again on the run.' He shot a look of gratitude to Grumio, the young, freckle-faced explorator. 'He has no sooner arrived at

Remorum in a shambolic flight than he prepares to flee once again – this time peeling back towards Parisiorum.'

A groan spread amongst the legions. Men cursed Gratian's name and spat into the earth. 'The craven cannot run forever!'

Maximus held both hands in the air for calm. 'Do not despair. For it is clear now that the struggle is edging in our favour even before we meet him and what forces he has. More, I do not want to risk his reaching Parisiorum. I have seen city sieges in my time, and I know that victory in such an assault comes at a terrible price – and your lives to me are priceless.' He pointed with one finger, sweeping the tip across the assembled masses. 'For you are my eagles. Thus, I ask you to fly with me, at haste, on past Remorum and to Parisiorum. Yes, it means another few days of brisk marching. But we have a chance of reaching Parisiorum before our enemy can bed in there – or perhaps we might even run him down before he manages to reach the place.'

The army rumbled and jostled in approval. Pavo felt realisation surge up inside him like fire. Justice was calling… at last.

'Come, march with me…' Maximus whumped one gloved fist against his plated chest, 'to *glory!*'

The hilltop exploded with a roar of polyglot voices – Latin, tribal, Greek and many more tongues acclaiming their chosen emperor. Thousands upon thousands of spears rose high, catching the torch and firelight like the peaks of a night sea, and thousands more drummed rapidly on their shields as if thunder loomed. Grumio and five of his speedy exploratores riders burst away first to scout the route, splaying out like the fingers of a hand ruffling through hair as they roved westwards. Next, Maximus leapt down from the wagon and mounted his war horse – the beast draped in an iron apron and mask. Dragathius, a dozen Sarmaturum horsemen and a century of golden-garbed Victores legionaries quickly arrayed around him like a shield as he moved off in the wake of the exploratores. Next, with the snap of whips and shouting mule handlers, the wagon train bucked and swayed into life. Scores of shrill and braying commands rang over every unit's camp space and – like a great argent lake draining, the legions began to fall into place behind one by one. In turn, Opis held the eagle standard and the ruby bull banner high, Libo at the head of the ranks, Pulcher and Darik heading up the cohorts behind, all waiting on the order from their tribunus.

Pavo filled his lungs and bellowed: 'Claudia, Ad-*vance!*'

Young Valentinian sat on the sill of an arched window in a high chamber of Remorum's acropolis. A commotion rose from the camp below, just outside the Gate of Ceres, where Gratian's forces were assembling for the march to Parisiorum in the pre-dawn light. But he ignored this din of shouts, clattering equipment and rumbling boots. Instead he gazed upwards. The night sky was always so peaceful, he thought, silken blackness studded with stars, gently winking like jewels, the new moon a thin crescent of smooth silver. In his earliest years he had often watched the heavens when he could not sleep. Such innocent times, he thought – times when he had been unburdened with this terrible stinging invisible cloak that now hung upon his shoulders. A mantle of shame. For never in his thirteen years had he harmed another living creature: not an insect, a bird, any animal. Certainly never a person. True, that would not change tonight – *his* hands would be unstained with blood in what was to come. But the feel of those words on his tongue earlier, those simple, deadly words that would allow it to happen – *I will see to it* – now remained like the acrid taste of blood that lingers after eating undercooked meat.

He stared at his armoured suit in the corner of the room, standing like a person on a wooden frame. The silver vest, pale blue pteruges and cloak shone brightly in the moonlight. The empty shadows beneath the brow of the silver helm stared back at him, asking him one question, over and over. *Who are you?*

'I had to do it,' he spoke quietly in reply.

'My love?' a sleepy voice asked from inside the unlit chamber.

He twisted to look inside, having almost forgotten he was not alone. His mother Justina was reclined on a couch, draped in a light stola that left her shoulders bare, her milky skin ghostly white in the moonlight, her usual loving expression spoiled with concern. Her delicate frame had once been a part of her beauty, but now they served only to make her look old and frail. With every moon that passed, her narrow, sculpted face seemed more lined and her once dark hive of hair more threaded with silver.

'What's wrong, my love?' Justina repeated.

Valentinian ran his fingers through his dark brown locks. 'No man – no matter how hard he tries to do what is right and good... *no* man is innocent.'

She frowned, rising and coming over to him, her stola trailing on the floor and giving the impression that she was gliding. She sat by his side on the sill and smoothed his hair back into place with a sigh. 'The greatest sin is that a boy of your age needs to consider such matters. Tell me what has happened?'

'I'm not a boy anymore. Neither am I innocent.'

'What have you done?' Justina said, cupping his face to tilt his head so he could not escape her loving gaze.

'I... I might have found a way for us to be free,' he said. 'And the many armies who converge on this land – they might not need to give battle.'

Justina's face paled a fraction more. 'You must tell me.'

His lips moved a few times, but he made no sound. With a sigh, he slipped down from the windowsill onto the floorboards, taking his mother's hand. 'I cannot bring myself to speak the words. Instead, come with me and I will show you.'

He led her through Remorum's stony passageways. Gradually, the air became tinged with the slightly musty odour of water and the sweetness of precious eastern resins burning in sconces. The corridor bent at a right angle ahead, and the walls and ceiling there were uplit by a dance of turquoise light and shadow. Valentinian placed a finger to his lips and slowed to creep towards this part. He edged his head around the corner, taking in the view of the deep teal waters of the bathhouse pool down below this small viewing balcony. The pool room walls were painted white with pale blue scenes of mermaids and leaping dolphins, their dance orchestrated by a triumphant Neptune. In small arched niches, statues of the old gods stared out blankly, clean water trickling from their open mouths like silver ribbons. The pool itself was empty.

'I don't understand,' Justina complained in a whisper.

Valentinian crouched, gesturing for her to do the same, so both were hidden behind the balustrade, yet the roundel-shaped holes in the decorative stonework afforded them a perfect view of the pool. 'All the way from Augusta Treverorum and during the chaotic journey here, and even while the soldiers set up the camp last night,' he explained. 'There was a man. A messenger, riding wide of the column. He was one of many, and I thought nothing of him. But then I noticed that while he looked busy – riding up and down between the marching units as if delivering orders – he never actually spoke with anyone. I lost sight of him after that. But last night, after my stepbrother's address in the hall... I came up here, alone. Or so I thought. For when I turned to close the door behind me he was there: the rider.'

Just then, Gratian entered the pool chamber down below.

Justina suppressed a gasp of fright, and Valentinian placed a calming hand on her shaking arm. 'He always bathes like this, before dawn,' he explained.

Gratian dropped his cloak and peeled off his Alani leathers before stepping down into the waist-deep waters, wading through the curls of steam, the muscles of his well-trained body flexing, the solar plexus rippling like a furrowed field. A withered old man followed him, carrying a bag of grooming tools. Next came Arbogastes and a pair of Alani, standing by the side of the pool, watchful as always.

Valentinian realised that he was trembling too now. Suddenly he felt like a fly, shaking the outer strands of a spider's web.

'Who was he, this rider?' Justina said in the merest whisper. 'What did he want?'

'He had come from the camp of Magnus Maximus.'

Justina's eyes grew moon-like.

'He had been shadowing the retreat here for days in the guise of a messenger, all the while looking for a way in,' Valentinian replied. 'Looking to... to...' he could not finish the sentence. 'To free us. To free all who cower in my stepbrother's shadow.'

Justina's face paled as she at last understood.

Valentinian gulped. 'The rider asked of me only one thing – for the slave door to the cellar below this pool room to be left open. *I will see to it,* I replied. I may never had spilled another creature's blood, Mother... but with those words...'

After a time she clasped his hand and squeezed. 'To fight evil, sometimes one must descend to its level. Do not fret over what you have done, my boy,' she assured him. 'Now where is this rider? When will he strike?'

Valentinian stared despondently down at the pool and the withered body slave. 'Here,' he whispered. 'Now.'

The waters were pleasant and the rising mineral vapours sharp, stinging Eborius' nostrils. It was like a stinging slap to remind him that he had to be on his guard here, all the while maintaining the well-practiced demeanour of a beaten, humble slave. Gratian walked a few circles in the pool, tracing the waist-deep surface with his fingertips. 'Six legions and three vast cavalry wings,' he said quietly. 'They *will* make it here in time... won't they?'

Eborius kept his eyes down on the tiled floor near his feet, but his ears pricked up.

Arbogastes – the strange-looking general – sat on a bench at the poolside, stretching out his legs and folding his arms, resting his wigged head against the piscine fresco wall and toying with the coppery braids. 'Domine, I don't know what more I can do now. We can only hope they are on their way.' Suddenly, he sat upright. 'Send *me* to find them. I personally will ride south and locate them. Then you can truly trust the reports I bring back.'

Gratian lifted a handful of water, watching droplets of it spill through the gaps in his fingers, before dropping the rest. 'No, there is not enough time. I need you – my most dependable general – here with me.' He reclined in the waters, moving his arms to stay afloat before plunging underwater to soak his hair, then rising and wading towards the semi-circular tiled steps near Arbogastes. 'Once I am bathed and clean, I will lead the withdrawal to Parisiorum and bed in there. If God is with us – as I know he is – then we will fight off the usurper there with what meagre forces we have.'

He sat on the steps, and Eborius quietly took a clay urn from his bag, plucked the cork free and tilted a coin-sized blob of clove-scented olive oil into his palm. He spread the oil over both palms then began working it into Gratian's shoulders and back. The Western Emperor sighed with pleasure. Eborius had trained in this very art for months. It had to be convincing. All the time his mind was trained on the other thing in the leather bag…

Arbogastes sat forward, his braids swinging like plumb bobs. 'But Domine, at least give me permission to prepare the Sequana fleet… in case things turn against us at Parisiorum.'

Gratian again denied his general, leaning back to lie supine, crossing his hands behind his head. Eborius began running his hands up and down the emperor's chest, then he moved to the thighs, applying more oil and expertly massaging out knots there. It would soon be time. Once more he glanced towards his bag, glimpsing the curved shape within. Just the lower legs and feet left to oil. Now he began to fret. What if the other part of the plan did not come off? He glanced at the pool chamber door, thinking of the stairs outside and the cellar they led to.

'Is there a problem, slave?' Gratian said, raising his head a little to scowl down at Eborius. 'You are too slow and time is not on my side today. Get on with it.'

'Yes, Domine,' Eborius whispered respectfully, then hastened his efforts. Pinching each of Gratian's toes, he gulped, watching the pool chamber door with the corners of his eyes. Still nothing.

'Ah, finished are we?' Gratian sighed, sitting up. 'Now, get this oil and dirt off of me,' he demanded, patting his own back.

Eborius reached over to his bag, annoyed by a slight tremble in his hand as he did so. He rummaged in the pack and all the time he was sure that Arbogastes' eyes were upon him. *Believe in yourself, or no one will believe in you,* he chanted to himself inwardly. It was the key tenet of the small school of spies Maximus had been training in Britannia for these last few years. *If you are to aid me when the time comes for me to take the Western throne,* Maximus had drummed into them, *then you must be more shrewd, deceptive and all-seeing even than Gratian's Speculatores.* Eborius might have laughed had the situation not been so tense – for here he was with his fingers wrapped around the handle of a concealed strigil, with Gratian's neck an arm's swipe away and Arbogastes, not just Gratian's general but also the Optio Speculatorum – highest of them all – staring at him.

With a thin façade of calm, he drew the strigil out of the bag. The hooked bronze blade caught the sconce light, and at once he cursed his lack of thought for not tarnishing the metal so as to make it less conspicuous. Gratian tilted his head forward. Eborius placed the strigil blade at the top of his spine. Them with deliberate, expert strokes, he dragged the cleaning blade downwards. The oil sheeted down onto the tiled floor, carrying with it specks of dirt and the contents of blocked pores. Eborius gulped, stealing a glance at the pool chamber door. Still nothing. He delayed by pulling a white towel from his bag and cleaning the strigil then mopping at the excess stripes of oil left on the emperor's back.

'Leave that. Come on now: the neck,' Gratian said, tilting his head back to expose his throat.

Eborius, kneeling behind Gratian, felt his legs tremble. This was the moment, he thought, shooting a furtive look at the door. It was supposed to have happened by now. What was going on? What had gone wro-

'Fire!' a voice pealed through the doorway of the bathing hall, followed by the beating of a stick on a pan as a crude means of alarm. Gratian sat tall, Arbogastes jumped to his feet and the two Alani with him jolted to attention. Over the scent of the minerals glowing in the sconces and the cloves in the bathing oil, a dark stink of smoke snaked into the pool chamber.

'Trouble,' Arbogastes growled. 'Go, see to it.' He flicked his head and the two Alani guards sped off through the door.

A few moments passed and the stink of smoke only grew thicker, visible black tendrils of the stuff puffing into the pool chamber now. Arbogastes rocked on the balls of his feet, agitated.

Gratian's nose wrinkled. 'You go as well, sort it out,' he snapped.

'And leave you unguarded, Domine?' Arbogastes said.

Just then the smash of an amphorae sounded from beyond the door along with a panicked shout.

'Go!' Gratian snarled.

Arbogastes sped off to investigate.

Eborius felt a great cold wash of relief. The smouldering incense he had set down near the empty, piled sacks in the storage vault below the bathhouse chamber had taken longer than expected to set the cloth alight. But it had happened, and it had drawn Gratian's guards away as he had hoped. Now Gratian and he were alone. Careful not to betray his elation, he moved the strigil round to Gratian's throat. *For Magnus Maximus... for freedom,* he mouthed, closing his eyes and tensing his arm.

Just as he tried to wrench it back, he felt the lightest sensation on the side of his own neck – as if a butterfly had flown past and a wing had beaten against his jugular. He saw now what he had been blind to before: Gratian's hand, raised, the tip of the fang ring spotted red.

With a gasp, Eborius dropped the strigil, fell backwards against the bench on which Arbogastes had been sitting, his left palm slapping against his slit artery. A hot pulse of liquid squirted between his fingers. In a breath it was all over his robes, flooding across the floor tiles, spraying on the walls. He felt a sudden coldness in his limbs, rapidly eating its way up to his torso.

With a low laugh, Arbogastes and the two Alani stepped back into the bathing chamber, along with another Alani guard carrying a copper basin filled with burning kindling – the carefully-prepared source of the black smoke.

Gratian stood over him, wrapping a towel around his waist. 'You stole into my camp and this city, right into my bathing hall. And through it all, we watched your every step, snuffed out your fire in the basement. I *let* you get this far, you see. For isn't it the most terrible thing to fail right on the cusp of victory?'

Black spots began to prickle Eborius' field of vision. 'You live today only to die tomorrow, Tyrant,' he rasped. 'Parisiorum will be your tomb.'

Gratian pulled a look of mock surprise, then turned his head towards Arbogastes and laughed. 'He believed every single word, didn't he?' With the look of a cobra towering over its prey, Gratian twisted his head back to stare down at Eborius. 'We're not going to Parisiorum. You see, the missing legions – the Celtae, the Petulantes, the VIII Augusta, the I Noricorum, the I Julia Alpina, the II Julia Alpina. The riders of the Armatura, the Gentiles... the vast wings of the Moorish cavalry,' he crouched to stare pityingly into Eborius' eyes. 'They're not in Hispania or Italia or Africa. They're here. They're all *right* here.'

Eborius's eyes widened in horror, his legs kicked weakly and a pink foam ballooned from his nostrils, lips and throat wound.

Gratian lifted the dropped strigil by the blade, tossing it and catching it by the handle. 'You could ride back to Maximus' camp and tell the usurper this.' He placed the blunt tip against Eborius' right eye. '... you *could*. But then dead men don't ride or talk,' he finished, driving the broad strigil blade through Eborius' eyeball with a pop, then deep down into his brain.

Justina clamped a hand over her mouth, fighting the urge to scream and vomit at once. Valentinian pulled her close, shaking. 'Come, mother,' he whispered, 'we must not be seen anywhere near this place.' Still crouching, they both turned away from the balustrade. 'We must tell Merobaudes, and get word to Maximus' army. We must-'

'I watched his *every* step,' Gratian repeated down at the poolside as if talking to the twitching corpse of Eborius. Then the direction of his voice changed, clearly being directed up at the balcony. 'Every single step... do you hear that, whelp?' Valentinian and Justina halted, a terrible chill creeping across their backs. Both turned back towards the balustrade, neither daring to rise from their crouch.

'Come now, you should be proud, for I am impressed by your efforts. Were I a dullard then this dog might even have harmed me.'

Valentinian's mind sped in a thousand different directions at once, like messengers racing out into the countryside, every single one of them bawling: *Merobaudes! Where are you, my shield?*

'I would abandon hope, stepbrother,' Gratian said calmly, gesturing with one hand towards his Optio Speculatorum and the Alani. 'For I am a creature with one thousand ears... I hear everything. I uncovered Merobaudes' attempts to misdirect my far-flung legions some months ago. I was informed about his forged ring shortly after news of the invader arrived.'

How? Valentinian panicked. Even as the thought flashed through his head, he smelt the cloying scent of rose and cinnamon. The smell of the perfume sent horror through him as Laeta slinked into the pool hall, staring up at the balustrade. She had been watching, listening, all this time.

Gratian admired her momentarily, then clicked his fingers. A sudden commotion exploded behind Valentinian and Justina. Valentinian felt his mother being torn from him, then a sharp, ripping pain as his arms were twisted up his back, forcing him to stand, another hand gripping the hair at the back of his head to force him to look at Gratian.

Gratian looked up at them, the thick pools of Eborius' blood gathered around his bare feet. 'Throughout all the days since, I have played you and Merobaudes for fools. My legions were all that time converging on this place. The legions in Hispania crushed the rebellion there last moon. All the while, Merobaudes believed the false reports I arranged. The oaf even sent messengers to Maximus telling him of my weakness, luring him... right here.'

'No! You lie!' Valentinian bawled. 'I do not know about the legions in Hispania, but the Italians, the Moors, I know for certain they have long been waiting for the chance to turn against you. They are not here. For they obey Merobaudes, *not* you.'

'Some of the legions of Italia and Africa *were* probably minded to follow Merobaudes' plan. But when I told them – *months* ago! – that the big oaf was dead… that their patron was no more… they were swift to change their minds and heed my call.'

'No,' said Valentinian. 'Merobaudes is here, well and…' his words faded when he saw Gratian's smile rise horribly.

'Not anymore,' Laeta smiled. 'The giant has fallen.'

Arbogastes jostled with triumphant laughter. 'Long overdue.'

'He served me well, though – unwittingly luring the invader all the way here. But now it is over for him,' Gratian said breezily, then calmly smiled up at Valentinian. 'And now it's over for you and your mother too, and for Maximus and every cur who marches with him.'

Part 4

Clash of Eagles

Chapter 21
August 383 AD
Gaul

The army of Magnus Maximus moved across a pan-flat sea of green, the grasses shimmering in the hot morning sun. Grumio and the exploratores roved on ahead, while the Tigrisienses led the main column as a light and fast vanguard. Maximus' elite palace legion – the golden-shielded Victores – headed up the main infantry march. Just behind them came the thousand-strong blocks of the Primani and the Secundani, all silver, amber and white, followed by the huge supply train of mules and wagons – and that strange fleet of covered vehicles. Rectus, riding on Ocella, joined the medical staff marching here. The cohorts of the Lingona, the Batavorum and the Tungororum marched like a screen on the right of the train, while the double-strength Frixagorum and Pavo's depleted Claudia shielded the left. The II Britannica and the VI Victrix anchored the rear, watchful and numerous. Finally, the mighty riders of the Sarmaturum and the Dalmaturum roved wide of the infantry column, taking a flank each – like slow thunder crawling alongside the lightning-strike of infantry steel. Every now and then, lone exploratores would bolt ahead or rove wide to survey the lands in those directions.

The sun grew hotter and hotter as they moved with a *clank-clank* of mail and weapons, their tunics soaked-through with sweat and their mouths growing dry. Cicadas sang endlessly as if proclaiming their impending triumph. They passed streams and brooks – tributaries to the great Sequana. Orders echoed down from the front: time was of great importance and so no unit was to halt to refill their drinking skins. Instead, baggage handlers moved up and down the column, offering fresh skins to soldiers who needed them. Corks popped and the refreshments were glugged away. They halted only when the mules and horses needed to drink.

For a time, the plain seemed endless. But then he saw the hazy outline of low hills ahead – and a thin, sparkling stripe of water running along the base of the hills. The river Vidula, Pavo deduced, combing over the mental images of the many maps he had studied as a boy in Constantinople's library. Something else emerged from the hazy mirage, something that gradually fattened in the silvery heat to take shape – a city standing like a sentinel just before this river, high and dominant.

The whispered name rippled back down the column. 'Remorum!'

Pavo eyed the place. A sea of wards and tenements, wrapped like a halo around a high scarp mound. Up there sat 'The Round Fortress', studded with fine, protruding turrets and stocky walls. But all those parapets were bare. A few unmanned imperial banners stood up there, fluttering gently in the hot wind. It was like Augusta Treverorum all over again.

When a felt-capped explorator rider came bolting in from that direction and approached Maximus' retinue, all necks stretched a little and hands cupped behind ears to hear what the man had to say. But there was no need to listen carefully, for the message spread in a series of excited cries. 'All four of the citadel gates lie open. The Tyrant fled at dawn.' The rider himself galloped up and down the length of the column, pointing west, his cape billowing behind him.

Even here, a half-mile behind the head of the silvery column and through the veil of dust cast up by the legions ahead, Pavo could see across the Vidula and down the long vale that stretched out beyond Remorum. A narrow route linking Remorum's Gate of Venus to the city of Parisiorum, several days' march away. The floor and sides of the vale were carpeted in lush grass that shimmered in the fierce noon heat, dotted with golden buttercups and purple irises. Two more exploratores sped into the vale and up onto its southern and northern banks.

'Clear!' Grumio yelled from the brow of the southern valley side, waving his spear back and forth.

'Clear!' yelled another from the northern edge.

Horns blared, and Maximus boomed from the front: 'Onwards, my legions. Our enemy hastens for Parisiorum. We must move quickly, pursue him all the way there, deny him time to set up defences.'

The entire army picked up into a full-step march and rolled past Remorum, across the broad stone bridge that spanned the Vidula then into the westwards vale like a great rivulet of quicksilver. Pavo could see a small hummock on the vale floor further ahead but no sign of the valley end, everything melting into a warping heat haze in that direction. The thrum of cicadas grew intense, the sound intensified by the high vale sides. Over this and the thunder of boots, Pavo heard the Claudians behind him rumble in tense excitement, and the Frixagorum Cohort, marching just ahead, chattering eagerly too. The enormity of it all – what these men would be facing in just a few days time – struck him.

He fell back a little to march alongside Darik. 'This oath of yours,' he said, 'no matter what happens over the next few days – promise me you will consider it settled.' He fully expected the stubborn big Maratocupreni to scoff at the notion, but Darik didn't even react. Lost in some other thought, seemingly. His handsome face was pinched in puzzlement as he rose on the balls of his feet with each step to see over the many heads in front.

'One final push,' Sura cajoled the Claudians. 'Then we're at Parisiorum. That's the last major stronghold in the region that Gratian can fall back to.'

Just then, a gentle wind blew from the west and the valley's far end. 'I smell bastards,' Libo mused, peering that way, sniffing the air as if a foul stench was blowing from that direction.

'This particular bastard is running out of places to flee,' Pulcher rumbled.

While those nearby laughed gruffly, Darik still remained silent.

'What's wrong?' Pavo asked quietly.

'This vale,' Darik said, still frowning and peering ahead down the valley. 'If Gratian fled this way then why... why are there no tracks?'

Pavo looked down the valley and saw what Darik meant. No

flattened grass, no churned earth. No army had come through here. Why hadn't Grumio and the exploratores noticed this?

'Tribunus,' Opis agreed, his voice wavering, pausing for just a moment in which the cicada song in the valley seemed to grow deafening, 'something isn't right.'

Pavo heard the standard-bearer's words and saw a strange thing happening up on the brows of the valley sides at the same time. Grumio and his exploratores up there were no longer riding. They were still, and facing down into the broad floor of the vale, watching the army, their horses' tails swishing while they calmly held the reins.

'Grumio?' Maximus' voice echoed up through the valley. 'Move onwards, to the west.'

Neither Grumio nor the riders replied.

'It's a trap,' Pavo croaked.

Just then, an odd sound rose. It was like a faraway, rolling thunder. The sound of a distant summer storm. But the noise grew and grew rapidly, rolling towards them from south and north at once. Pavo staggered forward to his place at the head of the Claudia, his eyes scouring the valley sides. His men yammered around him, asking what was happening, some shouting to others in nearby legions. Mounted officers snapped and brayed at their charges, turning their horses in tight circles to look north then south then north again.

First, the green southern ridge roiled, the heat haze bending and warping as if a silvery smoke was pouring across the heights behind the three silent riders up there. Then the smoke became real. A broad mass of steely-grey shapes that seemed to unfold like impossibly wide wings, dominating the valley top for almost a mile. Finally, Pavo saw the mass of shapes for what they really were: the Celtae, the Petulantes, the VIII Augusta, The I Noricorum – the four Western legions supposedly faraway in Hispania – were here, gleaming, replete, staring down at the army of Maximus. The Heruli too.

Next, the northern vale-side rippled too, as the legions of Italia arose up there: the I, II and II Julia Alpina. Then ahead of Maximus' column the sweltering haze further along the valley bulged and swirled, before the thousand white-clad riders of the Armatura walked into view, spreading ominously across the valley floor like a plug. There they too halted, silent, staring. Pavo heard the same rumble from behind, and knew what was there before he turned and saw them: the Gentiles cavalry, spilling round from behind the scarp mound of Remorum, arraying across the valley end behind Maximus' column like a second plug, horses rearing up, whinnying, riders holding spears aloft. Finally, streaming along the heights of the southern valley top came a great mass of dark-skinned Moorish horsemen from Africa: long-haired, lightly armoured but bristling with javelins, bows and slings, carrying bright round buckler shields. Four thousand riders if not more, spreading out in a great front next to the legions already arrayed up there. The entire Army of the West was not scattered and distant. They were here, all of them. Two spears for every one of Maximus'.

The Sarmaturum and the Dalmaturum – Britannia's two great horse schools – fell into disarray, the riders struggling to control their mounts, panicked at the sudden sights and smells of so many strange men and beasts. Dragathius yelled and barked at them, demanding one wing pull ahead and one behind to face the two enemy cavalry wings. Maximus barked some command that few heard – so tight with shock was his voice – but his officers relayed it over and over.

'Square, form a square!'

A chaos of clattering iron and shouts filled the valley as the column of Maximus rapidly transformed, drawing tight into a square, protecting the mule and wagon train and using the small hummock as a centrepoint, every man shooting anxious glances up at the huge forces all around them, fearful that they might fall upon them while they were in disarray. Pavo shoved and guided his men, shouting for the three tiny Claudian cohorts to draw tight. At last, the din of the formation change ebbed and the Claudia, moments ago a flanking unit in the column, now found themselves as the face of the square on the side facing the southern valley side. The Frixagorum Cohort stood to their right and the II Britannica their left.

Pavo stared up at the southern valley brow and the wall of steel there, and tried to block from his mind the thought of the equally huge enemy forces arrayed behind and on either flank. Despite the huge number of living, breathing souls in this valley, the only sounds now were the cawing of interested carrion hawks – well-used to the spoils that usually followed such gatherings of steel-clad men – the continued screaming of the cicadas and the occasional eerie whisper of the summer wind.

Slowly, Grumio the explorator turned and calmly joined the enemy ranks. The two up on the southern banks with him followed and the three on the opposite height did so likewise. Then, from the centre of the wall of legionaries up on the southern valley side, a lone horseman guided his mount a few steps proud with a slow, relaxed gait. The rider wore a diadem, canted to one side on his blonde-haired head, winking in the sunlight like his bright bronze armour, his black cloak lifting gently in the high, hot breeze.

Pavo's heart thundered.

'Greetings, Maximus,' Gratian said, his voice carrying well across the great green trench in which his opponent was pinned. Two mounted men moved forward to flank the Western Emperor. Bishop Ambrosius and the coppery-wigged Comes Arbogastes. A cohort of Green-cloaked Alani tribesmen fanned out behind them. Lurking close by stood a hundred or so men in hardened leather armour and dark cloaks; they had the look of personal bodyguards... but Pavo knew what they were, even saw the glint of the rings on their fingers. Some of them were accompanied by mighty Molossian attack dogs, clad in spiked armour and held on leashes.

'It has been some time since last you visited me,' Gratian continued. 'Not terribly wise, I would say. Now you *do* come to my seat of power, uninvited... with an army in tow. And what an impressive attempt at an army it is.'

The vultures overhead were now numerous, sensing the slaughter to come.

'Your scout riders did well... for me,' Gratian continued. 'Remorum remains garrisoned by my Alani guards and, as you can see, these hills are certainly not "clear". Were they your best exploratores? They only cost me a few bags of silver. Thus, I can afford to spend lavishly on some monument to commemorate your defeat. What would you like?' Gratian asked playfully. 'A nice arch telling of your folly? Perhaps a column depicting your decapitation?'

Pavo saw Maximus, sitting proud in his saddle, wearing a mask of courage, staring up at his nemesis. What reply was there to give, Pavo realised, when a wall of steel dominated the high ground either side of them, with wings of riders poised and pointed at their fore and rear like executioners' axes. Gratian raised a hand, ready to give the signal that would turn this pleasant vale into a sepulchral ditch. Fear swept through Maximus' ranks like a mist. Pavo felt it too, cold, strength-sapping. He saw faces around him drain of colour, heard prayers, oaths of anguish and steely silence as each man faced his fears in his own way. He stared into the summer sky, knowing it was over, whispering an apology to the legions of the fallen who would never now have their justice, to the distant Izodora and – heartbreakingly – to his unborn child.

Maximus stared up at his nemesis, and Gratian peered down. Two eagles, poised. One had to die.

'Destroy them,' Gratian said at last, dropping his raised hand. 'Kill them all.'

One thousand horns wailed, filling the sky like a growing bruise, and the Western legions came alive.

Thwack! The sound was sickening. The noise of bare knuckles cracking against cheekbones, echoing around the cellars of Remorum. *Thwack!* Now it sounded wet and loose, as if the bones had broken and there was little left but mulch. But whenever Valentinian dared to look up from the dark cellar corner in which he sat, naked and hugging his knees, he saw not a broken man on the end of this relentless punishment, but an immortal giant.

Beyond the wall of bars separating Valentinian from the ongoing torture, Merobaudes stood tall, arms outspread as if he was the master of the bronze manacles pinning him like that and not the other way round. He too was naked, but he looked stronger and more powerful than the brute in the leather breastplate who was beating him. Indeed, the torturer had to leap to land every strike on Merobaudes' fire-scarred face. His head snapped left or right with every punch, then slid back to face the torturer. His cheeks and forehead were split and bleeding, and teeth lay around his feet. His thin brown hair hung in blood-matted locks around his face. But through that curtain of hair and gore his eyes were like silver brooches, bright, staring at the torturer.

'You might have reduced legionaries to quivering wrecks with your freakish height and ugly face,' the torturer sneered. 'But now you are nothing. You are in chains that will never be unlocked. This – the feel of my knuckles ruining your face – will soon seem like a pleasant memory. When Emperor Gratian gets you back to Treverorum and we ship you down into the underground chambers...' he stopped talking, the words tumbling into a gleeful laugh. 'Have you ever seen a man twisted until his body ruptures. The stink of every organ tearing and bursting at once, spilling from one great wound like a soup. Disgusting... delightful.' He jabbed a thumb over his shoulder. 'The young Caesar – he will be executed like this before you are, so you can watch him die and know that your years of protecting him were for nothing. The bitch mother also – she will be raped like the whore she is before we kill her too.'

Valentinian pulled madly at the thick rope trussing his ankles, but it was knotted securely to an iron ring in the cellar wall. He pulled and growled in frustration, before falling limp, exhausted. He hated himself for the fact they had shackled Merobaudes in what looked like a ship's anchor chain, while deeming rope sufficient to keep him restrained.

The torturer swung a fresh punch, catching Merobaudes on the jaw. The two Alani guards watching the torture, resting their weight on their spears, whispered at one another, then one suggested to the torturer: 'Perhaps we should bring the bitch down here now. It has been some time since I rutted. It would be quite something to watch the runt in there squirm while we do it,' he said breezily, flicking his head in the direction of Valentinian's cell.

The torturer swung round, annoyed at this one telling him what he should do. But then his lips quirked at both ends, and he wiped his bloodied hands on a rag carefully and deliberately, his eyes searching the space between them as if playing out in his head what the Alani had proposed. 'Yes... do it.'

Valentinian felt his body jolt round as far as the ropes would allow, felt the cold, grime-coated steel of the cell bars on his palms as he gripped two with shaking hands, felt the same bars press against his face as he stared madly at the pair of Alani ascending the cellar stairs to the ground floor rooms where she was being held, sure there had to be someone here who would stop this. Lady Justina of a long and noble line, widow of Emperor Valentinian, regent of the Caesar of the West... *Mother.*

He heard the dull murmur of exchanged words, rising hotly, then the echoing sting of a slap, followed by a harrowing scream. They returned to the basement carrying her like loot, her scant gown ripped at one shoulder, the skin streaked with three bloody scratch lines.

As they carried her over towards a table, big Merobaudes' chains clanked, his huge muscles useless against the thick bronze. Valentinian shook madly and he stretched out a forlorn hand through the bars and towards her. 'No... *no!*'

But his cries were drowned out by the plaintive moan of one thousand war horns, somewhere outside the city.

As the wailing of the Western horns faded, Pavo stared, transfixed. Gratian's legions streamed like molten silver, pouring down the southern side of Remorum Vale towards the hastily-arranged square of Maximus. *Crunch! Crunch! Crunch!* Closer and closer and – scenting victory – growing faster in their stride. A moving wall of iron: the VIII Augusta, the Celtae, the Petulantes and the I Noricorum. Comes Arbogastes, the strange barbarian distinctive even from this distance thanks to his copper-coloured braid-wig, led this infantry descent down the slope on horseback with a personal guard retinue of twelve ironclad cataphractii, the legions in tow like great, outstretched silver wings.

'The wagons!' Maximus yelled over and over, rearing up on his horse, waving to the centre of the defensive square. 'Get the wagons onto the hummock!'

Pavo twisted his head just long enough to see commotion there amongst the panicked mules. Whips snapped in the air, dust puffed up. On the northern valley side also he saw the trio of Julia Alpina legions descending like a reflection of Arbogastes' advance.

The zing of a sword being drawn snatched Pavo's attentions forwards again. He saw the glint of sunlight on steel, and could even see Arbogastes' wretched visage uplit by the blade. The Western General held the blade aloft and then lowered it to his left – a signal to the Armatura riders blocking the western end of the valley, walking ominously. When he chopped the blade in towards the army of Maximus, those riders read the signal and broke into a canter. He then did the same to the left, and the Gentiles sped up too.

Pavo, head switching to the death rolling towards them in every direction, felt Libo's shoulder jam against his left and Sura's against his right as they backstepped a fraction for a tighter square and greater cohesion. Closer and closer the enemy came. Now he could see individual faces, banners and colours.

'Shields!' he cried, raising his, the men beside him clacking theirs into place likewise, then levelled his spear over the top right edge, thousands more spears falling level like this at the same time, all along the Claudia, the Frixagorum, and the II Britannica – both of those regiments had heard his order and taken it as their own. The Claudia – few as they were – were the keystone of this edge of the square, he realised.

When the braying of mules and rumble of wagon wheels behind them eased, Pavo shot another look over his shoulder to see that some of the wagons had drawn up onto the low hummock. Not the supply wagons, just those strange covered ones. He snapped his head front again, peering at Arbogastes and the sea of enemy legionaries coming down the slopes for them, judging the distance, the time left. Four hundred strides, each one eaten away by the quick, aggressive *crunch-crunch-crunch* of their advance. Something winked and dazzled, high up on the vale side behind the enemy advance. Gratian, remaining safely up there with his retinue and the Alani, the Heruli legion and the vast Moorish cavalry wing too. A tremendous reserve.

Mithras, give us hope, he mouthed.

Arbogastes raised his sword again, this time making that double swiping motion once more, but faster. The enemy cavalry horns either side blared, the sound filling the valley with an echoing moan. At once, the cantering Gentiles and the Armatura picked up from their canter into a trot.

At this, Dragathius spurred his two cavalry wings. 'Horsemen of Britannia!' he howled, his black steed rearing up, his sword held high. 'Protect the true emperor! Dalmaturum... ad-*vance!*' He swiped his hand towards Gratian's Armatura, coming for the right flank. Next, he swished his hand towards the Gentiles, coming for the left flank. 'Sarmaturum... *forward!*'

With a fresh paean of trumpets, Maximus' two wings of horsemen rumbled and mixed, each like a murmuration of starlings, before splitting into two wedges. The land shook madly as they trotted out east and west to close with the enemy horse advance in a storm of thrown-up dust.

'They don't stand a chance,' Libo said quietly, watching the Sarmatura go. 'Even if they gain an upper hand or look like breaking through...' his words trailed off and Pavo looked up with him at the Moors, arrayed like hawks up on the vale side.

Pavo knew the centurion was right. The mighty riders of Britannia would die in this vale. They all would. He saw that mind's-eye idyll of himself with Izodora, the pleasant Thracian farmstead, his lips on her sweet neck, their babe in a crib of loving arms.

Gratian's Gentiles exploded into a full gallop, then Dragathius and the Sarmaturum reflected the move, drifting to intercept them at an oblique angle. They met like two great broad swords clashing – the tips of each wedge screaming just past each other, the sharp edges ploughing together, mangling and wrecking the silvery formations. Passing shields *rat-tat*-tatted together, sparks flew and puffs of red leapt into the air. Horses screamed and fell to their knees, whinnying piteously. Riders cried out, thrown or torn, arms outstretched, backs ripped open or bellies slashed. Within moments, the Dalmaturum and the Armatura collided likewise just west of the defensive square.

'He's committed his riders just to draw ours away,' Pulcher growled, staring across the valley floor ahead and then behind as the Western legions spilled down onto the flat ground on both sides, each infantry front much wider than Maximus' square and some thirty ranks deep too, and now just two hundred paces away from the square. Ahead, Arbogastes now lazily held out his sword to eye the edge, then kissed the flat of the blade with villainous eyes. The Western General wore a cold grin – the look of a man who has fought in many battles, and knows when victory is a certainty.

Pavo felt his mouth drain of moisture and his bladder pulse as if he had just gulped down a skinful of ice water – one last bout of the Soldier's Curse, he thought with a wry humour – as Arbogastes had the I Noricorum and Celtae regiments level their spears, training the tips on the Claudian front. The Celtae Tribunus' face was bent with malice as he issued a hateful war cry. 'Death to the usurper!' he cried, and the thousand with him roared the same in reply.

So many, too many…

He noticed that Sura's shield, instead of meeting the edge of his own like the tiles of a wall, was overlapping by a hand's-width, as if to afford him extra protection. 'I need but one shield, Brother,' he said with a mask of a smile, easing Sura's shield away.

'The dream… it was of battle,' Sura whispered, staring at the enemy lines as he confessed at last. 'Battle far from here and in years to come. In it I stood like this with the Claudia. I have dreamt of battle many, many times.' He gulped, as if swallowing a rock. 'But in this one, for the first time… you were no longer by my side.'

Pavo felt a coldness streak across his skin.

Sura pushed against his shoulder even closer to Pavo's, chasing the coldness away. 'But I spit on my dreams. We live together… or we die together.'

'Archeeers!' cried several of Arbogastes' men.

'Archeeers!' Libo bawled in riposte, bringing the bows of the Claudia up. Many such cries echoed from all sides of the square and the enclosing enemy walls.

'Loose!' cried scores of voices, friend and foe.

Arrows whistled up from both sides – loose and wild shots from Maximus' men and dense, concentrated salvos from Gratian's bowmen. 'Shields!' many commanders bellowed as the arrows plunged down. Hundreds died on both sides. One arrow smacked into Pavo's shield, a finger's-width from the top rim. A man behind him screamed – shot through the cheek – and a pulse of black liquid leapt onto Pavo's shoulder, soaking through his ringmail and his tunic. The stink of blood was sharp and it played tricks with his mind – and the minds of his men too. He heard them panting, sucking in quick and ragged breaths, sharing panicked whispers. Worse, although Libo and Sura and most of the front rank stood firm, he noticed some in the rank behind edge back a half step, saw men in the neighbouring cohorts and legions edge back too, crowding together. A tight square was a good thing, but a crush was a sure way to bring about a defeat. He heard the dry-mouthed prayers of the Claudians behind him, felt the square contract a little more... then he looked back up to the top of the valley side and at Gratian. Resting in his saddle with the ease of a man on a country ramble. It was as if lightning had lanced down from the noon sky and exploded within him. He shook his shoulders free of Opis and Sura, taking a stride forward, out of the contracting square, and held up his spear like a giant finger, towards Gratian, twisting his head back towards the Claudia. 'See the bastard up there? Do you see him?'

The fearful and tearful eyes of the Claudia stared up, wide and worried. The Frixagorum too and the II Britannica.

'This is it. This is all we have worked for. Here, Now! Up there stands the man who has taken so much from each of us. Libo,' he said, 'tell me, is there anything you would not do to be up there now, your hands around his lying neck?'

The tears escaped Libo's good eye and flooded down his cheeks as Arbogastes' force advanced briskly to within one hundred strides, the thunder of their boots drowning out the shrieking of expectant vultures and the din of the cavalry embattled on the flanks. 'I would walk through fire for eternity for just that single chance,' he rasped through a cage of teeth, stepping forth like Pavo.

Pavo saw the red-rimmed eyes of Indus. 'Is it not the same for you? And you?' he asked Durio. He called to them all, seeing them swell with pride as he spoke their names. 'The hatred, the sorrow, the loss, all of it. That bastard up there is the beast that brought it upon us... *all* of us!'

The Claudians edged forward a step now, returning to their original shape, resting their weight on their front feet. So too the Frixagorum and II Britannica took up a more confident line, even as the enemy masses thundered to within eighty paces and the ends of their wide lines began to fold around the square.

'If I die here today, then I will die without regret,' Pavo raged, 'but I will not die meekly. And I will pass into Elysium happily, if only to know that one of you brave and brilliant men will smash through these jaws of steel and fight your way up that hill and strike down the whoreson up there. Just one man, that is all we need to spare all of our loved ones from his tyranny. Will it be you... or you – or you?' he said, picking out men from the ranks. 'Are you with me?'

They exploded in a furious and guttural *barritus* cry, rattling their spearheads on their shields.

'Primus Pilus,' Pavo bawled to Sura, sinking back into place on the front line and scowling at the wall of Gratian's men, now just fifty paces away. 'Give me a storm of iron and lead!'

Sura stretched a little taller. '*Plumbatae...*' As one, every Claudian legionary plucked one of the three lead-weighted darts clipped onto the back of their shield and raised it overhead. The same command rose from almost every other of Maximus' regiments and the entire square bristled like a threatened porcupine. 'Loose!' Sura bellowed in time with a score of similar commands. Some ten thousand weighted darts spat outwards from the square in every direction at the oncoming army of Gratian. When the darts plunged into Gratian's front lines, blood pumped up in small bursts in hundreds of different spots along the front, and it was as if the Western soldiers had hit an invisible wall. Men sank to their knees, darts jutting from their eye sockets and faces, others pirouetted, screaming, grabbing at broken shoulders, more still bundled over, darts having crashed into their shins or thighs. Some behind the fallen tripped, fell forwards and were struck in the back by the last of the falling darts. Many hundreds of Gratian's finest lay dead or screaming, but the many thousands more now surged over or around the dead, closer, closer.

'Ballistarii!' Maximus bawled now from somewhere within the square. Pavo shot a glance over his shoulder. Beyond the many wide-eyed Claudian ranks behind him, he noticed activity around the strange convoy of covered wagons up on the hummock. Men were crawling over the vehicles like ants, pulling on ropes, hauling the leather sheets away. Rectus was with them, seemingly understanding what was going on, hobbling around with the aid of his stick, helping to peel the covers from the vehicles.

'*Spiculae!*' Comes Arbogastes roared, snatching Pavo's attentions front and centre again.

The enemy lines slowed a fraction, lifting countless long, slim javelins and when the next order came – 'Loose!' – discharged them in a shining shower, sailing towards the legions of Maximus.

'Shields!' Pavo roared.

The Claudian shields rose, Pavo and the others on the front rank holding them like men walking into a head-on gale, those behind lifting theirs overhead as if to shelter from a deluge. The javelins battered down in a horrible thunder of iron striking wood. Men jerked and shuddered, screaming wetly where missiles found gaps in the shield roof. Timber shredded where shields were struck with three or more missiles, the legionaries under such compromised wooden boards helpless when another javelin plunged down upon them. Slings burred from small units of *funditores* near the wagons, and the shot whirred over Pavo's head, punching black holes in the faces of the Celtae men dead ahead. Some spasmed and kicked, falling in stages, others pressed on for a time before their bodies understood they had been shot through. But again far too few fell and far too many remained. The legions of Gratian stomped ever closer and the Celtae Tribunus' face was bent in hatred as he brayed his men forward and seemed to lock eyes with Pavo as if choosing him as a first opponent.

Forty paces… thirty.

'Ballistarii!' Maximus cried out again – his voice almost a croak now. But this time it was followed up with: *'Loose!'*

From behind Pavo, a mighty groan and shudder of ropes and timber sounded. Pavo risked a final look back, just in time to see the now-uncovered wagon fleet: each and every one of them was a *carroballista* – a wagon with a mounted onager or a bolt thrower upon their backs. Crews of three stood upon each vehicle, Rectus aiding one team. The wagons trembled, the torsion handles wound to their greatest extent, then – on hearing Maximus' command – one of each crew batted down on a peg, releasing the stressed throwing arms and ropes, catapulting head-sized rocks up and over Maximus' defensive lines, over Pavo's head. Some three dozen such rocks soared outwards from the square. Pavo's gaze swung forwards to the face of the Celtae Tribunus coming for him, seeing the shadow of one rock growing over the man.

In that instant, Pavo's and his eyes met. He was a man. A Roman. He was not Gratian.

And within one beat of the heart, he was gone.

The rock dashed the Celtae man like an over-ripe fruit, casting his blood, innards and ribbons of his body in every direction. The rock plunged on through the Celtae ranks, bouncing angrily, snapping legs, crushing chests and bursting heads, leaving a great red furrow in that legion. Simultaneously, the rest of the rock shower pummelled down on Gratian's army. The I Noricorum front exploded in a shower of dirt and debris, men snapped like twigs. Howls rang out as, somewhere nearby, Molossian hounds were struck too, and then one rock hammered into the group of twelve cataphractii riding with Comes Arbogastes, dashing those iron-shelled horsemen like eggs. Man and horse were cast back across the ground like unwanted toys in a flail of broken and torn limbs. When the dust began to thin, a broken front-half of one horse still kicked and whinnied – the poor beast believing its back legs were still attached. Seven of the dozen stout horse guards had fallen. Arbogastes, glowing with confidence a moment ago, now flailed, struggling to control his panicked horse, his copper wig sliding and almost falling off, the sunlight gleaming on a section of his bald pate.

A trice later, a second batch of these carroballista wagons creaked and groaned, then the ballistae aboard were loosed, sending long, thick, iron tipped bolts whooshing at a low trajectory. Three sped *just* above the heads of the Claudians from behind, drawing a 'what the?' from Libo. The bolts plunged into the spaces where the onager rocks had not, smashing into the enemy legionaries' chests, pinning Celtae and Petulantes legionaries to those behind and snapping the legs of those behind again like stalks of dry grass. Another ruinous volley, centuries more of Gratian's army dead or broken.

But that was it. No more time. Pavo watched the now vengeful, blood-spattered Noricorum and Celtae men surge over the last few steps separating them. Arbogastes knotted the coppery braids of his wig under his chin like the straps of a helm, dipped his head like an angered wolf, pointed his sword like an accusing finger at Maximus in the centre of the square and roared: 'Take the usurper's head!' The Western Army now dashed for the square, the earth shaking, the vultures overhead shrieking in delight.

'Claudia... *braaace!*' Pavo screamed as the entire defensive wall bristled, feeling Sura and Libo push up against his either side, shoulder-to-shoulder.

'Together!' Sura and Libo cried in unison.

'For the legion, for justice!' Pulcher and Opis roared.

'Stand with us, Mithras!' Indus and Durio bellowed together.

Darik and Betto bawled some unintelligible tangle of expletive war cries as the gap between the two armies vanished.

Bang! ten thousand shields whacked together in a rolling thunder that filled the green trench of land and rose up to the heavens. A thousand more spears clashed. Swords skittered across shields, blood jumped up in great gouts as spears were driven home. Molossian hounds sprang and clamped onto the throats of men, tearing out stringy masses of flesh and windpipes.

The defensive square swayed and Maximus' men screamed and fell as the great weight of Gratian's men quickly began to tell. Pavo felt the mighty advantage of the enemy and at once knew it was too great. Far too great. Driven by several enemy shields pressed against his, he staggered back a step then two then three in quick succession, and the hoped-for counter-push from the Claudians behind him did not come as they were too few. More and more the line buckled as spears jabbed and poked over the rim of his shield like berating fingers, the sharp tips swiping and slashing all-too close to his eyes and neck. One scored his cheek and nose, sending a sheet of salty-tasting blood down across his lips. He speared back at the attacking Noricorum soldier, knocking him off balance, then speared again, plunging the lance into the man's exposed shoulder. The man's face paled as mouthfuls of blood and chest-matter burst from his lips. Pavo ripped his spear back, the runnels of Roman blood cascading down the shaft and staining his hand.

At the same time Opis, by his side, fought manfully against two Celtae veterans, using the legion standard like a fighting staff while also slashing with his sword. He smashed the jaw of one veteran then plunged his blade into the chest of the second. Blood puffed into the summer air. But the sword blade stuck. Opis twisted madly to try to pull it free, only for a Noricorum legionary to run him through, armpit to opposite collarbone. Opis, gurgling, staring, astonished, slid away while the killer grabbed the Claudia standard with a gleeful cry.

'No!' Pavo roared. '*No!*' He surged for the killer, only for a screen of four other Noricorum men to block him, whacking their swords down upon his shield, splinters flying. Pavo, driven back by the concentrated attack, fell onto his back.

'Quiet, traitor,' one of the attacking quartet hissed, 'time for a long sleep.' As this one and the three with him made to slash down for a killing frenzy, Pavo swiped his spatha through the shin of the one who had spoken. The man's lower leg popped clean off and he fell, screaming, while Sura hacked into the neck of the second, Pulcher ran the third through the belly and Darik's spatha chopped through the air and robbed the fourth man of his sword arm.

'Argh! You Persian bastard!' the man screamed, aghast, clutching his arm stump as blood pumped from the wound.

Darik seemed to rise an extra foot, drawing his spatha towards his shield shoulder for a backhand cut that sent the man's head spinning clear of his body. 'I am a Maratocupreni!' he roared like a bear.

The headless body fell like a log, revealing the one who had killed Opis and captured the Claudia standard. This Noricorum man was about to swing the standard at Darik when Betto surged in from the side to headbutt Opis' killer – the fin ridge of his helm slicing through the iron of the enemy's helmet and sinking through forehead and brain. The Noricorum man's face twisted in anger, then confusion, as blood rained down his face from inside his helmet, and then he slumped to his knees and vanished in the press of battle.

Betto wrenched the standard from the falling enemy's grip and barrelled forward to where Opis had been standing, the dead foe's blood streaking down his helm and face in thick stripes. *'Non omnis moriar!'* he screamed, swishing the standard in a broad arc, knocking over three more attackers and half-braining a fourth.

The Claudians roared in support, pushing back as best they could.

Pavo thrust his shield at one attacker and heard the man's face collapse as the iron boss caught him on the cheekbone, then kicked another away and stabbed up through the armpit of a third. In the rain of blood and din of screaming, he found himself shoulder-side with Betto: 'Hold that staff as if it was one of your poetry scrolls! You have earned your promotion, just make sure you live to honour the standard.'

Betto laughed maniacally. 'Live? Is it not fine and honourable to die for one's brothers?' With that, he plunged into the fray, cajoling the Claudians nearest, slowing the gradual collapse of the square. Yet at the same moment, a great wail of dismay rose up from the Primani – one of Maximus' elite legions on the western edge of the square. Gratian's VIII Augusta legion had pierced their ranks and were flooding into the heart of the defensive square, and spilling along the exposed backs of the legions of Britannia. Pavo saw the knot of dark-cloaked Speculatores go with them. They sped up onto the hummock and over the carroballista wagons like lizards, slicing down the crews there with expert, single-stroke kills. He saw Rectus – still on one of those artillery wagons – grab a spear and shield. It had been years since he had been injured, years since he had fought, but he killed two of the agents before the rest converged on him and slew him in a frenzy of downward stabbings.

Somewhere deep inside, Pavo wept madly. But the soldier's skin was like a cold, inhuman armour. As the square collapsed, the soldiers of Gratian swamped and overran them, parting him from Sura, from Libo, from Pulcher. He spun, fending off attacks from every direction. Blades streaked down his back, breaking the mail rings of his shirt. Flats of blades hammered against his helm, dazing him. His shield became a useless rag of half-shredded wood and so he tossed it down, using his spear two-handed to keep enemy soldiers back. He found himself stumbling around the foot of the hummock, and he saw a Speculator there – one of those who had killed Rectus. Realising this might be his last act, he sprinted at the agent, pinning him through the gut and driving him at a run backwards and against the broken carroballista wagon on which Rectus' corpse lay draped like a discarded red robe. Pavo recognised the bald agent – and in particular the huge boil on his nose. The drunk from Antioch... the killer on the ramming ship. The Speculator's eyes widened in shock, then in matching recognition. 'You... how?' he croaked through a soup of blood, before he sagged, pinned against the wagon by Pavo's spear. Pavo used the dead agent's shoulder like a step, leaping up onto the wagon, tearing his spatha from his scabbard and beheading a second Speculator with one strike.

He swung to seek out the third of Rectus' killers, but could barely tell ally from foe. There was no square anymore, no order of battle, just a huge chaotic press of Roman slaying Roman, all centering around the hummock. Nearby, the two cavalry wings were still obliterating each other. He spotted in the midst of the infantry battle, Maximus rearing up on his war horse, man and beast dripping red, many of his golden guard of Victores gone. Then he saw Libo, Sura and Pulcher fighting together just a short way from this wagon, backing up the hummock towards him, driven by a quartet of Speculatores hacking at them. Betto and Darik too were being driven like this. At least, he thought, he would die near his brothers. But all the while, a sickening sight hovered over it all, up on the southern valley top: the relaxed Gratian up there, watching the last throes of his would-be usurper's army. *It was not meant to be this way!* he screamed inwardly.

A low animal growl snapped him from his momentary trance. He turned his eyes to the foot of the hummock. A crow-faced, grey Speculator held a slavering, bloody-faced Molossian dog on a taut leash. In a breath, dozens more of the dark agents emerged from the fray all around the grassy hummock, closing in on him and the small clutch of Claudians backstepping up the hummock slope. Impossible odds. Crow-face grinned horribly.

Pavo closed his eyes, saw again that vision of the quiet farmstead, of Izodora and their child in his arms. The image faded from his mind like ashes blown from a pyre, for now it would never be. His eyes slid open and he fell into a crouch on the edge of the wagon. He and his few comrades had the high ground at least. With his free shield-hand he tore the Hun rope free of his belt, whirling it by his side, and clenched his spatha tight in the other. 'Come on then,' he growled low at the enclosing ring of Speculatores, 'who wants to die first?'

'Oh that'll be you,' a voice replied from behind.

Pavo swung round to see the brutish Speculator who had spoken, smirking as he bounded up the hummock ahead of the others. The brute drew his arm back, a small throwing dagger held by the blade. Pavo had seen the Speculatores' skill with these lethal iron knives. With a jolt of instinct, he cast out his left arm, sending the Hun lasso licking out like a serpent's tongue. The brutish Speculator's eyes widened as the noose sailed down over his head, the throwing knife still in his palm. In the instant it took the agent to realise what this strange rope-weapon was, Pavo wrenched his arm back. The rope drew tight around the Speculator's neck and his eyes and tongue bulged from his head before, with a *crack* of breaking vertebrae, he fell. Crow-face and the ring of Speculatores further down the hummock stared, stunned for an instant, before their faces bent with predatory grins and they surged up the slope at speed.

Libo, Sura, Pulcher, Betto and Darik halted near the hummock top, coming together in a hasty defensive ring, bracing their spears – and Betto holding the standard like a weapon – for the onslaught. Just before the Speculatores swept in, Pavo leapt down from the edge of the wagon to join his men, all of them roaring like thunder: 'For the Claudia!'

Chapter 22
August 383 AD
Remorum

To Valentinian's ears, the tumult of battle from outside sounded strange down in these stony chambers: muted, unreal. But the torturer and his two Alani did not care about the battle, for they had only one thing in mind. They tried again to press Lady Justina down and bind her to the torture table but it was a mistake, for she kicked out, catching one Alani square in the nose with her bare heel. The crack of breaking cartilage echoed around the cellar like the wings of a speeding bat, and a thick soup of blood pulsed down the soldier's face. He moaned, swaying backwards, clutching his nose with one hand and going for his sword with the other. 'Stupid bitch!' the second Alani hissed, pulling out a dagger from his belt, creeping towards her like a hunter cornering a deer.

'No no,' the torturer said, stepping between the two Alani and Justina. 'You tribesmen would use a hammer to kill a butterfly! Think,' he tapped his temple, then turned to Justina. 'You *will* submit to us… or I will throw your boy over this table instead.'

Justina bunched up at the wall end of the table, teeth in a rictus, shaking with rage and fear.

The torturer's grin stretched wide as he paced over to Valentinian's cell and carefully unlocked it, then entered to crouch by his side. Valentinian could almost taste the torturer's fetid breath crawling over his skin as the man stroked his hair.

'The two tribesemen might not care for boys… but I have more eclectic tastes.'

Justina's face sagged, horrified and still shaking. Slowly, she let her body slide away from the wall, laying herself across the table. 'I will not struggle,' she said.

'Mother, no!' Valentinian roared.

'Very wise,' the torturer whispered, stroking Valentinian's hair one more time then rising, walking back towards her.

'Work on me instead!' Merobaudes raged as the torturer slinked past him like a cat on the prowl. 'You have been striking me all morning and still I feel no pain. Was that your best, worm? Come back, answer me!'

But the torturer had eyes only for Justina. She met his gaze, and even reached up to pull the ties holding up her high tresses of hair. The silver-black locks tumbled down in a cascade, swishing across her chest. At the same time she extended and slightly parted her legs.

'Oh yes...' the torturer purred, running his tongue around his lips slowly, reaching out to take the hem of her robe, slowly lifting it. The two Alani set their spears to one side to take up a good position to watch.

A cold sickness rose in Valentinian's belly and his eyelids slid shut as the torturer's throaty rhythmic groans rang out. Even worse was the horrifying and total silence from Mother. He wanted to stuff his fists in his ears to block it all out. His mind spun, and he found some cave of solace in an almost forgotten memory: a day from his ninth summer, when he had been travelling with big Merobaudes' patrol along the Rhenus frontier. They had stopped in at a town to eat, only to find that an execution was taking place. A man stood crying on the edge of the town acropolis rock, the point from which criminals were thrown to their death. Below, the man's wife had wept, hands reaching up towards him in futility. 'Stop this,' Valentinian had begged Merobaudes. But the big man had said nothing. The two garrison sentries had barged the man from the precipice with the hafts of their spears. The fellow had plummeted, flailing, screaming. With a horrible *whump* of his body breaking on the rocks, it was over. 'Why did you let him die? His wife will be bereft,' Valentinian had continued to protest. Merobaudes had seemed angry about this, and near dusk that day, he had snapped.

'Because that was his lover, not his wife. He poisoned his wife and his three girls so as to acquire her estate. He was a terrible man. Some men deserve to die.' Valentinian had only realised later that the big Frank had known all along that the execution was to take place that day, and he had brought Valentinian there to witness it… to understand.

'I never understood that cruel lesson,' he whispered, 'until now.' He ran the pad of his thumb over the edge of the eating knife he had stealthily plucked from the torturer's belt. It was sharp enough. With a short sawing motion, he worked at the thick rope. With a quiet *snap* the last twines of the rope parted, the bonds falling away from Valentinian's ankles. It was with not a droplet of fear that he rose, strode from the cell's open gate and over to the table. The torturer's head swivelled round to gawp at him, chin wet with saliva, face scrunched up in an ugly contortion of ecstasy.

'Boy?' the man groaned in part-frenzy, shuddering as he thrust at Justina. 'How did you get out of your bonds-'

Valentinian swung his arm up and plunged the knife into the man's temple. With a thick *clunk* the blade sunk deep. The torturer's eyes rolled in his head and blood showered from his nostrils and ears. He slid away from Justina and collapsed to the floor, spasming wildly.

Merobaudes stared, wide-eyed, proud and horrified at once. The two Alani who had been watching the rape in lazy excitement now staggered towards their spears, but Justina scrabbled from the table to grab one lance and guard the other. Just as the broken-nosed Alani opened his mouth to raise the alarm, she sprang from the table and at him, growling like a wolf, running him through the belly and driving him back against the wall next to Merobaudes. The second was about to pounce on Justina's unguarded back, when Merobaudes snapped his manacled hand shut around the man's flowing blonde hair. The Alani jerked backwards, halted. Justina turned to him, Valentinian took up the second lance and together they speared the tribal guard like a salmon before letting lance and man collapse. Panting, wet with sweat and blood, Valentinian staggered into his mother's embrace. In times past, he had always done so for his own comfort, now he did so for hers.

'The keys,' Merobaudes whispered.

Valentinian fished around the dead torturer's body, finding the keyring and unlocking Merobaudes' manacles. The Frankish general's great arms swung down, shaking with numbness.

Just then, the sound of voices echoed down the stairs. 'What's going on down there? Need any help with the bitch?'

Merobaudes stooped to strip one of the Alani corpses of its green cloak, drawing it over his shoulders then took the sword from the torturer's belt, his eyes fixed all the time on the stairs, his wounded and fire-scarred face feral. 'Get behind me,' he growled, pacing towards the bottom stair.

'But there are four more Alani posted up there,' Valentinian whispered.

Merobaudes crept on as if he had not heard. Valentinian walked in his wake, part-crouched like the big man, leading his mother by the hand. He saw just shapes and shadows at the top of the cellar stairs. The sentries there must have seen the green of Merobaudes' cloak, he realised, and by the time they grasped that it was not one of their Alani comrades ascending, it was too late. Merobaudes lurched like a lion up and into the ground floor vestibule, striking down the two up there, then running for a third and breaking his neck. The fourth spun away to run for help, only for the big man's sword to whir through the air and plunge between his shoulderblades. He fell without a sound.

'Now,' Merobaudes said as Valentinian and Justina ascended onto the ground floor, pointing at the two slot windows looking out onto Remorum's citadel ward, 'watch for reinforcements.'

Valentinian moved to the window and gazed over the tight districts of marble, stone and gardens, bright and majestic in the midmorning sunlight. The streets were bare apart from the small knot of Alani Gratian had left behind to watch the place while he set his valley trap. From the windows of the terraced houses and villas he saw other pale faces of citizens looking out fearfully. The nearby and raucous din of the battle sailed over it all like a terrible dream.

A clank of iron from behind sent a jolt of fear through him. he swung round to see Merobaudes emerging from a side room, bedecked in his iron armour shell, a large silver shield strapped across his back, his

345

long, thin hair swept back behind his ears for once, proudly displaying his fire scars and the very recent marks of the torturer's beatings. He handed Justina her stola, then tossed Valentinian's white tunic and boots across the vestibule. Valentinian caught the garments and hurriedly put them on. Then the big man gave him his silver vest and helm and pale blue belt of leather pteruges. 'You'll need these too,' he said gruffly, tossing them each a green Alani cloak. 'Hoods up.'

When all three were equipped and wrapped in Alani green, he led them through a doorway, out into the bright light of day. Valentinian and Justina drew up their hoods as they stepped into the daylight, using Alani spears like walking staffs as they had seen sentries do. The three passed a pair of Alani guards, lazily playing dice in the deserted market square. The two tribal sentries merely squinted in the sunlight and offered a grunt of greeting as the green-cloaked trio of Merobaudes, Valentinian and Justina passed.

They entered a stable house near the southern gates. Two more Alani stood guard here.

The first opened his mouth to ask the hooded Merobaudes his identity, but the big Frank's blade passed through his throat before the words did. With a swing of his elbow, he flattened the face of the second. 'Now, we ride.'

Quietly, they saddled three horses, and slipped from Remorum's Gate of Dionysus without challenge. As they emerged onto the city's scarp mound, Valentinian's flesh crept at the sight in the vale just a short way west. It was a broiling sea of silver and red. Screams of horses and men filled the sky and horns moaned plaintively. Out here, the hot wind carried a tinge of leather and armour oil, the smell of horses too – and the stink of blood and torn-open guts.

'We must take care,' said Justina. 'We must bear well wide of that trap.'

Merobaudes said nothing for a moment, once more with that dead-eyed look. 'Come with me,' he beckoned. He rode down through Remorum's lower wards then out into the open country. He headed east – away from the fray – and they followed. They slowed after a time, soon after they came within sight of a small vinyard estate, a mile from the fray and sheltered in a dell. Merobaudes steered his mount down and met with a man who was tending to his grapes. A few moments later, he came back to Valentinian and Justina.

'Lady Justina,' he said, 'Firminus here is a long-time friend of mine. You and Valentinian should stay with him for now. You will be safe here.'

'Where are you going?' she protested.

He looked back west for a time, then back to her, the hot wind of noon blowing his hair across his disfigured face. 'To do what I must.'

'The trap?' she spluttered. 'Then you ride to your death! You saw how it was – Maximus is doomed. You are strong and brave,' she said with a humourless laugh, 'but you cannot better Gratian and all his forces. Do not throw your life into the same pit as Maximus. Gratian has won. We cannot hope to change things.'

Valentinian edged his horse between the two. 'But we have to try.'

'We?' Justina glowered at her boy, now guiding his horse over beside Merobaudes.

Merobaudes too shot him a shocked look.

'*You* will come with me to hide in this farmhouse until it is all over,' Justina demanded. 'After a few months we might find passage south, perhaps to Africa. I have good trade relations with a tribe beyond the southern imperial borders of Mauritania. They will take us in. In the deserts there we can lead good lives and-'

'The summer after next will be my fourteenth, and I will take the *toga virilis*,' Valentinian interrupted, sitting taller in his saddle. 'I will be a man. More, I will have no more need for a regent, for I will be true Caesar of the West.'

Justina glared fire at him. 'Yet next summer is not yet here. And you will not see it if you blunder towards your stepbrother's trap with this overly-proud fool,' she said, flashing a hand at Merobaudes.

Valentinian stared at her. It was an imperious but loving look. 'Mother, today I killed a man. For the first time, I took the life of another. All these years I have avoided bloodshed, even of the smallest creatures. But today I was put in a position I never again want to be in... and the only way out was through the shedding of blood. Again, I find myself with another choice: a pitiful hope of a life in exile in the burning deserts of Africa… or to ride on the winds of Fate, to stand and face my stepbrother, the black-hearted bastard whose veins pulse with my father's blood. And so I have chosen the path of honour.' He began to turn his mount away from her. '*Vale,* Mother,' he said, before heeling his mount into a trot towards the West and the faint clamour of battle.

Likewise, Merobaudes circled his steed and broke away after the boy, the pair soon riding abreast at a gallop.

Over the hot wind of the ride, Valentinian was certain he heard his mother's harrowing cries sailing into the air in his wake. He felt hot tears speed backwards across his cheeks, and lay low in the saddle, pelting at full speed.

'You are a fool, lad,' Merobaudes said. 'But I have never been so proud of you.'

Valentinian saw from the side of his eye the giant's feral rictus, fixed on the way ahead. They came to the Remorum Vale's eastern end. The valley floor, once green, was more silver and scarlet now, and the battle was a shapeless, horrible mess. The only thing he knew for certain was that Maximus was on the cusp of obliteration. Mother was right.

'How do we do this?' he asked Merobaudes, slowing as they approached along the vale.

'It is simple. You do everything I say, you hear?' Merobaudes replied.

Chapter 23
August 383 AD
Remorum Vale

A pungent stink of ripped-open bowels floated up from the battle and across the southern valley top. Gratian pinched his nose between gloved forefinger and thumb. 'I say,' he chuckled, 'next time I watch an enemy being crushed, I'll be sure to position myself upwind of the fray.'

The Alani regiment guarding him rumbled with laughter.

Bishop Ambrosius, mounted by his side, remained piously expressionless.

'Something wrong?' Gratian asked him, irked by his failure to laugh.

'You are winning, Domine. Everything is *right*. I am merely letting my mind wander to the future.'

'How so?' Gratian eyed him sideways.

Ambrosius tilted his head back a little as if to bask in the sunshine and stare up to God's realm. 'This victory means something great: that the Isle of Britannia will be returned to you from the usurper's hands.'

'I suppose,' Gratian shrugged.

Ambrosius shuffled in his saddle. 'The thing is, the discussions and plans for this battle were hasty. Much was said and decided in such a short space of time and I wonder how many of the decisions actually made it onto the scribes' scro-'

'Spit it out,' Gratian sighed.

Ambrosius shuffled again. 'As... as we agreed, once Maximus falls,

Britannia *will* be placed under my episcopal jurisdiction, yes?'

Gratian gave him a sideways look. 'That scrap of rock in the north? If you wish to try to tame the savages there then by all means, do so. I will need *someone* to be the steward of that forsaken place once I have Maximus' head on a pole.' He chuckled and wagged a finger down at the red smudge of battle. 'Seeing this is a good lesson for you or any who might serve me and rule parts of my empire in my name.' He twisted in the saddle, meeting the eyes of the smattering of officers and advisors with him, casting a sour look over the Heruli legion – armed for the first time in a year and standing back in reserve. 'That, down there in the vale... *that* is what happens to those who defy me.'

The Moorish cavalry mass, a stone's throw along the valley top, listened attentively too, their long dark manes of hair wafting in the hot wind. He turned back to the battle and picked out the best sights: the invading Tigrisienses archers, being pulverised easily by his Julia Alpina ranks; the carnage of the twin cavalry battles at either end of the fray, where horses now bolted, braying in panic, wet with blood, dragging decapitated bodies by the ankles or slumped, ripped open riders away down the valley; and the huge heaving infantry showdown around the hummock. While the original order of battle was all gone, there was some kind of pattern to the fray – one of decisive and imminent victory: his own legions vastly outnumbered Maximus', and the advantage was only widening. 'The carroballista wagons were his big ruse,' Gratian remarked to all around him. He pulled his hands up near his face and adopted a mock-terrified expression. 'I was petrified that his sticks and rocks might even reach halfway across the valley floor, cast up a puff of dust and spoil the air up here for me.'

The Alani again rumbled in sycophantic laughter.

At this distance, Gratian had to work hard to pick out Maximus himself. Gone was the white armour, for now the usurper fought on in a shining coat of blood, one arm hanging limp as if he had taken an injury. The mounted Arbogastes hacked and sliced through the infantry melee towards him. *It won't be long now...* he thought.

He spotted his Speculatores amidst the fighting. It had been a tough decision to commit them to battle, but they were the ultimate fighters, the best hunters. Even if half of them died or suffered terrible injuries, he was sure that the remainder would be the ones to bring Maximus' head. So why were they instead entangled a good javelin's throw away from the usurper, atop the grassy hummock? He saw that his agents had encircled and were overwhelming a clutch of men from one of Maximus' legions.

'Leave them, leave them,' Gratian called out jauntily as if they could hear from this distance, laughing and swiping a hand jovially. 'Go, get me the usurper's head!'

The Alani chortled at this.

But Gratian's laughter tapered off as he noticed the blood and dust-stained banner swaying amidst the beset and encircled knot of legionaries up on that hummock. A silver eagle on top, with a ruby banner hanging from the crossbar, emblazoned with... a dark bull? His mind raced over the many legionary emblems. There was only one regiment who marched under that insignia, wasn't there? The Claudia? But they were surely by now lying in a damp mass grave in faraway Thracia. Yet another thought struck him: what had become of Zeno and Crassus and those two cohorts he had recalled? He had never witnessed their return. In the rush of anticipation as he had orchestrated this ambush, he had not even noticed their absence at all. He stared harder at the red banner. It couldn't be, could it? No, no, he convinced himself, there must be others – rag-tag auxiliary units raised from Britannia. Whoever they were, they were stubborn, he thought, tracking one figure amidst the baying Speculator ring, fighting like a demon.

'It seems Maximus has a champion down there,' the Alani Tribunus laughed.

But Gratian did not laugh this time. His eyes tapered to slits. He could not see the faces of men at this distance, but the way this one fought – the speed, the strength. That deft reading of each of the Speculatores' moves, and his clever strikes at the great Molossian hounds... like one who had fought them before. It sent his mind spiralling back through time... to the clifftops at Dionysopolis. His hands tightened on the reins of his stallion and he straightened a little in the saddle.

The sunlight flickered and flashed on the gory iron garb of the 'champion', and so he could see nothing to affirm or disprove the fanciful thought. He laughed, understanding just how preposterous it was. The corpse of that wretch, Pavo, lay on the sea bed of the Mare Internum, dead like the other Claudians in their cold mass grave. In any case, the soldier down there – whoever he was and no matter how skilled he might be – could not beat all of his hundred Speculatores. The notion brought him a moment of calm. But then from nowhere, he heard that sound in his head. A sound that rasped over the ebb and flow of battle din, that swallowed the heat from the sun and drained every speck of confidence from his veins. The wet, rattling breaths of the dark creature on the moorland, coming for him, sword drawn.

'No… I prayed last night,' Gratian hissed through caged teeth. '*I was penitent!*'

'Domine, something is wrong?' Bishop Ambrosius said.

Gratian swung to him, annoyed that his lip felt stiff, as if it might quiver when he replied. A few of the Alani looked up at him too, confused at his sudden change in demeanour. The huge bank of Moorish riders too squinted, confused.

The thing is not here. It is a dream, a dark fantasy, nothing more, he told himself. As if to convince himself, he twisted his head in every direction: looked up at the skies – nothing. Across his retinue and the Heruli – nothing. Down into the fray – nothing. Then off to the east and…

There it was.

A giant, part-silhouetted by the mid-afternoon sun. A colossal thing, swaying along the valley ridge, past the Moorish lines, its thin hair wafting in the summer wind. All too real. Something hung from one of its hands. A sword? He could not be sure. He blinked and rubbed his eyes twice. How could nightmares walk like this?

'Archers!' he called to the bowmen amongst the Moorish riders. 'Shoot that thing. *Shoot* it!'

Everyone around Gratian rumbled in confusion. All looked east in the direction he was pointing, but none reacted as they should have. Gratian kicked one of his horse's flanks angering the beast but bringing it round towards the archers albeit in an agitated state. He brought his knuckles across the nearest bowman's face. 'Do as I say or I'll have you killed. Shoot that thing!'

But the struck man and his comrades seemed more confused than afraid. 'But, Domine, it is Merobaudes? I thought... I thought you said he was dead?' All across the Moorish cavalry wing, thousands of voices rose in a confused jabber. 'He lives... the shield of Valentinian, the colossus of Gaul *lives.*'

Gratian's lips moved, spelling out the name as he saw that it was not the moor creature of his dreams but the giant Frank. *Merobaudes? How?* He saw now that Merobaudes carried in his hand not a 'sword', but a buccina. At last, he regained his composure. He flicked a finger at the Alani. 'Finish him, *finish him!*'

The Alani Tribunus jolted into action. 'Do as your emperor commands,' he snarled, then levelled his spear towards Merobaudes. The rest of the five-hundred green-cloaked tribal guard did likewise, swinging to face Merobaudes.

Yet on Merobaudes came, calm, confident, colossal, alone, carrying just that bronze trumpet. Shafts of sunlight caught his face as he went, betraying the swollen eyes and split cheek to go with the old fire-scars. The Alani stalked along the valley top, along the Moorish front and towards the giant Magister Militum, the wind casting up their long blonde locks. Gratian watched them fan out around the shadowy colossus. His heart thumped in anticipation. The last of his great rivals would die up here too, along with Maximus down in the valley. 'Do it,' he hissed.

As the words were spoken, Merobaudes' shadow split into two as a smaller figure stepped out from behind the big general. Valentinian's silver vest and helm sparkled like a treasure.

Confused by this, the Alani halted between Gratian and the two newcomers. 'Are we to slay him too, Domine?' they called back. 'In front of...' the man said then slid his eyes towards the watching Moors.

Before Gratian could answer his Alani, young Valentinian addressed the Moorish cavalry. 'Riders of Africa. Long has General Merobaudes urged you to hold your tongues and keep your swords sheathed. For too many years Gratian has gone unchallenged. All because of the fear that we were not strong enough for a rebellion to succeed, that I – the only other with a blood-claim to the throne – would be executed.'

Gratian's skin crept as the massive wing of dark-skinned riders sat proud in their saddles, hanging on Valentinian's words.

'But my life is worth nothing compared to the tragedies my stepbrother has directed,' Valentinian continued. 'Gratian: the man who upon his accession cut off the head of Theodosius the Elder, your erstwhile patron and worthy lord, father of the Eastern Emperor; the man who lied to you, telling you that Merobaudes had fallen. In truth he had Merobaudes and myself on the edge of death in his cellars just a short time ago. Too many have suffered and died under my stepbrother's reign. No more. *No more.* The time has come.'

Slowly, the Moors nearest Merobaudes and Valentinian walked forward, forming a protective ring around the pair, blocking off and surrounding the Alani. Gratian was suddenly acutely aware of the complete absence of guards around his own person. He glanced over to the nearby Heruli reserve. 'Lanzo!' he snarled at the red-moustachioed Heruli Tribunus. 'Come forward, guard me.'

'Brave Lanzo and the descendents of the Heruli of the wild lands,' Valentinian spoke over Gratian. 'The time is now. This one chance is yours… *ours.*'

When the Heruli legionary front rustled, ready to take a step forward to answer Gratian's call, Lanzo held up a hand and spoke in an ancient Germanic tongue. Not a single one of them moved.

Gratian stared at Lanzo.

Lanzo stared back. 'I gave you all my support,' he said in Latin now. 'I prayed you could be the emperor your father was. In every way, you have failed. My Heruli will no longer obey the commands of a false emperor.'

The hot summer wind whistled. Gratian turned back to Valentinian, staring into his stepbrother's eyes, seeing a strength in there that he had worked so hard to repress for so long. So many years of ridiculing the boy, of telling him he was nothing, of having those who grew close to him tortured, maimed and murdered. Now he realised it had all been like whetting his blood-rival's blade.

'Riders of Africa,' Merobaudes boomed. 'Maximus, our liberator, is in dire shortage of men,' he pointed down to the valley floor. 'I ask you to fight for him as you would fight for me.'

Gratian heeled his stallion, causing it to rear up, the whinny half drowning out Merobaudes plea. 'Riders of Africa,' he countered. 'Cut this pair down, then pour down into the vally and end this battle. Do as I command... or I swear to you that I will have your desert villages torched, with every single child, wife and parent still inside.'

Silence. The lead Moor – an older man with a gaunt, puckered charcoal face, switched his old head from Merobaudes to Gratian, back to Merobaudes then finally to Gratian.

Pavo kicked a Speculator away from the crest of the grassy hummock like a sailor on a raft fending off a hungry shark. He carried his helm in one hand like a shield of sorts and his spatha in his numb and shaking sword hand, his mail vest ripped and hanging around his waist, his chest sliced from shoulder to hip and bleeding. Sura and Libo were with him, pressed back to back. Pulcher, Betto and Durio had scrambled back up there too, slipping and sliding as they tried in vain to backstep away from the ring of black-cloaked ones.

Just then, a great cry rose from the southern valley side; the shrill, ululating voices of foreign riders. The sunlight danced and sparkled on the Moorish reserve up there as they reared up and shook their weapons aloft. Then, like a smith's urn tilting to spill its contents, they raced down the slope like poured bronze. Pavo's heart froze. This was it, the death strike.

A cry from close by ripped his attentions back to the here and now. 'It is him,' shouted the silver-haired, crow-faced Speculator who seemed to be leading the others and who restrained a giant Molossian dog on a taut leash. 'It is Pavo! Tear him apart! Tear all of his men to shreds! For Emperor Gratian – before the Moors come to claim his head as their prize!'

The crow-faced Speculator roared with laughter, reaching down to unclip his Molossian's leash. The attack hound lunged towards Pavo and Crow-face and his ring of agents pounced like wolves too, blowing the small group of Claudians apart. The dog leapt for Pavo but he sank to one side and kicked out to catch the beast in the chest with his heel. The creature rolled away, winded and whining. Crow-face pounced for him next, catching his defensive spatha strike on some black-painted iron bracer, then grappling with him. The pair fell to the bloodstained grass, rolling past ripped-open bodies and cleaved, staring heads. They tumbled wildly down the side of the hummock, past packs of fighting men, guts and skin clinging to them like mud and leaves. Pavo swung the fist clutching his helm at the man's midriff, but the Speculator was nimble, bending his body to avoid the strike. Worse, the helm flew from Pavo's grip and tumbled away.

When they rolled down onto the valley floor, Crow-face sprung to his feet first and booted the still-prone Pavo's sword hand. Pavo cried out, the strike causing his wrist to spasm and the fingers to open, the sword flying away. The Speculator ripped out his own spatha and twirled it once to expertly catch it overhand, standing over the still-grounded Pavo, his silvery hair wafting in the wind. 'So what's it to be, traitor?' He said. 'Heart or belly? I could even let my dog chew on your neck.' The winded Molossian hobbled over, growling, blood and saliva rolling from its huge yellow fangs onto his face.

Pavo spat the gloopy filth of saliva and blood from his lips, the mess coating the Speculator's boots. The man blinked and grinned. 'Ah well, belly it is.'

He tensed his arm, lifting the sword back for the ruinous strike... and then a Moorish horseman saddled on a great white mare burst across the air behind the agent, bringing his curved sword expertly through the Speculator's neck. It was like a warmed knife sliding through a block of fat. Crow-face's head spun up into the air, mouth agape, and then the black-cloaked body toppled to one side like a pushed-over broom, sword still held up over where his head had been. All around Pavo, the ground shook madly. Confused, panicked, he rolled onto one side and then all-fours and took in what was happening all around him. Like a fisherman's knife ripping upwards across the scales of a salmon, the Moors were tearing through the fray, spearing down and cutting through not Maximus' men, but Gratian's. Dragathius rode with them, his Sarmaturum riding in formation with the African horsemen. Maximus' cavalry general was plastered with gore, but smiling evilly – his eyes and teeth terrifying in contrast to the blood, his long hair flailing in his wake. Pavo rolled to one side as a Moor on a powerful stallion almost trampled over him accidentally, then he swung round to see a wing of the African riders swarm up the hummock, trampling over the Speculatores up there. The black-cloaked agents fell with a chorus of screams and snapping bones, and those who dived clear were speared like fish. All along the fray, the cavalry charge blew everything apart. More, a strange clarion call now rose from the southern valley side. Pavo peered up there. A giant figure stood, blowing into a horn, and a smaller figure stood by his side. Where was Gratian?

Some of Gratian's legions seemed to be reading the continued cry of the horn from up there, and now they were turning upon other regiments of his.

'For General Merobaudes!' he heard the Moorish riders cry, and the men of the turning legions echoed the call. 'For Valentinian!'

Now Petulantes officers turned their charges against their erstwhile comrades of the III Julia Alpina. 'Death to Gratian!' they cried.

Arbogastes, almost having fought his way to within striking distance of Maximus, heard this latest cry and twisted in his saddle, eyes wide, the coppery wig sliding askew again, his jaw slackening at the colossal wave of riders tearing his forces apart. Like a startled deer, he kicked his horse into a frantic gallop, trampling over his own men, grabbing one of the ironclad cataphractii with him and pulling the man from his saddle so he might slow the oncoming Moors, then breaking clear of the fray and speeding west, up the valley and towards Parisiorum. A band of Moors gave chase, but Dragathius called them back. 'No, with me, the

Dalmaturum are still beset on the right flank!'

As the relief riders swept on to smash apart that other cavalry battle between the Dalmaturum and Gratian's Armatura, Pavo gasped in exhaustion, seeing Gratian's legions breaking apart, men fleeing in crazed runs, or kneeling and surrendering, held at spear and sword point by the legionaries of Maximus or those who turned to his cause.

He swayed back a few steps until he bashed against an upturned carroballista wagon at the foot of the hummock. His gaze slid around, seeing the carpet of broken-open, steaming bodies of the recent dead and the twitching, slithering bodies of the not-yet-dead. Vultures and flies gathered in thick black crowds, feasting. He heard a low growl, and realised the Molossian was still nearby… between him and the nearest dropped sword. His skin crept as the beast padded towards him. But, almost in apology, the great hound dipped its head before him, then clamped its jaws around the severed head of Crow-face the Speculator, lifted it and calmly carried it over to a sunny spot where it sat down and began licking hungrily at the bloody neck stump. Shuddering in relief, he twisted to look around the low hummock behind him. He saw Libo and Sura, Pulcher and Durio, Darik and Indus – crimson-spattered visions of Hades. Betto too stood with the Claudia standard, his blood-covered face streaked with white lines where tears poured as he planted the staff in the hummock top. 'Woe… to the vanquished,' he said quietly, the ancient doggerel of Livius understood by all.

Shaking with fatigue, Pavo looked over to see Merobaudes and Valentinian descending into the valley, approaching the remains of battle. Even from this great distance, young Valentinian spotted him, rose tall and mouthed his name. *Pavo?* Merobaudes too halted in his tracks, staring at the Claudia banner.

Finally, close by, a great rumble of concern arose. Maximus, dripping red and with curls of steam spiralling from man and horse, slid from his mount and landed on his knees, gasping for air. His remaining golden Victores guards helped him to his feet. Another lifted Maximus' standard and pumped it into the sky. 'Mag-nus Maxi-mus!' he bawled.

Many thousands of voices soared into the sky, echoing the cry over and over. '*Mag-nus Maxi-mus! Mag-nus Maxi-mus! Mag-nus Maxi-*

mus!'

'Tribunus Pavo,' Valentinian said, approaching.

'Caesar,' Pavo quarter bowed. When he rose again, he looked beyond the sea of bloodied men and the rising paean of triumph, up to the southern valley side. 'What happened to Gratian?'

'He fled,' big Merobaudes answered. 'When we turned against him he rode like lightning.'

Pavo felt a great chill and noticed a distant stain of dust, fading away to the south. He thought of the far-reaching network of noblemen, spies, garrisons and legions entire no doubt still loyal to the fallen emperor. 'Then it is not over. We must not cry victory until we know he has been seized.' He swung his gaze across everyone nearby: Maximus, Merobaudes, Valentinian, the Claudians, the Victores, all of them. 'While Gratian remains at large, every one of us – and our families – are in danger.'

Chapter 24
August 383 AD
Central Gaul

Gratian hunched over his stallion's neck for speed, his black cloak flailing madly behind him as he pelted south, alone, away from the valley. He heard shouts, saw thrown javelins quiver in the earth, wide or falling short of his flight. His mind flashed with all that had happened, and none of it seemed real. In the space of moments, everything had turned. He glanced over his shoulder to Heruli legionaries giving chase on foot but then giving up. Being alone felt cold, terrifying. For a moment, he thought he understood how those masked slaves might have felt on a 'hunt'. But then he spotted a thicket of ash nearby.

'With me!' he snarled. A turma of equites stationed in the shade of the thicket cantered into view then broke into a gallop to fall in around him like an arrowhead.

'What happened, Domine?' the decurion asked, face pale with shock.

'A complication, nothing more,' Gratian snapped.

Behind him, the distant but clear chant rose up from the vale: '*Magnus Maxi-mus! Mag-nus Maxi-mus! Mag-nus Maxi-mus!*'

The decurion looked that way, but dared not speak.

For the rest of the day Gratian kept his horse moving south at frantic speed, heedless of the lather on its hide or the foam streaking from its mouth, or the concerned looks on the faces of the thirty equites riding with him. All the time, his eyes raked the horizon like a plough.

'Domine,' said the decurion, his black plume blown flat by the wind of the breakneck ride, 'we should stop – rest and water the horses. Perhaps we could then veer due west, towards Parisiorum or the waystations on the *Via Agrippa*? There, we could collect fresh steeds and supplies.'

Gratian canted his head a little, like a gull hearing a morsel of food falling to the ground. 'No, we ride for Aurelianum,' he snapped. It was a day's ride away, but that great stronghold city on the banks of the Liger would make for a good stronghold to take stock and organise his retaliation, he thought. It was stronger even than Treverorum, and he had stationed the Septimiani legion there last winter to watch the city... and the movements of Governor Isauricus. The man had been seen talking to Merobaudes one night at an imperial symposium. Shortly after that report, Gratian had arranged for Isauricus' body slave to fall down a well, and for a well-disguised Speculator to take his place. He imagined in his mind's eye riding in through the great grey walls, giving his Speculator body slave there a single look, and watching Isauricus' big, obsequious face widening in shock as a blade slammed into his back. Once Isauricus was dead, he would rally the Septimiani. They were palace elites and they would form a new core. After that, he could send word south to Lugdunum. There, two wings of the Brachiati cavalry school were stationed, along with the Regii legion and a new legion he had been raising secretly – the Gratianenses. They could form the core of a stronger, more loyal army. More, Laeta would be there soon too. He had sent her there by fast wagon just after the events in the bathhouse at dawn. He thought of her sweet-scented skin, her wanton lips... and the delightful things she could do. Yes, he thought, southern Gaul and the neighbouring Diocese of Viennensis would be a perfect launch site for reprisals. 'Ya!' he snarled, heeling his horse into a faster gallop. Next, he could despatch further riders to Italia, to gather up the garrisons and patrols of the peninsula. The Misenum and Ravenna fleets too. This was not over. It had only just begun.

They rode on at that incredible pace as the light began to slip away. Soon, the flat and endless heathland ahead became painted in long stripes of amber light and charcoal shadow, then it all melted into a veil of deep blue and indigo, and finally the sunlight was gone, the moon and stars casting everything in an odd, ghostly grey. Gratian noticed every dark shape ahead. Bushes, stands of trees, high mounds – ancient ruins of Gallic oppida, low bluffs and thick woods. Despite the arrowhead of steely riders around him, he felt a strange, horrible sense of nakedness. He began to hear his horse's laboured breathing and it mixed with his own, turning into something else in his mind.

The low, rasping breaths… the whisper of death… the closeness of that thing.

Just then, one shadow ahead seemed larger than those of the bushes elsewhere. Was it… was it moving, swaying, towards him? Gratian stared, and stared again: it *was* the moor creature from his nightmares, he realised with cold terror. It had not one face but one thousand faces. He yanked on his reins in panic and his silver stallion reared up and slumped onto its hindquarters, exhausted, whinnying madly. He fell from the saddle, the equites parting expertly around him so as not to trample over him. They slowed, circling back and sliding from their mounts to surround him, worried.

But Gratian remained on his knees, not daring to look up in the direction of the thing. The words of the Prayer of Penitence poured from his mouth in a rapid stream, almost without pause:

'*O Almighty God, merciful Father,*
I confess to you all my sins and iniquities,
with which I have ever offended you.
But I am heartily sorry for them and sincerely repent of them,
and I pray you of your boundless mercy…'

'Domine? Are you hurt?' the decurion said, helping Gratian to rise.

Gratian's head switched around the black land. Nothing. No creature. 'Where did it go?'

'Who?'

'You did not see it?' he croaked.

Blank faces in the gloom.

He seized the decurion by the collars of his cloak and pulled him nose-to-nose. 'Do not try to make a fool of me! Who put you up to this? Was it Merobaudes? Was it?'

'Domine, I, I don't understand,' the decurion wailed.

Gratian seized the man's jaw with one hand then flicked the fist of the other past the decurion's neck. The two parted and it seemed that the moment had passed... until the first spray of dark red pulsed from the decurion's jugular vein. The man himself did not notice at first, but the other twenty nine riders did, each taking a step back in horror. The decurion, confused, looked around his fellow cavalrymen, then noticed the light patter of blood hitting the grass below his feet. In the light of the stars and the waning moon, one half of his body glistened wet, and his face lost all colour. With a weak groan, he fell to one knee as if genuflecting before Gratian, then toppled to his side on the bloodsoaked grass.

Gratian swung around the other twenty nine riders. 'Any other traitors here?' he said, his fang-ring hand dripping red as it moved to his jewelled spatha hilt.

The twenty nine – stunned – silently shook heads. Only one dared to speak. 'I saw it,' he said, gulping, shaking. 'The thing you saw. *I* saw it too.'

Gratian crept closer to this one.

'Yes, I saw it,' he repeated hurriedly, licking his dry lips.

Gratian came nose to nose with this one now, then gestured at the dead decurion's body. 'Take his plumed helm. You are decurion now.'

The one who had spoken could barely mask his relief and delight at the promotion. He seemed entranced by the helm, prizing it off the dead man's head without care for the body and sliding it onto his scalp.

With a violent wrench of the reins, Gratian tugged his horse back to standing and vaulted onto its back. 'Stay loyal to me and all of you will be well rewarded,' he said to the riders as he patted the purse on his hip. 'Do you hear that? I have mere bronze and silver now. But I have a vault in Aurelianum and another in Lugdunum, both stacked with gold solidi. Now get back onto your horses. We ride throughout the night.'

The horses fell into a stupefied canter during the blackness, but Gratian scarcely noticed. His mind was fully-occupied with the dark lands ahead, watchful for the dark creature.

Near dawn, they came to Aurelianum, a buttress of creamy stone sited atop one of those ancient Gallic oppidum mounds. Gratian scoured the battlements, spotting the white banner and blazing red sun of the Septimiani, and the lustrous iron helms of the men of that elite legion patrolling the walkway and the stout towers. The watchmen peered over the battlements in disbelief as their emperor led his wayworn knot of iron horsemen through the shanty-wards of the vicus outside the city walls and up the broad flagged ramp-road towards the open northern gates.

'D-Domine?' A Septimiani officer called down.

Gratian ignored him, leading his band inside, wading through crowds of early-rising citizens still clutching bread and jugs of freshly-drawn water, blinking in incredulity. They came to the stable area near the city forum – a large stone warehouse open on one side and divided inside by timber partitions to make individual animal quarters, the floor scattered with straw and the air reeking of dung. Stable boys sped to their aid, leading their exhausted horses to the water troughs. Gratian snatched a jug of fruit juice from one slave and glugged it down.

'Majesty!' a familiar voice echoed throughout the stable house.

Gratian turned to see Governor Isauricus sweeping towards him, his long blue robes trailing on the floor, arms outstretched, that jovial face wide with a welcoming smile. His long flowing grey-blonde hair and beard hung like octopus' arms around his shoulders and chest. 'This is a most unexpected visit.'

'Is it?' Gratian said curtly. *Or did you and Merobaudes collude?*

Isauricus' face twitched in surprise. 'What happened?' he said, seeing the state of Gratian's garb – dusty and spattered with crimson.

'Battle,' Gratian lied, gesturing to the encrusted patches of the murdered decurion's blood. 'Battle happened.'

'Then it is over? The invaders have been repelled?'

Gratian considered the consequences of his answer, and chose to phrase it carefully. 'I oversaw the main swing of victory, but I was chased from my position by a band of traitors.' He noticed thick crowds gathering – civic staff and soldiers of the Septimiani close by and citizens congregating at a respectful distance outside the open side of the stable house.

Isauricus' face flagged. 'But... you did *see* the moment of victory, didn't you?'

Gratian stared at him, feeling the tense stares of the many around him. For a moment he considered another flat lie, but then he noticed the bald, scrawny body slave lurking behind Isauricus. A distraction was as good as a lie, he thought. His eyes met the slave's, and the slave read the tacit command.

Isauricus gasped. All heads turned from Gratian to the long-haired governor. Isauricus gazed around them all as if a profound truth was on the tip of his tongue. But all that emerged was a pinkish foam and a low, hollow rattle. He staggered towards the watering trough, gripping its edge, his weight tipping the whole thing over. Isauricus fell and, with a gurgling crash, the trough and a huge cascade of water came tumbling down over him. The heavy trough staved in his head, but it was of no matter, for the blade sticking from between his shoulders had been fatal anyway.

Gratian stepped away from the spreading water and blood as the Septimiani jolted to their senses and turned towards the body servant. The scrawny man merely placed a staring eye ring on his finger, kissed it, then closed his eyes and spread his arms out wide like one awaiting transportation to Elysium. With an explosion of shouts and hissing of drawn swords, the Septimiani legionaries pounced upon the servant. In a flurry of hacking arms, blood leapt up. The watching citizens screamed, backing away and then fleeing – uncertain if this was the start of a civil massacre.

Gratian waved his turma of dismounted riders back from the chaos. He noticed the Septimiani Tribunus speeding through the city towards the stables, white cloak and plume flailing as he drew his own sword. 'All is in hand,' Gratian said, stepping out in front of the legionary commander. 'A traitor slew poor Isauricus – but he is now in ribbons.'

The tribunus blinked, looking past Gratian's shoulder to the stable's open side and the red tangle of flesh and bone that remained of the body servant, then at the prone corpse of Isauricus, then finally at Gratian himself. 'Domine? How... *what* happened here? A few of my men sent a call around the walls saying you were here. Why?'

Gratian opened his mouth to feed him the same lie, when a horn blared, muffled – coming from somewhere outside the city walls. Shaken even more, the tribunus backed away from Gratian with a salute. 'Domine, I must see who approaches our city.'

Gratian watched as the man climbed to the northern battlements and began signalling with the Septimiani banner, then waving, then shouting some challenge at whoever was approaching. 'Identify yourself!' the tribunus bawled again.

'Trouble, Tribunus?' Gratian called up to him.

'A legion approaches, Domine,' he called back, 'but… but not one of yours. It's, it's the Victores. It's *Maximus'* legion and… and his riders. The Primani and Secundani too… more coming in their wake.'

'They march in victory,' said another sentry with a tight gasp.

Gratian felt the ground fall away beneath him. He thought instantly of his finest agents, the Speculatores, and almost had the call to bring them to his side on his tongue before he realised that they were most probably all dead now. He saw the fleshy mess of the body slave and realised he might just have carelessly thrown away his last agent's life.

The tribunus up on the walls turned to look down into the city at Gratian, his stiff and panicked stance easing, the Septimiani staff sagging in his grip. 'You were beaten. Maximus routed your army,' he said in a tone dripping with disgust and disdain. The many citizens cowering and watching from windows and doorways now gasped, necks lengthening, eyes widening. The Septimiani gathered near the stables gradually turned to stare at him too.

'The usurper won,' said a legionary flatly.

'The "usurper" is now Emperor of the West,' agreed another.

Gratian saw how they all still held bloody swords in their hands. '*I am your emperor, you dog,*' he screamed. 'I have a fresh army waiting in the south, and Maximus and his men will be turned back. Any man who so much as speaks another word of the usurper will be executed. But kneel before me and – once order is restored – each of you will have ten gold solidi.'

Another muffled cry sounded from outwith the city. 'Magnus Maximus offers a donative of thirty solidi for each soldier of the Septimiani. Come, march with the new Emperor of the West in his quest to find Gratian, the fallen tyrant.'

The eyes of the Septimiani glittered like jewels. The low thunder of boots and hooves approaching Aurelianum's northern ramp sailed through the city streets.

The Septimiani tribunus stared at Gratian for a few heartbeats, then fully drew his spatha. 'Kill the riders, seize the fallen emperor,' he burred, flitting down from the battlements, a dozen more coming with him.

It was like a sudden downpour of steel. Javelins flew from the most prepared of the Septimiani. Six of Gratian's equites shuddered and clutched their chests as the lances punched through ringmail, bone and flesh. Three more equites leapt for the Septimiani legionaries closest to them, striking them down before they could be struck down themselves. A pair of the riders sliced through the tethers of a dozen fresh horses, leaping on the backs of two and driving the rest out in a stampede. Gratian poised himself and lunged to grab the reins of one and haul himself into the saddle. Eleven of his men managed to take a horse. The rest became swamped with Septimiani legionaries before they could mount, but their struggle opened a path through the city, towards the southern gates – away from the approaching forces of Maximus.

'Ya!' Gratian screamed as his black mare burst into a gallop along the flagged streets. The Septimiani Tribunus moved to block his way, only for Gratian to ride over the man without a second thought. Javelins spat and whizzed overhead and by his sides. One more of his equites fell but within moments they were halfway across the city and in sight of the open southern gates. The watch here was roused by the noise from the far side of the city, but as-yet oblivious to its meaning.

'Domine?' Septimiani men here called down, not quite sure they could believe their eyes.

Gratian ignored them and sped on out of the southern gates, raced down to the Liger River bridge and thundered across it with a furious rattle of hooves on flagstones. Once onto the softer ground of the far banks they pounded on up a low rise and sped into the network of low hills and vales beyond.

'To Lugdunum,' he rasped to his remaining ten riders. Seven days away, he thought. Forget the treacherous Septimiani. The Brachiati riders, the Regii legion and the Gratianenses would be his new bedrock. Laeta, waiting for him there, would be a fine outlet for his anger too. 'There my new army will rise up and – by the Will of God – the traitors will beg for a quick death.'

For seven nights they rode. On the third night they crossed the diocesal border from Gaul into Viennensis. Soon after they came to a waystation, guarded by six auxiliaries. At first, the auxiliaries would not let them approach, saying they had heard that the fallen emperor was on the run in these parts and demanded that the party identify themselves. It had been their death warrant. Gratian led his ten riders away from the burning waystation upon yet another set of fresh mounts. Word had spread, he realised. Like fire, it would travel fast. But Maximus' lumbering army could not hope to move as speedily as he and his small band. They would reach Lugdunum before the rumours took hold there. Lugdunum would be the great dam, the turning point, the start of the reconquest... the first spots of a red deluge that would rage northwards across Gaul.

On the fifth night – as the riders slept by their horses on the open ground by the road, man and beast exhausted, Gratian remained awake, staring at the black countryside. Now the shadows of bushes and trees moved as if all were walking, swaying towards him. The rattling wet breaths of the moor creature grew louder and louder in his head, along with the squabble of a thousand voices. Children singing then screaming, women laughing then sobbing, men crying out in pain, slaves weeping, hooves thundering, and the ongoing sizzle and rasp of torture instruments, the iron song of war and the screech of carrion birds. Maddened, he knelt, praying over and over.

'*O Almighty God, merciful Father,*
I confess to you all my sins and iniquities,
with which I have ever offended you.
But I am heartily sorry for them and sincerely repent of them,
and I pray you of your boundless mercy...'

He halted and looked up and around. The squabbling voices and terrible sounds seemed to be gone... only for them to return like a roaring gale. Eyes wide as moons, he clasped his hands over his ears and fell to his side, staring, until dawn came.

At noon on the seventh day, they moved along a narrow deer trail across the top of a conifer-lined massif, the trees mercifully blocking out the blazing sun and lending a fresh fragrance of pine resin to the air. Squirrels darted up and down the tall trunks as they passed, from and to dreys, woodpeckers drummed and insects hummed. They emerged from the trees and onto the southern slopes of the massif. Gratian shielded his eyes from the sun, looking downhill at the confluence of the great south-flowing rivers Rodanus and Arar. Nestled securely in a loop of the joined river rose the vast walled metropolis of Lugdunum. The silver battlements sparkled in the noonday heat, uplit by the foaming cobalt river waters lashing around the northern, eastern and southern sides, and from this high approach Gratian could see the greatness of the place: the imperial barracks and cavalry school, the tall, domed basilica and the grand mint; the wool and arms factory; the huge theatre cut into the slopes of the acropolis mount in the centre of the city and the majestic bathhouse and palace up there. It would be a fine bulwark and perhaps a new capital, once things were put right.

They came down to the foot of the massif and crossed the low, arable river lands: fertile wheat and barley grounds criss-crossed with streams, irrigation ditches and – in places where the land had been left untended – moors and swamps. The heads of workers dotting the crop fields rose up like interested rodents, staring at the tarnished emperor and his weary riders.

'See?' he said to the ten horsemen with him, pointing to the jagged sun banners on the city parapets as they clopped over a wooden tributary bridge and approached the northwestern gates. 'The Regii legion lines the walls here. Even if Maximus' lies have stretched this far, they will remain loyal to me. And we can rest assured, thanks to our great efforts and days and nights of riding, that the usurper's lumbering forces are at best days behind us!'

'Domine!' the Regii on the walls bawled, thrusting up their spears as one in a grand salute. Almost five hundred voices. The summer air filled with a paean of buccina song – heralding the presence of an emperor.

'You hear that?' he smirked to his riders. He fished in his bag for his jewelled diadem and slid it onto his long-unwashed blond locks. 'You were wise to stick with me. You will live good lives as rich men. I need a core of good men to replace my school of agents, you see. And I-'

His words tapered off, drowned out by the groan of the city's huge, bronze-strapped gates. Out came a quartet of Regii legionaries, carrying on their shoulders a litter, the semi-opaque drapes wafting lazily in the breeze. Gratian recognised the fabrics, even caught the sweet scent of rose and cinnamon in the air.

'Laeta,' he whispered wetly, his lust rising alongside his sense of triumph. 'Bring her here,' he commanded the Regii.

The four soldiers obediently trooped over to him.

'We have much to discuss,' he called to her, 'troubles in the north, and I know you have sharp ideas about how the Western Empire should be shaped – ideas I want to hear. But that is for later. First, I have other needs that you must see to.'

The four Regii drew up beside him, presenting the side of the litter.

'It is never my intention to hurt you, but in the throes of the bedchamber some things cannot be helped. And when we get into the city palace, it *will* hurt,' Gratian said as he dismounted and reached up to pull the drape back.

From within, Dragathius stared back at him, crouching on one knee like a sprinter, his evil face glinting with menace, his long grey hair hanging either side of his wide grin, shuddering slightly with anticipation. 'Hurt?' Maximus' cavalry commander whispered. 'Oh yes, it *will* hurt...'

Gratian staggered back, arms milling for balance. Dragathius sprung from the litter, drawing a spatha in one hand and a tribal axe in the other, shrieking, long grey hair flailing up behind him. The four Regii dropped the litter and drew their swords too, flanking Dragathius. It was only the instinctive leap of one of Gratian's dismounted equites to block their combined strike that saved him. The eques sank to his knees, skewered by five swords, his head nearly halved by Dragathius' axe, blood pulsing from each wound.

As Dragathius struggled to wrench his sword and axe free of the dead eques, Gratian clambered back onto his horse. A shrill laugh toppled down from the walls of Lugdunum. 'I've already taken good measures to rectify the Western Empire,' Laeta called down from those heights.

'Laeta?' Gratian gasped, then roared. '*Laeta!*'

'You should have known I have a knack of backing the strongest. Once it was you... now it is Maximus. I paid the legions and riders here with coins from your vaults. Forty solidi per man to open the gates for Dragathius and swear fealty to the new emperor.'

'Aye,' Dragathius growled, ripping his sword free and working the axe almost free of the eques' corpse too. 'Magnus Maximus and the legions may be days north of here. But my riders and I got here yesterday. Now... step down from your horse and fall to your knees. It is over.' He lifted his axe – dripping with brains and blood – and held it ready to throw like a hunter might, the keen edge trained on Gratian's chest.

Gratian's top lip curled into a hateful sneer. 'Have Lugdunum, you cur,' he cried, wrapping his arm around the shoulders of the nearest eques and pulling him across his front like a shield. Dragathius reacted, loosing the axe. The weapon whirled into the eques' midriff. The horseman let loose a dreadful cry of pain, before Gratian shoved him away and kicked his own mount round in a tight circle, speeding east – directly across the wheat fields, sending workers scrambling out of his way. Behind him, the cry of men and clash of swords sounded as the last of his equites blocked Dragathius and the Regii four. A lethal whir sounded – arrows loosed from the city walls. He glanced back to see all but three of his riders pricked with shafts, and the remaining trio dropped their swords, slid from their saddles and fell to their knees in search of mercy.

Facing forwards and lying low in the saddle, he set his sights on the Rodanus bridge, powering across it before any could give chase. The low meadows on the far banks made for speedy riding, and soon the gentle hills and vales were between him and Lugdunum. The loss of the great city and its forces bit at him like rabid dogs. But soon he clopped onto the flagged way of the pine-fringed *Via Compendium*. It was a quick road south, towards the Alpes and beyond: Italia. He gazed up at the hazy grey and ethereal range hovering above the southern horizon. So the mountains would be his great dam now. All the garrison and levy forces still in Italia and Africa could be summoned to block the mountain passes before the reconquest began. A winter in preparation and then a summer of revenge, followed by long years of reprisal. 'Reprisal and penitence,' he seethed. 'The two will swing like a corpse on a rope.' He glared south and was about to lash his horse for more speed, when...

Glinting steel, a burst of leaves, a thunder of hooves. The horsemen surged from the treeline to the right of the road and spread across his path like a barricade. Three of Dragathius' Sarmaturum riders. Stationed here, he realised, to catch him in case he somehow escaped from the litter trap. His head pounded. A troop of enemies not far behind and these three ahead. Nowhere to run. As he grabbed his spatha hilt and pulled it awkwardly free, he realised how long it had been since he had been in true battle without a thick ring of protectors. Those swordplays with his Alani were good for keeping him quick and skilful, but they did not truly test him. The lead Sarmaturum rider heeled his horse into a walk, then a canter, levelling his sword for a strike – no dialogue, no demands for surrender. Panicked, Gratian kicked his own mount, causing the stallion to whinny and rear up. The action caused the creature to take the Sarmaturum rider's sword strike across the belly. The stallion fell to the ground, thrashing in a mess of its own guts. Gratian rolled clear and just managed to swipe his sword round to hack at the lower leg of the attacking rider's mount. This war horse plunged to its knees, screaming, throwing the rider like an onager would hurl a rock. The rider flailed but landed on his head, his neck breaking instantly. The other two riders – one broad and older, the other young and bright-eyed – circled the now horseless Gratian. He eyed each with darting looks. Finally, he realised he had the answer. 'My crown,' he stammered, taking off the jewelled diadem and holding it up so it caught the sun. 'It is yours. Let me go and it is yours.'

'I think I'll just take it anyway,' the broader Sarmaturum chuckled. 'You're in no position to bargain.'

So Gratian smiled instead at the young, bright-eyed rider. 'So *he* will take this prize, when you have done just as much as him to capture me?'

The young man laughed once and sat tall in his saddle. Gratian knew it was but a mask of indifference, for he saw the younger one's furtive glance at his elder. He tossed the crown past both of them, into the grass. 'Go, have it – whichever of you is fastest.'

The two Sarmaturum glared at each other over Gratian's head, then the young one scrambled down from his mount and leapt onto the crown. The older one howled at him for being a fool, and Gratian used the man's momentary distraction to lunge upwards and sink his spatha into the fleshy part of his belly, just underneath the rib cage. The blade plunged upwards, splitting lung and heart. The older rider sagged forward in the saddle, dead.

The young man swung round, horrified, dropping the crown. Gratian smirked at him, shoving the dead rider aside and clambering into the saddle. The young one came at him, tear-streaked, sword cutting round for Gratian's trailing leg. But Gratian pulled his leg up and the strike tore the horse's neck. Gratian leapt clear as this proud steed fell too, landing on top of the young man. The youngster cried out. 'My legs are broken! Help!'

Gratian walked round to stand over him, lining his spatha over the man's face. 'With pleasure,' he purred, driving the spatha tip down through his cheekbone. The young rider's dying screams scared off his horse – the last steed alive and present. As the beast thundered off the left side of the road and into the nearby pine woods, Gratian cursed, knowing a horse was his best chance of speeding to safety in Italia. Distant cries and blaring horns sounded from the direction of Lugdunum, not far behind him. He realised the roads would soon be thickly awash with pursuing enemy soldiers. So he wasted no time, lurching into the woods on foot in pursuit of the horse. Branches snapped and bracken crackled underfoot as he forged roughly westwards through the musty forest. The horse that had fled would stop near water, he guessed. Yet hours passed and the light faded, and he realised he was lost. In the darkness, he stumbled through brakes of fern, struggled through gorse thickets and scraped between closely-packed pine and silver birch trunks. In the depths of night, the forest began to hiss all around him as a tepid summer mizzle fell. Soon, it soaked him through, making every step heavier. Mist rose in coils around him, giving rise to a thick, earthy petrichor, and there seemed to be no end to this damned wood. But then he realised something: the horns and the shouts in the north had vanished hours ago. Nobody was chasing him. Dragathius must have sped on down the Via Compendium like a fool. More, the first light of dawn – grey shafts of light weakly penetrating the cover of cloud – shone down, showing him the way from the woods. He emerged from the pines onto a rain-soaked moor, the low roiling cloud above hiding the tops of the Alpes mountains which rose just an arrow-shot south. He stared east, across the moor. A narrow but deep river ran down from the mountains and across the moor, cutting across his path. It was spanned by an old timber bridge – wet with the rain and shining, a single length of ragged rope hanging limp from the rail at one side. *Over the bridge and along the rough eastwards track,* he thought, *a way along the edge of the Alpes range. A way towards the next southwards pass through the mountains.* Best of all? Not a soul in pursuit. Not an enemy in sight.

He took a small horn from his belt and held it to his lips, issuing three shrill blasts. The sound echoed eerily through the smir of rain and across the moor. How far was the fort from here, he wondered? He had kept the Genevan scout riders very well-paid over the years. Those few hundred horsemen would come to his call. They would usher him along this path then through the Alpes and into Italia. He watched the moor and listened intently, wondering if fortune might be with him and the Genevans might be riding close by. But the Genevan horsemen did not appear or reply to the horn call with a call of their own.

Instead, from behind a rock on the far side of the bridge, the thing that had been waiting there for him, the thing that had haunted the chambers of his mind for so long, rose and stepped out.

Gratian's breath stopped. For a moment, his heart did not beat. The thing moved across the moorland on the far side of the bridge, coming towards that timber walkway. Gratian's eyes alternately narrowed and widened with each quickening breath. The mizzle made strange shapes of the figure. It was a shadow of a man, with a spatha hanging from one hand, the head was dipped, and his mind projected first one face then a thousand more upon it: Merobaudes, Dragathius, Maximus, Gallus, the hundreds of animal-masked slaves he had hunted in the woods, the scores of rivals he had tortured, the entire legions who had been sacrificed to further his ambitions.

Gratian stared at the thing that had haunted his dreams for so long. 'Who are you?'

The creature halted at the far bridgehead, blocking the way across. When it looked up, its true face was eagle-like and baleful, its hazel eyes searching deep inside him.

'You know who I am.'

Chapter 25
August 25th 383 AD
The Geneva Bridge

The warm rain hissed down on the bridge timbers, splashed into the river in silvery bursts, ran from Pavo's sodden scalp, down his nose, lips and chin and dripped onto his poorly-repaired mail shirt. The chest cut from the Battle of Remorum Vale – nine days ago – was bandaged but still raw and hot, and his muscles ached from the relentless pursuit, first with Maximus' marching army, then on the speedy ride with Dragathius' advance party, Sura, Libo and big Pulcher coming too. He had been there, in Lugdunum with Dragathius' other men, waiting to spring from the gates and assist the Regii four who had carried the litter. When Gratian had fled that snare, he had been quick to take mount and ride in pursuit with Dragathius. They had shot across the Rodanus bridge and down the southerly Via Compendium, and soon they had found the slaughtered Sarmaturum trio Dragathius had posted there. The big cavalry master had bawled at the dozens of riders with him. 'To the south, before he reaches the mountains!' But Pavo had let the others go, hanging back, staring at the dead three and at the trio of slaughtered horses – one of which was the steed Gratian had been riding. The Western Emperor *might* have escaped on the third Sarmaturum horse… but if he hadn't. Pavo's eyes had been drawn to the pine woods at the edge of the road. Half-snapped branches hung there. Something had plunged into those woods. He had entered the trees and, just before dawn, arrived at this bridge. Seeing no recent bootprints on the dirt road leading to it, he realised Gratian had yet to reach this point.

'You,' Gratian blinked, swiping the rainwater from his face. 'How can you be alive? I threw you to your death at Dionysopolis. I had your galley riven in the Mare Internum.'

Pavo took one slow step forward onto the bridge timbers. 'I was pulled from the waters underneath the cliffs of Dionysopolis by one of my legionary brothers. And after our galley was rammed, he was with me also. We clung to timber fragments as if they were life itself. Then we trekked across Anatolia, moved like fugitives back through Constantinople and our homeland of Thracia. We found the foul island where you had my men imprisoned. We chose to join our brothers incarcerated there. We shared their unlawful punishment and unpardonable pain. It was with the aid of Gothic allies – truer and more noble than any of your kind – that we sent your men, Zeno and Crassus, to their deaths. Next, I led my legion across the breadth of the empire. Some of my men have faced you and know what you are. All have suffered the consequences of your wicked orders. Some are orphans, and know only that their fathers died needlessly on the plains of Adrianople. To a man,' he spat, stabbing a single finger downwards as if claiming the bridge as his own, 'to a *man*, they begged me to bring them to Maximus, to let them take their place by his side on the day that you finally met justice.'

Gratian spread his hands, grinning triumphantly. 'Justice?' he said, stepping onto the bridge and looking around at the cloud-swamped mountains and pines. 'Maximus has spent thousands of lives in grabbing Gaul. He will not hold it for very long. By next summer, his head will rest on a pike and Gaul will be mine again.' He gestured across his own armoured body. 'Look, I am the Emperor of the West. I live, and so Maximus has failed. Given time, I can wring more than enough troops from Italia and Africa to crush him.

Pavo shook his head slowly. 'What forces remain in Africa and Italia are – like the horsemen and legions who turned upon you at Remorum – loyal to your stepbrother. Valentinian has taken oaths from the commanders in the dioceses and provinces. More, your Speculatores are dead. All dead. Their time is over.'

Gratian issued a single, barking laugh. 'I can simply snap my fingers,' he did so, 'and Emperor Theodosius is obliged to answer my call – sending his spare legions from your sorry Eastern homeland.'

Pavo took another step forward, letting the tip of his spatha drag on the bridge timbers, the low grumble of steel chewing against wet wood causing the bridge to shiver a little. 'There are no spare legions in the East that he can send,' he burred. 'The great armies who once controlled those parts now lie in a great grave of bones near Adrianople. Your doing, *Domine,*' he spat the honourific like a knot of gristle. 'And your undoing. Did you know that Emperor Theodosius gave Maximus his blessing? The East was against you throughout all of this too.'

Gratian's top lip twitched and curled back like an angry dog showing its teeth, and he stepped further onto the bridge, closer to Pavo. 'So be it. There are still legions and cavalry schools loyal to me. If the East is as impoverished as you say, then perhaps I will lead them there. I will drag Theodosius from his chair and I will personally behead *him* as I beheaded his father.'

Pavo halted now, spreading his feet, bringing his spatha up in a two-handed hold. He shook his head slowly. 'You will die on this bridge.'

Gratian's face flashed with malice now. He drew his sword slowly and deliberately. 'You forget, Legionary, I have been trained since boyhood by the best swordsmen in the empire. And when we fought before, I won. I cast you from the cliffs!'

'You fought well... *with* the support of your bastard Speculatores,' Pavo said flatly. 'Here and now, it is just me and you.'

Gratian's face flickered with some dark emotion. Pavo stared into his eyes, unblinking.

From nowhere, the ground began to shiver. Pavo glanced past Gratian and into the woods in the direction of the Via Compendium. *Riders... Dragathius?* A thrill travelled up his spine. But the woods were not shaking, and there was no sign of movement in there. Now the thrill changed into a shiver as he realised the noise was coming not through the thick woods but from behind him, from the east.

Gratian laughed like a jackal. 'An audience!' he cried, just as the distant rumble changed into an eruption of hooves, pouring across the moor.

Pavo risked a look over his shoulder. *Equites sagittarii* – horse archers. Scores and scores of them, coming towards the bridge and his back.

'Horses!' Gratian quailed theatrically, raising his sword hand and free hand in a gesture of mock terror. 'But… they're coming from the wrong direction, aren't they? That's right. An *ala* of scout riders from Geneva. Most *definitely* loyal to me.'

The riders slowed around the bridgehead at Pavo's back, trapping him on the walkway. They milled and stared for a moment, uncertain as to what was happening. When one spotted Pavo's drawn sword, he shouted: 'The emperor is in danger,' drawing his bow, nocking an arrow and training the tip on Pavo's back.

'No!' Gratian halted them with a raised hand. 'This dispute is for me to settle.'

The groan of the archer's straining bow eased, but only a little.

Pavo turned his gaze back to the central stretch of the bridge and to Gratian, just in time to see the Western Emperor's lips flicker at either end and rise sharply into a shark's smile. With a shrill cry, 'Haaa!' Gratian sprung forward, jabbing his spatha tip towards Pavo's neck. Pavo sank to one side to dodge what would have been a killing blow, and in the same motion brought his sword up to bat Gratian's strike away then swished it back down and round for the Western Emperor's left flank. Yet Gratian was just as agile, dropping his sword mid-air and catching it blade-down to use it as a guard. Sparks flew as Pavo's strike clashed off of the blocking sword. Both recoiled from the force of the collision.

Gratian took just two steps back before speeding in again, chopping towards Pavo's neck. Pavo slashed upwards to parry, but Gratian feinted, bringing his strike downwards to streak down Pavo's chest, ripping his mail shirt open – the crudely repaired links spraying loose through the rain. Pavo stumbled back from the strike, crashing against the bridge rail, winding himself. Gratian drove in for a death-strike, bringing his sword chopping down like an axe, and Pavo only just spun away from the spot before the blade hacked into the rail timbers. It stuck there for a mere trice, but long enough for Pavo to spear his sword at Gratian's midriff.

The strike was hard and good, but Gratian's cuirass was made of the finest bronze, and the force of the blow merely dented the moulded metal.

Gratian's nostrils flared in irritation as he eyed the damage, then pulled his sword free of the rail and twirled the weapon, sinking into a slight crouch. He came at Pavo like a dancer, fast and spry, slicing for his left then his right. Pavo realised then that Gratian had been trained by the Speculatores, for only they moved as lithely as this. He licked his sword out once, but Gratian batted it away, so he dropped into a squat and tried to strike for Gratian's thigh, only for the Western Emperor to vault the strike and land near Pavo's side. As Pavo hurriedly tried to rise and swing to the threat, Gratian lashed his sword across Pavo's back, the blade ripping away the rag of mail left there and slashing his skin.

Pavo suppressed a cry, staggering up and away as the two swapped places. The wound was skin deep but hot as fire. His armour now hung in useless ribbons. Worse, his bandaged cuts from the Battle of Remorum Vale had opened. Hot blood rolled down his chest and back like a grim water clock. Gratian rocked on the balls of his feet, fresh, eager, strong, blade flicking and flexing like a snake's tongue tasting the air, looking for the moment to attack. It was then he realised he could not beat this creature with a blade. So when Gratian came for him again, he feinted as if going to strike Gratian's left shoulder. When the Western Emperor faded away from the blow, he curled his free fist into a ball and unleashed a powerful hook, catching Gratian on the side of the jaw.

It was like the kick of a mule, largely because it had been so unexpected. Gratian flailed backwards, saliva and a gloop of blood leaping from his mouth. He lost his footing, toppling onto his back and dropping his sword. The sight was like a thousand thorns of lightning through Pavo. He lunged forward, bringing his spatha up for a killing strike. *For justice...*

In that instant, the supine Gratian twisted his head and caught the eye of the lead Genevan horse archer.

Thrum...whack!

The arrow took Pavo in his right thigh, sent him crashing to one knee. He cried out, every part of him desperate to clutch the wound. But that would mean dropping his legionary sword and foregoing this chance, and his heart would not allow him to do so. He rose, swaying, using the bridge rail for support, the arrow shaft jutting from his flesh.

The Genevan's bow groaned again, the archer winked and took aim.

But Gratian rose between the bowman and Pavo. 'No, I will do this,' he said placidly, his chin streaked with blood. 'But keep your bow trained on him. The rest of you – prepare to ride for the mountain pass. We make for Italia just as soon as I am done here.'

Pavo heard his breath grow ragged. The fibres of his tunic felt heavy with blood and from the lower edge of his vision he saw that the skin of his right, arrow-pierced leg was red and slick. He felt his heart pumping crazily to work with what strength it had left.

In contrast, Gratian walked as if he were weightless, padding towards Pavo then deftly spinning on the ball of one foot, pirouetting past and striking hard for his left arm – still clutching the bridge rail for balance. Pavo threw up his sword to block. Sparks puffed up through the rain in a sudden white shower. But Gratian's strike skittered free of the block and he drove the blade on down to bite through Pavo's sleeve, deep into his shoulder. The crack of breaking bones rang out. The arm at once lost all feeling and fell limp. Gratian drove his sword point down and the tip only just failed to break into Pavo's rib cage, but it did glide through the flesh from shoulder to belly, opening up a dreadful wound. Now he swayed, left arm useless, right leg shaking, blood pulsing from the cut to his chest. The crimson runnels pit-pattered down on the bridge timbers, audible over the drizzle, rolling into and staining the river.

'Oh, I would say you are done,' Gratian sucked air through his teeth. 'You cannot even balance, can you?' He shimmied left then right deftly as he said this. 'It's taking everything out of you to even remain standing.'

Pavo tracked his movements groggily. Dark spots began to grow and burst before him, very gradually eating away at the edges of his vision. He blinked hard, trying to conjure again the image of Izodora, her scent, the summer winds caressing them both by the Thracian farm, the sensation of the swaddled child in his arms. It served to remind him what it meant to be here, with this chance to put things right.

'Kneel before me,' Gratian cooed.

'Never,' Pavo rasped. But his voice sounded odd, slurred, distant.

'You have no choice. You can feel the coldness in your limbs, can't you? Death is coming ...'

Pavo felt his legs shaking. Then, with a wave of cold horror, he dropped and felt the dull thud of one knee hitting the bridge. His sword arm trembled as he tried to keep it high, as if it alone kept alive the image of Izodora and their unborn child.

Gratian visibly grew at this, stepping closer and standing taller. With a deft flick he smacked Pavo's sword flat, batting the blade downwards.

Pavo tried to lift his weapon high again, but found that it would only come halfway before his arm shook madly and fell once more. He felt the cold touch of Gratian's sword on his neck.

'I have spoken with my Speculatores in recent months – after I heard rumours that you might still be alive,' he explained as he strode around Pavo. 'They told me much about you and why you have been so rash to pursue me. I hear the Goths killed some Eastern whore of yours?'

'Her name... was Felicia,' Pavo said, looking up the length of Gratian's sword. 'She was killed by one of your Speculatores. My half... brother.'

'Ah, Dexion! Yes, he was a skilful agent. I know all too well how much of a pest half-kin can be,' Gratian said tunefully. 'Then there was Tribunus Gallus. I hear he died like a dog, buried alive under the blazing ruins of a Thracian farmhouse?'

'Tribunus Gallus died... a hero,' Pavo said. His vision was more darkness than light now, and he felt a terrible coldness creeping through his body. He tried again to raise his sword, but the blade felt like a marble block. 'Now he lives on in the heart... and mind of every man he... ever led. Every Claudian I have trained has been instilled with his values: justice and tenacity... against all and any odds. They will go on to train others. Our spirit, like his... will never... die.'

Gratian arched his eyebrows. 'Poetic. But meaningless. Nobody will remember Gallus' name. And once I have struck your head from your shoulders, nobody will remember yours either. I will find a way to gather fresh followers and I *will* restore order to my empire.' He lined up the edge of his sword against Pavo's neck like a woodcutter. 'Everything you have done, everything you have endured. It has all been for nothing.'

Pavo looked up, seeing Gratian's sword lift away from his neck in a powerful backswing, the drumming rain half-blinding him. In that moment, he saw the faces of one thousand fallen brothers and felt a final spark of strength – the strength of a legion – rise within him. The marble block became a legionary spatha once again. It rose to meet Gratian's killing blow.

Clang!

The sound echoed like a thunderclap around the moor and the Western Emperor's sword spun crazily through the air. Pavo found himself rising to his feet, defying the coldness spreading through him, face to face with Gratian again. With a thick *plop*, Gratian's sword landed in the river. At the same time, Pavo brought his spatha up to the Western Emperor's throat. Gratian stepped back, wide-eyed, clutching the sword hand and fingers – the bones shattered from the ferocity of the life-saving parry.

'For nothing?' Pavo burred down the length of his blade in that cold, distant voice. All of him was numb now. 'No... for Gallus, for Felicia, for Avitus, for Felix, for Zosimus, for Quadratus, for Bastianus, for Trupo, for Cornix, for Rectus, for Opis...' he chanted the long list of names as he staggered forwards, using his body weight to push Gratian back against the bridge's wooden rail.

'Shoot him!' Gratian – pinned against the rail, head arched back and away from Pavo's sword tip – cried to the Genevans. But he and Pavo were so close the archer did not risk shooting. As they dithered, a new thunder rose, this time from the western woods. When Dragathius and his squadron of horsemen burst into view there, the Genevan archer became suddenly less loyal to Gratian, letting his bow slacken.

But Pavo cared not. He lowered his sword for just a trice to snatch the wet rope hanging from the rail and flick it up.

Gratian's eyes bulged as he saw the Hun-style noose on the end falling over his head then slapping down around his shoulders. 'No!' he cried out, swinging his good hand up for Pavo's neck, the fang ring jutting proud. Without a speck of emotion, Pavo sliced upwards, chopping off Gratian's hand at the wrist. The hand fell to the bridge's wet timbers. Blood pumped from the arm stump. Gratian issued a hideous scream that melted into some panicked verse of prayer, the noose resting around his neck.

'O Almighty God, merciful Father,
I confess to you all my sins and iniquities,
with which I have ever offended you…'

Pavo, stared through the Western Emperor, speaking over him. 'When I was a boy… my father told me about the one time he and his legion… were in the presence of an emperor… about how he wept with pride. I strove to be… everything he was. I trained and I learned, I marched and I fought… and now here I am, with you on this damp, forgotten piece of land. For me there… will be no pride, no tears… simply the long, low toll of Justitia's scales falling level once more. Here it ends for you… Gratian, murderer of the innocent.'

He yanked the noose tight. Gratian's jabbering prayer ended with a croak as he gagged, eyes bulging with terror, searching madly across Pavo's face. 'It is you after all, isn't it?' he rasped. 'The dark creature from my dreams. The one with countless faces.'

Pavo's distant stare sharpened suddenly onto Gratian's eyes. 'No. Those are the faces… of those you have killed. But rejoice, for they will trouble you no longer… in Tartarus.'

With a sharp swing of his good arm, his elbow cracked against Gratian's chest, sending him pitching over the bridge rail, cloak flailing. There was a moment of nothing, before the entire bridge juddered. A retching sounded, along with the rubbing of the rope on the timbers. Pavo, swaying, cold, stared downriver through the rain. From the bottom edge of his fading vision, he could see Gratian looking up, clutching at the rope and the air with his broken hand and the bleeding stump of the missing one, legs kicking. 'I… I… I repent!' he hissed over and over.

But Pavo heard nothing of those final words, seeing in his mind's eye the many who had fallen. The spark of strength fell away from him like the thick runnels of blood and rain. The coldness was all-pervading now. He saw more with his mind than with his eyes, as he began to fall into a hall of memories. He barely saw those who ran from Dragathius' squadron to surround him. Sura, Libo, Darik and Pulcher too. They were there for him when he fell, as always. They caught him. Sura cupped the back of his head and roared at him like a drillmaster, voice choked with emotion, demanding that he awaken. But despite their shouts, they could not draw him back from the realm of memories.

A long, rattling breath escaped his lips, and echoed through the corridors of eternity.

Epilogue

October 383 AD
Constantinople

A warm autumnal haze hung over Constantinople. The Eastern capital's streets were packed, the forums crammed with people drinking wine and talking of the great significance of this day: the troubles in the West were over, and today it would be confirmed. Tonight, they said, the most joyous celebrations would fill every corner of the capital. All eyes looked every so often to the First Hill and the rising marble domes of the Chalke Hall, waiting for the announcement.

Inside the Chalke Hall, the eyes of the many hundreds were all fixed on the throne dais and Emperor Theodosius. Consul Saturninus watched the swell of visitors from a high balcony – the many bright robes and livery down there like moving tesserae. There were dignitaries, nobles, generals and priests.

The Gothic reiks from the *haims* settlements had travelled to the Eastern capital too. With them stood Eriulf and Faustius, the two highest Goths in the land. Together, yet clearly not united, one sporting his proud, spiked tribal mane, the other draped in senatorial robes and crowned with a carefully-sculpted Roman haircut. Saturninus thought of the muddled message one of the Claudia men had passed on to him this morning as he had approached the hall. A message about something that had happened on the legion's journey to the West. It still made little sense. How could the Vesi – that dangerous and clandestine sect – still be active within the Gothic populace? He hoped that he had picked the Claudian soldier up wrong.

The young braid-haired Goth, Alaric, stood between Eriulf and Faustius, carefully expressionless, his gaze gliding around the hall. Saturninus glanced to his left. Stilicho, up here beside him on the balcony, smiled proudly, watching Alaric as if he were a younger brother. Since his return from Persia, Stilicho had made efforts to cement the Gothic peace, even offering to take Alaric under his wing – allowing him to train with the legions and observe the art of imperial military strategy. It was a start, but Stilicho's progressive outlook was not shared by many.

Bacurius One-hand stood on the other side of the hall, scowling at the Gothic trio and at the rabble of tribal soldiers they had brought with them...even at Emperor Theodosius' Gothic general, Modares *and* the Goths amongst the emperor's shaven-headed Inquisitors.

With equal levels of belligerence, Bishop Gregory peered at the Goths and those noblemen amongst the Romans whom he knew still clung to the old Gods or the Arian word of Christ, while they in turn muttered and whispered about him and his Nicene Christ-God.

Yet the high tensions within the Eastern court were but one concern. Every single pair of eyes was trained upon the doors, awaiting the visiting embassy. The new regime in the West was to come here today to pay homage to Theodosius. Once beholden to Gratian, he would now be recognised irrefutably as the senior of the empire's twin stewards.

The doors swung open, drawn apart by two of Theodosius' gold and blood-red Lancearii. A bright shaft of hazy late afternoon light speared across the hall and a warm autumnal breeze floated in too. In came one man, sheepish, head bowed. Not the man they all expected.

Saturninus' neck lengthened as he craned over the balcony edge to get a better look, to be sure his eyes were not tricking him. A haggard man, bald but for a U of hair around his ears and the back of his head. But that face... it had to be.

'Arbogastes!' the crowd whispered in a thousand voices.

Without his copper-coloured wig, he looked twenty years older. He approached the throne with round shoulders, sinking to his knees, his sleeveless mail shirt jangling. 'Domine, I submit to you,' he said, head bowed.

Emperor Theodosius stared down his nose at the Frankish general. 'How was it? Leading Gratian's cavalry into battle?'

From here, Saturninus could not discern much about Arbogastes' expression other than the crags of age and his honey-gold eyes rolling up towards Theodosius. 'I did only what my cruel master demanded of me, Domine. But as soon as Merobaudes' signal horns blared, I called on my cavalry to desert him. You could say that with my flight from battle, I *turned* upon the tyrant!'

Theodosius eyed Arbogastes for a time, the only sound in the hall the crackling of incense burners and the squabble of gulls outside near the sea walls.

Saturninus noticed Bacurius One-hand's lips move, as if willing the emperor to agree to his earlier-offered advice. *Throw the barbarian hound from the land walls!*

'You will stay here, with me,' Theodosius said calmly. The inference was clear – that he did not trust the man. Few did. But then he was useful – clever and well-connected with the many tribes beyond the empire. 'You will join my *sacrum consistorium* and contribute to my meetings of state.'

Bacurius let loose a disgusted groan. 'Another bloody barbarian?' he said to one of his attendants in a derisive whisper – only for the supposedly disguised words to sail up and around the Chalke Hall like a herald's cry. Theodosius pinned the ferocious-looking general with a look of rage. The many Goths within the hall muttered and shuffled, stances hardening, all of them now well-aware of Bacurius' prejudices.

Saturninus noticed a brief but clear look between Arbogastes and Eriulf. Eriulf gave him a nod of welcome. An expression of gladness that another tribesman would join the emperor's sacred council? For a moment, Saturninus almost understood Bacurius' rigid viewpoint. Modares and Eriulf – two of the emperor's six-strong council – were Goths. Arbogastes and old Richomeres were Frankish by birth. Of the Romans within the council there were...

'Just you, me and that ball of rage, Bacurius,' Stilicho said quietly by his side, as if reading his thoughts. 'And even I'm half-Vandal.'

'Don't forget Bishop Gregory,' Saturninus mused.

Stilicho arched one eyebrow. 'Actually, I rather would.'

Saturninus laughed despite himself. 'Interesting times lie ahead,' he said, 'that is for sure.' His eyes searched the crowd until they found the groomed knot of XI Claudia officers: the wild-haired Libo, big greasy Pulcher, pristine Darik and a knot of junior soldiers. 'We should speak with the Claudians. They have a solid relationship with the Gothic settlers. More, some of them have served or fought in battle alongside me, you and most of the emperor's sacred council at one time or another. I'll arrange to meet their Tribunus.'

He spotted Sura amongst the Claudians. It was an odd thing to see him wearing the red cloak that had once been Pavo's. Even odder to see the haunted look on his usually mischievous face. Saturninus could not prevent a sad sigh passing through his lips.

'The legions have lost a great man,' said Stilicho quietly, feeling Pavo's absence just as keenly. 'There are so few left.'

The rumble of boots from beyond the open doors brought all attentions back to the entrance. Magnus Maximus swept in, bedecked in his beaming white battle armour, pteruges, helm and purple cloak. Dragathius walked by his side, long grey hair combed back with a braided circlet holding it there. Eight Victores legionaries marched in mini columns of four either side of the pair, bedecked in full palace livery, ribbons trailing from the tang of their spears, cloaks pinned with glistening jewels, ornate noseguard helms and gilt shields polished like mirrors.

The rest halted a respectful distance from the dais, while Maximus swept on ahead, confident, ebullient and almost glowing with energy. He threw up a hand in salute. 'Domine,' he boomed, then sank to one knee gracefully.

'Rise,' Theodosius said with a rare warmth in his voice.

Maximus stood, beaming still. 'The news may have reached you more than a month ago, Domine, but I must say it aloud for all to hear: the tyrant has been thrown from the Western throne.'

A joyous roar filled the hall.

Theodosius examined his fingernails until the clamour died, before rolling his eyes back up at Maximus. 'I hear you left the body of Gratian unburied?'

Maximus dipped his head a fraction, as if swallowing a stone. 'I was not present at the moment he was slain. It was Pavo, the Tribunus of the XI Claudia,' he halted glancing round the hall until he spotted Sura. '... the former Tribunus of the XI Claudia, who struck Gratian down on a bridge near Geneva.'

'Pavo... yes,' Theodosius grumbled under his breath, 'and I could have sworn he was on the other edge of the world.' He drummed his fingers on the arms of his throne. 'Still, you might not have been present, but you could have sent a party along to the bridge to honour Gratian's body,' he said.

Saturninus recognised the emperor's tone. He was testing Maximus.

Maximus looked up at the Eastern Emperor, his eyes full and sad. 'Did he deserve such an honour, Domine?'

'No, but young Valentinian deserved the resolution of seeing his tormentor committed to the soil.'

Maximus nodded slowly. 'I am learning with every day of my new role. Indeed, I have entered full orthodoxy to follow God's path like you. I have been cleansed of my sins by the most pious Bishop Ambrosius. He remains in the West, singing hymns of praise to God, thankful for the end of Gratian's reign and,' he paused and resumed with a fuller voice, 'for the high-stewardship of the empire passing to you.'

Saturninus might have laughed were the situation apt. Like Arbogastes, Ambrosius 'the Pious' was clearly something of a survivor. Some said many of Gratian's dark deeds had been blessed – even encouraged – by the man. It was little wonder that the bishop had chosen to stay in the West.

'Where is Merobaudes?' Theodosius asked as the clamour died, casting his eye over Maximus' retinue. 'It was he who turned the day with his call to the Moorish riders, I hear.'

Maximus tilted his head to one side for a moment in a gesture of respect. 'He risked his life for us. He is a colossus, and for that reason he chose to remain in the West also, to watch over the lands while I am absent. He will be my Magister Militum.'

'And young Valentinian?'

Maximus looked a little confused for a moment. 'The young Caesar? Why, I have invited him to come to Treverorum to live with me. I can help prepare him for when he becomes a man in the next year.'

Theodosius let a short pause pass, then replied very clearly. 'Valentinian is to return to his seat in Mediolanum with Lady Justina. There he will govern Italia and Africa, as is his right.'

Maximus dipped his head in acceptance. 'So it shall be.'

'And I must ask you to make an oath: your foray into Gaul was brave and stirring. Your defeat of Gratian will be talked of for centuries. But your ambitions... they must end there. Valentinian suffered under Gratian's reign – virtually a hostage to his stepbrother. Now, I decree that he remains lord of his lands and you of Gaul, Hispania and Britannia... but that each of you shall hold the position of co-Augustus. Neither of you will be senior to the other, nor will he or you seek to expand your territories at the expense of the other.'

Maximus' smile only broadened. 'This is your will, Domine?' he extended his arms to either side. 'Then so it shall be!'

The hall exploded in another round of cheers. Guards, workers and slaves near the great doors passed the word outside and in moments the cheers were spreading around the city streets. A mighty wall of sound rose up: singing, drums and lyres, along with the throaty cry of wine sellers looking to capitalise on the jubilant atmosphere.

'Interesting times ahead indeed,' Stilicho patted Saturninus on the back, withdrawing from the balcony as bounteous trays of food and jugs of wine were ferried into the hall, 'but this is a good start. Now... I fear I must do my bit and drink a trough-load of wine,' he laughed.

As Stilicho departed, Saturninus turned back to watch over the festivities in the Chalke hall. The ordered groups from before had now melted into a frenzy of dancing and feasting, the faces sanguine and the voices high. At long last, the empire knew peace from corner to corner. Yet there was something in the air – an odd taste, or a strange pressure, like that before a storm – that told Saturninus to stay sober tonight... and to remain watchful in the times to come.

November 383 AD
The Thracian Countryside

Izodora gazed around the farmhouse. It was a simple stone home of a few rooms and a small estate of wheat fields. Elm logs snapped and sparked in the hearth fire. Golden bars of sunlight shone through the open shutters and spread across the floor. It was growing cold outside, the mornings frosty and the evenings bitter, but in here all seemed warm and safe. She sat upon a cherrywood bench and turned her gaze upon the tiny bundle in her arms, sliding one shoulder of her robe away, allowing the babe to suckle. The boy's eyes were still shut tight, his arms waving and legs kicking as he issued the most pathetic of squeals. 'Your father gave up everything for you,' she said softly. 'He was a legionary, a hero.'

The babe squealed again, the fire sighed, and all was silent.

'A hero? No, the fallen – they are the heroes, they truly gave everything,' Pavo replied quietly, watching her from the bedroom doorway. He was dressed just in his loincloth, his good shoulder resting against the oak frame, his doting gaze fixed on mother and child. 'Without them I would not be here with you now.'

Awkwardly, he moved away from the support of the door frame, shuffling across the flagged floor, the immobility of his shield arm still strange and draining. The long wound was now sealed in a white stripe of scar tissue that ran from shoulder to belly, but it burned madly when touched, and the badly-healed bone beneath ached in these colder days. A single white whorl of scar tissue on his right thigh was all that remained of his arrow wound, but the muscle damage had been acute. Walking slowly felt like standing on a swaying ship – indeed, harvesting just a small tract of the wheat outside had been something of an ordeal. With great care, he sat down behind her on the bench, his thighs encompassing hers, drinking in the scent of her hair, wrapping his good arm around her waist slowly, enjoying the softness of her bare skin on his. 'Both of you are heroes too. Out there in the West, I thought only of you, of this.' A ludic smile rose on his lips. 'You crowed about saving me... *how* many times before?'

'Three,' she replied without hesitation.

He held her a fraction tighter. 'Well the fourth time was the most vital. I don't know if I would have been strong enough out there had it not been for the promise of this.'

Memories of the frenzied quest to Gaul seemed almost surreal now. The return journey to the East had been a patchwork of unconsciousness and feverish agony, travelling in the backs of wagons and aboard ships. The young Claudian medicus, Verax, had proved himself as a worthy successor to Rectus, though. He had stayed by Pavo's side the whole time, staunching the blood loss, dressing the wound every few hours. Verax had granted him these moments, and granted the baby boy a father.

Pavo recalled little about the Claudia's return to Constantinople, but when he had come to in a bed within the Neorion barrack *valetudinarium*, it had been to the sight of Saturninus sitting there, watching him. The consul had stuffed a stamped scroll into the crook of his numb arm and a bag of coins in his good hand.

'Go, be a husband, a father,' the consul had insisted.

Pavo had ignored the coins and stared at the scroll, recognising the seal and the contents even from the first line. A *missio causaria* – medical discharge papers. He had tried to sit bolt upright and throw the papers back at Saturninus, only to moan and collapse with pain. It had taken him days to realise he could never fight again. He thought of his and Sura's parting embrace. Both had held back tears – badly – and been unable to speak. Sura had accepted his officer's cloak with no more than a single nod. As he had hobbled in crutches across the drill square to leave the barracks for the final time, the hectoring cries and clatter of training fell suddenly silent. To a man, the Claudians stopped what they were doing. Libo, Pulcher, Betto, Durio, Indus and Darik at the fore, wearing that same glassy-eyed look as Sura. Betto, as always, found the right words. 'Hail, Tribunus Pavo... *Semper Invicta,*' he said, raising his spear.

The rest of the legion raised their spears likewise in a valedictory, iron salute. '*Semper Invicta!*' they cried as one, an explosion of noise that must have startled the multitudes all over Constantinople's sprawling wards. He could barely breathe, so strong was the hand of emotion choking his throat as he had walked out of the barracks, out of the capital, out of the great game of empire... to take wagon to this quiet farmstead in the countryside of southern Thracia.

In the three months since, he had known little but safety and silence. The absolute joy of waking next to his pregnant wife. The elation when the obstetrix had delivered the babe. Now this – his sixth day of fatherhood – was the brightest yet.

But he did not feel deserving of any of this new comfort. Home for so many years had been a tent or a draughty barrack house. The absence of clattering armour or chisel-like voices from a drill-square or bawdy laughter echoing through stony halls seemed deafening at times.

Izodora stroked the babe's head, and the sight softened his thoughts.

'I never thought I would be a father,' he said. 'It always seemed like something other men might do, but not me.'

Izodora smiled. 'My grandmother once told me that bringing a child into the world was like whispering your greatest secret aloud for the very first time. Once the words are spoken, the world will never be the same again.'

'My world is golden,' Pavo said, holding her a little tighter, kissing her neck and stroking one of the baby's cheeks. They both gazed lovingly at the mite.

'We should name him,' she said quietly.

'Marcus,' Pavo replied almost immediately.

Izodora noticed his glassy gaze, and followed it over to the small ox-hide box beside the hearth. For a moment, she didn't understand the significance. Then she remembered the box's contents: Tribunus Gallus' belongings, including a small wooden toy soldier that had belonged to his son – years ago murdered by Gratian's men. She squeezed the babe's hand. 'Marcus,' she repeated softly.

He leaned over, kissing her head and the child's, then held them both in a lasting embrace.

'Darik claimed he will pass by here to visit before the month is out,' she said.

Pavo half-smiled. 'Darik must now get used to the drudgery and tyranny of *real* legionary life. Under Sura too – can you imagine? Even as a centurion, he'll have no time to preen his reflection in the flat of his sword.'

'Are you suggesting that my brother is vain?' She gasped.

Pavo laughed, stroking her arms. 'He'll come by. He'd better.' He thought of the bloodstained moment, mid-battle, when Darik had helped drive off a knot of Noricorum legionaries who had captured the legion standard and were set to butcher him. The oath had been honoured.

They remained like that, in silence, for a time. Pavo's mind drifted. He thought of Eriulf's matching promise to come and visit. Another brother of different kin, just like Darik. After receiving his discharge scroll, he had given one last order to Betto – to pass word to Saturninus of the strange Vesi goings-on up near the river border. He had considered sending the news to Eriulf too, but something held him back: Runa, Eriulf's sister, had been part of that sect, and the Goth was still inwardly grieving for her. It would have been callous to dig at those old wounds with such impersonal means as a scroll. Perhaps when Eriulf visited though, he could broach the matter.

His gaze glided through the bars of sunlight and the floating dust motes trapped within it, over to the window. Outside, the stubble of the recently-harvested wheat field shook gently in the breeze. Two crows circled in the blue winter sky out there. It made him think of the crone and the vision of the two eagles, one white, one dark… then both blood-red. She had been absent from his dreams ever since Gratian's demise – save for fiery repetitions of the eagle dreams during his feverish return from the West. He wondered if he had seen the last of her. Silently, he thanked her for her guidance over the years. These last seven years in particular had been such a strange and tangled time.

'You will not miss it, will you?' Izodora said. 'Life with the legions?'

He found his gaze turning to an oak chest in the corner, within which his boots, spatha and armour were packed away. He recalled again that last moment before he had left the barracks, the faces of his closest comrades. The thought of it all conjured a thousand more memories, of marching through the wild barley, joined to the brothers by his side as if by some invisible cord. As they marched, they sang – a golden song of camaraderie.

'Can you hear the sound of soldier boots,
walking proud and tall on the ancient routes?
See a silver eagle gliding low,
and a great red bull on a legion pole?
We are the Claudia, sworn to Rome,
to guard this sweet, green land that we call home.
We shine and clatter like soldier kings,
With the wind of Mithras under our wings...
His lips moved silently, in the shape of the booming crescendo:
...for we are the watchmen of Thraaa-cia!'

A tear gathered in the corner of his eye as the remembered song faded away gradually. 'No,' he replied to Izodora at last. It was a lie, but the right one. This was his life now; the empire was at peace and justice had been done.

November 383 AD
Treverorum, Gaul

Snow battered the eastern turret of Treverorum's mighty gatehouse, plastering the north-facing sections of stonework in white. Up on the roof of one of the two gate turrets, Merobaudes shielded his eyes from the whistling blizzard, his long, thin hair flailing out to one side like a banner, his bear cloak, thick woollen tunic and trousers caked in snow too. The Heruli – reinstated to their previous station as a true palace legion here in the capital of Gaul – shivered and shuffled along the parapets nearby, walking and stamping through the wintry squall just to try to keep warm.

'Still no sign?' Tribunus Lanzo chattered, his red moustache heavy with ice crystals.

'None,' Merobaudes grumbled. 'And the light fades,'

'Another day passes,' Lanzo said. 'Emperor Maximus *should* have returned by now.'

Merobaudes said nothing. Maximus had set out for Constantinople well over a month ago, to meet with Theodosius. Six days ago, advance riders from his return party had arrived back at Treverorum, bringing news of the outcomes of that meeting in the eastern capital. More, they reported that Maximus himself was only a day or so behind.

'Magister Militum,' Lanzo said, his voice heavy, reluctant. 'My men were discussing the emperor's lateness last night around the hearth in the barrack house. One of them suggested something that has troubled me all night and all day today.' The tribunus stared off into the wintry squall for a time, as if afraid to continue. 'Gratian... Gratian was never buried. His body was left hanging by the Geneva bridge. What if... what if he was not dead?'

Merobaudes turned his great frame to peer down on the Heruli leader. 'I was not there. I did not see him hanging, nor did you. But those who did described his face turning black, his tongue bulging from his mouth. He had but one broken hand. No man could have survived a noose in such a state. You think he saved himself and now stalks the roads? You think he has waylaid Emperor Maximus?' he scoffed.

Despite his outward confidence, Merobaudes felt a terrible dance of cold, invisible fingers inside his thick clothing. *What if?*

Lanzo said nothing. The blizzard screamed to new heights around them.

Merobaudes laughed falsely, waving a hand. 'Go back to the barracks. The darkness is almost here. Tell your men on this Gods-forsaken stretch of the walls they may retire too. I will keep a lookout until the next shift begins.'

Lanzo made to argue, but the blizzard picked up again, and instead he simply chattered his teeth, then nodded. 'As you wish, Magister Militum.'

Alone, Merobaudes cast his mind back over the colossal Battle of Remorum Vale. So much risked by so many. Surely fate could not be so cruel as to snatch Magnus Maximus away now during a simple journey across a land at peace? His mind drifted to the moments after the battle. Pavo, the callused leader of the XI Claudia, had been a mess of blood and sweat, consumed by that strange mix of elation and sadness that comes after any battle. It was with watery eyes that he had told Merobaudes of his strange dreams. Two eagles, tearing each other apart. The dark eagle and the white one, Gratian and Maximus, he reckoned. Yet the two had fought so fiercely that both had soon been stained red. Come the end of it, when one claimed victory, snapping the neck of the other, he could not tell if it was the dark bird or the light one that had prevailed.

This riddle simply stoked fresh visions of Gratian – somehow still alive. *What if?* He twisted to look inwards over the snowy wards of Treverorum, seeing the demolished heap that had until recently been the Office of the Speculatores. So too had the notorious dungeons been filled with rocks and sealed up. Yet still the remembered screams of men dying in those dreadful places echoed in his thoughts. Gratian had been a nightmare when he was alive. Yet now that he was dead – surely? – it seemed he had grown more terrible in the minds of those he had tormented. He thought of young Valentinian, who would by now nearly be back in his southern capital of Mediolanum with Lady Justina. It had been one of the outcomes of the meeting in Constantinople, according to the advance riders. A wise decision, Merobaudes knew. The boy had suffered terribly at his stepbrother's hands, but he would learn from that. He would be a fine leader, perhaps one day even the senior Augustus of the entire Roman world as his father had once been.

When he turned back to the countryside, a small blur of movement down there blew his thoughts away. His eyes widened, fixed on the white-blanketed spot. He could not see who or what it was through the blizzard, but he heard the soft crunch of something moving across snow and tracked the shapes as they approached the city. Men on horseback, he realised as the shapes entered the weak orange bubble of torchlight cast down from the walls. A trumpet sang from the adjacent gate tower and the gates were dragged open. Merobaudes heard the voices of the few guards still on duty at ground level as they welcomed the new arrivals. His heart surged with hope, and he heard the thump of feet ascending the stairs.

Maximus emerged onto the tower top, beaming despite the freezing journey, spreading his arms wide to throw back his thick woollen cloak and reveal his polished white armour. A thrill of elation pulsed through Merobaudes, chasing away the whispery doubts about Gratian. Gratian was gone, Maximus was here. His golden reign could now begin in earnest. Merobaudes laughed aloud, extending his arms to accept the embrace. Maximus strode towards him, and the two clapped together like gloved hands – just as they had done in the moments after the Battle of Remorum Vale.

'You pulled me from the fires, Merobaudes,' Maximus said. 'In that green valley, when Gratian had us trapped, surrounded... I thought it was over, I truly did. I was sure I had led the soldiers of Britannia to their deaths, and that I would fall with them, forever to be known as the fool who thought he could challenge the mighty Gratian.'

It was a tight embrace, Merobaudes thought. Despite the perishing cold, there was a real warmth there. Yes, a real warmth... in his chest... just by his armpit.

'You played a vital part in my victory,' Maximus continued, parting from Merobaudes just a fraction. 'But now, your part is over.'

Merobaudes looked down at the dagger embedded to the hilt in his armpit, then looked into Maximus' eyes. 'Why?'

'Theodosius made me swear an oath,' Maximus said joyously, his eyes brimming with tears like a proud father. He tore the dagger free, then plunged it into Merobaudes' side just below the first wound. 'An oath I have no intention of keeping. To rule just a patch of the West? Meekly deferring to Valentinian... a *boy*... in all matters regarding Italia and Africa?' He sucked in a winter breath through his nostrils, his eyes narrowing in a momentary trance. 'Never.'

He plunged the dagger in again, this time piercing Merobaudes' kidney.

Shaking, aghast, Merobaudes' lips moved but he could not muster a reply. Thick, black blood poured from his lips and down his chin. Over Maximus' shoulder, he saw the thickly-snow-coated roofs and streets of Treverorum, and the struggle going on in the empty lane near the gatehouse. Lanzo, being pounced upon by Dragathius and his men, fighting, losing, falling... gone.

Maximus ripped the dagger free again and plunged it in three more times in rapid succession, his white armour turning red as he kept Merobaudes in that partial embrace. With slow, steady steps like the leader of a dancing pair, he walked the giant back towards the turret's outwards-facing edge.

'You were Valentinian's shield, and now you are broken. Your strongest allies are all dead. Those Moorish riders are right now being dealt with by my followers in Africa. And the legions who turned against Gratian in support of you? They will be told a sad story of your accidental demise. Thus, the boy and his lands will fall to me. Once the West is united under my banner, Theodosius and his crippled East will shake at the sound of my armies' trumpet calls.'

Merobaudes tried again to reply, but with one lung filled with blood, a wet, rattling hiss was all he could manage. His legs began to shake and Maximus released him from the embrace. His giant body swayed, and he pitched backwards over the outer parapets of Treverorum, falling silently for a few breaths before he thumped down on the snow outside, a bloody star of red exploding around him.

Maximus scooped up a handful of snow from the merlons to clean the blood from his armour, then a Victores legionary who had followed him up here handed him a cloak of black feathers to further conceal the stains. Maximus threw the cloak on, giving the legionary a pre-arranged nod as he did so, then left the tower top. Once Maximus had descended from the tower and was well inside Treverorum, the Victores legionary stepped over to the turret's inward-facing edge.

'Bring help!' he called out across the city. 'The Magister Militum has fallen from the walls!'

Down on the snow outside the city, with his final pulse of life, Merobaudes thought of Pavo and his odd dream. Now he understood, all too well...

...the Dark Eagle had risen.

The End

Author's Note

Dear Reader,

Thank you for joining Pavo and the Claudia men (once they were eventually reunited) in their latest adventures. Their journey was long and brutal, but I trust it made for an enjoyable read. 'Dark Eagle' is based on the events in and around the Roman Empire in the years of 382 and 383 AD, so a lot of what you read is true (horrifyingly so in the case of the Persian 'boats' torture). There are also plenty of speculative threads and scenes where I have tried to craft the whole thing into a smooth and enjoyable narrative. Here's the background to these ingredients of fact and fiction.

Let's start with Persia. Around 382, Emperor Theodosius sent an embassy to Shapur II, the new Persian King of Kings, seeking a lasting peace and a formal settlement to the long-standing territorial struggle over Armenia. Stilicho was just twenty four years old and very much a man on the up, having married Theodosius' niece and having secured himself the coveted office of *Comes Stabulari* (Count of the Stables). He was selected to travel east to take part in the talks, under the leadership of a certain Ambassador Sporacius. We know nothing about Sporacius other than that he led the talks... and that he was never mentioned in history afterwards. Thus, I chose a hopefully unforgettable end for him.

Meanwhile, in Thracia, the ashes and dust were still in the air and only just beginning to settle following the resolution of the Gothic War. As Saturninus observes in the volume you have just read, it was certainly no triumph for the Eastern Empire (despite Themistius the Orator's hyperbolic speeches). More likely it was a truce agreed between two sides who were almost broken after some six years of relentless conflict. Historians debate about whether the Goths were integrated into Roman society, or allowed to settle in their tribal groups and retain their culture and customs. Having followed the debate, it seems to me that the latter argument is most plausible – hence my description of the Gothic *Haims* dotted around northern Thracia. You can read more about my thoughts on this on my blog (web address at the end of this note). Whatever the nature of the peace deal, we do know of some general laws that were applied. The Goths were apparently exempt from taxes, but on the condition that they would muster and march at Emperor Theodosius' call. Also, *conubium* – marriage or sexual union – between Roman and Goth was forbidden – hence my scene early on in the tale with the poor Roman lad and his Gothic lover. Tellingly, it seems that the Goths were granted gifts of grain and gold, and that some of their misdemeanours went unpunished by fearful Roman officials.

There are no clear records of Roman legionary strength or positions in Thracia at this time, other than a high likelihood that they were few and far between. Given my depiction of northern Thracia being a patchwork of Gothic villages, it would seem likely that there would be some kind of imperial policing system there – cautious but watchful, tasked with seeing that the Gothic settlers were indeed sticking to the peace treaty. Thus it had to be the XI Claudia who got this unenviable assignment!

Their tormentors, Zeno and Crassus, are entirely fictitious, but the island to which they were taken is – despite it's rather Tintin-esque name – real. St. Thomas Island, just off Bulgaria's Black Sea coast, was and still is known as 'Snake Island' for the grey water snakes that slither around in the grass and rocks there. As described, the isle is a rather bleak place, and in Roman times was topped with only a lighthouse and an old statue of Apollo, a wind wall to block out the sea bluster, and a barrack house on the southern edges. Gratian's order for extermination of the Claudians is an invention, but there is a semi-historical precedent to this. In 286 AD every single man in the 6600-strong Theban legion was put to death by the emperor because of their stubborn refusal to give up the Christian faith.

Of course, there were bigger dangers brewing in Thracia than Zeno and Crassus. It is thought that, underneath the delicate façade of the Gothic peace, there was a strong sect of tribesmen who resented the settlement. Edward Gibbon says:

It was generally believed that the Goths had signed the treaty of peace with a hostile and insidious spirit; and that their chiefs had previously bound themselves, by a solemn and secret oath, never to keep faith with the Romans; to maintain the fairest show of loyalty and friendship, and to watch the favorable moment of rapine, of conquest, and of revenge.

Two Gothic factions emerged: one loyal to Rome and another bent on destroying the empire. Faustius (née Fravitta) was the champion of the former, and Eriulf (sometimes referred to in the historical texts as Prulfius) of the latter. The 'Vesi' as I have entitled Eriulf's sect, represent the seed of the Visigothic identity that would later arise and shed its cloak.

Now, onto the West. In this and previous volumes, I have certainly painted Emperor Gratian as a detestable and cruel leader. His fondness for torture and bullying are my invention, though there are signs that he was not averse to brutality: when his father died and the Western throne was up for grabs, many of his potential rivals were swiftly executed – almost certainly at his behest. More, regarding his fondness for hunting and games (often to the detriment of running his Western realm), Gibbon said that Gratian:

Reminded the numerous spectators of the examples of Nero and Commodus…

…but also went on to claim that he restricted himself to the slaughter of animals – so I am certainly cherry-picking. As for his first wife, Constantia, we know only that she died young and in mysterious circumstance in 383 AD, and that Gratian married Laeta very soon afterwards. Concerning Gratian's prayers of penitence to cleanse him from all sin, I have used an adapted Lutheran version of the Prayer of Contrition.

Regardless of Gratian's sins or otherwise, by 382, there was a strong desire amongst the Western subjects to overthrow him. The historian Zosimus quotes a chief priest who, disgruntled by Gratian's refusal to wear the ancient robes of the Pontifex Maximus, said:

If the emperor refuses to become Pontifex Maximus… we will make one.

It was Magnus Maximus – ambitious and reading the mood of the people – who stepped forward from this cloud of discontent, roused the legions and riders of Britannia, then sailed them across the channel. He steered his forces some way up the Rhine before disembarking and setting foot in Gaul, Gratian's heartland.

Of Maximus' departure from Britannia, Gibbon says:

The youth of the island crowded to his standard, and he invaded Gaul with a fleet and army, which were long afterwards remembered as the emigration of a considerable part of the British nation.

Many identify 410 AD as the formal end to Roman control of Britain, but I see it as more of a gradual process, and this moment – the stripping of the island of its best armies, leaving local officials to rule in his stead – marks its beginning. Those left behind would go on to form the Welsh and Scottish dynasties. Indeed, Welsh legend still talks of Maximus – known in those tales as Macsen Wledig, Prince Macsen, or Imperator – leaving much of the organisation and protection of the northern part of Britannia to a man named Coel Hen, whose territory came to be known as the Kingdom of Northern Britain, based at Eboracum (York).

Anyway, back to Gaul and the impending showdown between Maximus and Gratian: Details of where they faced off are sketchy. We know only that it was somewhere in the vicinity of Paris, and for this reason I have chosen 'Remorum Vale' – one of many valleys near modern Reims, a short way east of the French capital, as the site of the confrontation. The sequence of events portrayed in my battle are mostly fictitious, with the exception of the moment when Gratian's troops deserted him, putting him to flight. In 'Theodosius: The Empire at Bay', Williams & Friell postulate that Maximus must have made thorough preparations, with secret agreements about the suborning of Gratian's armies. They and other historians suspect that it was Merobaudes who betrayed Gratian at the critical moment, rallying the Moorish cavalry to turn to Maximus' cause.

Thus, Gratian sped south with a small cavalry escort, but found doors and gates closed to him at successive potential safehavens.

Eventually, he arrived at Lugdunum (modern Lyon) to be greeted by a litter containing his new wife, Laeta... only for Andragathius (or Dragathius as I have called him to avoid the alliterative and occupational similarity with Arbogastes) to leap out and attack him. Some say Gratian perished here, or that he escaped this trap only to fall near a bridge on an eastwards track. Wherever he was killed, his body was left unburied. Gratian's reign was over.

In the aftermath, Emperor Theodosius acknowledged Maximus as Augustus of the West, but only on the strict condition that he shared the title with young Valentinian. It must have seemed that the empire was – as Pavo hoped – at peace for the first time in years. But history never relents and generally loathes a happy ending. Shortly after Gratian's demise, Merobaudes was killed, and the culprit and circumstances are not at all clear. More, just a few short years would pass before Maximus publicly tore up his oath to Theodosius, bringing disaster and war back to the empire on an unprecedented scale.

So where does this leave Pavo and the Claudia? I have yet to decide: Pavo is in a good place – for the first time in years. There is a short period of relative calm to come. Yet – as mentioned – history shows this will not last. I will let you, my loyal and valued readers, decide. So get in touch – tell me if you want to set out with the Claudians again, to sing their song and march into the storm that awaits. Just don't bet on a happy ending...

Yours faithfully,
Gordon Doherty
www.gordondoherty.co.uk

P.S. If you enjoyed the story, please spread the word. My books live or die by word of mouth, so tell your friends or – even better – leave a short review on Amazon or Goodreads. Anything you can do in this vein would be very much appreciated.

Connect with me! I always enjoy chatting with my readers. Get in touch at: www.gordondoherty.co.uk/contact-me

If you enjoyed Legionary: Dark Eagle, why not try:

Empires of Bronze: Son of Ishtar, by Gordon Doherty

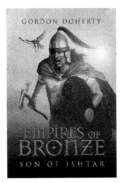

Four sons. One throne. A world on the precipice.

1315 B.C. the world is forged in bronze, and ruled by four mighty empires. Tensions soar between Egypt, Assyria, the Mycenaeans and the Hittites, and war seems inevitable.

When Prince Hattu is born, it should be a rare joyous moment for all the Hittite people. But the Goddess Ishtar comes to King Mursili in a dream, warning that the boy is no blessing, telling of a bleak future where he will stain Mursili's throne with blood and bring devastation upon the world. Thus, Hattu must fight against the goddess' words and prove to his kith and kin that he is worthy. Yet with his every action, the shadow of Ishtar's prophecy darkens…

Strategos: Born in the Borderlands, by Gordon Doherty

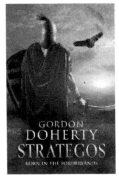

When the falcon has flown, the mountain lion will charge from the east, and all Byzantium will quake. Only one man can save the empire . . . the Haga!

1046 AD. The Byzantine Empire teeters on the brink of all-out war with the Seljuk Sultanate. In the borderlands of Eastern Anatolia, a land riven with bloodshed and doubt, young Apion's life is shattered in one swift and brutal Seljuk night raid. Only the benevolence of Mansur, a Seljuk farmer, offers him a second chance of happiness.

Yet a hunger for revenge burns in Apion's soul, and he is drawn down a dark path that leads him right into the heart of a conflict that will echo through the ages.

Glossary

Aquilifer; Senior standard bearer of a Roman legion and carrier of the legionary eagle.

Auxilium Palatinum (pl. Auxilia Palatina); These elite infantry regiments (or palace legions) of the late Roman Empire served as the emperor's core guard in his Praesental Army.

Ballista (pl. Ballistae); Roman bolt-throwing artillery that was primarily employed as an anti-personnel weapon on the battlefield.

Buccina (pl. Buccinae); The ancestor of the trumpet and the trombone, this instrument was used for the announcement of night watches and for various other purposes in the legionary camp.

Cataphractus (pl. cataphracti); Heavily-armoured cavalry used by the Roman and Sassanid Persian Empires.

Clavii; Long, decorative, coloured arrow-shapes adorning late Roman garments.

Chi-Rho; One of the earliest forms of Christogram, and was used by the early Christian Roman Empire. It is formed by superimposing the first two letters in the Greek spelling of the word Christ, chi = ch and rho = r, in such a way to produce the following monogram;

Comes; Commander of a field army of *comitatenses* legions.

Comitatensis (pl. comitatenses); The comitatenses were the Roman field armies. A 'floating' central reserve of legions, ready to move swiftly to tackle border breaches.

Conubium; Marriage or (informally) sexual union.

Curio; Herald or head priest of a priesthood.

Decanus; Legionary rank, denoting the leader of a tent-group (contubernium) of eight men.

Decimatio; A military form of punishment, where one man in ten would be clubbed to death by their comrades.

Decurion; Leader of a *turma* of Roman cavalry.

Diocese; An administrative and geographical division of the later Roman Empire. Each Diocese was subdivided into a collection of provinces.

Djinn; Supernatural creatures in early pre-Islamic Persian and later Islamic mythology and theology.

Dominus (voc. Domine); A respectful honourific indicating sovereignty.

Draco; A type of legionary standard that became popular in the era of our story. It comprised a bronze dragon head that would groan when wind passed through it and a flowing cloth tail that would ripple in the breeze as if alive.

Dromedarius (pl. dromedarii); Swift and hardy lightly-armoured Roman camel scout cavalry, used primarily in desert regions such as Syria and Egypt. These riders were commonly recruited from the native populace of those areas.

Eques (pl. Equites); Roman light cavalry, used for scouting ahead and screening the flanks of a marching legionary column.

Eques Sagittarius (pl. equites sagittarii); Roman horse archers usually well-armoured in mail.

Explorator (pl. Exploratores); Swift, skilled advance scout cavalry, tasked with ranging far ahead of marching armies and into enemy territory to ensure the route was clear.

Fibula; A Roman brooch for fastening garments.

Foederati; Broad term for the variety of 'barbarian' tribes subsidised from imperial coffers to fight for the Roman Empire.

Haim (pl. Haims); A Gothic region or settlement.

Hexareme; A Roman galley with six decks.

Hortator; Member of a galley crew, responsible for the oarsmen keeping time. Commonly they would beat on a drum or sing a rhythmic chant to keep the oar strokes smooth and in time.

Iudex; The fourth century Goths did not have kings as such. Instead, the tribes – each led by a *reiks* – would unite and elect a 'judge' or 'iudex' who would steer them through a period of migration or conflict.

Intercisa; Iron helmet constructed of two halves with a distinctive fin-like ridge joining them together and large cheek guards offering good protection to the face.

Justitia; Roman Goddess of justice

Kalends; The first day of the month in the ancient Roman calendar.

Labarum; A Christian legionary standard.

Liburnian; A small, swift and nimble galley with just a single bank of oars.

Limitaneus (pl. Limitanei); The limitanei were the empire's frontier soldiers, light infantry spearmen who served in the legions posted along the borders.

Magister Militum; Roman 'Master of the Army'.

Medicus; Medical officer attached to a legion, the most senior of which would hold the title *Medicus Ordinarius*.

Miliarense; Large 4th century AD silver coin.

Mithras; A pagan deity particularly loved by the legions – probably something to do with the belief that Mithras was born with a sword in his hand. He is thought to have evolved from the Persian Mithra, the God of Light and Wisdom.

Molossian; An ancient and now extinct breed of hunting hounds, bred in southern Europe. Modern mastiffs are probably descended from these large and formidable creatures.

Navarchus; A Roman admiral or fleet commander.

Odeum; A Roman amphitheatre, used to deliver performances of poetry or plays.

Optio Speculatorum; Commander of the Speculatores.

Pallium; A rich man's robe. In the times of the later empire, this was equivalent to the older-style toga.

Plumbata (pl. Plumbatae); A lead-weighted throwing dart carried by Roman legionaries, approximately half a metre in length.

Pomerium; The outermost road in a Roman city, running just inside its walls. The word originated from the sacred boundary of the city of Rome.

Pontifex Maximus; High Priest of the College of Pontiffs in ancient Rome.

Primus Pilus; The chief centurion of a legion. So called, because his own century would line up in the first file (*primus*) of the first cohort (*pilus* – a term harking back to the manipular legions).

Principia; Situated in the centre of a Roman fort or marching camp, the principia served as the headquarters.

Reiks; In Gothic society, a reiks was a tribal leader or warlord. Whenever the Gothic tribes came together to fight as a united people, a 'council' of reiks would elect one man to serve as their *Iudex,* overall leader of the alliance.

Sacrum Consistorium; The Roman Emperor's 'Sacred Council' or inner circle of advisers.

Sagittarius (pl. Sagittarii); Roman foot archer. Typically equipped with a bronze helm and nose-guard, mail vest, composite bow and quiver.

Schola Palatinum (pl. Scholae Palatinae); The elite cavalry regiments of the later Roman Empire. Typically, these crack riders would serve in the Emperor's *Praesental Army.*

Shahanshah; The Persian King of Kings.

Signaculum; a leather necklace and pouch bearing two small lead discs with the legion's name on one side and their own name on the reverse.

Solidus (pl. Solidi); Valuable gold coin in the later Roman Empire.

Spatha; The Roman straight sword, up to one metre long and favoured by the late imperial infantry and cavalry.

Speculator (pl. Speculatores); A shadowy secret police employed throughout the Roman Republic and Empire. They tended to focus on internal affairs and domestic threats, carrying coded messages, spying, and assassinating on command. Similar to, but not to be confused with, the *Frumentarii* or the *Agentes in Rebus.*

Timpani; Also known as kettledrums, these instruments consist of skin stretched over a copper bowl.

Toga Virilis; The "toga of manhood" was a plain white toga, representing adult male citizenship and its attendant rights, freedoms and responsibilities.

Tribunus (pl. Tribuni); The senior officer of a legion. In the late 4th century AD, a *tribunus* was usually in charge of one or more legions of *limitanei* or *comitatenses*.

Trierarchus; Captain of a trireme.

Trireme; A war galley with three banks of oars.

Turma (pl. turmae); The smallest unit of Roman cavalry, numbering thirty riders.

Valetudinarium; A medical building in a Roman camp or fort.

Printed in Great Britain
by Amazon

70258557R00246